UNTRAMMELED DESIRE

In the beautiful and brutal world of twelfth-century France, a woman's desires count for little, but young Solange de St. Florent submits meekly to no man. Not to her rapacious stepfather. Not to the cruel baron who vows to take her. And not to the henchmen who try to imprison her in a convent, as she escapes into the night, naked but for a cape.

UNPARALLELED LUXURY

Seeking protection at the court of Queen Eleanor of Aquitane, Solange instead is betrayed into wedlock with Aimery de Montvert . . . the Queen's own lover! Her only hope now, against intrigues aimed at her life, is the blonde Viking chosen to lead France on a fated Crusade.

ROMANTIC SPLENDOR

Across Europe, to Imperial Byzantium, into battle with infidel hordes, Solange would live to see ruin befall her tormentors. And, in a palace with a breath-taking view of the Golden Horn of Byzantium, she would live to see that the man who had given her his hand in marriage, had given his heart as well.

Other Avons books by
Jocelyn Carew

Follow the Shadows

Jocelyn Carew

AVON
PUBLISHERS OF BARD, CAMELOT AND DISCUS BOOKS

FOLLOW THE SHADOWS is an original publication of
Avon Books. This work has never before appeared in
book form.

AVON BOOKS
A division of
The Hearst Corporation
959 Eighth Avenue
New York, New York 10019
Copyright © 1979 by Jacquelyn Aeby
Published by arrangement with the author.
Library of Congress Catalog Card Number: 78-67750
ISBN: 0-380-41921-1

First Avon Printing, August, 1979

AVON TRADEMARK REG. PAT. OFF. AND IN
OTHER COUNTRIES, MARCA REGISTRADA, HECHO EN
U.S.A.

Printed in the U.S.A.

Follow The Shadows

Book One
France, 1146

1

The hounds were hot on the scent.

In a clearing in the Belvent Forest, gilded by the afternoon sun, Solange de St. Florent stood in an arrested attitude of listening. The pack, in full cry, passed near her but out of her vision.

Knowing well the green woods and tawny fields of Belvent, as these had belonged to St. Florents for three generations, Solange could see in her mind's eye the great full-throated pack, tracking its prey to a shallow graveled ford by Petitmer stream.

She had not expected her new stepfather, Mehun de Mowbrai, to hunt this afternoon. She certainly did not wish to face him! The jangling echoes of their most recent quarrel, only a couple of hours before, still rioted in her thoughts. The next time she saw him she must be calm. She must keep her flaming temper to herself, no matter how difficult that might be.

She could still see her pretty, silly mother, cringing against a narrow window in the great hall, her hands pressed to her face in dismay at the sight of Mehun, her husband of two months, and her sixteen-year-old daughter, Solange, snarling at each other. It had become a familiar scene.

If only Raoul would return from court and claim Solange as his promised bride. She would then be free of Mehun.

Something in the hounds' cry now caught her attention. The distinctive bay of Mehun's boar-hound was not to be heard. Now that she listened for it, she could not detect Beau's distinctive, hoarse bark at all.

Then this could not be Mehun's pack! He would never leave the castle without dark and dangerous Beau by his side. Whether Mehun were hunting for fun or just ridding the forests of wolves, he always had Beau with him.

Her reckless gallop away from the castle, letting her

3

mare, Marchedoux, take her as far from Mehun as she could get, had carried Solange close to the limits of Belvent. She was dangerously near the boundary line, marked by blazes on the trunks of ancient trees. Beyond that line lay the lands of the Baron d'Yves.

Her knees trembled. Her peril was great! The baron's hunt, hot in pursuit, had heedlessly crossed the Belvent boundary. She was close to the Baron d'Yves—the devil himself!

She made the sign of the cross, glancing down for comfort at the wildflowers she was holding. Her mother's gardens had been blighted by an early October frost, and the bouquet would please her.

The pack's cry was fading away. The hunt had passed her by. She breathed a bit more easily. But she dared not linger longer—not this close to d'Yves. Hastily she gathered two more sprays of goldenrod and a handful of lavender Michaelmas daisies. Quickly unsheathing her vermeil-hilted dagger, which she always carried on the slender belt around her hips, she cut a tendril of wild grapevine for binding the flowers together.

She must hurry. The rays of the westering sun, slanting across the clearing, told her there was little time before dark. She had been more than ordinarily foolhardy this day.

Solange hitched up the skirt of her flowing bliaut, the bright yellow of the silk matching the goldenrod she carried. She had been so furious with her stepfather that she had not even paused to change into riding dress. She started toward the spot where Marchedoux was tied.

Suddenly, at the opposite side of the clearing, there exploded a crackling of dry sticks and the thrumming of desperate hooves. The hunters' prey burst into the open space like a closely-shot arrow. Glaring at her, his gray sides heaving, gasped an enormous wild boar. He was crazed by fear and rage. His square feet dug their wickedly pointed hooves sharply into the forest dirt as he galloped to a stop.

Standing tall at the shoulder, as high as her hips, he regarded her with furious little red eyes. He was the largest boar she had ever seen. Might he be the one they called *le Meurtrier*, the Murderer? Over the years, many dogs and men had fallen victim to his vicious attacks.

His long head terminated in a broad snout, now sniffing the air with flaring nostrils. His tusks, dark and glistening with fresh blood, curved sharply upward. She shrank away. Once she had seen tusks, not quite so large, disembowel her father's best boar-hound with a single upward toss of the massive head.

The dogs had apparently lost the scent. Here was their quarry, terrible in rage, ancient in cunning. Fear rooted her to the ground like a quivering larch. She reached for her dagger. She would die here, in this softly lit forest glade, on the tusks of a wild boar. Her stomach turned and her mouth became sour. Die she might—but the beast would suffer too. She crouched, clenching the dagger in her fist, ready to plunge it deep into the underbelly of the savage boar. But the beast seemed to come to his senses. The brief breathing time had given him energy. He gathered his wits again, sensing that she was not the enemy. It was the hounds, baying and yelping, who had driven him here. Now the air behind him was silent.

With a soft snort, the animal wheeled and ran from the clearing by a path leading off to Solange's right. In a few moments, the rustle of his passing had faded entirely. She crouched still, stunned by relief, and breathed a prayer of gratitude to the saints, whose intervention had saved her life.

The prayer, half-spoken, died on her lips.

The dogs had lost the scent, but the hunter had not. Into the clearing he stepped, a man of middle years, dressed in a dark blue tunic of Champagne velvet, flamboyantly embroidered with gold thread. He carried a fur-lined mantle over his arm. In his gauntleted right hand he held an ugly boar spear, and in the other he lofted an ivory hunting horn, suspended from his neck by a long, braided silken cord. He stopped in astonishment at the sight of Solange, letting go of the horn.

His thin lips twisted into a smile. "I swear I have a better nose for the most delectable prey than old Vraidux," said the hunter, coming closer.

A breeze sprang up, tossing the leaves that canopied

the clearing. By a chance the golden sun fell full upon Solange, revealing her silver hair, her charming face, her lissome form. She held her ground, facing the man defiantly. A long, low whistle escaped him. There was a knowing light in his pale eyes.

Her heart beat wildly. She feared he could see it thumping through her thin gown. She dared not show him the fright that turned her bones to jelly. "Your boar went that way," she said steadily, pointing toward the other side of the glade. "Your hounds are poor things indeed if they cannot follow a trail as clear as that one."

"Vraidux is dead," explained the hunter. "My best hound, torn on the tusks of that beast. I will settle my accounts with the boar, never fear."

He dismissed the subject with a jerk of his head, as though the great boar already lay dead.

"Only one hound of value?" she scoffed. She must keep his attention on the hunt, while she edged the few yards to her horse. Once mounted, her advantage would be sure, but it would not be very long. She dare not make a mistake.

For she had no doubt about the man before her. That slim face, lean cheeks framing an arrogant beak of a nose . . . the cruel, thin lips that made a slash across his otherwise handsome face . . . the black eyebrows peaking in an expression of perpetual scorn . . . the knowing, weary look in his pale eyes . . . she had no doubt about the identity of this cynical man. It was the infamous Conon d'Yves.

"Don't run away," he said. "I am d'Yves. And I know who you are." He smiled his cold smile.

"You are the man they call the Wicked Baron?" Her voice quavered, and she saw a leaping spark in his eyes. It told her that he noted her fear. He enjoyed seeing her tremble.

He moved a step closer. "Not so wicked," he purred. His voice was surprisingly pleasant. "You must not believe all you hear. Come, let me show you that I am not such a bad fellow."

She had no clear idea of what he would do to her, but she was sure that her name and rank would be no protection. Yet she had to try. "I am Solange de Saint Florent," she told him firmly, her voice steady now. "Daughter of Odo de Saint Florent, Baron of Belvent."

His smile mocked her. "Who else would you be?" he asked. "The fame of your beauty has spread far . . . and still did not tell the half of it, as I see now. I regret that I have heard of your loveliness only quite recently——"

"That matters not," she said, dismissing his flattery.

An unpleasant smile lurked around his bloodless lips. "To tame a lass of your mettle——"

"Is not your affair," she pointed out.

His smile broadened, as though a private thought amused him. He straightened his girdle, and Solange seized upon the moment. She turned to flee.

But she was too late. He caught her before she was out of the clearing. Pinioning her by the wrist, he brought her sharply around to face him, twisting her arm cruelly behind her. He forced her close to him. Panting for breath, she could feel the fine cloth of his tunic rubbing against her.

His eyes burned down into hers. She could see strange yellow lights in them, like will-o'-the-wisp lanterns in the bogs on summer evenings—the devil's own lights, leading the unwary traveler to his destruction.

His free hand stroked upward from her waist, cupping a firm breast. A smile touched one corner of his mouth.

He thrust her backward against the trunk of a great oak, and the hard bark poked her painfully. "Now then, my child, I think you will not escape from me. I will bring you a foretaste of the delights of—You little devil!" he cried.

She had kicked him. The toe of her pointed leather shoe made little imprint upon his leather boot, but her knee found its mark.

His grip faltered only for a moment. Then his mouth came down, savage with his pain, upon hers. He forced her head back, pressing her against the tree. She could not escape. She writhed against his embrace, but he held her in an iron grip. His free hand, still searching over her, now clenched her flesh in cruel fingers. She cried out against his hot mouth.

His grip upon her wrist turned her fingers numb. She

7

had forgotten she still held her small dagger, drawn against the boar, until she heard the weapon drop from unfeeling fingers to the forest floor.

Still, there had to be a chance . . . her left hand stole out, lightly touching the baron's clothing—the smooth tunic, the heavy, studded hunting belt. The baron pressed hard against her whole body until she could feel the imprint of the gold embroidery against her skin, the rough weave of his hunting stockings against her thighs.

She found what she wanted. His enormous hunting knife was heavy in her hand. It was too heavy to slide in secret from its sheath. The time for caution was past. Wrenching the knife from its scabbard, she held the blade high over him and plunged it downward into his shoulder with all her might. She felt the blade penetrate the heavy folds of his tunic, and then rapidly, slide into living flesh.

His yellow-flecked eyes mirrored shock, then pain. His grip loosened and he staggered back.

Quickly she whipped away from him, panting with her terrible fright, not quite realizing what she had done.

"You witch of Satan!" he snarled, bringing his hand away from his shoulder and studying his palm. "You've drawn blood!"

"And was not that your intention?" she countered. "Your treatment of me was far from gentle!"

His eyes kindled, and he started toward her again, his unharmed arm groping for her. He stopped short. She was still holding his hunting knife, threatening the middle of his chest with the point.

"That's *my* knife," he joked grimly. "Good Toledo steel, and well worth the cost, since there is no rust on the blade to bring me to my premature death. Do you wish, fair maiden, to be hanged as a felon for stealing a knife?"

"You're on Belvent land," she said, "and you are more likely to hang than I when Mehun hears of this day."

The baron laughed. "You mistake your friends, lady, if you count on Mowbrai. But remember this. I do not forget an injury of any kind. One day or another I shall exact the last copper of revenge. From the boar who killed my hound." He took a shuddering breath and frowned with pain. "And from you."

Without another word he turned and left the clearing. She began to shake. She must get home while she still could. She did not trust him not to return.

Forcing herself to breathe deeply, she staggered toward Marchedoux.

She was halfway home on the road along the bank of the Petitmer, leaving the dark forest behind her, seeing the towers of the castle rising against the saffron sky, before she realized that she had dropped the flowers but still held the baron's hunting knife in her free hand.

Better this souvenir than another he might have left her! she thought with grim humor. She fastened the weapon by its loop onto her belt.

2

The castle battlements scraped the sky. The castle promised security in the worst of times.

As she drew closer on the road paralleling the Petitmer, additional turrets grew out of the gray stone mass perched formidably atop a rocky outcrop at the bend of the river. The staff on top of the flag tower on the donjon now held Mehun's banner, a black bear on a scarlet ground. It snapped in the evening breeze, proclaiming defiantly that Mehun was in his castle.

The usurper! It is *my father*'s castle! she railed, though Odo de St. Florent lay in an unmarked grave in the Holy Land. Mehun had been over-quick to establish his possession of both St. Florent's widow and his castle! Solange's heart twisted inside her like a turn of the hunting knife dangling heavily at her hip.

She crossed the bridge over the stream, wider here than in the forest. The clear water purled in eddies along the rush-bordered bank, but the center stream was deep and strong.

She was in time. The barbican gate still stood open, and

she pulled Marchedoux to a walk as she passed through the great gate. For once she was anxious to see Mehun, to warn him of d'Yves's attack on her. In Mehun's woods he could allow no insult to his villeins or his family. So would his reason run. A lord who did not protect his own was no lord at all.

How different, if her father had lived, would be the scene that met her now! There would be activity around the great oven, the dairy, the cookhouse. There would be preparations for her wedding.

Before her father had left for Outremer, five years before, he had betrothed her to Raoul de Puiseaux. She had turned sixteen only last month. Her father—if he had returned—would have sent for Raoul even before her sixteenth birthday, and she would now be getting ready to be married.

How often had she dreamed of her wedding! The feasting, the baking, the games laid out in the lists below the curtain wall, the brightly colored tents set up for the honored guests. Her father and mother moving among their friends, receiving congratulations on their only daughter's fine marriage to the heir of the large de Puiseaux estate. Raoul himself taking her hand in his and repeating the solemn vows of betrothal made for the first time five years before.

Her thoughts could go no further. What would happen when she and Raoul rode away at the head of his armed retainers and courtly friends? These were not part of her dreams. Strangely, she had almost forgotten what Raoul looked like.

How would he have changed? He was only fifteen when his beloved mother died, and although he had ruled as his father's heir for five years, he had not yet done homage for his fiefs. The year after his mother died, when Raoul was sixteen and Solange only fourteen, he had ridden away to the court of King Louis VII to do homage and be confirmed in his fiefs. And there he had stayed.

He had written no letters to his betrothed. But it was time—past time—that Raoul returned for her, even though the wedding could not be as she had dreamed it.

Her father would never place her hand in Raoul's at the

wedding ceremony before the chapel door. Odo de St. Florent had fallen, fighting the Turks in the Holy Land.

Dark-browed, land-obsessed Mehun had passed by on his return from Outremer to Normandy. He lingered in the fair lands of Belvent, and told the lady of Belvent that her husband was dead.

"I saw him fall with my own eyes," Mehun had said, "and the Paynim swarmed over his body." In a month, Mehun had wed Petronilla de St. Florent.

Solange trembled anew. Instead of easing, as her old nurse, Mahaut, had told her it would, her rage and grief had grown until the mere mention of Mehun's name brought a scarlet curtain of fury to blind her sight.

She passed through the lists, where Mehun's new black destrier snorted from his paddock at the sight of dainty Marchedoux, stepping lightly through the dust, hooves echoing on the wooden drawbridge over the moat. Once inside the bailey, she slid from the saddle and handed the reins to Bernier, the second groom.

"Late, Lady Solange," he chided. "The forest is right dangerous after dark."

"Wolves?" Solange said lightly. "Marchedoux can outrun them all. But I did see the grandfather of all boars. Do you think it might have been *le Meurtrier?*"

Eyes shining with excitement, Bernier exclaimed, "The Murderer? I've heard he was back in Belvent Wood. And you saw him?"

"Indeed I did. Foaming at the mouth." She sketched a quick account of the incident. "Back, you said? Where had he gone, then?"

"Who knows the ways of the wild?" said Bernier solemnly. "They come and they go, the boar do, and likewise the foxes in their dens. But the hounds can catch them. Yon great Beau of the master's—"

Her sudden scowl brought him up short. "Nay, Lady, no offense. It's only that the Lady Petronilla told us we must give respect to the new master."

"And since my father is not here to give Mehun his deserts, then I suppose I must not blame you." Solange suddenly spat out, "My father would hang Mehun from the tower gibbet!"

"Nay," the lad said again. His cornsilk hair was nearly as light as Solange's, and rumor had it that they shared the same blood. Bernier never presumed upon Solange, but he dared, once in a while, to chide her. "Your father was not harsh. He would have laughed at him and then sent him on his way."

"My father," said Solange with proud fire, "would not have allowed such a stain upon his honor."

Bernier lowered his eyes. He stood submissively, thinking better of remonstrating with Solange. At last he said, "Mehun de Mowbrai has been asking for you."

"And you said?"

"All I knew. Which was that you had gone out to ride." He had not informed Mehun that she had ridden out as though the demons were after her.

It was later than she thought. The work at the armory had been halted for the day, and the smith's fires were banked. The cows stood in long rows for the milkmaids, and the fresh scent of hot bread filled the bailey. She quickened her steps.

She burst across the main court and through the arched door at one side of the angled *palais* wall. This part of the castle was newer than the great keep. The first fortification was stern and comfortless. Odo's father, in times of peace, had built the newer residence apartments. Real glass covered most of the windows, and tapestries woven on Arras looms hung from the walls during festive occasions.

Mehun was waiting for her, seated on the great carved chair on the dais, under an intricately decorated wooden canopy, Beau at his feet.

Resolutely, Solange stepped forward to stand before him. "I must tell you, sir, what befell me this afternoon," she began. "I was in the far wood—"

"Gathering wildflowers, to judge by the sorry state of your gown," Mehun finished for her. "A pretty occupation for a pretty lass, eh? Except that you seem to have wallowed on the forest floor. I have no interest in your girlish adventures. I have news for you."

"For me?" She turned in inquiry to her mother, across the room, gazing down into the embers of the day's fire. The news could not be good, she thought. Her mother's feelings were always inscribed on her face and in her gestures.

"Your mother agrees with me," said Mehun hastily. "You are past sixteen, she tells me. Time you set up your own establishment."

Sheer surprise held her speechless. Then the great news burst upon her. It could be nothing other than her marriage! "Raoul is returning!"

Petronilla made an involuntary movement that rippled her long sleeves like drooping golden banners in a fitful breeze. It was a strange gesture, more protest than rejoicing.

Solange whirled in giddy joy, and ran to her mother. "You must have sent for Raoul! How good you are!" Petronilla looked away. Solange put her arm awkwardly around her mother's shoulders. Caresses were not common between them. "Come, Mother! Raoul's home is not so far away. We will see each other often."

"Solange!" Mehun interrupted sharply. "I have not finished."

"Raoul is coming and I am to be wed, as my father wished," she said gaily. "You must forgive me if I reflect the happiness you have brought me with your news."

She had not had happiness from Mehun's doings before. She would regret leaving the St. Florent lands, the castle of Belvent, and her mother. But nothing was the same since Mehun de Mowbrai had laid his grasping hand on Belvent.

"Tomorrow," Mehun announced, "the groom will come in the morning. You will be wed at once. Perhaps then this castle can live in peace."

His words rankled. Peace when *she* was gone? When he himself was the sole disturber of their happy life? She held back her angry retort. With escape so close at hand, only one more night beneath the black bear rampant on its scarlet ground, flying over the keep, she must take care lest the gate close before she could slip through it.

Her smoldering eyes, though, revealed her thoughts. He laughed shortly, a braying noise echoing to the corbeled ceiling. Beau raised his great head, and remained watchful.

"We must have fresh rushes on the floor," he said.

"Flowers throughout the hall, my good wife tells me. The tapestries must be hung. See to it, Solange."

She turned bewildered eyes to her mother. "Why not you, my lady Mother? Methinks you do not like this haste? Tomorrow is too soon," she added, turning to her step-father. "It is not decent to wed with such speed."

Her mother's words, if she had spoken at all, were lost in Mehun's growl. "I wish you to do it. Your mother has not the heart for it." His sidelong glance at Petronilla held speculation. "She feels your loss already."

"There is hardly time for all—"

Mehun went on as though she had not spoken. "There will be garments to be gathered, I suppose, and your maids must set to work. I will give orders for the wedding feast myself."

"We have no chaplain," Solange remembered, "Father Jean went to the Holy Land with my father."

"Fortunately, that will not delay us," said Mehun. "A traveling priest has this day come begging alms. He has agreed to sing a marriage mass for his supper."

Mehun's dark eyes were watchful. Ordinarily, Solange would examine his every word, turning them over to find the maggots beneath. But he seemed at last to be playing fairly with her.

"You have things to do," Mehun reminded her, and she realized she had been dreaming. With a muttered word she picked up her yellow, mud-spotted skirt in both hands and scurried from the hall.

Calling to her nurse, Mahaut, as she ran toward the tower steps, she raced up the winding stairs to her own apartment in the donjon. The rooms set aside for her as the daughter of the house were comfortable, far removed from the *palais*. She was allowed privacy here, and she guarded it jealously. Mahaut, and sometimes Jehane, were the only attendants allowed to enter.

Simply furnished, holding only a narrow bed, a table, a chest under the window for her clothes, and a footstool covered in red velvet, her quarters were always a haven in time of trouble. Now she was to leave her sanctuary.

"Tomorrow?" echoed Mahaut. "Why such speed?"

"To get me out of his sight," explained Solange gaily.

"Mahaut, did you know about this and didn't tell me? You wretch!"

"By the Virgin, I did not!" protested Mahaut. "There's been nary a word in the courtyards about your marriage. Tomorrow? Impossible! He's a madman to suggest it!"

"You will carry this suggestion to my stepfather?"

"And get a hiding at the least, if not the branding?" The old woman grinned, gap-toothed, and suddenly her wrinkled face crumpled. "It means losing you, my only chick, that's been mine since a week old. . . ."

Her last words were lost in sobs. The old shoulders shook, and she brought her reddened hands up to hide the workings of her lined face.

"Come now, Mahaut," said Solange softly, "you mustn't grudge my happiness."

Strangled syllables escaped from between Mahaut's gnarled fingers. "Happy, you say. Will Raoul comb this long pale hair, fine as Lilles silk? Will he bring you possets when you're ailing? Hush you when you waken from bad dreams?"

"I'm sure he will treat me well," smiled Solange, on her knees before her nurse. "You wish to come with me, my dear Mahaut? I could ask it as a favor."

Mahaut rocked back and forth on the red velvet stool. Tears pricked behind Solange's eyelids. She threw her arms around Mahaut, and abandoned herself to weeping. "What will I ever do without you, Mahaut? You've been my true mother, all this time."

It was true. Frivolous Petronilla, aware of her charms and her attraction for her luxury-loving husband, had turned the baby Solange over to Mahaut. From then on the sturdy peasant woman, with an unbounded supply of love and common sense, had been Solange's whole young world.

Solange dried her eyes. "Come now, darling Mahaut. No need to cry. You will come with me."

The bent old woman shook her head, sniffed loudly, and wiped her nose on the towel she produced from a hidden pocket in her sleeveless brown apron. "My child, nay. These old bones could not travel as far as Puiseaux or to the great court." She sniffed again, much restored.

"I longed to hold your first-born son in my own arms. But it is not God's will, and there's an end to it. Now, for your wedding dress, I think the new deep blue will do well."

After the two had chosen Solange's wedding finery, the bride added, "And pack everything else. My stepfather tells me we will be leaving at once."

"Then," said the old woman with a final sniff, "let us pray for fair weather."

3

𝕿heir prayers were answered. Solange woke to brilliant sunshine, and Mahaut's cheery cracked old voice.

"Come, fair bride, waken!" she cried in the words of a song popular with traveling performers. "Rise and greet the sun," the song went on. "Say farewell to maiden's joy, and hail love's true delights."

It was a complicated business to get the bride dressed, and the activity soon took all their attention. Mahaut called Jehane from her work in the great hall to help them dress Solange.

First, over the bride's slim white body was dropped a chemise of finely woven linen, tinted pale blue. It fell airily to just below her knees. Then came the pelisson, made of saffron-hued wool from the Belvent sheep, with an outer layer of deep blue sendal silk.

"Mahaut, lace me tighter!" gasped Solange. "Raoul must be proud of me this day."

And then came the finest of silk bliauts, deep violet to match her eyes. It had the longest possible sleeves. The cuffs would touch the floor unless she held her hands out gracefully at waist level. There had been no time to add the gold embroidery the dress needed to set it off properly, but this lack was more than made up for by the girdle Petronilla had sent Solange. Of broad gold links cunningly fastened in supple rings, like Saracen armor, it was set with stones of good fortune.

"Sardonyx—that's for fever," mused Solange, touched by her mother's gift. "And agate is for good health."

"You're telling them like beads of a rosary," complained Mahaut. "A heathen practice."

"But you believe in the powers of the stones," smiled Solange.

A horn sounded brightly over their heads, the silver notes tumbling down like falling doves from the top of the watch tower. The sentry had caught sight of travelers on the road.

"It is Raoul!" cried Solange, dashing to the narrow window-slit, eager to catch first sight of her bridegroom. He came promptly upon his word, she thought, eager to carry her away.

From this window in the great keep, Solange could see far across Belvent lands. The beech woods in their October coppery hue at the horizon, the tilled strips of land, brown and tan after the harvest, lying close to the protective walls of the castle for shelter, all were ruled by the lord of Belvent. Stone towers at the four corners of the enclosing twelve-foot-thick curtain walls stretched out on either side of the watchtower where Solange stood. She was looking down upon the road from the south, the road taken by her father. He had been the last Odo de St. Florent and a stranger to the bellicose energy of his ancestors. Her mother had sewed the cross of red wool on the front of his tunic and watched him set out on Crusade. It was five years ago, the year of our Lord 1141.

Now her bridegroom's train approached, at first only a shadowy movement at the edge of the wood. The troop of armed men came on apace. Jehane jostled her at the window, excited by the approaching spectacle. It was a brave sight, and Solange's heart beat faster as she watched. The sun glinted on the great helms, on the lance tips and shields, sending sparkling bits of sunlight dancing over the fields.

The horses came on steadily, trotting under their heavy burdens as freshly as though they had come from just over the hill, instead of on the long journey from Puiseaux. Strange, she thought, that their banners were not yet unfurled. The absence of red and white, blue and green pennons fluttering in the breeze made the approaching retinue seem somber and harsh in the bright autumn sunlight.

They drew nearer, but not near enough that she could see the device on the leader's shield. He sat his saddle well, that much could be seen from the tower window. But with his visor pulled down halfway over his face, she could not make out his countenance.

Mahaut was clapping her hands for servants. Soon the chest was strapped and fastened and carried down the winding stairs, ready to be loaded by Solange's husband's servants. Solange watched still, feasting her eyes on the means of her escape from the once-beloved Belvent. She remembered Raoul's gentleness, his amiable sweetness. How could she fail to be happy with Raoul?

"Come now, Solange," said Mahaut. "Your lady mother will want to see you before you go out to meet your bridegroom. Come away from the window now. Plenty of time later to feast your eyes upon the man. You will tire of him soon enough."

"Now, Mahaut," ventured Jehane boldly. "Not all loves are done with as fast as that. Just because your own didn't last doesn't mean that a wilier woman can't keep her man in thrall."

Solange eyed Jehane speculatively. The girl was fresh from a village, far out at the edge of the oak forest. Her father and brothers had a small holding and the privilege of letting their two pigs rummage along the forest floor for acorns. But there was never enough food for them all, and Jehane had been lucky enough to be taken into household service. Room—shared with four others but nonetheless with a good roof over their heads—and meals, and a new suit of clothes once a year at Michaelmas were not to be taken lightly. But Jehane was too outspoken. Petronilla might well send her back to her father if her wrath were aroused.

"Mahaut," said Solange sharply, "I will not have you hitting Jehane, not on my wedding day. I do not wish to take my vows with crying servants around me. Come then, forgive Jehane."

The moment passed, without the buffet on the ear that Mahaut clearly believed was appropriate punishment for the young woman's disrespect. She lowered her hand and sighed. "How can I keep these girls in their places with you—" Then it came over her again that her darling Solange was about to leave her forever.

Solange had turned back to the window, and did not see her nurse's valiant struggle with tears. No crying servants, she had said, and Mahaut was determined to do her mistress's bidding.

She did not see what caused Solange's sharp exclamation of dismay.

"Mahaut, did you see? That little brown dog ran under the horses, but Elie got him out again."

"Elie lets the puppy run too much," said Mahaut. The boy was her grandson, and she grumbled daily about the puppy, but no one was fooled by her complaints. She doted on the boy, and on the puppy as well.

Mahaut moved to the window, looking over Jehane's shoulder. The train of riders had reached the stone arch over the Petitmer. Impatient of restraint, Brun the dog wriggled free of his master's small arms, jumped to the ground, and raced toward the visitors, barking at the first horse. Without losing a step, the rider wheeled his mount toward the dog. The horse's hoof struck the puppy and sent him rolling over the ground, down the incline to the stream's edge. Elie scrambled in a frenzy after his pet and cradled him gently, sitting on the ground.

The boy lifted his head and looked after the riders, the last of whom was just now clattering over the lowered drawbridge. The boy's shoulders sagged, telling his story clearly.

"The dog's dead," said Mahaut, in a strangely expressionless voice. "Why did he have to do that?"

There was no possible answer. A gray mist fell over the landscape, like a fog, although there was still no cloud in the sky. Solange raised horrified eyes to Mahaut. "That's not like Raoul," she said at last. "He was always so gentle. It must have been Raoul's man riding at the head of his troops. Raoul could not have been so horribly cruel."

She turned away from the window. The room looked stern and bare, now that the rainbow colors of her garments were packed and gone.

She patted Mahaut's shoulder, an attempt at comfort. There was nothing more to say. Dogs were plentiful at Belvent, and Elie would soon find another pet. But the horror of seeing his dear Brun killed in such a wanton fashion would not be so easily remedied.

Petronilla was waiting for Solange in her rooms across the great hall. She was dressed in a turquoise pelisson edged with miniver, under a bliaut of deep rose shot with gold and intricately embroidered with pearls. Ready lay her mantle of turquoise silk lined with white marten, a recent gift from Mehun.

Petronilla was not alone. Mehun stood nearby, almost like a guard. "Your mother wishes to tell you the benefits of married life," he said heavily to Solange, "so that you will know how to submit to your husband's wishes, how to delight him in every way. Where did you get that hair, Solange?"

The abrupt change of subject surprised her. Automatically she touched one of the braids that Jehane had carefully interwoven with gold ribbon to match the ornate girdle.

"From her grandmother," supplied Petronilla sharply. "Odo's mother looked much like Solange. Hair the color of moonlight, and eyes the color of wood violets in spring, or so it was said."

A faint smile touched Solange's pale lips. "And a temper, so I have heard, that would set a thatched roof ablaze."

Mehun grunted. "Not much different from her granddaughter," he mumbled.

There was no answer for that. Solange turned toward her mother, whose eyes brimmed with tears. In a rush the two of them locked in embrace, and Solange hugged her mother as though she could never let her go. Petronilla's lips were close to Solange's ear, and she whispered three words. Solange could not quite make them out.

She felt a warning pressure from her mother's hand and pulled back with no sign of having heard anything. Petronilla said with a tremulous watery smile, "Let me look at you. How pretty you are! Remember, Solange—oh, *remember*—that I will always love you!"

"And . . ." Solange choked and could not finish. Hand in hand, with Mehun hovering behind them, they left the room and descended into the great hall. Bare-floored, newly swept, it was waiting for fresh rushes and garlands of flowers to be brought in while the marriage ritual was taking place.

Solange asked, "How is it that none of the servants knew about my wedding? Usually the whole courtyard seethes with news before it gets to me! This time it was such a closely guarded secret that none knew."

"Your stepfather wished no advance word to come to you. He wanted to tell you the news . . . the good news, himself."

Petronilla's words were flat, and Solange looked curiously at her. Now, close at hand, she noticed her mother's red-rimmed swollen eyes. What had Mehun done to her? And what had she tried to convey in whispers?

Through the great oaken door, thick enough to withstand all but the heaviest iron-tipped battering ram, there came the jingling of hundreds of little harness bells, the clamor of many voices, harsh and masculine, the heavy ringing sounds of gauntlet upon iron, of metal sabaton upon gray stone.

"Come," said Mehun. "Let us hurry. The bridegroom is growing impatient."

"But—no greeting? No cup of welcome?" Solange pulled back. "You do not do the honors of this house as they should be done."

Mehun turned his hot brown eyes upon her and she quailed. Mehun in anger was formidable and unpredictable. She had once seen him hurl his lance through a servant's shoulder for bringing a basin of water too hot for his hands. "I will take care of the honors of this house, Solange," he told her. "Get you hence, and heed well your tongue."

The small procession left the great hall. All the gala trappings of a noble wedding were missing, the black mule with gold and scarlet trappings to carry the bride the few yards to the chapel, and the long troupe of servants, kinfolk, and neighbors to follow her as she progressed through the main court. Accompanying her now were only

Petronilla and Mehun, Dermot the seneschal, and Mahaut and Jehane trailing humbly behind.

The tiny party made its way through the gate in the court wall and into the bailey. Solange's wonder deepened. Where were the servants? There should have been a hundred of them, spilling out of the workshops and the barracks, clustered around the storehouses and the cooking house. Everyone should be in gala dress for her wedding day. Even though the notice had been short, the servants should still have been anticipating a fine feast and a token coin, at the very least.

But she passed through quiet men, women with lowered eyes and restless feet, and strangely subdued children. She glanced around, hoping to see young Elie, but he was not in sight.

Mehun jerked her forward. The chapel was situated almost at the barbican wall. A strange priest with weathered cheeks, age-bent shoulders, a border of windblown hair encircling his tonsure, stood before the door. She longed for the comforting presence of Father Jean.

This was an odd sort of wedding. She searched the faces of the men standing in their armor, visors only partly lifted. Why had they not taken off the heavy metal? Surely they could not expect trouble? A chilling menace, the more frightening for being unwarranted, emanated from the silent, mailed men.

Where was Raoul? She did not see him among the knights. Perhaps he had changed so much in two years that she did not know him.

Her mother pulled at her sleeve. Solange knew she must approach her wedding with downcast eyes. She quickly dropped her gaze and suffered Mehun to lead her the last few steps. Before she knew it they had halted. Immediately the priest began intoning the words of the binding promises.

She was suddenly cold. She ached for Raoul to at least take her hand. This was such a frigid reunion.

She looked, pleading, into the face of her bridegroom. It was not Raoul.

Not Raoul! The soft wild cry of a hurt creature escaped her lips.

"Come now," said the Baron d'Yves, smiling at his bride-to-be, "give me your hand."

She snatched her fingers away from his touch as if they were seared and reached automatically for the dagger she usually carried at her belt. Too late, she remembered it was still lying on the forest floor.

"You!" she screamed. "Where is Raoul?"

Crouching like an animal at bay, she turned sharply to Mehun. "What have you done? Where is Raoul? You think to wed me to this—this monster! I will kill you first!" Her hands bent into claws and she reached for his face.

With insulting ease Mehun grabbed her wrists and held them before her. "You will cease this display," he gritted between tight lips.

She jerked with all her strength, trying to break his grip. He twisted her arms around behind her, while she kicked uselessly at him. At length, somewhat breathless, he presented her once again before the priest, not relaxing his hold on her.

"Get on with it," he ordered gruffly.

"May God strike you dead if you do!" shrieked Solange. "This is blasphemy!"

The priest, torn between his promise to perform the marriage and his terror at Solange's curse, wavered.

"Blasphemy?" D'Yves, eyes narrowed and suddenly intensely interested, commanded. "Explain yourself."

"I am betrothed by solemn vow to Raoul de Puiseaux," she flung at him. "My father made the contract and his chaplain pronounced our vows. Raoul and I made a contract in Holy Church!"

Behind the principals at the chapel door rose a murmur of agreement from the servants. Most of them had been present at the betrothal ceremony. Mehun turned to stare at them. There was silence.

"A contract in Holy Church?" echoed the baron. "Where is this chaplain? I should like to question him about this."

"Why?" demanded Solange. "To put him to the torture?"

"How little you know men, my dear," murmured the baron. "There are other ways to persuade a man to change his mind besides torture—ways less grisly and much neater." He turned to Mehun. "I do not see your chaplain here."

"Father Jean went with Odo de Saint Florent on crusade," said Mehun. "He too was killed on the field at Adana."

"But the contract—," began Solange.

Her mother pulled at her sleeve. "Leave this," she said. "You cannot mend what is past."

"The contract cannot be enforced," said Mehun. "The man hasn't been seen here for two years. The girl must be wed."

"For my dowry," she said scornfully.

The baron's eyes glittered with a cold amusement. "Your dowry? I had no idea. Mowbrai, have you stolen it?"

"The wench lies."

"Lies?" Solange took advantage of her stepfather's distraction and twisted out of his grip. Whirling quickly around, she put Petronilla between her and the two men and cried out, "Lies, say you? I scorn to lie. There are gold coins set aside in a secret place. My mother knows—"

Something in the quality of stillness that fell upon the three watching her told her what had happened. "The gold coins went to Mehun, didn't they, Mother?" guessed Solange. "You could not honor my father's memory even that far."

Suddenly the baron threw back his head and laughed, loudly and long. "Gold coins! Solange, you will laugh when I say I paid for you. *I paid.* Two fat fields and a goodly wood, simply to have your hand in marriage. The fair Lady Solange, whose beauty is beyond compare. Yet a virgin."

"You attacked me yesterday. I barely escaped. This is your idea of courtesy toward your bride? And would you have failed to wed me, had you already violated me?"

Petronilla stirred, startled. "You did not tell us this, Solange."

"How could I? Your husband would not allow me to tell my story."

The baron interposed. "Whether your virginity were lost yestereve in the wood or on our marriage bed, or wherever I chose, it would be lost to *me*. That is all that matters. You are mine. Mark it well, Solange. I will get my money's worth."

Solange quivered with rage. She knew it would be wiser to keep her peace, but she could not hold her tongue. "Was that what you thought you would get, the thrill of forcing me?"

"I was merely an overly eager bridegroom," he said silkily.

Solange turned again to Petronilla. "My lady Mother, *this* is the man you wish me to wed? I had not thought you cared so little for me. Why do you not hang me from yonder gibbet yourself, instead of waiting for d'Yves to do it after he has tormented me?"

"Solange, you exaggerate," quavered Petronilla, her face ashen.

"Lady de Mowbrai," said d'Yves, "your daughter is impetuous. I imagine she means only half of what she says. I find her delightful." Turning to the priest, he added, "The maid's objections are merely so much sauce to increase her value to me. Get on with your work."

The priest had finally gathered his wits. "I dare not go further in this until the rights of it are clear. My bishop——"

"To the Paynim with your bishop!" exploded Mehun. "Get on with this marriage!"

"Without the bride?" mocked Solange, a safe few feet away. "Bring me Raoul and I will wed in ten minutes. But not this monster of depravity!"

Petronilla protested. "Solange, you are rude to the baron. You know nothing about this man, and he is a member of the king's council. Take care lest you insult him past forgiveness."

"Insult!" Solange turned on her mother savagely. "I fear you have gone blind, Mother. This is the man who kept one wife in a cage through the winter, outside the watchtower. The cage dangled from the gibbet."

"A caged bird sings the sweeter," murmured d'Yves.

"She died that next spring, didn't she?" demanded Solange.

"A sad thing, I vow. It was her own fault, you know. She was with child, and she didn't tell me. You would not be so foolish," countered the baron.

"Her fault! Next you'll tell me that she teased your dogs to attack her?"

"No, no. That was not my first wife. I forget which one she was. My third, perhaps? At any rate, she was stubborn about turning over her dowry to me. But if you think—as I surmise Dame Rumor insists—that I set the hounds on her, you are gravely mistaken. I swear to you I did not." Turning yet again to the old beggar-priest, he repeated, "What are you waiting for?"

The priest quavered, "I dare not. To break a contract made in Holy Church is a sin."

Suddenly Mehun loosed his temper and roared, "Priest jackanapes! Out of my sight! Begone before I give you the buffet you have earned by your nice scruples!"

The priest scuttled away, frightened out of his wits. He knew he might remain safe if he forswore his conscience, yet he would not.

The baron stepped forward, his arm preventing Mehun's fist from descending. "Do not invite trouble on your soul, Mowbrai, by striking an honest man of God." His tone was bantering, making light of the priest's terror. "More trouble than you already have," he finished in sterner fashion. "You swore to me there was no contract of betrothal."

"Her mother did not tell me."

"Not likely," said the baron sharply, "when you already have possession of the dowry. But not my lands—yet. Since the priest has a tender conscience, I would not force him. Find a priest, Mowbrai, and right speedily. The fields and the wood remain mine until the maid and I are truly wed."

D'Yves turned to Solange who was panting with fear and anger. "Do not worry, my dear. You will think better of this foolish defiance. For I will have you . . . make no mistake. You will remember that d'Yves always gets what he wants."

"Even if it takes shutting your wife up in chains?"

He frowned. "She—well, no matter. That is past. But you will do well to mend your ways. My memory is long."

Turning to Mowbrai, he asked, "How long will you need

to find a willing priest? A week? I warn you, I am impatient."

He turned again to Solange and swept over her slowly with his kindling eyes, possessively, as though he already owned her. "One week," he repeated. "No more." A smile touched his thin lips. "Stay out of the woods, Solange, lest some other man come upon you. I choose to be the first to sample, at great length, your very evident charms. Mark me well."

She gave him stare for stare, feeling her skin tingle with shame as his eyes penetrated her clothing and seemed to feast upon her very flesh.

Never would she let this corrupt and evil man so much as place his hand upon hers.

And so she told Mehun, later, after the baron's troop had left with clatter of hooves and jingle of harness and mail. She and her parents had repaired to the great hall, and she dropped to a stool before the fireplace.

"Solange," Petronilla advised, "don't be so stubborn. D'Yves isn't what you think. Much of what has been said about him is simply gossip."

Solange turned her violet eyes solemnly upon her mother. Petronilla could not sustain her daughter's scrutiny, and turned away. It took Mehun to break the deadlock that had developed.

"I will speak once again—forcefully—with the doddering priest who failed to pay for his supper," Mehun planned. "I suspect the man's conscience is not strong enough to withstand a few days in a cell without food."

"His conscience," retorted Solange with triumph, "is beyond your reach. Did you not see him passing hastily over the drawbridge before that monster left us?"

"So he is gone. A trifle. You will wed d'Yves in three days nonetheless—"

"A week!" cried Petronilla. "You cannot find a priest in three days."

"I'll find one," he promised grimly. "And d'Yves will return betimes. I wish to parcel out my new fields before the snows come."

"I will not wed the man," vowed Solange, "in three days or in a week. Or in ten years."

"Quiet! You will wed the man in three days or you will spend your life in a cell in the Convent of Saint Vergillia."

"Mehun!" screamed Petronilla.

Solange turned to ice. The Convent of Saint Vergillia lay a day's journey away. It was run by nuns of an excessively strict regime, with vows of silence and penitential scourging beyond the ordinary. Those members of noble families who once entered the gates of the convent were rarely heard from again, until the Superior sent word of their demise to the ungrieving family. The regime was so harsh that few delicately nurtured women survived it long.

"Make up your mind," Mehun said. "I have no doubt as to your decision. But it should be made quickly." He left the great hall, turning at the door to repeat, "Three days, Solange. That is all the time you have."

4

The weather broke and rain drove hard against the colored glass windows of the *palais*, sweeping in curtains across the courtyard, turning the lists into inches of mud. It hammered so hard against the wooden shutters of the older part of the castle that it was often hard to hear even a raised voice. The Petitmer ran full to its banks, and the moats filled with roiling water.

On the third day the weather cleared and the sun shone upon a frosty world. Autumn was past. Winter was upon the land.

The small, well-armed caravan escorting Solange to her new home at the Convent of Saint Vergillia set out just after daybreak of the fourth day. The ground was near to freezing, and rang harshly under the trotting hooves.

Puddles left from the rain carried a thin covering of ice, and the rising sun struck green and gold rays from frozen raindrops clinging to the underside of brushy twigs.

Sunrise turned the eastern sky to apricot under the low-hanging bank of clouds that fell almost to the horizon.

This would be her last sight of the world. Mehun had told her so, and against her will she believed him. The convent was a few hours away. Solange wished she were dead. She had stormed for one day after Mehun's ultimatum, raved like a mad dog the second, and given up hope on the third.

Now she sat her horse listlessly, slumping forward in dejection. Around her was the guard Mehun had sent with her, four men. Not a large force, for he feared no rescue attempt, but ample to keep her from escaping.

Escape was, on the face of it, futile. Where could she go? She had heard something recently, an overheard scrap that she pursued in her echoing mind now until she caught it again. *The king.* That was it! Louis and his queen were coming to Bourges. And Bourges was not far away.

Raoul, whose place was with the king, would doubtless be part of the court that traveled with the monarch! If she could get to him, tell him of the fate Mehun planned for her, he would marry her at once. She would then be safe.

Her spirits lifted slightly. The gates of the convent were not yet in sight. Perhaps something could be contrived.

It was a measure of her despair that she had not remembered until now that Raoul could champion her. The massiveness of her stepfather's threats, and the baron's icy eyes had blotted out thoughts of Raoul. But now there was time for hope.

Glancing furtively around her, she saw that her companions were oblivious to her. The journey was simply a chore for them. These men, who had come with Mehun from the Holy Land, knew hard experience and rough living. This journey meant nothing to them.

They stopped late for nooning. Gervais, the leader, ordered a halt at a place where the road climbed above the river plain. She took her bread and cheese away from the others to a small outcropping near the side of the road. She spread her mist-gray cloak, the only one of her bridal garments she had brought, upon the sun-warmed rock and sat alone.

She could see far from here—to the frosted meadows, the narrow stream meandering through lavender-tipped water grasses. Catching a glimpse now and then of blue sky reflected in the pools, she drank in the heartrending beauty of the world she was about to leave forever.

She did not look back the way they had come. She needed to know more about the way ahead. Gervais approached.

"What is that wood before us?" she asked. "Will there be wolves?"

"Not until dark," he said, trying to reassure her. "We'll be through the wood long before nightfall."

"It looks," she said casually, "as though it stretches for miles."

"Actually," he said, glancing at her suspiciously, "it does. But on the other side of it is the convent."

An expression flickered over her face that made him wish he had not spoken. "Sorry," he said. "It may not be as bad as you think."

She cut off a piece of cheese with her tiny knife, before looking up angrily at him. "You think my stepfather is in the right?"

The contemptuous remark was a mistake. Gervais moved back. She might have gained his help if she had not sneered at his lord. She had learned something, she reflected, turning back to her horse, but it was little use to her now.

She lingered long at the side of her mount, as though reluctant to take up the journey again. When at last Gervais came, she accepted his help and swung cautiously into the saddle.

The road led directly into the forest. The afternoon light in late October did not linger, but seemed to plunge from day into night without warning. The ancient forest, its mammoth trees stretching their heads toward the light, lacing their limbs together far overhead, allowed only dim illumination to penetrate below the lower branches.

They moved briskly into the dusky wood. Gervais shifted uneasily in his saddle, and brought his lance to the ready. He gestured them into a faster pace. She calculated swiftly as they cantered along the track. Once she looked back and could see no sign of the open country they had just left.

Now? Not yet, she counseled herself, but farther into the forest, which Gervais said stretched for miles. Could she believe him? Or was he giving her the illusion of a few hours extra freedom?

Finally she could wait no longer. She could hardly see a dozen yards ahead of her. With a quick thrust of booted foot against the strap she had cut nearly through earlier, the strap broke. The saddle slipped beneath her and she cried out.

She had not counted on hitting the ground so heavily. Breath left her, and she did not have to feign helplessness.

The men reined up and Gervais came running back to her. She stretched, sobbing for breath, on the ground.

Infrequently she allowed a groan to escape her lips. The moan was more than half-real, but she had to be careful not to overdo it, or the men might feel they could not leave her alone.

Gervais gave quick orders. "Get the blanket from the pack. Find a stout branch, Stephen. You help him, Gauthier. You, Baldwin, come with me. We'll have to make a litter."

With her eyes closed, her ears followed their progress. She could picture them hustling through the forest brush, following orders—Stephen was so serious, otherworldly. It was said that he had studied to be a priest, but had failed in his purpose at the last moment. Baldwin was so portly that his armor chafed his beer-swilling stomach. He had loose lips and greedy eyes. Gauthier, mournful, moody, unpredictable, was the one she distrusted the most of the four. When a savage mood rode him, he left human emotion behind.

A great crashing through underbrush marked their progress, and once, some distance away, someone fell heavily over a snag hidden in the dark. She dared to look, then, through half-open eyes. She could still hear Gervais's voice, far off. She listened for the others. One by one she heard them, following their leader, looking for sturdy tree limbs within reach of the ground.

Cautiously, without moving her head, she scanned the small clearing around her. She was alone.

She must move quickly. Closing her thoughts to visions

31

of wolves and panthers and even *le Meurtrier*, she pulled herself to her feet. Holding on to a nearby sapling, she tested her ankle. She had felt it twist under her when she fell, and she would be lost if it were broken.

A sharp pain shot through it, but she did not fall. She could make it. She had to.

She had taken one step toward the brush when she realized she was not alone. Fear seized her, such a blood-draining fear that she dared not look around.

"So . . . you are better?" mocked Baldwin from the other side of the clearing. "Gervais will be glad to know this." He licked his lips with a wet tongue.

She sighed. She must abandon her attempt at escape, but only for the moment. The sanctuary that Raoul would provide had become an obsession with her. She cared not what she must do to escape Mehun's men.

"I shall tell him myself," she said coldly.

Baldwin started toward her, but Gervais was right on his heels. Throwing down a pair of straight branches, he said, "I see our effort was wasted. You will not need a litter."

"I cannot ride farther," she said flatly, holding out her ankle. Gervais eyed the swelling with tight lips and grave eyes.

"We'll see about that," he said grimly. "It is too dangerous to stay the night in this forest. I might almost think you planned this mishap."

"Why should I?" she said. "My life is over. There is simply no place to go."

"You could go back to Mehun and marry the baron," said Gauthier. "It seems little enough to me."

"It would to you," she snapped. "It is no use to tell you how I loathe that man."

Baldwin giggled. "That's no barrier to marriage," he chortled. "Many a maid has loathed her man until he taught her better!"

"Enough," said Gervais quietly, and Baldwin returned to sullenness. "We'll camp here for the night," said Gervais, "and I should like your word that you won't give me any trouble, lady."

"Why should I?" she said sweetly. "The injury that keeps

me from riding will also prevent me from venturing into the jaws of wolves. A campfire and supper will appeal mightily to me."

She turned to look into the mysterious darkness of the forest behind her. The great oak trees and silver-gray beech trunks stretched like pillars to heaven, curtaining the forest floor against the light of the soft blue twilight sky. Here at hand the shadows interlaced ominously, like a horde of evil spirits.

Her shiver was not feigned.

Long after their supper of cheese, a knife-hewn loaf, and a freshly caught rabbit, Solange lay awake. Not until she heard the separate noises of four men snoring, did she dare to move.

She had feared Gervais might tie her wrists for safety's sake, but he had evidently believed she feared the wolves. That was true enough, but she feared Saint Vergillia more.

She had inched a yard away from the fire when she became aware of an alteration in the breathing around her. She froze, waiting until the wakeful one would lapse into sleep again. Soon the breathing all returned to subdued regularity.

Sending up a prayer of gratitude, she began to edge away again, still lying on the ground. A yard and one more, and she would chance rising to her feet and fading into the terrors of the dark forest. She turned her head toward the shadows, to estimate the distance between her and the end of the clearing.

And he was upon her.

Baldwin, feigning sleep to deceive Gervais and Solange both, stretched his length upon her with a rush, pinning her to the ground beneath him, covering her open mouth with his hand.

He began to pull with his free hand at her bliaut, and she felt the fine silk tear. There was soon nothing between her flesh and his padded leather undershirt.

5

The rough leather was cold, chilling her to the marrow of her bones. The shock lasted as long as a heartbeat, holding her immobile for a fraction of a moment. Feeling his greasy tongue lapping like a dog's around her lips, loathing swept her. Rough, calloused hands kneaded her breasts, a bruising knee butted incessantly against her legs. She fought back mutely. Baldwin invaded her mouth with his disgusting tongue, and she could not breathe. Her thighs writhed against him, but her movements only inflamed him.

She twisted her head from side to side, but his mouth clung to hers like a limpet on a rock, gagging her. A tide of nausea swept over her. Suddenly she tasted blood and realized that her teeth had penetrated Baldwin's slobbering lip. With a muffled curse he fell to one side, wiping his mouth with the back of his hand. She heard herself begging, "Please leave me alone!"

"You vixen! You'll not balk me! You'll cry for mercy this night. Many's the wench begs Baldwin to take her. You're no better than they, for all your fancy airs!"

His hot breath whispered words in her ear that she didn't understand, but their import was plain enough. He finished, "Let the nuns have what's left of you!"

He arched his body and, even in the darkness, she knew he was jerking at his leather shirt and pulling down his chausses. He fell against her, already hard and pulsing. His hand clamped over her mouth, bruising her lips against her teeth. Horror gripped her mind.

She did not know exactly what happened then. She had only one thought—*escape*. With the strength of one last desperate wave of loathing, she twisted beneath him, hearing the tearing of cloth where his knees pinned her torn bliaut to the ground. She clawed at his back, his shoulders, wherever her fingers could reach, feeling the skin rip beneath her nails. Her knee came up.

She was free. It took a moment to realize that Baldwin's weight no longer imprisoned her. She grabbed at the ground for a weapon, but could feel only cloth. Her fingers closed upon wool and fur—her mantle.

Baldwin groped for her, catching her arm. His fingers tightened in fierce anger. His purpose had changed. She was sure that he now cared only to kill her.

She could not twist loose this time. Baldwin was on his feet, dragging her up to stand swaying beside him, her arms pinioned behind her. She clung to the cold comfort of her mantle.

"Now, you she-devil, you won't get away again. I'll have you, no mistake about that, until I'm weary. And you'll beg me for death."

He panted more threats, but she no longer heard. He forced her to walk, dragging her away from the campfire. Hadn't anyone heard the terrific struggle?

They must have heard. No doubt they feared to interrupt Baldwin at play. A dangerous animal at bay, even *le Meurtrier* could be no worse. What shivering cowards were these? There would be no help for her.

She stumbled, but his grip kept her from falling headlong. At last he stopped. He threw her to the ground and her cloak fell beneath her. The impact of the fall knocked her breath away. He dropped to his knees beside her and ripped the last of her shredded bliaut away. Shivering with terror, she moaned, writhing in anticipation of pain. The cloak worked from under her, and twigs pushed into her bare back.

The light from the campfire did not penetrate this far, but Baldwin could see. Like a predator he had night vision. His hands moved roughly over her, pinching, cruel.

If Baldwin had turned beast, then she must be as alert as any prey. Quick as a leveret, she pulled a corner of her cloak over her thigh. The touch of her own familiar cloak gave her hope. She had but one chance. She must not fail.

She put all her strength into one sinuous movement. Swift as the eels in the Petitmer, she clutched the cloak and tossed it over his head.

She darted away, her naked body milky pale in the darkness.

"By the Cross," came Baldwin's muffled voice, as he clawed at the cloak, "I'll teach you a lesson you won't forget."

She ran. Baldwin pounded heavily behind her. In the darkness, it was like running under a blanket. She fell headlong more than once, the dry sticks of the forest scraping her skin, thrusting at her body. She felt blood from one long gash, sticky along her thigh.

She ran and ran, with leaden feet and without direction. Finally, pain like a dagger in her side stopped her. Her breath came wheezing, in shuddering gasps. She could do no more. She fell over a fallen limb, and sprawled her length upon the ground once more. Instinct prompted her to roll into a ball, revealing her whiteness as little as she could.

Holding back a sobbing breath she listened for Baldwin, inexorably behind her, stumbling nearer and nearer.

Something was hard under her cheek. Her fingers closed upon it. It was a dead limb, twice as thick as a man's finger. Cautiously, she felt the end of it. Small pieces of decayed wood shredded under her fingers. Though the limb was brittle and old, it might serve her.

Baldwin's footsteps thudded near. She was used to the darkness now, and she could see, against the faint redness of the faraway campfire, the bulk of the man. He moved erratically, like an animal in pain, head swinging from side to side, his breathing gross and labored. He did not see her. He stopped a yard away to search the darkness, to listen for her breathing. He started forward again.

Now!

She thrust the limb, holding it steady with both hands, between his feet. The crack of the dead wood sounded like a cannon in the night. Baldwin's feet shuffled frantically, and he fell, headlong, like a giant oak in a storm. Fell— and lay motionless.

Relief crept slowly into her mind. Baldwin lay, harmless now, so close she could reach out and touch his booted heels. Now that the danger was past, she felt the icy wind of winter on her overheated skin. She began to shiver uncontrollably and could not stop.

At length she stirred. She must move lest she freeze.

Having escaped from Baldwin, she must not throw her life away now. She longed fiercely for her fur-lined mantle. Dared she go back for it? No. She did not know where Baldwin had dropped it.

She moved to her knees, hugging herself for warmth. She must escape before Baldwin stirred. She listened for the sound of his breathing. All was silent. After what seemed a long time, she crept from her hiding place, on hands and knees until a pitiful whimpering sound stopped her, and she trembled. Careful to avoid touching his body, holding her breath, she listened again. The whimpering stopped, and she understood it had been her own voice.

She listened again, this time for sounds of pursuit from the campfire. They were indeed her stepfather's men. She was convinced that the sound of her struggle with Baldwin had wakened at least one of the other three. No one had interfered with Baldwin. Indeed, she would be lucky if they did not each want a turn, after Baldwin had had his!

She shivered but kept moving. She must escape. But she would not get far in this cold night, clad only in her own skin. The wind, even gentled by the forest around her, was as sharp as a boar's tooth.

She could not think very clearly. A part of her mind told her she must flee, that Gervais would find her and drag her back to the campfire and probably finish what Baldwin had left undone.

The cold seeped up through her bruised knees, into her bones, and she could not stop shaking. She lost her balance and fell forward, thrusting out her hands involuntarily to break her fall.

Her fingers fell upon soft fur. A scream rose in her throat as she snatched her hands back. She must have touched a night creature scurrying on the forest floor. But the creature did not move.

Her cloak! Baldwin must have carried it, unthinkingly, after he freed himself from its folds.

But Baldwin's body pinned the cloak fast beneath him. She tugged gently at first, and then with increasing violence until she feared the fabric would tear. So close to the life-giving warmth, and yet she could not reach it.

She must! She crept forward on her hands and knees.

She touched, very gingerly, the hulk of her assailant. The bare back, the torn woolen hose, the leather boots. Painstakingly she worked her cloak from under Baldwin's boots. It took a long time, and she stopped often to see whether he was waking.

All the while Baldwin did not move. She could not even hear his breathing. Was he dead? It was but a whisper in her mind. With a catch in her breath, she crossed herself. It was not the first dead man she had seen, but it was the first to die—if he indeed were dead—by her hand.

Another fit of shivering seized her. Tightening her courage, and thinking firmly of the rigors of the convent which awaited her, she worked at the inert body. She did not know how long it took her to push the huge bulk onto its side.

Only once during that long effort did her heart fail her. His arm, limp as she seized it, seemed suddenly to stiffen, as though gathering itself to grab her. He was not dead, then! But, sorely wounded in his fall, he might yet die. But she could not call for help for him. Soon enough they would miss him from the campfire and start a search.

With renewed desperation, she gave one last great shove, and the hulk fell over on its back. The groan that lingered in the air could have been hers. Or Baldwin's. She could not tell.

But the cloak was free! She snatched it up, trembling with excitement, and covered herself. The fur was soft against her bare skin, around her shoulders, hips, thighs. With her nakedness covered, and Baldwin at her feet, hope began to soar again.

With shaking fingers she fumbled for the silver clasp at the throat but found only shredded cloth where the clasp had been. Holding the cloak together with hands at throat and waist, she edged away from Baldwin's prostrate frame and into the darker shadow of the trees.

Keeping the faint light of the fire behind her to serve as direction, she moved cautiously farther into the deep woods. Fear of Gervais, of Baldwin, momentarily receded. It left room for other fears.

She paused often to listen. There were no sounds of pursuit behind her, and no sounds of heavy bestial breathing either. She stumbled over a fallen log. The mishap started an unwelcome train of broken thoughts. Vivid pictures jostled each other in her mind, one replacing another in quick succession. Fox dens abounded in the rocks near the edge of the forest. She could fall into one and break her leg. She would then die a far-from-merciful death. Saint Joseph, defend me! she cried silently.

The moon rose, touching the upper reaches of the forest with echoes of light. The lower regions, where she felt her way, were by contrast even darker than before.

Her thoughts circled again. *Baldwin had lain so quietly.* Dead? She did not think so. There had been that sudden tightening of the muscles in his arm. Just so did a rabbit shudder convulsively in the throes of death. She shook her head to free her mind of morbidity. She needed every bit of her strength.

She had been told that a road somewhere in the forest crossed the road to Saint Vergillia's. She had no idea how far away that other road might be, but it was said to lead to Bourges, where the king was. Where Raoul was.

She was so tired. She fell again, and this time could not get up. Her exhausted limbs refused to obey. She would rest just for a minute. She had fallen into a hollow left by the uprooting of a great tree. The trunk itself still lay at the edge of the depression. Numbly, but as meticulously as though she were sleeping on her own pallet in Belvent, she arranged herself on soft fur, pulling the rest of the cloak over her. It felt like a shroud.

She slept.

But she wakened. The moon looked quite red in the distance. Red? The moon was the wrong color and in the wrong place. Unless she had walked in circles, as one does in the forest, and returned to Gervais's campfire. Her mouth went dry.

Rising to her feet, joints stiff, she staggered toward the moon that was not a moon. She must find out whose campfire it was. Were these travelers who might help her? Or was it the campfire she had left?

She drew closer until she could study the campfire. It was smaller than Gervais's. There were three men sleeping near the fire for warmth. But she did not know them.

Who were they? She could not tell. But she knew—yet did not know *how* she knew—that if she could just get to the fire, she would be safe.

She reached the edge of the tiny clearing. The sleepers did not move. A horse whinnied then, nearby, startling her. She gasped.

The three men awoke instantly, leaping as one man back from the firelight. The tallest of the three, half in shadow, stared in her direction. She was not conscious of her wraithlike appearance, the pale gray cloak flowing like mist from her shoulders, her tangled silvery hair.

Pointing his lance steadily in her direction, the tall man spoke. "Who are you? Mélusine? The witch of the wood?"

6

Of the three men around the fire, clearly the knight with the lance was the leader. Taken aback by his accusation, she tried to speak. But her throat was dry and, though her lips moved, she could not make a sound.

"Speak!" adjured the knight. "Speak, lest I see whether you are real or spirit. My lance—"

"Aimery!" said the second man. His voice was gentle in admonition but held a certain authority. Suddenly a small gust of wind bent down to the embers of the campfire, stirring the ashes and making the coals glow again. The breeze brought to Solange the strong and unmistakable scent of roasted leveret.

"I'm hungry!" she croaked helplessly.

The knight's lance lowered, and he chuckled. "Come to the fire, then, my lady witch. Do you, Garin, give place to our guest. Rainard, bring food."

Solange hesitated but then, moved by the aroma of roasted meat, stumbled closer and sat on the billet of wood beside the fire where the second man indicated she should sit.

The meat was cold by now and the ale was tepid, but she wolfed it down as though she had not eaten for days. That was the simple truth, she realized. Except for bread and cheese this noon—how far away that seemed!—she had sent away her meals untouched ever since Mehun had threatened her, half a week before.

Now she licked the last grease from her fingers with deep concentration. Then she gave a sigh of contentment and looked up at her hosts. There were the three she had seen first, and apparently no others. The knight looked her over. The second man, Garin, wore a long friar's robe. Rainard was a squire. They sat in a protective half-circle before her, watching her with vibrant curiosity.

Their intent gaze struck her with amusement. "Do you think I will dissolve into thin air," she chuckled, "like a vision of Mélusine?"

"Not very likely," said Aimery with a reluctant grin. "I have never understood that the witch of the wood ate like a man home from the hunt."

"Aimery," protested the friar. "Do not jest so. I believe this lady suffers, else she would not be roaming the woods at this time of the night."

"My quip was ill-timed. Lady, if your appetite is satisfied," he said with faint sarcasm, "do you think you could tell us who you are?"

She sighed. She must think quickly, decide how much of her story she wished to tell. She did not know these men. They were a strange troop of travelers, to be sure. A knight, a squire bound to Aimery, and a man of God. She remembered something strange, too. When Garin made way for her to sit at the fire, she had caught a glimpse of metal through a slit in his woolen robe. A mailed friar? How could this be?

She must go carefully. They could send her back to her stepfather. They could turn her over to Gervais, in whose custody she should be, by law. They could even take her on to the convent themselves. She feared to reveal too much, even the fact that she wished now to make her way to Bourges.

"I do not think my story would interest you much," she said with an easy air. "I am on my way—" Confusion overtook her. She did not know the name of any town far enough away from Bourges to make a safe lie.

"On your way where, my child?" prompted the friar gently. "Perhaps," he added, when she remained silent, "we should not ask of you what we are not, ourselves, willing to impart. I was born Garin de Montvert, third son of the count of Montvert. I have been home—that is, to my former home—to be at my father's side when he died. Now I return to my order's mother house at Citeaux. You may call me Brother Garin. I have chosen the church as my life."

"Brother Garin," she acknowledged the introduction.

"My oldest brother has succeeded to the estates and honors of our father, and my next brother, Aimery, whom you see before you, is at one with me in leaving our home."

"She is not interested in this," scowled Aimery. "My squire, Rainard de Nivelon."

It did not help to know their names. What manner of men were they? That was the real question, and she had as yet no answer to it. She searched Aimery's face for some clue.

Aimery moved restlessly, conscious of her gaze on him. His face was in shadow as he bent forward, leaning his elbows on his knees, purposely preventing her from reading his thoughts. His apparent skepticism, ready to tarnish her story, made her falter. The words died on her lips.

Suddenly, reaction set in. From the depths of her despair —hounded by d'Yves, sent captive to a convent, escaping Baldwin, weary and starved—she was now fed, and, for the moment at least, safe. Nettled by Aimery de Montvert's clear suspicions, she felt indignation rising in her. How dared he presume to judge her? She was not bound to him.

She needed only a safe conduct to the king's court. Her reasons for going there were not subject to Aimery's approval. She would show him how little she regarded his opinions. Moved to retaliate in the only way she could, she turned away from him, pointedly, and addressed the friar. Fixing her eyes on Garin, she began to tell her story.

"My father had vowed, for reasons I don't know, to go on pilgrimage to the shrine of Saint James of Compostela in Spain, which was not too far away. Soon afterward some pilgrims, returning from the Holy Land, stopped to rest with us. Their tales—well, my father could not rest until he set out to see the wonders of the holy places in Outremer."

"Only one set of pilgrims?" queried Brother Garin mildly. "There must be hundreds on the road going to Jerusalem and returning, year in and year out. Why did he heed this set of travelers?"

"Belvent is not on the main track of the travelers," explained Solange. "It is rare that we see company, except for pedlars."

She continued earnestly. "My father betrothed me, for my safety, he said, while he went on pilgrimage, since he was going much farther than he had at first planned. That was five years ago and we have not seen him since. He hasn't returned from Outremer, nor—," she added in a low voice—"will he. My stepfather says he saw my father die. But that doesn't change my betrothal, does it?" She stretched her hand out to Brother Garin. "You would know. My betrothal stands as a contract, does it not, even though my father and his chaplain, who went with him, cannot bear witness?"

"It surely seems so," said Brother Garin, fingering his lower lip in a thoughtful manner.

"So far," interrupted Aimery harshly, lifting his head, "I see no reason that explains why you roam the forest, quite far from Belvent, as I believe, dressed in a tattered cloak. And nothing else."

His glance lingered expressively on her bare leg. Quickly she covered her knees. But it was too late to hide the fact that she wore nothing under her squirrel-lined mantle.

"I'm explaining," she said with a touch of asperity. She had nearly reached the end of her endurance, and while the meat had restored her somewhat, the additional strain of convincing a man she was sure did not want to be convinced of her honesty was nearly too much.

"My father, as I said, had betrothed me. My mother remarried in unseemly haste and now my stepfather, without any right, broke the betrothal contract."

Both brothers stirred. She had captured their interest. A contract, especially one blessed by the Church, was the basis for all dealings in their world. One did not dishonor such a contract lightly.

More confidently, she went on. She told of the baron's arrival and of the assumption that she would tamely submit to a bridegroom not chosen by her father. She told of Mehun's threat, and of the beginning of her journey to Saint Vergillia's convent.

Brother Garin said sharply, "Saint Vergillia's? They would not take a girl, especially one well born, simply to punish her."

"I think," said Solange simply, "I was meant to stay there. You see, Belvent has no heirs except for me. My stepfather would therefore have a free hand."

"But," said Aimery, "you have not arrived at Saint Vergillia's. Your escort?"

Voice lowered, she said, "I escaped."

"From four armed men?" exclaimed Aimery, in disbelief. "You're sure you're not a fairy spirit but, in truth, flesh and blood?"

With grim humor, she answered, "Too much so—that was much of the trouble!"

Aimery looked directly at her and she caught what might have been a smile. She had no need to tell him, or the friar about Baldwin. But her eyes darkened as she remembered that she had probably killed the man. Somewhere soon she must find a priest to absolve her—

"She is exhausted!" said Garin, with quick sympathy. "See, tears course down her cheeks. Truly, Aimery, we must take her under our protection and get her to a safe place."

"To the court? Take this . . . this, as she herself says, very earthly woman with us on a three-day journey? I doubt not tongues will wag at both ends!"

"Nonetheless," said Garin firmly, "we cannot turn her over to the nuns at Saint Vergillia's. She would not do there at all."

"Nor can we restore her to her armed guard," said Aimery, grudgingly agreeing. "If she has been able to outwit them, then I will not deliver her again to their care."

Rainard spoke then, eyes alight. "She is so beautiful."

Aimery glanced at him. "Very true. We must get her

clothed decently, so I can think better what we must do."
He laughed ruefully. "I am not sure, after all, that the
noble lady is not at least kin to Mélusine. She sets my
senses reeling, in truth."

Brother Garin said dryly, "That is surely a very human
quality. I begin to have some hope for you after all. I've
wondered how long you would live a monk's life."

"I have not forsaken women!"

"Might as well have done so, for all the good you get."

Solange noticed that Aimery stiffened in resentment.
"Enough, Garin. You do not understand."

"Forgive me," Garin said, inflexibly, "but it seems to
me that you are indeed bewitched. But not by this lady
here."

What might have happened next, Solange never knew.
For the brothers stopped short in an attitude of listening.
Solange could hear nothing, but Aimery's hearing was
more acute. He made an urgent gesture to Rainard. The
boy leaped to his feet and swiftly took Solange by the
wrist, pulling her to her feet. "Hurry," he said, "away
from the fire."

He dragged her into the shadow of the trees. "You'll
have to turn squire," he whispered urgently. "I'll get you
some clothes. We're about the same size."

He rummaged in saddlebags. She could hear the
scratching sounds of scrambling in the leather pouches. He
handed her garments as he found them.

"Here, put these on. Chausses, I think they'll fit. Here's
a chemise. Hurry!" She took the white linen garment.
Turning away from the youth, she dropped her cloak from
her bare shoulders. With fumbling fingers she dropped the
chemise over her head. Rainard was taller than she by
half a foot, and his undershirt fell halfway between knee
and ankle.

Then came the chausses, two legs of woven linen joined
at the waist. Over these, Rainard made her pull on his only
pair of *braccae*, the trousers he kept to wear for the hunt,
or in battle. A simple tunic, over the head, with sleeves to
her fingertips, finished her attire. Thank goodness Rainard
had a larger frame than hers!

The last item Rainard found was his round felt cap.

45

"Take this; cover up your hair." Roughly he pushed her long pale hair under the hat. Finally he pulled upward at the crown and turned down the small brim to make more room for her hair.

For a diffident lad, he was remarkably dictatorial, she thought grimly. But she obeyed, knowing her safety depended on these men. She had no doubt that the sound Aimery had heard was Gervais, searching for her. Even if it were not he, she could little afford another stranger's eyes resting with speculation upon her.

It was, after all, Gervais.

She could hear his voice greeting the two men at the campfire. Rainard enjoined her to silence with a finger on her lips and then, with a gesture, ordered her to stay where she was. He slipped back to the fire.

"Your business?" Aimery addressed the newcomer with cool courtesy.

"I seek a runaway," said Gervais. "Gave us the slip, and I dare not return empty-handed."

Brother Garin said, "How old is the lad?"

"Lad?" Gervais turned to him, noting the friar's habit. "It is not a lad, Brother, but a troublesome girl."

"You could not keep track of a girl?" jeered Aimery.

"This maid is not ordinary," explained Gervais. "She feigned an injury. I had not thought her so deceitful." Thoughtfully, he added, "Nor so desperate. Have you seen her?"

Aimery said, "I do not recall a child alone on this road. Do you, Brother?"

"We were not on this road," interrupted Gervais. "On the road yonder, from Belvent toward Saint Vergillia's. And no child is she!" He laughed sharply. "A temptation to Saint Anthony himself! Have you seen her?"

"No," said Aimery flatly.

"Are you three alone?" Gervais demanded, clearly suspicious.

"You question me?" added Aimery softly. "I said I do not recall a woman alone."

Gervais stood his ground. Apparently, thought Solange, his fear of Mehun was greater than his respect for Aimery.

"Your squire, I see. But there is someone else moving in the shadows."

"The horses, sir," said Rainard stoutly.

"I know a horse from a slim lass," said Gervais with contempt.

"My own servant, a foolish boy," said Brother Garin, surprisingly. "For a misdeed, I have imposed upon him a vow of silence."

"I wish to see him."

"Now, this is beyond tolerance," protested Aimery, his hand dropping toward his sheathed dagger.

"But I do not believe," said Brother Garin, hastily interrupting his brother, "that you would wish to be the cause of the boy's breaking his vows?"

"Only to see him, Brother. I will not require him to speak," said Gervais stubbornly.

Aimery moved toward Gervais. Solange crept to the shadow of a tree where she could see better and still remain hidden. The two men, Aimery the taller and better built; Gervais more stocky, faced each other.

"You will not force your wishes upon us?" said Aimery very softly.

Gervais appeared to consider doing just that. But at last, he drew back. "My men and I will perforce return to Belvent," he said slowly. His brow furrowed in indecision.

"Without the girl," said Brother Garin.

"Without the girl," agreed Gervais. Then he smiled. Surprisingly, he raised his voice. "I believe I can persuade my companions—all *three* of them—to return without a further search. We shall start in the morning, since one of my men cannot mount his horse until morning. At least."

Solange, hidden in the dark, sent Gervais silent thanks. Gervais had not been fooled by her rescuers. Instead, he was setting her at liberty, so to speak, and telling her that Baldwin had been found and would live.

She was not a murderess. She would sleep better tonight.

7

The sun was just tipping the eastern horizon with gold when they took the road. Solange, still wearing Rainard's squire's clothing, had taken her share of the preparations for the journey.

"Watch out for a trap," Aimery cautioned roughly. "I am not at all sure we persuaded your knightly guardian that we spoke the truth. If they see you taking your ease while we labor, they might wonder what manner of squire possesses such privilege." A frown darkened his face, and her heart sank. "If I were chief of an escort whose hostage was missing, I think I might well investigate such a strange arrangement as a squire who did not serve his master."

She faltered. "And ambush us on the road? Oh, no! I must not be caught!" She looked wildly around her for an avenue of escape.

Aimery grabbed her arm harshly. "You're under my protection now. I won't let them take you. What kind of man do you think I am?"

"I don't know," she said sincerely.

She bent to lift the weighty leather pouch at her feet. It must be filled with rocks, she thought as she struggled to get it off the ground. With a supreme hoist, she raised the pouch waist-high. It began to slip toward the ground again, and she brought one knee up to help support the burden.

Balancing the load precariously, she measured with her eye the formidable distance between the hook on the saddle and the handle of the pouch. She tried to swing her burden as high as the hook. She missed. The pouch began to slide to the ground again. Suddenly, her hands were empty—Aimery held the pouch.

She released her breath in a puff, white in the chilly air. "What's in that bag?" she demanded. Then she remembered. "What if someone saw you doing my work?"

"Don't scoff," he warned, "lest I think the nuns could mend your manners!" The words were sharp, and she started with sudden alarm, but the light in his deep-set gray eyes reassured her. "Besides," he continued, "anyone watching you struggle might think the bag is full of gold, and believe it better in his hands than in mine."

As though he held a mere handful of dry leaves, he hooked the pouch onto the harness on the pack horse.

"Th-thank you," she said in a small voice.

He frowned, looking down at her. "Did you think I would hand you over to the nuns?" he asked, serious now.

"I didn't know," she said, eyeing him thoughtfully. "A week ago I did not expect to be on my way to the convent yesterday. Nor did I expect anything else that's happened." Her voice faded away and he had to stoop to hear the last words.

He dropped his hand lightly on her shoulder, "Don't worry," he said. "I'm aware that you're not fashioned for convent life." He chuckled. "Besides," he added, "I've gone to some trouble over you already. I'm not anxious to see my efforts wasted."

She turned away. She did not understand him. One moment he was kind to her, and the next, he seemed to think no more of her than he would of a stray dog. A nuisance, that's all he considered her. No more. But, she bit her lip in vexation, what more did she want from him?

She busied herself and Rainard came to help her with the pack horse. "You're not pulling the straps tight enough," he told her. "Here, do it like this."

She smiled at him. "Thank you. I'll be glad to get started and away from this place."

Rainard watched her for a moment. Quickly casting a sweeping glance behind him and seeing Aimery busy at the far side of the campfire, he said, "Do not let my lord's manner distress you, my lady. He is always a-fret when he is separated from the object of his devotion."

She stammered, "I . . . did not know Sir Aimery was wed."

Rainard gave her a look of pity. "No more is he. But his chosen lady has smiled upon him, so of course . . ." His voice trailed away.

Aimery suddenly stood within earshot. The man moved like a cat, she thought. "Explaining me, Rainard? I need no intermediary with any lass, boy!" Rainard vanished. Aimery surveyed Solange from head to foot. She was conscious suddenly of her garb. Unreasonably, under the glittering eyes of her rescuer, she wished she were clothed in silvershot white samite. And she was conscious of an overweening curiosity. She would like to see his "chosen lady"!

Abruptly he turned away. Over his shoulder he shot the words. "I'll brook no more delay. We must travel on at once."

Prodded by their impatient leader, the little troop was quickly on its way. Aimery led, on his dappled gray palfrey, a mettlesome Gascon horse. This was peacetime, by which it was meant that, for the moment, no barons in the neighborhood were in arms against their neighbors, so Aimery wore only light armor on the road.

Rainard followed his knight on his own palfrey, leading the great war-horse Falcrone, bearing only a high saddle, unadorned, and stirrups of silver. It was a modest set of trappings. Aimery was landless, she surmised, hoping to make his fortune by his prowess in battle. But somehow the simple description did not entirely fit him.

"You must ride behind me, lady," said Brother Garin apologetically, as he mounted his shiny black mule. "It is not seemly, but we must maintain our little game. You understand?"

"Of course, Brother Garin," said Solange. "I am grateful for the opportunity to ride, even on this *ronçin*." She surveyed the ill-favored animal, an ordinary horse, fit only for servants. Her lips twisted sharply. "I feared your brother might make me walk!" she added waspishly.

Lifting an eyebrow, Brother Garin said, "Do not make a hasty judgment of him, lady, I beg you. My brother is without peer, except for a few minor faults."

"He could not be your brother, otherwise," said Solange. "Don't worry, Brother Garin. I will do my best not to gall him." She mounted the nag. "Although," she added thoughtfully, "the need to teach him a lesson cries to heaven."

She glanced at Brother Garin. His expression was full of wrinkled apprehension. She burst into ringing laughter. "Don't worry, Brother Garin. I'll be good."

To demonstrate, she cast her eyes down in a pose of demure meekness. Brother Garin was moved to say, "Thank God I'm a vowed celibate. The man who marries you will wish he'd never been born, I don't doubt. We'd best take the road. Aimery's already out of sight."

They rode for some hours toward the rising sun. The troop, burdened as it was, could keep up with Aimery only by hard, concentrated riding. The *ronçin* was unused to such a fast pace and, though willing enough, lagged farther and farther behind the rest. Solange, lost in thought, did not notice until she was brought up sharply by Aimery thundering back to meet her. He raised his helm, and she could see the dark mood that rode him, mirrored in his rugged features.

"Planning to escape as soon as you're behind me, out of sight?" he said, reining up and turning to ride beside her.

"Escape?" cried Solange, her voice husky. "On *this?*"

"I'm glad to see your spirits have revived so much that you feel no need for gratitude."

Feeling her cheeks warming, she could think of nothing to say. They rode on together, Aimery holding his mount to her pace.

"Of course I am grateful," she said finally, in a low voice. "I admit I am not overly used to the feeling, but you must give me time."

"What were you thinking about when I came back?"

"You would not be interested."

"On the contrary," he asserted with a sincerity that surprised him. "I want to know."

"I was wondering what I would do first when I see the king. How far is it yet?"

"Three days' journey."

"Three days!"

"If we keep a smart pace."

They were already traveling faster than before. Brother Garin and Rainard were in sight again, ahead of them.

"I wonder how soon I shall be wed," she ventured, but she had lost Aimery's attention. A frown creased between his heavy eyebrows. She followed the direction of his gaze across the valley. Reining to a halt, she saw the tawny grass in the valley below. The road, wending east from their camp of the night before, cut across the woods and emerged at the east edge of the forest. The stream through this valley was not the Petitmer. Suddenly she was a stranger, in a land far away from all she had ever known.

Bells rang in the air. Across the valley, situated in a wide plain, stood a square, solid building. From here she could see only two slits of windows, and a stumpy belltower. It was more like a fortress than any other kind of building, and yet the harsh bells told her it was Saint Vergillia's convent.

"Damp, unhealthy air in the bottomlands," pronounced Brother Garin, joining them. "And your stepfather was sending you here?"

"To die, I have no doubt," agreed Solange in a light voice.

"We're wasting time," Aimery broke in harshly.

They set their horses into a smart canter, and no further word was spoken until they made camp for the night.

They turned aside from the road to a rocky ledge above the valley. Solange, unused to riding hours at near gallop on a breakbone nag, nearly fell when she slid down from the saddle. Brother Garin caught her. Again she felt the hardness of mail beneath his friar's homespun robe, but she was too tired to wonder at it now.

They feasted on freshly-caught hare. "A fine repast," said Brother Garin. "When one thinks of all the folk in the world who have nothing so fine . . ."

"Then don't think of them," said Aimery good-naturedly. "There are pleasanter things to think of. You agree, lady?"

"Assuredly," she said quickly. "I could be dining on black bread and water at this moment." Involuntarily she looked over her shoulder in the direction of Saint Vergillia's.

Even before she was finished eating she was overcome by the warmth of the fire. Her flight of the night before had left its traces in sooty shadows beneath her eyes. She forgot the meat held in her fingers, and the voices of her fireside companions faded into faraway sounds. Phrases drifted to her.

"A temptation . . . she's been sent to you. . . ." That was surely Brother Garin.

"A child," said a scoffing voice. Was it Aimery? "No comparison with the queen, whom I worship."

"Take care, lest your idol take your soul into pagan ways."

Solange was nearly asleep. The leg of hare dropped with a thud from limp fingers. Someone lifted her, laid her down, and covered her with a blanket. Aimery. His hand brushed away the fair hair from her forehead. She slept at once, and did not hear Aimery's muttered remark when he returned to the campfire.

"You are righter than you thought, Garin. If I had met her but a year ago, well . . ."

"There is a time for all things," rejoined Brother Garin. "And the time for this will come."

Aimery glanced sharply at him, but seeing his brother's serene face, stifled a cutting retort.

They traveled on the next day, always tending to the east. The road wound around hills, over rocky scree, through fords.

Other travelers appeared on the road now that they were closer to the great city. Solange pulled her felt cap closer about her ears, making sure her long, silvery hair was securely tucked inside. Few whom they overtook heeded the small mounted troop that passed them at a hard canter.

But toward noon on the second day, they were overtaken by a small army, riding as though devil-driven. The leader slumped in the saddle of his palfrey, slouched as though to cosset a wounded shoulder. Five knights rode with him, and an assortment of ill-favored retainers brought up the rear. Horses and riders filled the road, the thundering of their hooves resounding in the air.

"By the saints!" muttered Aimery. "They intend to run us down!"

Hastily he herded his small troop aside to let the swifter travelers pass. Solange watched them come. As they pounded nearer, suddenly she pictured again the escort accompanying her intended bridegroom a week ago. Her eyes narrowed against the bright light as she edged closer to Brother Garin. Now she could make out the device on the shield of the leader, the rider favoring a recent injury. She saw, as her mouth dried, the hawk of d'Yves.

In breathless panic she averted her face. The Baron Conon d'Yves swept past. She could not mistake that cruel slash of mouth; the beak of a nose, the duplicating hawk on his pennant. She could almost feel his eyes penetrating her disguise, recognizing her. She was not sure she had turned away in time.

Later, over their meager supper of bread and cheese, she timidly suggested that d'Yves might have seen her. Brother Garin stoutly denied the possibility. "I do not think he recognized you at all. He did not stop, and he would have, don't you think?"

Aimery agreed, somewhat absently. During the day his spirits had seemed to droop ever lower. But if he were the queen's lover, should he not be more cheerful, coming closer to his paramour? There was much about love, Solange reflected, that she did not understand.

"But if he had," pointed out Aimery, rousing from his abstraction, "what then? He would not take you from us by force."

"Would he?" seconded Brother Garin anxiously.

"Truly, I do not know," said Solange. "There were six of them all armored. I do not wish you to run into peril for my sake." She looked at her rescuers anxiously. "Perhaps I had better leave you."

"And go where?" said Aimery. "Truly, methinks you are more of a fool than even I thought!"

"Aimery!" said Brother Garin sharply.

The apology came hard to Aimery, but he got it out at last. "I am sorry, lady. I spoke too harshly. There is no question of your leaving us. We have charged ourselves with this duty, and we will see it through."

Small comfort, thought Solange, her eyes filling with tears. A duty. That was all she was.

"What will you do, lady, at Bourges?" asked Brother Garin. "We will arrive tomorrow. Do you have someone to go to?"

"Only the man I am to marry," she answered. "I am sure Raoul will arrange something until we can be wed."

"I had forgotten that you were betrothed," confessed Brother Garin.

"I had not," said Aimery. "I will see you to his care. Raoul, you said?"

"Raoul de Puiseaux."

Aimery and Garin sat as though paralyzed. Neither spoke for some minutes, while she stared at them in bewilderment. Rainard, too, glanced uneasily from one to the other.

"You have not seen him for some time?" suggested Brother Garin in a flat voice.

"Not since he left for the court." She started to her feet. "What is the matter? Is he *dead*?" Her voice rose shrilly.

"No." Aimery's voice was dull.

"Then what?"

Garin said, with the obvious intention of soothing her, "It is only that he is so often gone on errands for the king. He travels the length of the royal domains." He fell silent.

"Then he is a trusted servant of the king's!" Solange cried. She sank again to the ground, and leaned with relief against the saddle behind her.

"Let us hope," added Brother Garin, "that he may be found at Bourges when we arrive. Have you any special knowledge, Aimery, of his whereabouts? Would the king have sent him traveling again?"

Aimery looked levelly at his brother. "I have none, as to his traveling. Nor do I know anything more about the man."

His remark seemed curiously framed, and Solange studied him for a moment. He met her eyes, finally, and said, "Best sleep now. A long day tomorrow. Don't worry, lady. You will find your Raoul."

She had to be content with those words.

8

On the afternoon of the third day, their pace slowed. The road was increasingly clogged with travelers journeying in the same direction as they.

The king had many vassals, and he and his court traveled constantly from one to another, as food and supplies demanded. His reluctant host now was Pierre de la Chartre, the archbishop of Bourges, whose ecclesiastical palace was bursting with "guests."

The king's court was enormous, of course, and a multitude of mouths had to be fed. Just now Aimery's troop were overtaking cart after cart, laden with foodstuffs. Two-wheeled carts, small enough to be pulled by women, were filled with pale green cabbages, packed in hay which itself might bring a penny in the bishop's town. Live chickens and geese, even an occasional swan were tied together by their legs and slung from a pole held on a woman's shoulder. There were baskets of fish, freshly caught carp, bearded barbels that just this morning had been swimming in an icy stream.

Drovers herded pigs to town, making the animals transport themselves to the butchers. Four-wheeled carts lumbered noisily down the rutted roads, ungreased axles protesting, under loads of hay and fodder, piled high until they looked like moving ricks, suddenly possessed by a mad desire to journey to greener fields.

Aimery clove a way through the moving throng. In spite of her weary spirits, Solange grew intensely interested in her surroundings. She had never been very far beyond the borders of her father's lands, and the sights and sounds and smells were new and stimulating.

For the moment she could put aside her grave anxiety, generated by her companions' reactions to the name Raoul de Puiseaux. What was wrong? What would she find when she arrived at Bourges? Raoul was not dead—Aimery had said so. Nor married. This dreadful possibility had not occurred to her until later. Brother Garin had asked, "Is he the kind of man to break a contract and not let you know?"

"No!" she had answered vigorously, and that had satisfied her on that score. Now, with Bourges so near, she would see for herself before nightfall. In the meantime, there was no use in further speculation. She believed Raoul would be at the king's court, and, greatly delighted by her eagerness for him, would insist upon wedding her at once! How happy she would be!

Before them the widened road dropped abruptly into what appeared to be marshland, bordering a river that wound almost in a circle, holding the town of Bourges in its close embrace. The flowing water lapped at the foot of the wall itself. Two rivers met here at the base of the town, both streams flowing through broad water meadows stretching to the hill on which Solange stood.

Now frozen, the marshy lowlands were safe and passable, but she guessed that, in spring freshet time, the entire valley in which the town lay would be a reedy sea. This, she recognized, was the reason for the town in the first place. Nature had provided a secure fortress commanding the valleys of the Yèvre and the Auron, impregnable to foes.

Bourges itself was built upon raised ground at the juncture of the two rivers, growing upward from the water into a conical bulk like a strawstack made of stone and thatch.

Thoughtfully, Solange considered why her heart was not beating faster. Just across the lowland was Raoul. Within sight of her destination, she was conscious now only of a dampening of spirits, not the elation she had expected.

Her low feeling was *not* an omen, she insisted fiercely. Happiness certainly waited for her across the river. If only she weren't so tired.

The setting sun encarmined the jumble of roofs rising toward the crown of the hill and gilded the cross on the spire of the wooden church crowning the city. Bourges was larger than she had dreamed. There were probably hundreds and hundreds of people within those walls. How would she ever find Raoul?

"Don't worry," said Aimery gruffly.

She managed a shy smile, but he turned away. With a sharp command he set his Gascon into motion, and the rest of them galloped down the slope behind him across the tawny, sedgy valley on the causeway to Bourges.

They entered the city over a bridge and through an ancient gate that Brother Garin told her was built atop an old Roman fortification. There were still to be seen, if one knew where to look, the Roman towers, nearly a thousand years old, now parts of other buildings.

Aimery led the way through narrow cobbled streets. Her senses were attacked by strange bewildering sights, by a stench that made her gag after the fresh air of the countryside. The houses overhung the streets so far they appeared ready to drop on her head. Rotten vegetables lay thrown into the street. Dogs barked. Frightened horses plunged in their harnesses.

Steadily, through many interruptions and delays, they made their way toward the bishop's official residence at the summit of the town. Pierre de la Chartre was host to the king and his court for as long as the king willed it. Full of sinful pride, the king's armed men tramped the streets, ruthlessly thrusting aside all in their way—even the bishop's own men—who raised mailed fists impulsively before capitulating to the men with the royal insignia.

Her eyes grew wide with wonder and fear. It did not make her easier in her mind to notice that both Aimery and Brother Garin rode very close on either side of her.

The front gate of the bishop's castle was open, as it would be until vespers, when the great iron-sheathed doors would be closed against the lawless rabble of the town.

A knot of people clustered before the gate, dark as hiving bees against the light stone of the wall. Aimery grimaced and turned off the main street into one of the stinking alleys that spewed running filth into the main way. They made their way quickly through lanes and alleys that Aimery seemed to know well. Always the castle wall lay to their left as they circled through the town. Night was falling with the abruptness of a winter sunset. Already they rode in near darkness. Torches lit the night as they occasionally passed an open door, but these infrequent flashes were the only illumination in the streets.

At length they turned sharply to the left, and followed along the grim castle wall for a way until they reached an almost invisible door set flush in the wall. Only a man with a keen eye could have found the concealed postern gate. Or, Solange thought wryly, a man who had used the gate often, in stealth.

Aimery rapped twice with ironclad fist, and the door creaked open a mere crack to permit someone to peer out. A few words were exchanged before the door opened wide enough to let them enter. They were inside the curtain wall, and the postern closed behind them with a dull thud.

The clamor of the city faded abruptly, sounding now like a faraway battle. Turning over the horses with a word of instruction to Rainard, Aimery led Solange and Brother Garin on foot through ways he seemed to know well. They must have bypassed the bailey, Solange guessed, and would soon emerge into the courtyard proper. But soon she forgot to speculate, trying only to keep up with Aimery's long strides.

Finally, they entered the castle itself by an obscure door at the base of the larger tower. Warm air welcomed them. It smelled of burning wood, stale roasted meat, and the odor of human habitation. Somewhere in this brooding hulk of stone, people lived and breathed. And, Solange devoutly hoped, ate.

They traversed a labyrinth of small corridors, turning sharp angles cunningly designed so that one armored swordsman could hold an army at bay. Flaming pine torches were set in niches at intervals along the wall, sending sooty smoke upward to stain the stone ceilings.

At length she reached out to pluck Aimery's sleeve. "Where are you taking me?" she asked. "To the queen?"

The half-light showed her Aimery's sensitive mouth

twisted into a wry smile. "To Her Grace?" he repeated. "No, not to the queen." He glanced at Brother Garin, looming like a guardian behind her. "To a *safe* place."

Why would she not be safe with the queen? Or perhaps it was safer for Aimery himself if he hid the woman he had ridden with for three days! Another puzzle among so many, and she could not solve any of them.

They reached a cross-corridor, well lit and wider than those they had just traveled. At one end of it a door stood ajar, and from beyond the door came women's voices, laughter, and the sound of a lute. A boy's voice was raised in plaintive, lonely song. Even here the scented heat from that room touched Solange's cold cheek. They hesitated. Through the door emerged a stocky figure of such great muscular strength that he looked misshapen.

"Trotti! He must not see me here!" Aimery whispered, and when she turned to him in surprise, he was gone.

"Who is Trotti?" she wondered aloud, turning to Garin.

"The queen's servant. She brought him with her from Aquitaine. Servant, I said," Brother Garin laughed without real amusement, "but some say, the queen's familiar."

She fell silent. A "familiar" meant witchcraft. She shuddered.

Brother Garin said ruefully, "My brother has a maggot in his head. But no matter." He took her past the hall leading to the queen's apartments. Then he said abruptly, "He is not for you, lady. Not now."

Appalled by his mistaken assumption, she retorted, "Brother Garin, I never thought Aimery de Montvert was for me. I do not break my vows so readily. I am betrothed, if you remember."

"I had not forgotten," said Brother Garin in an odd voice. "But, forgive me if I say too much, I thought sometimes on our journey that you were not indifferent to him?"

Solange's weariness vanished. "Indifferent? How could I be?" Her eyes, anger-darkened, flashed violet sparks. "I dislike him intensely. He drove us like swine, he treated me like the lowliest page, he—" She sputtered in helpless indignation, but before Brother Garin could speak, she crumbled, apologizing. "I'm sorry, Brother Garin. I'm grateful to him, and you, for bringing me here and protecting me in the forest. For saving me." Her eyes filled with tears as she looked up at him. "I don't know why I said those things. You three gave me back my life."

Brother Garin, who thought he knew very well why she was upset, patted her shoulder. "Never mind. Let us just be on our way now."

At last they arrived. Brother Garin rapped at a door and then opened it. She followed him into the most luxurious apartment she had ever seen. There were tapestries on the walls and a fire crackled in the grate. Arrases over the slit windows kept out the cold fairly successfully. And there was an intricately designed rug on the floor instead of rushes.

A lady-in-waiting was seated before the fire, her maid kneeling before her. Both looked up. The lady rose and welcomed Brother Garin with a glad smile. "Brother Garin! Back at last! All went well at home?"

"Lady Sybille!" He took the lady's hands in his and shook them warmly. He glanced with a smile at the servant-girl timidly standing aside, glancing curiously at Solange. Solange felt the heat from the fire stealing upon her. "How is your husband?"

A shadow passed over Lady Sybille's face. "As well as ever. He is here at Bourges. But you have brought us a page! How thoughtful!"

Lady Sybille's dark eyes narrowed as she examined Solange more closely. Solange felt her cheeks burning. Her tongue felt dry and she could not speak. Besides, she recalled, she did not know what Brother Garin wished her to say. She remembered with a start that she still wore Rainard's clothing. She spared a fleeting wish that Aimery had not deserted them and then blushed even more fiercely.

"Not a page, I think?" queried Sybille, head cocked to one side like a curious robin.

Brother Garin agreed. "Not a page. A lady in distress whom we have rescued."

"We?"

"Aimery, of course." A look of sharp intelligence passed between them. "But the poor child has had much trouble, and I have brought her to the countess."

Sybille smiled with warm radiance at Solange, and

pressed her into a chair before the fire. "You, Meg, fetch a posset for the lady, quickly. I shall inform the countess. She will be surprised!"

The maid scurried away, and the lady disappeared through an inner door. Events were moving too rapidly. Solange felt she was being swept away by a spring flood. "Where is this place?" she demanded. "Who was that lady? What am I doing here? Who is the countess? I confess, I am addled!"

Brother Garin said quickly, "No time to explain. But she is Sybille de Nannes, an old friend of mine. And the countess is Alis de Dreux, wife of the king's brother Count Robert."

Solange's eyes grew round. "But why should I come here?"

"She will keep you here until it is decided what is best for you. You need have no fear while you are with the countess and her ladies."

Solange had no time to ask more questions. The inner door had opened and the countess entered. She was a dumpling of a woman, in deep pink, with bright eager blue eyes. Her cloud of hair was fluffed beneath a pink veil, held in place by an engraved golden circlet set with rubies.

" 'No fear,' Brother Garin?" mocked the countess, advancing toward them. "I should hope no one in my suite would be afraid of anything."

She smiled at Solange, a kindly smile of great charm, and Solange felt all her doubts fade away. She managed a tremulous smile and stammered her thanks.

"Now, my dear," said the countess with a motherly twinkle, "we must find you suitable clothes. Really, Garin, how could you think it fitting to clothe the child thus?"

"She is not a child, Countess," said Brother Garin wryly. "Believe me, it was for the best."

Meg arrived with the posset and Solange drank the fiery liquid. It brought tears to her eyes.

"She'll be all right," said the countess shortly. "Now, Garin, you said she need have no fear while she is with me. Fear, my dear friend, of what?"

Brother Garin sank into the chair indicated by a wave of the countess's jeweled hand. He had had a more strenuous journey than he had anticipated, and his relief at delivering his charge into the safe hands of Countess Alis was evident.

"Wait," he said, settling down for a long story, "Wait till I tell you!"

9

As Brother Garin finished his tale, Solange began to believe that he was talking about someone else. This was only the fourth day of the week. And the first day of this week she had started out from Belvent, in the custody of four armed men, on her way to a living death in Saint Vergillia's convent.

And here she was, scarcely four days later, sitting in a comfortable chair before the fire in the grand apartments of Countess Alis, the sister-in-law of King Louis VII! With a great effort, she gathered her straying wits together and paid stricter attention to the discussion.

"And now what shall be done?" mused the countess. "Quite obviously, the girl must not be sent to a convent when she has no vocation for the religious life. But there is a knotty problem here."

"I agree," said Brother Garin, adding cryptically, "I had great hopes of her. She spent three days in the saddle with us, under my brother's protection."

The countess raised an eyebrow as she pondered the meaning beneath his seemingly ordinary words. Their talk was in a kind of a code. A word meant what it meant, but also meant something else besides.

"And now you have lost that hope?" said Alis softly. She glanced sideways at Solange, still clad in her squire's jerkin, rumpled woolen hose, and pointed boots. She spread her fat hands wide in a gesture of dismay. "My dear child, whoever dressed you thusly did you no favor!"

"My rescuers felt a squire's clothing was better than none at all!" said Solange, with returning spirit.

Alis's laugh rang forth. Plump as a capon, visibly fond of the good things in life, she considered good humor of above-average importance. "You're quite right!" she cried when her wheezing chuckles subsided. "Well, we will fix this sorry state of affairs. There is much to do, my old friend, and an idea has just struck me, one I wish to share with you. Later, Brother Garin. Later."

So saying, she rose and gave her hand to the friar, who bent over it and kissed it lightly. It was an odd gesture from a friar, but evidently his knightly upbringing still held him. A knight was the highest rank in secular society, and this man had received the coveted title or else he would not be wearing mail. A friar he might be, but a knight he certainly had been once.

"Leave us now," Alis said, "and I will think on . . . all you have told me, although I believe there may be things you have deemed it wiser to keep to yourself. Eventually I will learn of them, you know."

"Believe me, I have told you all I am sure of." Brother Garin paused before Solange. "Do not worry, my child. You will find no greater friend than the Countess de Dreux."

Solange clung to his hand for a moment, loath to see him go. It was not that she feared the countess, but Brother Garin was her final link with her past existence. What would become of her now?

Then she remembered that, somewhere in this vast castle, lived her own betrothed, hers by right of Holy Church.

Once Brother Garin had gone, the countess clapped her hands, and the room was transformed. Two maids scurried in, carrying hot water and a vast wooden tub. Meg brought fresh garments, and Sybille de Nannes appeared with an enameled box of fragrant herbs.

Sybille tilted her dark head and looked with bright curiosity at the countess.

"There are strange rumors already, floating through even the empty halls," she announced, "and if only half of them are true . . ." She pursed her lips and shook her head slightly.

The countess laughed, but her eyes blazed. "I suppose I can guess how the rumors started. Sybille dear, there is no time now to relate the child's story to you. Make haste to get her clothed decently. I imagine we may expect visitors shortly."

The maid, Ratonne, had already stripped Solange of her squire's clothes, and Solange was immersed in the tub. The countess took the box from Sybille and, lifting the lid, took out a large pinch of potpourri and dropped it into the steaming bath. She considered the perfumed results for a moment and then impulsively dropped another generous pinch into the water. "Don't linger too long," she admonished Solange before leaving the room.

Ratonne began at the top with vigor—scrubbing Solange's long hair, muttering at the twigs and dead leaves that had fastened themselves to the silver strands.

After a bit, Sybille began to watch the proceedings with interest. Solange felt her pale skin become rosy under the frankly curious eyes of the countess's lady-in-waiting. "It is not so long since I bathed," Solange offered in apology, "but I have not had even a comb during these last few days."

Sybille said, "My only thought was that the countess erred when she called you a child. You are very definitely a woman. And I do not wonder that you have had . . . adventures."

"None that overwhelmed me," returned Solange dryly. "But I should not like to repeat them, I admit."

Impulsively, Sybille offered, "I hope your youth will not be wasted. I wish you happiness."

Surprised, Solange glanced up. The shadow over Sybille's face, she thought, was not due entirely to the firelight.

Solange was dried, perfumed, and dressed. She had almost forgotten how deliciously soft a fine white linen chemise could feel against clean skin, how comforting a pelisson was—especially one lined with red marten, an edging of the luxurious fur contrasting with the blue wool of the garment itself.

She almost felt that the shaming hands of the baron and later of Baldwin, the wracking doubts and fears of this past week, had all been scrubbed away with the brush Ratonne wielded with such energy. She could nearly believe that her old self was being borne away this very moment with the dirty water in the wooden tub, carried out by the two struggling maids.

Her new self waited docilely while Sybille dropped a bliaut over her head, draping it skillfully, holding it in place by a girdle of woven silk cords. The rose-colored silk, shot with gold thread, settled like a cloud over Solange's slim hips. Blue leather boots completed her costume, and Sybille brought the countess's hand glass and placed it carefully in Solange's hands. "Take care," she warned. "There are only two other glasses in the castle, and the queen does not lend her possessions. Not to *anyone*."

Solange hardly recognized the thin oval face, bracketed by hair the color of moonlight, straight and shiny. The rose bliaut brought a touch of pink to her cheeks, but nothing could dispel the shadow in her eyes. Nothing but Raoul.

"I often braid my hair with ribbons," she began, but Sybille shook her head vigorously.

"Not now. Your hair looks lovely this way."

"But it makes me seem so young."

"Exactly," agreed Sybille.

There was no further explanation. A knock interrupted them, and the door was opened from the outside by the same stocky man Solange had seen standing outside the queen's apartments.

He nearly pushed his way into the room, but Sybille de Nannes stood squarely in his way. "Yes, Trotti? What is it?"

"My lady wishes me to speak to the countess." His voice was rough and growly, as though he were speaking from a cave. His words were humble enough, but his darting eyes searched out Solange, and she knew that he had come about her.

The countess entered from an inner room, and swept regally toward Trotti. "Yes?"

"My lady wishes the visitor to come to her."

The countess hesitated for only a fraction of a moment before replying, "Tell Her Grace that my visitor,"—there was an emphasis very slightly on *my*—"is too fatigued from her journey to sustain the pleasure of seeing the queen."

She stood steadily, closing the door inexorably on Trotti

until he had no choice but to leave. Alis shut the door quickly behind him.

"My lady, I could go," cried Solange in some agitation. "I am not at all fatigued—I do not wish you to be troubled."

"Hush, my dear," said the countess. "I am not in the least troubled."

The twinkle in her eyes meant that she told the truth. "Would you not like to inspect the bedchamber? But leave the door ajar. You may be interested in developments!"

Obediently, Solange went into the next room. Through the open door, she heard the countess say, "I'll give him five minutes to relay the message."

"Surely not the right message?" suggested Sybille lightly.

"There's always a first time for one to tell the truth," said the countess, "but probably not that one."

The countess underestimated Trotti's swiftness. In less than five minutes, the door was flung open. The deep husky voice of Eleanor, duchess of Aquitaine and queen of France, carried clearly to Solange in the inner room. "Bring out the maid so that I may see her."

"Maid, sister?" said the Countess in a silky menacing tone. "My honored guest?"

"I do not know her name or quality. The woman Garin de Montvert brought to you. I confess I should like to see what manner of child roams the forest at night like a charcoal-cutter's brat!" The queen laughed lightly. "Mere woman's curiosity, after all!"

She spoke lightly enough, but surely no trifle brought the queen here with such promptness.

The queen's scorn scalded Solange's pride. She was herself nobly born, daughter of conquerors, of no less value than Eleanor. Suddenly violently angry, Solange, head high, back straight, left the shelter of the bedroom. She shot the queen a challenging look before lowering her glance and making a deep curtsey. Somehow, the exaggerated obeisance mocked rather than submitted.

Had she been looking into Eleanor's eyes in that moment she would have seen the hot fury of a jealous and unforgiving woman. But Solange did not see. She glanced up under her meekly lowered lashes. The queen was far more beautiful than she had dreamed. No wonder Aimery was enthralled. Solange had time only to note blond hair, more golden than Solange's own, and a pervading scent of musk, before the countess spoke.

"Sister Queen, may I present to you my guest, the Lady Solange de Saint Florent of Belvent."

"Your father," demanded the queen, "What rank is he?"

"The Baron Odo de Saint Florent, your grace. Dead, so I have been told, in the Holy Land."

"And you wander alone in the forest? One might think you would be safer in your home. Belvent, you said?"

"Yes, Your Grace. Belvent. But it is no longer my home."

"Indeed?" The queen's question seemed idle, but for the light moving deep in her eyes. She waited, forcing Solange to explain.

"You have much to learn," she said when Solange had finished her story. "There is more than one path to getting your own way."

"And what would you have done," burst in Alis with vigor, "had you been at the chapel door with armed troops at all sides?"

"The troops," said the queen, "would have been on my side."

A flirtatious slyness passed over the queen's mobile features and Solange could believe the boast was only the truth. The queen suddenly smiled enchantingly. "Dear child," she murmured. To Alis, she said, more briskly, "I wish the child to come to me. She will be better for my tutelage. She will enjoy my classes, I am sure."

"I sew, embroider, weave," protested Solange. "I play chess—my father taught me the game well—I have been taught to read, to sing, and to ride. If Your Majesty will permit me to say so, I see no need for further instruction in the skills a lady must possess." The queen's amused glance flickered over her and she fell into an embarrassed silence.

"And yet, methinks there are still rough edges. I wish to see you under my own tutelage, to guide you in your search for a husband. I know of many a knight who might find you attractive."

"But I am betrothed!" cried Solange.

The queen regarded her with a long, thoughtful look, her eyes darkening. She knew that this slim girl, her youth still upon her like dew, had spent three days with Sir Aimery de Montvert, whom the queen regarded with growing favor. "Betrothed?" she said lightly. "But, even so, a little courtly polish would not be amiss." The queen turned to her sister-in-law. "You cannot but agree, I think?"

"I will abide by the king's wishes," said Alis. "In the meantime, I would not dream of troubling you with the lady entrusted to *my* protection."

The queen eyed Solange thoughtfully. "What is your wish?"

Solange faltered. Dared she enlist the queen in her plans? On the other hand, did she dare keep her secret to herself? The answer was plain. "My wish is to marry him whom my father chose for me."

The queen nodded quickly. "I agree. This must be done at once. I shall myself see that the king arranges it." A wry grimace touched her lips. "It is the sort of small thing he delights in." She surveyed Solange from head to toe. Solange sank into a deep curtsey. The queen murmured "Yes. She must be wed, and quickly, before she addles the wits of—"

"Of whom, Sister?" prompted the Countess.

"Of the entire court!" finished Her Majesty plainly.

10

After the queen left, Solange reached out a hand blindly for support. Her knees shook so that her whole body trembled. Sybille put her arm around her and led her to a chair. "She is overpowering, isn't she?" murmured the lady-in-waiting. "Especially the first time."

"She is formidable," whispered Solange.

"But you stood up to her," said Sybille. The admiration in her voice was mixed with disquiet. "I hope nothing comes of it."

"What should come of it?" asked Solange. "I answered the queen's questions. I told the truth. What more should there be?"

Countess Alis intervened. "Do not frighten her, Sybille. The queen enjoys sending her ladies into fits of hysterics, that is all, Solange."

"And she will not rest," pronounced Sybille gloomily, "until she reduces every one to jelly."

Solange began to feel indignation stirring again. How dared one woman, queen though she might be, believe she held so much power over even the noblewomen of her realm? Solange was as proud in her way as the queen was, but she had never slighted attendants or servants at Belvent. An accident of birth made her what she was, nothing more. And she determined that she would not fall a-trembling again before Eleanor. Darkly, she suspected it might just take more strength than she had to hold her own.

"Don't do it," counseled Countess Alis anxiously.

Solange looked up, surprised. "Do what?"

"Whatever you decided to do," said the countess. "You looked very determined for a moment, and I warn you, the queen is not to be challenged, as though one were breaching a castle wall."

Sybille's bright eyes moved from Alis to Solange. Sybille was a timid person, overwhelmed by two burly brothers who rode roughshod over her feelings much of the time, and she had barely enough confidence in herself to choose her own clothing. Solange was, beyond all things, daring. Sybille was alternately fascinated and frightened.

Solange stroked her hair back from her temple, a mannerism which, her mother could have told Alis, meant Solange was deep in thought. "No, I shall not defy the queen," Solange said slowly, "But I am no vassal, who must account to her for my comings and goings." She drew a deep shuddering breath. Then suddenly she turned to Countess Alis and smiled brightly.

"I am most grateful to you," said Solange sincerely, "and I promise not to do anything rash."

Countess Alis nodded approval. The girl had been transformed in an instant, right before her eyes, from a cool, purposeful maid into a lovable and enchanting woman.

Alis was not quite sure which of the two alarmed her more.

Solange laid her head against the carved wooden back of the armchair in deep exhaustion. This day seemed to stretch backward into infinity. She had ridden far and hard since morning. Lunch had been sketchy and had left her very hungry. Now even her hunger seemed a thing of the distant past. Her eyes closed.

When she woke, she was alone. The ashes from the fire gleamed faintly, and for a moment she was back in the great forest, frightened, moving carefully toward Aimery's campfire.

She stirred in her chair—she was not in the forest, then! —and the sound carried to the next room. Footsteps came at once. She looked up to see a bouncy, bright-eyed girl carrying a taper in a tall silver candlestick. The girl's friendly smile revealed even white teeth and dark hair. She set the candleholder on the floor and surveyed Solange.

"You're the new girl," she announced, unnecessarily. "Solange? I'm Bertille de Savarin, one of the countess's attendants. Lady Alis said I should tell you it's time to go."

"G-go?"

"To dinner," said Bertille. "In the great hall. Surely you must be hungry? They said the queen came here to see you. When she talks to *me*, I'm always starved afterward. From fear, I suppose. Isn't that strange? But it's true. I'd take my oath on it!"

Such a prattle! thought Solange. But she could detect good humor beneath the chatter, a kindly intention to put her at ease. She smiled back. "I confess that a roast goose —*all* of it—would be most welcome."

The journey to the bishop's great hall was surrounded by ceremony as formal as that for a wedding, despite the mundane purpose. Solange's eyes widened. She joined the retinue of the Countess de Dreux, standing, where she was bidden, six steps behind the lady's left hand.

Ahead, torch bearers lit their way. There were men-at-arms bearing lances. Two small pages carried the countess's boxes of perfume vials and candied dates. Catherine de Charpigny, whom Solange had not met until now, joined the rest of the party. A second group of men-at-arms brought up the rear.

The countess glanced down the line of her attendants. Satisfied that all was as it should be, she nodded to Evart, her steward, and they got under way.

The party made its way down gray stairs, hewn in days long past. Once they were on the ground floor, they left the tower and entered the inner ward of the bishop's palace.

A cold wind greeted them from an open door, nearly extinguishing the torches. Someone shouted angrily and a door slammed. The torch flames steadied into a flicker, blown only by drafts stirring in the passageways.

They halted, waiting. A growing hum of voices, punctuated by laughter and occasional shouts, hinted that the great hall was not far ahead. Tantalizing aromas wafted out to meet them, promising roast goose, venison, and many other meats.

Solange forgot her fatigue in her excitement. Was the king truly here? Would she be able to see him? She expected her own position at the table to be well down from the dais, perhaps just above the salt, the division between nobles and lesser folk.

From far away came the silver notes of trumpets, causing movement all along the waiting line. Catherine whispered to Solange, "Three fanfares! That means the king is coming."

"I'm starved!" said Bertille. "I wish he'd hurry."

They moved closer to the great hall. The ceremonies attending a meal at the king's court seemed endless. No wonder all ate heartily when they got the chance!

Pages, dressed in velvet the color of new Gascon wine, approached each of them, bearing water jugs and small basins for the nobles and their ladies to wash their hands. Other pages followed bearing towels.

A cool draft swept down the hall and Solange unthinkingly moved to the countess. When she changed her position, she found she could look directly through the open door into the great hall. Such a commotion! She thought she had seen tumult at Belvent, but that was nothing compared to this.

Waiters dashed through clusters of men and of women wearing expensive garments and jewels that caught the torch light. And there were people she knew. Brother Garin stood near the dais. And behind him—surely she knew that head, slightly turned aside. Just before he moved out of her vision she caught a glimpse of him.

It was Conon d'Yves.

From the direction opposite Solange came a great procession, with trumpeters and armed guards. The stir was tremendous. As the new procession approached the wide-open door, all in the countess's party dropped to the floor in deep obeisance. The king!

She could see him only dimly, stealing a look upward through her thick lashes. A small, spare man, compared to Aimery a reed in the wind, nonetheless there was a certain unmistakable air of authority about him. The queen, fingertips resting lightly upon her husband's arm, walked beside him. The moment was gone before Solange could be positive, but she was quite sure she had seen Aimery standing just behind the queen.

Alis spoke briefly to the king as they entered the great hall, and then went to her allotted place at table. The king's court did not seem, now that Solange could look about her, to be as luxurious as she had expected. Plates of gold—perhaps she had expected these—and silver goblets encrusted with jewels. But there was little of that here, except at the king's table. The lavishness of the court seemed to be in the numbers of noblemen and their men who found it desirable to eat at the king's expense. There were more of these than the hall could hold at one sitting.

She was thankful to note that the benches above the salt were cushioned. She had had enough of perching on a stump to eat her bread and cheese.

Only the countess and her husband, near Solange, were given silver trays to place under their bread. The loaves were already hacked apart, though, so that the meat could be cut without delay and put upon the loaf.

She could not remember, later, the great variety of food paraded before her. There were slices of stag, a pasty of fowl, roasted meats. She passed up rabbit in onion gravy flavored with saffron. She relished the sweetness of baked pears.

Dinner was nearly over before she could sort out all the

73

people around her. She had been seated far above the salt, on the raised table just below the dais. Such was the privilege of those who lived in the countess's suite and were under her protection.

Now Alis plucked at her sleeve, rising from the table. "Come, my dear. The king wishes to see you."

Eyes wide with dismay, Solange had no choice but to rise and follow the countess to the dais while everyone stared. She tried to keep her knees from turning to jelly, and hoped her dry mouth would not prevent her from speaking.

His Majesty addressed her very kindly, and his kindness threatened to overwhelm her with tears of gratitude. Fighting for control, she lost the trend of his words. When Alis prompted her she realized he had asked her a question.

"Sire?" she faltered, cheeks burning.

"My child," said Louis, "no need to fear me. After what my sister tells me of your trials, I must take it amiss that you do not trust me. Your father was my own vassal, you know. I had not heard of his death, and I must tender my apologies."

Gently leading her on, questioning skillfully, he elicited the whole of her story—or almost the whole. Prudence prevented her from telling about the baron's assault in the wood and subsequent threat of revenge. Nor did she explain about Baldwin.

"But I was exceedingly fortunate, sire, that I was guided to the campfire where—Brother Garin and his party," she said carefully, feeling the queen's eyes upon her, "took pity on me and brought me here, sire, so that the king's justice could be invoked on my behalf."

No need to dwell on Aimery's role in rescuing her. She shot a swift glance toward him, and was unreasonably happy to see faint approval in his deep-set eyes.

"I see," said Louis. "And I will make sure that you, as my vassal's daughter, do indeed receive justice. My sister tells me you wish to be married. Is this true?"

"Yes, sire. I wish to marry the man my father betrothed me to before the door of Holy Church."

For a long moment the king was possessed by a wild

desire to be that man, the man who had the good fortune to claim this woman for his own. The moment passed. No one had noticed. Louis was long-practiced in keeping his thoughts to himself. It was a lonely business, but he was safer that way.

"Well, you are a maiden who should be married," he said finally, with a rueful laugh. "Lest you turn the heads of the men here in my household. I well know what havoc a strong-willed woman can cause."

He paused. A bitter thought traveled through his mind, tightening his lips. He shot his queen a glance, fleeting as the wind, but full of meaning. She appeared not to notice.

The king said, "Then you wish to marry your betrothed? I should imagine this presents no great problem. Tell me, child, his name, and we will have this done with at once."

Solange's face lit like a candle. She was incandescent with happiness, the king thought, and he put aside a longing wish that he could some day see that same look on the face of his queen. Might as well expect a goat to carry a knight, he thought. Not that the queen was a goat, of course. He rather thought he himself was the goat. Suddenly, the king felt very old.

The king was curious as to what sort of man merited the beautiful woman before him. He wished he could bestow happiness upon her, but his touch so seldom brought happiness . . . so seldom.

His thoughts ran their own course for some moments until, with a start, he returned to the great hall and the hubbub of many voices.

When he came back to the present, the delightful Lady Solange was still looking at him earnestly. "Raoul de Puiseaux," she was saying, as though she had said it before and he had not heard her.

"My clerk?" he said in surprise. He had surely not thought his clerk, a reliable but tedious poursuivant in his service, could have gained the devotion of a hound, let alone the dazzling Solange. But the ways of women are strange. "He is away just now. But," he added quickly, seeing her violet eyes darken in disappointment, "I shall send for him to return, posthaste."

Count Robert was hovering at his brother's right hand. "A messenger from Abbot Suger, sire, with urgent word—" His voice trailed off suggestively.

The king stirred, and sighed. "Yes, Robert. At once. Now, my child, we will work this all out to the best advantage for all. You see there are others who wish to talk to me now. I think—" he smiled kindly at her, but the smile did not quite reach his absent eyes—"I think I shall also send for your mother. And, of course, your stepfather."

Solange rose to her feet in a whirl. *Must you?* trembled on her lips, but she remembered in time that this was the king, and her only hope. "Yes, sire," she said obediently, eyes downcast. She turned to follow Alis out of the king's presence, but he suddenly called her back.

"The baron, too," he called. "I must send for him as well. For he has entered into a contract in good faith. Can you tell me his name?"

"Oh, but sire," she said with a rush. "He is already here."

"Here? In this town?"

She nodded vigorously, her long hair swinging. "Right here in this palace."

She searched the room, looking for the face she knew and hated so deeply. There, at last, against the far wall, she caught sight of him. His head was bent, listening to a woman. Solange turned to the king.

"There he is. Just going out the door now. With the dark-haired lady—"

The king followed her direction. Suddenly his face changed. "You mean *d'Yves*? Is *he* your baron?"

"Yes, sire. Conon d'Yves. His barony lies along one of Belvent's boundaries."

Count Robert joined the conversation. "My brother, I beg you to walk softly in this matter." His voice was so low that only the king and Solange, could hear him. "Take care that you do not misstep. I speak with due respect, sire."

"Yes," said the king. He took a deep breath. His eyes were fixed upon the door through which d'Yves had vanished. "Yes, you are quite right. D'Yves has much power in my council. But I think he can see reason."

He nodded. The audience was over. Solange followed Alis back to their place at the table, where the countess gathered her entourage to make the long trip back to her apartments. Solange did not notice that the number of armed men following behind them had grown.

She had hungered and had been fed. She had been frantic with worry, and the king had promised her justice. She was suddenly so tired that she nearly fell asleep on her feet. Up ahead, in the countess's rooms, was a pallet for her. She must stay awake until she got there. She very nearly didn't make it.

11

It was a week before Mehun jangled into the courtyard of the Bishop's palace at Bourges. The weather had turned colder, but there was little snow, so the trip had been accomplished fairly easily.

But the king's messenger must not have reached Raoul, for there was no word yet from him. From the summit of the old donjon, the round tower that would be the last stronghold of the defenders if the castle were ever besieged, Solange watched her stepfather's arrival.

"I suppose you must miss your mother greatly," the childless Alis had sighed.

Solange did not wish to go into the troubled tangle of her feelings for her mother. Alis would merely turn a puzzled face to her. Alis was so kind, and so uncomplicated. She had a sure grasp on the basic means of comfort—a warm blanket, a hot meal, a sweet repose. These things came first to her, and she thought surely these were the elements of solace. Alis truly cared about those around her, searching even into the town with a discerning eye for the neediest persons. These suddenly had food and blankets and even, sometimes, a new cloak of rough-spun Picardy wool.

Alis knew that Solange was deeply troubled, but wisely, she did not probe the tender places. "She must work out her own way," she told Brother Garin privately. "But I do fear that she will come to tragedy in the end."

"Perhaps not in the end," objected Brother Garin. "Tragedy, possibly, in the future. That may come to us all. But in the end, I think she is stronger than we are. And she will win out."

"Pray God you are right, Garin," sighed Alis. "That girl has captured my heart with her sweetness."

"And her courage," added Garin. "She has had need of that."

"And when she finds out . . ." Alis gazed into the fire, brooding. "Garin, should I tell her?"

"I fear she would not believe you. Or she might turn on you, just when she needs you most."

"You are doubtless right, dear friend. But it is so hard. Just to stand by. I am not accustomed to being helpless!"

A log shifted in the fire, ashes exploding around it.

"Brother Garin," she asked after a while, "is it true? Do you know for a fact that the dreadful rumor about that man is true?"

He shook his head. The question had bothered him too. How much weight could one put on appearances? On rumors, possibly started by envy of Raoul's high position?

"Only our Lord, with his infinite wisdom and mercy, can read a man's heart," he said. There was a note of deliberate pomposity in his voice.

Countess Alis laughed abruptly. "Garin, my friend, I have known you for many years, remember. You do not need to preach to me. I am past listening to sermonizers. I am not intruding on the Lord's province, my dear friend, and seeking to read anyone's heart. But I do believe that you might have seen some more earthly proof of what is alleged against him."

Brother Garin laughed ruefully. "You have me there. I have no proof. And yet I am gravely reluctant to see Solange wed to the man. Rumor or not, Raoul de Puiseaux is not worthy of the child. Raoul de Puiseaux is not the man who should wed Solange.

"For look you, my friend. He has been at court two years, and yet he is content with a clerk's duties. He struts vainly in his minor importance, and I swear he has no more brain than a peacock."

"There are few men of intelligence."

"And Solange deserves one of them. A brave man, with courage to match hers, and a strong man to curb her waywardness and teach her maturity. Raoul de Puiseaux, no matter what her father thought, is not the man to wed the child."

"You persist in calling her a child," said Alis dryly. I can assure you, she is no such thing."

Brother Garin nodded agreement. "She is, though, a child in this way, Countess. She does not know what effect she has on us poor males." He managed a wry smile. "Even those celibates . . . the ones who are not too dried up yet."

She put her hand out to cover his. "My dear, I can believe you. And yet Aimery was not stirred?"

"She is too genuine," Garin pronounced wryly. "She is impertinent to him, she demands responses from him. In short, she treats him like a man. Not a slave."

"And Aimery wants a queen on a pedestal," mused the countess. "How long will that last? Aimery is no born celibate."

"I hope it does not last so long that his veneration leads him into a trap he cannot get out of."

Alis glanced sharply at him. "You think he will betray his loyalty to his king?"

Garin looked shocked. "No, no. I could not believe it of him. And yet, the lady we speak of is most alluring, and I have not yet heard that she fights Temptation with a sharp sword. She may beguile my brother beyond his strength."

"Yet, if the lady yields herself to him, she is not worth serving," said Alis, "as Aimery may find out from the hangman, if the king deals with him."

"Think you there is real danger of this?" whispered Garin, horrified.

"No, I do not think so," said Alis robustly. "But it would be better were the question not to arise at all. I should wish. . . ."

The silence grew long and he cocked his tonsured head toward her. "What would you wish? Is it something you could pray for?"

She sighed and said, with resignation, "I do not wish to tell the Lord what is best. But I do think that our dear Aimery could do worse than wed this child." She peered closely at him. "This does not surprise you?"

"No, for our wishes march together. And I think it would be taken in the proper spirit if we simply prayed for a safe deliverance for Solange, and for Aimery. For her deliverance from the hazards that surround her now, and for the opening of his eyes."

"Is he happy, do you think?"

"No!" It was a forceful explosion totally at variance with the calm tenor of their discussion so far. Garin rose and took a turn around the room. "He is cross, stubborn, hasty. He gives the impression of a man riding an impossible trail, on a quest he cannot win. But there are other reasons for this besides the lady he adores."

"My dear, I do know. It takes courage to face the truth."

Garin halted in his pacing. "You mean about our mother? He faced that long ago."

"Do you think so?" Alis rose from her chair and crossed to Garin, peering up into his worried face. "Perhaps he is still running from his tragedy. This is why he pursues a will-o'-the-wisp, a hopeless love."

"I suppose you are right. And it is fruitless to think a mere inexperienced child could lure him away from his obsession."

The countess smiled, a secret smile with a hint of mischief in it. She looked no older than Solange herself. "I watched him tonight," she said thoughtfully, "and I think he is in a fair way to become besotted. And not with the queen."

Brother Garin stared. "But—"

"Never mind," counseled Alis. "Say nothing. But time will sort all things out."

"You're secretive."

"I mean to be."

Solange, of course, was unaware of that conversation.

She had in fact been kept quite close to Alis's suite, whether by the king's order or not she did not know. But she saw almost no one outside of the countess's retinue. Meals were taken in the suite now. The countess developed a series of mysterious pains, and she vowed she felt too unwell to leave her room. Solange, realizing that Bertille and Sybille were disappointed at missing the excitement of the great hall and the entertainment that usually followed, offered to stay with the countess.

"It means nothing to me, Lady Alis, to see so many people. I don't know them. In truth, I feel much happier here. Since the king has sent for Raoul, I must wait in patience for his return. How long it seems!"

But she did, with Alis's indulgent permission, slip away now and then to the top of the keep. It was quiet there, with only the strong wind to buffet her and in some magical way clear her thoughts away. She was used to the open air at Belvent, rain or shine, frost or heat, and she was stifled in the small tower suite that was all the bishop's palace afforded the countess and her ladies.

The constant chatter of the girls, like swallows under the eaves, the heavy fragrance of rouge pots mingled with stale underclothing, and the acrid pungency of old ashes, all drove her to the top of the keep.

The keep was a massive round structure, formidably built with stone, the last stronghold of a besieged army. There were few enough windows, merely slits, for the most part, and these let in more rain than light. The stairs inside the tower, rising from the ground floor to the top through complicated ways, were narrow and winding.

At the top, the tower opened up to a flat platform, capable of holding a sizable army with weapons, their vats of oil, and their food, for a prolonged siege. The platform was encircled with a stone parapet, high as a man's shoulders, but with regular notches to allow the besieged to drop stones, or shoot arrows at the attackers. Even vats of boiling oil could be poured through the notches.

But Bourges had not been besieged for longer than those living now could remember, and Solange found that the machicolations were convenient to lean elbows on and look out across the city. Only the watchman, who sometimes slept away his duty time, kept her company, nearby.

All would work out, she believed, in time. She must believe it, or else hurl herself from the top of the tower.

So things stood when she saw Mehun riding in, his banners with the black bear fluttering from lance tips. She strained her eyes to see better.

There she was! Petronilla, riding the white horse that had been Odo's last gift to her.

Even from this distance, Solange believed she could feel the violence emanating from Mehun. She could not reconcile her mother's submission to this terrible man with her love for Odo, that easygoing, unambitious, good-natured man.

Solange wrapped her new cloak protectively around her, consoled a little by the soft squirrel fur. One of Alis's comforts, she thought affectionately.

The gusting wind snapped the king's pennon, flying overhead from the top of the massive keep. It swirled, cold with fine new snow, lifting the hem of her mantle. She shivered, but not entirely from the cold.

Her enemy rode toward her on the street below. With permission from the king, her stepfather could draw her back into his power. She guessed he might be even more ruthless in his anger over having been put to so much trouble because of her. The choice would again be hers: marry the Baron d'Yves, and, if rumor told true, possibly spend her life in the dungeon loaded with chains, as his last wife had done; or die above ground at Saint Vergillia's. She would be given no time to consider which she wished to do, and beyond doubt she would not have a chance to escape again!

The procession from Belvent drew up to the barbican gate. The tumbling slopes of the roofs below her soon hid them from her view. She lingered long after they were out of sight, dreading the moment when she must come face to face with Petronilla and the dreaded Mehun. She was still standing on the battlement when Aimery came to get her.

"Solange?" he called, coming to stand beside her and

look out across the city. Beyond lay the ice-edged rivers, the water-meadows, tawny with dead reeds, and the brown tree-covered hills rising beyond. "What are you looking at?"

She didn't answer directly. Instead she asked, "How did you find me?"

"Sybille thought you might be here. They looked every place else for you."

"Mehun sent you?" Her voice frosty as the air. "I shall not come."

"Your mother has arrived," said Aimery, "and is asking for you."

"My mother?" said Solange, prey to a strange mood. "I doubt she remembers my name."

Aimery watched her with baffled eyes. What did this girl want? He was no wiser when she turned her violet eyes to him and let her hood drop, revealing her silvery hair. It smelled of meadow flowers. "What do you think the king will do?"

Aimery laughed sharply. "No one knows what the king will do. But we shall soon find out. He has called a meeting in half an hour in his council chamber. I came to get you, thinking you might like to see your mother first."

Belatedly, she realized that Aimery had done this out of sheer kindness. How badly she had repaid him! She put out her hand to touch his sleeve. "I thank you, Sir Aimery."

Surprisingly, he smiled. "You are quite frozen. You can't quite control those chattering teeth. Best come in, out of the wind."

"But not to speak to my mother. You see, *he* will be there."

Aimery nodded. There was no question as to the identity of *he*. Mehun, of course. Aimery could not enter into Solange's fears. To him Mehun was simply another knight —not highly civilized, in fact, quite possibly treacherous. But there was only one way for Aimery to deal with him, and that would be in knightly combat, an extremely unlikely event. Solange had no chance at all, dealing with a man like that.

"Yet," said Aimery, not quite realizing he spoke aloud, "you do not seem to me to be the kind of woman who scurries into corners when a man appears."

She looked up, surprised, into his face. "What kind of woman, then, do you think I am?" she asked at last, in genuine curiosity.

"I don't know," he said slowly. "The valiant kind of woman to defend her lord's castle when he is away. The kind to keep his serfs fat and prosperous. The kind who could even sit in judgment and give fair dealing."

She looked away, thoughtful. Was that really the kind of woman she was? Not like her mother, then. She was pleased. A sudden smile transformed her face. Lightly, she asked, "A worthy wife to some knight?" She laughed shortly. "But not to Conon."

"I confess," agreed Aimery, "I should not like to see you be the property of Conon d'Yves. I have heard much about him." He frowned. "But then, the king will be fair."

She could not be sure. But perhaps the good angels would convince Louis.

"Come," said Aimery, "we must not be late for the king's meeting."

They were in fact the last to enter the council chamber. Already the king was sitting on his dais, the queen only a step lower. Solange had heard that the queen had refused to sit with the king until her chair was raised to almost the same level as his. Eleanor of Aquitaine would not take a lower place to anyone except to her liege lord and husband, and then only enough to make a token difference.

Solange stiffened when she caught sight of her mother and next to her, Mehun, glowering. There was d'Yves too, with a strange secret smile, and Brother Garin standing beside the Lady Alis.

After her duty curtseys to the royal pair, Solange crossed to curtsey to her mother. Head down, she raised her eyes only sufficiently to look into Petronilla's eyes as she rose. To her surprise Petronilla's eyes held a kind of mute appeal that Solange could not understand. Begging her not to make difficulties? She must know Solange better than that. She had no time to puzzle over it, for the king began to speak.

"This is a matter," he said, "that I must decide, since Odo de Saint Florent was my vassal. And since he is not returned from crusade, then his wife and daughter and chattels are at my disposal."

He bent a regretful glance toward the usurping Mehun.

"I come to swear allegiance to Your Majesty," inserted Mehun, "and give fealty for the land that belonged, when he was living, to Odo de Saint Florent."

The king went on, laying out the circumstances upon which he must legally act, and then, at last, turning to Mehun. "Tell me, how are you certain that Saint Florent is dead?"

"I myself saw him die," said Mehun sturdily. Then, seeing that the king waited in silence for amplification, he obliged. "At the battle of Adana, he was in the forefront of the battle, as was his wont," said Mehun. "I would be glad, sire, if my lady were spared the details of Saint Florent's death. But I owe it to him to say that his death was a glorious one, fighting amain with all his might to free Jerusalem of the blasphemous infidel's rule."

"A glorious death?" said Lady Alis. "A useless one, more likely."

Her brother-in-law gave her a quelling glance, but she merely smiled. Mehun continued. "And since the Lady de Saint Florent has seen fit to honor me in marriage, then it follows that her daughter is subject also to my rule."

The king said gently, "You do not need to instruct me in the law. But if you are so well versed in it, I wonder that you did not seek my permission to marry the lady."

Mehun reddened, but he said, sturdily, "There was little time. The estate was threatened by its neighbors, and I saw there was no time to lose if they were to be repelled."

The king probed gently. To Petronilla—had she had any word about Odo besides Mehun's? To Solange—did she not wish to enter the convent? Or to marry the Baron d'Yves?

"What then?" he asked after her vigorous denial.

"I wish to marry the man to whom my father betrothed me," she said stoutly. "To carry out the contract entered upon in Holy Church."

The king said thoughtfully, "I remember this. But I wonder that he has not come to claim you by this time.

Lady de Mowbrai?" he added, turning to Petronilla. "You confirm this arrangement?"

Solange smiled confidently at her mother. Petronilla did not meet her eyes, being intent, so it appeared, on a curiously carved ring of carnelian on her forefinger. Then came the blow. The sheer force of it stunned Solange so that she could not think.

Her mother said, "There was no betrothal, Your Majesty."

"No betrothal!" screamed Solange, when she found her voice, stepping forward, forgetting the king and all else. "You stood there *with* me at the church door! Father Jean betrothed us according to Church law. There was even a sum of gold coins set aside in the chest for my dowry. But you—you spent that! Gave my father's gold over to *him*!" She finished bitterly, pointing an accusing finger at her stepfather. Tears smarted behind her eyes, but she would not allow her foes to see her humiliation. She glared at her ashen mother through watery eyes.

Out of the corner of her eye she saw Conon's face, satisfied, smiling. She whirled around, looking for aid in the face of her mother's apostasy.

There was a bit of help. "My lord," said Alis. "This previous betrothal makes the second one invalid, does it not?"

"If there were such a betrothal, it would of course prevail," said the king. "But you see there are two opinions as to a simple church rite. I should like to speak to the priest—" He turned to Petronilla. "The priest's name, please?"

"Father Jean, a priest who served my husband—my late husband—as chaplain for some years," said Petronilla stonily. "And if there had been a betrothal, he would have conducted the ceremony. But alas, Father Jean is dead. So I have heard from my husband." She looked at Mehun then, and smiled slightly, but it was not a convincing performance. Petronilla was as agitated as Solange.

At length the king spoke again. "I must rule in favor of the Lady de Mowbrai. She surely knows what happened."

"And so do I, my lord!" cried Solange. "I too was there.

86

My mother is so under that man's influence as to deny her own soul!"

Her knees quaked. She sank to the floor, and buried her head in her hands. Desperate sobs racked her body. She had hoped for so much from the king. Her own mother had turned against her. Her own mother!

Aimery lifted her up with a gentle hand. "Come now," he said soothingly. "This doesn't solve anything. Let us consider what is to be done. His Majesty will—"

The queen's voice cut like Toledo steel. "The king will wait until all the facts are sorted out," she announced clearly. "Take the girl away. Not you, Sieur de Montvert. She needs comfort in her disappointment. Perhaps the Lady Alis?"

Aimery's firm hand on her arm guided Solange to the countess. Solange was conscious only of a loud buzzing out of which came voices, raised in argument. The queen said, "Let the hubbub die down, my lord. Then the girl can be married quietly."

After Aimery had come to his senses! Eleanor thought. She suspected that he was far too interested in the girl he had rescued in the forest. And just what had happened between them? She considered herself a realist, and therefore believed the worst. She would deal quickly with this unforeseen threat to her claim to Aimery's sole devotion.

"Perhaps," suggested Brother Garin, "it would work out better if the decision were delayed until Christmas. Abbot Bernard will be here."

"And is his judgment so much better than mine?" asked the king with deceptive mildness. He held his temper with great difficulty. The queen had, once again, made him appear a fool in public.

"No, my lord," said Brother Garin quickly, if not quite truthfully. "But if he should consent to marry them, how happy an event!" The identity of the groom was still in doubt, but he preferred to ignore that.

Alis coaxed Solange toward the door. Solange involuntarily glanced up when she passed the glittering pale eyes of the Baron d'Yves. "I can wait," murmured Conon softly. "You will remember I told you that once."

Solange remembered. Wait for revenge, he had said then. And although he did not say so now, it was plain to read in his secretive, cruel smile.

The king spoke as Alis and Solange reached the door. "Lady Solange, your betrothed will be here in a few days. If you still wish to wed him, and he bears out your word, then the matter is settled."

"Yes, Majesty," said Solange, smothering a hiccup, and sketching a curtsey. Emboldened by his kindness, she made haste to add, "I am grateful for your justice. Raoul *will* bear me out."

She curtseyed again, and escaped into the hall, Lady Alis just behind her. If she could have read the king's thoughts, she might not have been so easily soothed.

The king told himself that the minute Raoul came back, Solange would be ready for another solution. And, although Eleanor thinks I am quite blind to her flirtations, I will deal with this latest one in my own way. The king's smile was as secret as the Baron d'Yves'.

12

Solange became resigned to the short reprieve. In a few days would come the Feast of the Nativity, and all of Bourges would celebrate. She could not become reconciled, though, to the continued absence of Raoul. The king sent word to her that Raoul was away on a royal errand, and would soon return. Solange fretted with impatience.

In the meantime, she remained in Alis's suite. Petronilla had sent word that Solange should come to visit her, but Alis would not permit it. "I do not like to have you out of my care," she said. "Your stepfather has much to lose by your marriage."

"I don't understand," said Solange. "He already has the bride money that my father promised Raoul. What more is there to lose?"

"You might marry someone who would fight for your share of Belvent," Alis pointed out. "Conon d'Yves was willing to pay for you, but your husband—assuming it is not the baron—"

"It won't be," interjected Solange with spirit.

"—might want to acquire some of your father's lands."

Solange nodded thoughtfully. "Raoul might want the equivalent of the bride money," she said sagely. "In fact, if it will embarrass Mehun, I shall insist that he does."

"My dear," began Alis, but she realized that Solange would not listen.

Over the next few days Solange made friends with the ladies of Alis's suite. She had met the girls when she first arrived, but she was then so intent on her own misery that she knew only that they were kind. Now she was learning to know them better, and for the first time in her life, she had friends of her own quality. At Belvent, she had had many friends, but they were all of a lower class, and there was no one to share Solange's love of poetry or her exquisite needlework.

She enjoyed the high spirits that filled Bertille de Savarin, an apple-cheeked, dark-haired girl with a bouncing figure and an eagerness for excitement.

Isabel de la Valle had unfortunately large features assembled without charm. She came from the queen's own duchy, Aquitaine. Her pale blue eyes seemed to notice much more than they should, and Solange felt ill at ease with her.

While she could amuse herself merrily with Bertille, she grew fonder every day of Catherine de Charpigny. There was something about Catherine that could only be described, Solange decided, as an inner peace. That was a quality Solange had never had. Catherine was affianced to Alis's nephew, and her days were spent in sewing shirts and embroidered bliauts for Henri, and in making lists of requirements for Castle Belin where Henri would take her once they were wed. The date had been fixed for a week before the beginning of the Lenten season, and Catherine felt ridden by the urgency of many details.

But Solange, happier than she had been, looked upon them all with affection and an amiable tolerance. For their part, the girls were struck with the romantic possibilities of her dilemma, and formed themselves into a sort of protective shield around her.

Since the king's audience, Alis felt danger surrounded the girl under her protection. Belvent was a handsome fief, and violence, thought Alis, rumbled in the distance like thunder. On rare occasions the countess would allow Solange to sally forth from their suite, if the girls and her nephew Henri went along. Often other young and gallant knights joined them, under Henri's watchful eye. One or two made a practice of joining them for these carefully escorted walks. One, Pierre de Cambrai, a pleasant-faced, uncomplicated young man, seemed to walk with Bertille more often than the others.

Surprisingly, Aimery frequently found time to join them. She sought an opportunity to speak to him alone, but it seemed impossible. Always at least one of the girls hovered nearby. She was amused by the idea that the frivolous Bertille could provide any protection, and she believed she needed none anyway.

At length she found a chance to talk privately with Aimery. The four girls and their escorts, hovering like hummingbirds, had gone into the palace courtyard to watch some squires tilting.

The young noblemen, having the great good fortune to be attached to the king's court for their training, were on the eve of their entrance into knighthood. They had undergone long, hard discipline in the study of war. And Queen Eleanor, it was said, made sure that the knights-to-be knew the finer points of how to treat a noble lady, as prescribed by the rules of her Court of Love. This was meant to soften the edges of warriors so that their ladies could live comfortably with them.

Now they were almost ready for their vigil, which would take place the next week. Perhaps the Abbé Bernard himself would pronounce their vows. Just now the young men were practicing amain, and, from sheer idleness, many members of the court gathered to watch.

Solange moved, entranced by the sight, along the rail that bounded the tilting yard. One lad at the far end had caught her eye, and she was intent upon his graceful sword play. She hardly noticed that her companions did not follow her. Suddenly Aimery stood beside her.

She glanced up and smiled. "Is that one not superb?" she said. "See his grace as he recovers? He nearly fell."

Obediently Aimery watched where she pointed. Then, in a more sober mood, she said, "I have not had a chance to thank you for your kindness that day in the audience chamber. I was behaving very badly, I know. I wonder that you did not scorn me."

"I would never do that," he said. "But you were making a bad impression on the queen."

"The queen!" said Solange sharply. "It was the king who made the decision to wait."

"Oh, no," corrected Aimery. "It is the queen who rules His Majesty. As she rules us all."

A note in his voice struck her sharply. "But surely it is the king who will give me justice?"

"Are you sure you want justice?" said Aimery, his lop-sided smile appearing. "Perhaps you confuse justice with simply having your own way?"

She was too stung to reply for a moment, but when she could she said simply, "Ask Raoul then, when he comes. Ask him if he wants justice—"

Aimery's face darkened surprisingly. "Do not speak to me of Raoul. Justice—"

He did not continue. With an obvious effort he controlled his tongue, leaving Solange mystified. What had he been going to say? She could not even guess.

"Justice," she said softly. "I suppose you are right. All we want is mercy, is that not correct? Surely one does not wish for justice. It might produce some very unpleasant results."

"You speak of my feeling for the queen, I do not doubt," said Aimery stiffly. "Believe me, it is beyond your understanding. Just as your feeling—," he said, suddenly much more human, "for Raoul passes my understanding."

"But—believe me," began the bewildered Solange, but Aimery interrupted her.

"It seems we both have need for mercy rather than justice," he said tautly. "But if we live for the moment, perhaps we can manage to survive." He smiled again. "Shall we be friends? And in the meantime, perhaps we shall be happier to join the others. The Lady Bertille seems to be the center of some jesting."

Justice—what a strange thing it was, thought Solange. Justice for Aimery might easily mean banishment from the court, for raising his eyes to look with human emotion on Queen Eleanor. As for justice for herself, she knew that the king did not look favorably on her rebellion. But there was truly no other way. Conon d'Yves would not agree, of course.

The baron managed, one night, to insert himself between her and Catherine at dinner at the long trestle table just below the dais where the king and his queen took their dinner. Catherine had caught sight of Henri, and in her haste to speak to him, left Solange alone.

Conon handed her to her place at the bench, and made as though to sit beside her.

"That place," said Solange icily, "is for the Lady Catherine."

"I am aware of that," he said. "That is why I have kept my eyes upon her, knowing that sooner or later her own affairs would come between her and her duty as your guard. For such is her function, is it not?"

He speared a piece of meat and set it on her loaf. "Do not trouble yourself with me," said Solange. "Your efforts are futile."

"I do not think so. I cannot believe, for instance, that any woman so deliciously desirable as you are, so made to be bedded, would voluntarily take the cold rule of Saint Vergillia to her bosom, when a warmer companion is available." He looked at her with unmistakable intent. "Available, and more than eager."

"I wonder," said Solange, too bitter to curb her words, "that you do not turn your efforts to other fields. Certainly there are many ladies here at court who would be willing."

"Willing, for one time only," he said, "I suppose you are right. But my fancy takes a more permanent turn. Once, believe me, would not be enough with you. Besides, I have bought you. You will come to me in the end."

"Once would be entirely too many times," she said. "Here comes Lady Catherine."

With apparent good grace, he left them. But she did not feel that she had turned aside his insane determination to have her. Why her? she wondered, and then, with some success, tried to forget him.

Later that evening, Petronilla made an attempt to make up the quarrel with Solange. She came to Lady Alis's rooms and begged for an audience. "I think you must see her," said Alis. "She is your mother."

"No longer," said Solange with bitterness. Nonetheless, she consented to see Petronilla.

"Why did you," she said, coming quickly to the point, after a hasty greeting, "mock me? Why do you deny there was a betrothal? You are lying for that man!"

"Believe me, my child," said Petronilla, in anguished tones, "I did it only for your good. I have heard something. Raoul . . ."

"Yes, mother?" said Solange sternly. "Don't stammer. What about my fiancé?"

"Mehun was right," said Petronilla at last, shaking her head. "You will not believe me. But if you weren't so headstrong, I could save you much grief."

"You could have done that before," said Solange hardily.

"When did you ever listen to me?" cried Petronilla. "No, you were your father's girl, or Mahaut's. But not mine. One might have thought you were a cuckoo in the nest, except that one look at you proves you're a Saint Florent."

At length her mother left her, saying only, "I wish to send you someone to serve you. You cannot take the Lady Alis's servants to do your own work any longer. If you will live here, then you must have Jehane. I will send for her."

"Don't bother," answered Solange sharply. But nonetheless she knew that Jehane, from Belvent, from *home*, would be welcome.

13

𝔄 day or two later, Solange had let her conversations with Conon and with her mother fall neglected into a corner of her mind.

The routine imposed upon her by the countess's care was stifling, though affectionate. Not that her duties were heavy. They were, in truth, very light. Solange's main task seemed to be sorting out the lovely silks for Alis's constant embroidery, and taking a few stitches herself when Alis wearied.

She had too little to occupy her thoughts, even though her hands were busy. Ceaselessly her thoughts skittered around the same questions: when would Raoul return? Why had her mother denied the betrothal? Why had God seen fit to let her father die and leave her without his protection?

At Belvent, she would have the remedy for these sleep-less nights. She would take Marchedoux from the stable and together they would gallop hard for hours. Cold air smarting against her cheeks, brushing troubled thoughts away, the numbing healing of sheer physical exhaustion— all these would bring sleep at night. But she was no longer at Belvent and it did no good to yearn for what was gone. She might as well try to hold fast a scudding cloud over-head.

One day, when the sun had shone brilliantly all day on the frost-covered roofs, she could stand confinement no longer. If I had wanted to live indoors, she thought, I could have gone to Saint Vergillia's!

Wrapping her fur-lined cloak around her, she slipped out of the suite. Instead of turning left toward the rising stairs, she went down, out of the tower. Fearing she would be stopped if she were recognized, she made her way by a devious route until she came, with luck, to the postern gate, where Aimery had brought them that first night. Her luck held. No one was on guard, and she slipped through the gate into the street beyond.

Down the hill through the narrow streets she went, carefully watching her steps on the frost-covered cobbles. From time to time she stopped and turned, to memorize the way she had come. Always the great bulk of the Bishop's Palace on its eminence rose above her, and at length she felt sure she could find her way back from anywhere in the city. One could hardly lose such an enormous structure!

The entire town was like a permanent market day, exciting, vivid, vibrant with life. Entranced, she wandered down the Street of the Glass-Workers, where the bright orange forge sent fiery light into the street. She turned into the Parchment-Maker's Street, where she nearly collided with a friar with a roll of new parchment under his arm. The Goldsmith's Lane, where the shop attendants seized the arms of passersby urging them with great uproar to patronize their shop, instead of being robbed by the thieves who worked next door.

Shaking off their clutching fingers, she pushed through the crowds, past the beggars with their uplifted crippled hands. She wished she had coins to give them, but she was no wealthier than they. She would have food tonight and sleep within doors, that was the only difference. When the king decided her fate, then she would know how poor or how rich she would be.

She wandered so far that she did not know where she was. The next corner looked familiar, and she turned. It was dark and dingy, only a few yards down the lane, and she knew she had made a mistake. Ahead was a tavern door, and she stopped short, intending to turn back. But suddenly, out of the door spilled a half-dozen burly men, clad in padded jerkins, clumping boots, very drunk. Two of them must have already begun to fight inside, for the quarrel was already in full swing in the street. Fearfully, she shrank back against the wall. The fight raged, back and forth. She darted glances to right and left, but the fight had summoned an immediate mob who gathered around, and she could not escape. One of the men from the tavern noticed her.

He shoved his fellows out of the way and approached her. "Come to see some real men fight?" he leered.

"Oh, get me out of here!" she implored him, gesturing with her hand. The movement revealed the fur of her cloak, and his eyes glittered greedily.

"Hola!" he shouted. "I'll get you out, my pigeon! Out of that fine robe!" He grabbed her roughly and pulled her toward a darkened doorway. She struggled with him silently but she knew she could not break away from his brute strength. He shoved her against the wall, pinning her with his stinking body. He pulled her cloak away from her shoulders, but he could not get it off for the wall behind held it.

"I'll have it," he muttered, "but I'll have my lady first!"

She thrust against his chest with both hands. He laughed, a brute snort. She felt fury course through her like a red tide. How dare he! She began to fight in earnest. She poked stiffened fingers at his eyes, and he dodged away. His hands were hard on her. She writhed out of his grasp. But she heard silk tear and felt cold air on her skin.

With one hand she grabbed at her falling cloak, and, stooping, flailed an arm against his groin. She missed. He grabbed her shoulders and straightened her, banging her roughly against the wall again. The blow took the breath from her body.

He was too strong for her. She heard fabric tear again as he rent her bliaut from neck to girdle, and she knew she was lost.

An unholy light lit his eyes.

Abruptly, his expression changed to alarm. A mailed fist appeared on his shoulder, and suddenly she was free.

The armed man hurled her assailant aside. He reached for her. Filling her lungs and screaming, she threw herself away from him.

"You idiot!" the newcomer exploded, grabbing her outflung arm. "Don't you have any sense at all?"

She recognized the voice. Aimery!

"How glad I am—," she began. "He—"

"Later!" he said angrily. "We've got to get out of here." Shielding her with one arm, he drew his short sword and eyed the menacing crowd. They were dangerous, and could overwhelm them both by sheer numbers.

"Back!" ordered Aimery. Instead, the crowd, forgetting the brawl that had brought them together, sensed greater loot and excitement in the pale woman and the single knight. They surged forward.

Solange was struck to her knees. A sharp pain shot up her thigh. Aimery's weapon found its mark on one or two at least, judging from the howls. Loath to face cold steel, the unarmed mob suddenly vanished as though they had never been there.

"I pity the man who weds you!" fumed Aimery. "He'll be wedding the devil's own trouble!"

They glared at each other angrily. She was too irate to speak.

A sound issued behind them and Aimery turned his head quickly enough to see that the crowd had not really vanished. They were merely skulking, watching, like rats in a cellar, for their chance to fall upon their prey. One or two or more of them might be hurt, maimed, even killed, if they attacked. But the rest would find loot enough to reward their daring.

Aimery grabbed Solange and thrust her ahead of him. "Walk!" he commanded through tight lips. He marched behind her, turning to guard the rear, and brandished his short sword in the air. "If you attack," he shouted into the darkness, "the king will send enough men to wipe you out. Burn your miserable huts with you in them! He's done it before!"

Solange scurried along ahead of her rescuer, not too far out of reach. She clutched her cloak tightly to her breast. They left the dank alley behind them. The danger was not past, but with every hurried step they moved closer to the main street where they might find aid.

The main street was jammed surprisingly full. Aimery drew Solange closer to him and put his arm around her. She drew a deep shuddering breath of relief, and wondered how Aimery had known where she was. Spying on her? She was pleased, somehow.

The press of the crowd pushed her gently against him,

and she could feel his body, even in its light armor, comfortingly against her. His arm hugged her tightly, and she discovered that her throat was suddenly dry. Too much danger, she thought quickly. It could not be this man's touch upon me, his breath close to my ear, not *this man!* Only Raoul should move her thus. She would not admit that there was a bit of regret in her thoughts of Raoul.

The reason the crowd was lining the main street soon became clear. At a distance came the tinkle of little mule bells, a sure sign that a dignitary of the church was approaching. No churchman would ride on a charger, the magnificent destrier. Those were proud horses, made for war. But the Savior Himself rode a mule into Jerusalem, and his priests were content to do the same.

The churchmen's mules, however, often boasted trappings of silver, blankets of scarlet, and even jeweled bridles. But the mule that now approached, was a beast of great simplicity. Monks surrounded the rider, monks of a strangely burly appearance, and Solange wondered whether there were weapons beneath those simple robes, or armor, like Brother Garin wore.

The rider himself, the famous Abbot Bernard, red hair turning white, blue eyes burning in his hollow-cheeked face, seemed to be contemplating another world, one far better than the one at his feet.

But his expression, whispered Aimery, belied his overwhelming interest in the world around him. He was thin beyond the ordinary, worn almost to a skeleton by fasting, by constant traveling, and by—some said—interfering with the politics of the western world.

He had dueled, and won, with Peter Abelard, a formidable teacher of what Bernard called heresy. He was said to speak with the authority of the pope himself—"and why not?" murmured Aimery. "Bernard singlehandedly made Eugenius the pope when Innocent died. Or so it is said."

The very sight of this man was enough to persuade his audience that they were in the presence of an extraordinary man. "He works miracles . . . he healed my aunt . . . he's more pious than the pope," ran the murmurs behind Solange. "They say that God Almighty speaks directly to Bernard. He is a saint."

At length the clamor of the peasants and townspeople wrested his attention from his meditation, and he turned to bestow benisons upon them, to the accompaniment of shouts and cheers. Bernard, the abbot of the Cistercian Monastery of Clairvaux, had come to celebrate Christmas at Bourges.

With silent accord Solange and Aimery, his arm still around her, slipped into the procession of monks following the abbot. Pilgrims thronged around them, clogging the street. The monk next to them was suspicious, nearly shouldering them out of the procession, but a level look from Aimery made him change his mind.

It took a long time to travel the short distance through the street to the gates of the bishop's palace. Solange was not tall enough to see over the shoulders of their cowled escorts, but she knew they stopped from time to time to answer the cries of the poor people of the town, seeking whatever blessing they could find.

And when the procession reached the wide-swung barbican gate and the abbot rode in, Solange wished it had taken longer.

For Mehun was waiting in the crowd in the courtyard. His eyes fell darkly upon Solange, and then flicked to Aimery. "So," he said. The flurry of welcome to the abbot, Bernard's slow dismounting, and the jostling of many who wished to touch the abbot's robe, kept him from saying more. At length he made his way to Solange, trapped in the crowd.

"So, daughter," he said. "You seek to put your lies first before the abbot, to turn his mind."

His voice was pitched loud enough to reach Solange, but he had not expected the sudden silence, commanded by Bernard's raised hand. Mehun's words rang out startlingly.

"So," said Abbot Bernard, with deceptive mildness. "You believe that my mind is easily turned?"

Mehun saw he had blundered badly. But there was nothing he could do, except to continue. There was no way back.

"No, Father," said Mehun, chagrined. "It is that I have more trouble than a man needs with this girl."

"And it is to come to me in the end? Well, then, let us hear about it."

"Not now," said a monk in the abbot's ear. "The king is waiting to welcome thee."

"Kings will wait upon justice," said Bernard, "if it is a question of a ruling. This is the girl?"

His eyes fell upon Solange. She knew she was not looking her best, clutching madly at her enveloping cloak, but she summoned sufficient courage to look the abbot straight in the eyes, and make her curtsey. "I am the girl he means, sir, but I am not his daughter."

"So?" Bernard turned to Mehun. "The girl lies, you said? Then she is your daughter?"

Mehun, shamefaced, said, "My wife's daughter. And therefore mine. But she will not obey me, and it is merely a matter of childish rebellion."

"Not quite, Father Bernard," interrupted Aimery unexpectedly. "A matter of an oath foresworn, in all likelihood."

"And you are?"

"Merely a friend. Aimery de Montvert."

"Ah yes, I know your brother Garin. But I will hear this later, since it appears a lengthy tale. In the meantime, I must greet my host. I fear that I must leave you now. In the meantime—," he glanced kindly at Solange, seeing her frightened eyes—"do not fear. Nothing will happen to you."

He swept on toward Bishop de la Chartre waiting on the steps of the great building. Left behind by the abbot's tide of men, Mehun glared at them. "I won't forget this, Montvert. You are interfering where you have no business. And you will suffer for it." He turned on his heel and followed the abbot until he was lost in the crowd.

Solange was suddenly shy in Aimery's presence. The memory of his arm around her was lively in her mind, and she could not raise her eyes to his. She said in a muffled voice, "Thank you for saving me back there."

Aimery's face was a mixture of emotions she could not read. Anger must have been foremost, for he said coldly, "Abbot Bernard promised that nothing would happen to you. I suggest, unless you wish to make him a falsifier, that you do not stray into the town again. Come along. I'll get you back to the countess."

He said no further word until he deposited her at the door of the suite she shared with the girls. She wanted to make him say something, anything. She said, "I could have saved myself back there. They would not have harmed a lady of the court." She deliberately ignored her ruined bliaut. Perhaps Aimery had not seen her nakedness. She devoutly hoped so.

"You think not?" said Aimery coolly. "Your cloak, your jeweled bliaut, and whatever else you may be wearing would have been torn off you for the value of the clothes. And then," he said with a wolfish grin, "who could tell you were different from any other woman in the streets?"

She fumed, sputtering helplessly. Then he was gone. She did not see him again until later that day, when he was at Queen Eleanor's right hand and did not look her way.

But she did not care. For Abbot Bernard was not the only new arrival at court that day.

When she arrived in the great hall for dinner, she met Brother Garin. He looked drawn, unusually tired. But the news he brought her drove the observation from her mind.

"Riders have come with dispatches from Paris," he said. "One of the riders was Raoul de Puiseaux." He eyed her narrowly. "Has he sent word to you of his arrival?"

"No!" she gasped. Delight lit her violet eyes, and her smile illuminated the room, so Brother Garin thought, his heart sinking. Was the maid truly in love with that . . . that *clerk*? He could not think she was—and yet she seemed to be. His thoughts darted for some way to aid her, but none occurred to him.

"Is he here? Where is he? I wonder why he didn't— maybe he didn't know I was here. That's it, isn't it, Brother Garin?" She didn't wait for an answer. Dancing on tiptoes, she demanded, "Where is he? I must see him."

In the end she did not see Raoul until dinner was set down on the table. She was searching all the faces, the new ones and the old, trying to catch a glimpse of Raoul.

The forbidding frown of Aimery rose before her mind's eye. Raoul was worth a dozen stern ill-tempered knights like Aimery. Nonetheless, the thought of Aimery's timely rescue, his gentleness in the king's audience room, on the tower when he had brought the king's summons, and the scalding scorn when he spoke to her at other times, all this bewildering mixture took a little away from her excitement over Raoul.

She saw her betrothed at last. As he knelt before the king to present, she guessed, the results of his mission, she had a moment to look at the man she would marry, the youth her father had looked on with favor.

He had changed. Of course he has, she admonished herself; it's been over two years. She herself had probably changed. But this Raoul seemed a little, well, *softer* was the only word she could think of, a little more rounded as to cheek. A little . . . unsubstantial. She remembered with relief that she was comparing Raoul with the knights who swarmed around the palace, dressed in light armor, bulky and stiff. Raoul was in maroon velvet, gold-embroidered, and she was positive that he wore no mailed shirt beneath his belted tunic.

The king was speaking to Raoul, and they both glanced in her direction. Raoul's eyes flickered in recognition as he made his way toward her. She could not contain her excitement. She left her bench and ran a few steps toward him. She was stopped abruptly by the look in his eyes. Pale blue, they held an odd dullness that she didn't remember.

He stopped before her, and put his hands on his hips. "I confess I did not expect to see you here at court, Solange. What brought you here?"

There was no love in his eyes, only a simple curiosity, perhaps, and surprise.

"I came—well, Raoul, it's a long story. But mainly, my stepfather seeks to give me in marriage—"

"Not to me!" said Raoul involuntarily.

"No, of course not. Mehun says there was no betrothal between you and me, and my mother agrees. If you can believe it, Raoul, my mother says we are *not betrothed.* Raoul, you must tell the king—"

The slightest of smiles rippled over his face, so quickly that she was not sure she saw it. "Your mother says there was no ceremony?"

"She lies, you know that."

"Well, now, Solange, I must consider. I should not like to put the lie to your mother. That brutish husband of hers might run me through."

"*Raoul!*"

"Well, I certainly must search my conscience. But the king beckons me and I must run." He swayed on his heels. "But if I were you, Solange, I should not begin sewing on my wedding finery."

14

*L*ater, she would remember that first flicker of dumbfounded recognition in Raoul's pale eyes. She had expected —she didn't know quite what—but certainly not this cold reception.

True, he hadn't written her, except that once, shortly after he had departed for the king's court. When he had left her at Belvent, he had been all smiles, full of gentleness. She could still feel his hand smoothing back her long pale hair, the chaste kiss he placed on her forehead.

Recalling every slight detail of their meeting, as she tossed on her pallet that night, she decided she must have embarrassed him with her country ways, running like a child to meet him. She squirmed with dismay at the recollection of how young she must have seemed. And yet, seeing him again, she had suddenly returned to the childhood they had shared. Solange would arrive at Puiseaux Castle, and Raoul would show her the newest litters of pink fat pigs, or the kittens cunningly hidden under the threshold of the stable door.

When Raoul had come to Belvent with his parents, she would suggest they ride out to follow the hunt, or to see her father's new falcon perform. But sooner or later, she remembered, Raoul would weary of such sports—or pretend to weary, thinking them too rough for her—and suggest a game of chess under the apple trees in the orchard.

Always, she remembered, he had chosen the quieter pursuits in deference to what he thought were her desires.

How shamefaced Raoul must have been this night, not supposing her to be so bold as to come to court to seek him out! He must have had a different idea of her. And strangely, for the first time, she wondered how could he have mistaken her so, all these years? Why hadn't he seen that she longed for the hunt, or to go hawking, or simply to gallop through the forest rides? Perhaps he had not understood her.

Tomorrow, she decided, she would decorously wait for him to send word to her, to come to see her. He certainly knew where to find her.

Perhaps he had found another love. That might explain his attitude. A new love, even though it hurt her, was something she could understand. But why didn't he just tell her?

The next day, she started up every time the door opened. Countess Alis was exceedingly popular, for her own comfortable personality, and also because she was married to the king's brother. Many thought to reach the king through her.

"If they only knew," giggled Bertille, "how little of what they say ever goes outside this room."

"The countess is a woman to be trusted," said Catherine. "If I had trouble, believe me, I would go to her at once."

Catherine looked kindly at Solange. Solange smiled weakly back. Surely all the world must know that her betrothed had scorned her, in public. How ashamed she was!

Isabel de la Valle had joined the girls at their sewing that afternoon. "Probably she wore out her welcome with the queen," whispered Bertille. She had no use for the queen's distant cousin, who heartily returned the compliment. "Sly as a cat," insisted Bertille secretly. "Don't trust her even as far as you can see her, Solange."

Isabel came over to where Solange and Catherine sat at the window where the light fell on their work. "Truly, I cannot believe you are in great trouble, Solange. From what my cousin the queen says, the problem is trivial, and will be easily settled. But one must wonder at it. First your mother denies your betrothal, and then the man himself certainly acts . . . *unbetrothed*! I wonder why you would insist on wedding someone like Raoul?"

Catherine looked up sharply. "I feel sure you will not wish to upset Solange further, Isabel. We must all feel she has put her problems into the right hands, and—"

"Oh, yes," cried Isabel, bridling with indignation. "I am sure that Solange believes her knight will come riding to her rescue! That will be a day to mark well!"

Solange bit her lip, fighting back the tears. But Isabel had not finished. "More like a cat than ever," Bertille exploded later, "playing with a mouse she had already wounded."

"Tell me, Solange, do you ever sleepwalk?"

"Sleepwalk!" exploded Solange. "Never! And I wasn't sleepwalking the day I was betrothed!"

"Has anyone seen my green silk thread?"

The countess's voice cut across Solange's bristling retort. By the time the countess had dealt summarily with the situation, sending Isabel on a totally fabricated errand to the queen, and setting Solange and Catherine to search for the elusive green floss, Solange's hot temper had subsided, and she knew that she had no need to explain her quick flare-up to the countess. The countess saw much more than she seemed to see.

But nonetheless, Isabel de la Valle's remarks rankled. Sleepwalking, indeed! There was a reason for Petronilla to deny the betrothal ceremony. She was under Mehun's rule.

But she could not quite understand Raoul's turning away from her. He knew where to find her.

If he wanted to.

It was clear to her now that he did not want to search her out. She wondered whether the expressions of love between them had all been one-sided. She was not sure, even though Raoul had seemed more awkward than she.

At length, toward the second afternoon, when the sun tipped the cross atop the wooden spire of the church on the hill above the palace, she thought she could not draw another breath. The chimney had decided to smoke, sending stifling gray clouds out into the room, causing the ladies to cough. Evart and the grooms, who were coughing as well, came to look and profess helplessness.

She snatched up her fur-lined cloak and disappeared through the door of the suite while they were still discussing the wayward chimney.

She started again for the courtyard of the castle. She knew she should not travel alone through the corridors, but she did not care. If she did not breathe fresh air, and soon, she would scream.

She had gone only a short distance when she neared the corridor leading to the queen's suite. Perhaps she might see Aimery coming or going. She had often done so, and many times he had joined her and the others for a stroll in the wards of the castle. This time, as she reached the cross-corridor, she saw a familiar figure coming towards her. It was not Aimery.

It was Raoul, dressed in Italian green velvet, a sheaf of rolled parchments like pipes in his hands. When he saw her he hesitated, turning back as though to escape her. But she stood stock still, watching him with level gaze, and he thought better than to escape.

"Raoul, I've been wondering where you could have gone to the other night," she began.

"Sorry, Solange. I am too busy to talk. The king's business, you know. I don't have a moment."

Hot temper flared up, but she swallowed it. She would take a leaf from the countess's book. "I should like to see you sometime, Raoul, soon." She cast her mind swiftly around, and fastened upon a lure. "We can talk about the old times. I'm sure you'd like to know how Bernier is, and how old Mahaut is faring. Marchedoux, too, you remember my fine mare?"

His face was softening a bit. "Well, I should like to hear about Bernier. Did he come to court with you?"

"No," she said puzzled. "I did not realize—"

His face changed sharply. "Realize what?" His lips tightened. "Sorry, Solange, some other time."

Without another word he turned on his heel and left, leaving her standing watching after him, mouth agape at his deliberate rudeness. She shook her head in bewilderment. Truly, she did not understand him.

This time she did not go down toward the courtyard. She had had enough of people for awhile. She turned, instead, in the other direction, toward the parapet at the top of the palace. There she had watched for her mother to come from Belvent, summoned by the king. She had seen the little procession wind down the far hill, just as she and Aimery and Brother Garin had done that first day, when she had thought that she would find her love and the haven he would provide here, in Bourges.

Now, she thought, spreading her cloak under her forearms and leaning on the gray stone, she had not even that faint hope. Her mother had turned against her, and Raoul was cold.

Abbé Bernard had agreed to render judgment. It was his right, of course. Being a man of the church, he was in a position to rule on a church ceremony. Was it valid? Or did its force die when Odo de St. Florent died? Now, thanks to her own mother, there was even a question as to whether it had taken place.

She moved restlessly along the parapet. She was not sure what she was looking for, until she found it. A place where a stone had broken off, a gap in the high wall so wide that a dog or a cat might fall through it. Or a human, a slim, desperate human, might wriggle through the restraining wall and plunge below.

She could not do it. She dared not commit such a sin, for God's eye was everywhere and whatever she had to endure in this world would be easier, so they said, than punishment in the next. She knelt by the gap.

Sharp metallic footsteps rang on the stone floor. She looked quickly around as she was pulled roughly to her feet. It was Aimery.

"Do you follow me around?" she demanded angrily. "Don't you have anything else to do?"

"Apparently you need a fulltime guardian," he said, making a rigorous effort to keep his temper. "But the Lady Alis thought you might—"

"Get into trouble again?" said Solange. Her voice sounded hot in her ears, but it did not shake. "I do not need any more trouble."

She did not think about how close she might have come

to worming her way through that gap in the parapet. If Aimery had saved her by his timely appearance, she would not give him the satisfaction of knowing it.

"A way out of your troubles," Aimery said. "That stone ought to be replaced. I don't know why you would want to jump."

"You know perfectly well that I was not going to jump," she said crisply, and quite untruthfully. "At least at Saint Vergillia's I would die in a state of grace. And it would not take much longer to die than to leap from this height."

He looked troubled. "What are you going to do, go into the convent?"

She shook her head. "But I don't understand what's happening," she said. "I don't understand Raoul, for one thing."

"I hope not," he said roughly. "I'm not much of a philosopher, but it seems to me that you don't know what you want out of life. You can't be in love with Raoul."

"Why not?"

"You give no sign of it to me."

"And you, of course, know much about love!" she said hotly.

"All I need to know," he said, his lips tightening. "You need to grow up. Life isn't a series of feast days and tournaments. Trouble comes to all, and you're just trying to say it doesn't."

To her horror, she felt tears coursing down her cheeks. "Well," he added more kindly, "I don't need to add to yours. But you do need to grow up."

"How?" she stormed. "Just how? By letting everybody hand me around from one man to another? From Raoul to Conon d'Yves? And all because a little narrow-minded brute says so?"

"You mean Mehun."

"Of course I mean him. But there's the king—he's going to decide. Or the abbot, and they all say they can tell me how I will live my life."

Aimery's glance turned sour. "It's the way of the world," he said at last. "Even queens must bow to their lords."

She didn't catch the bitter tone in his voice. Too intent

on her own hurt, she could only ease it by hurting in her turn.

"Not that queen," she said darkly. "That queen does exactly as she pleases. And you are a fool to believe otherwise."

"Watch your tongue!"

"Oh, there's no one to hear me. You're the only spy who follows me around. But if you think that you will succeed with her, you need to grow up as much as I do."

He was angry. She knew the little muscle along his jaw tensed, but she did not care. She could not stop.

"What is it I have heard the troubadours sing? 'I marvel —I marvel not—' Oh yes, now I remember. . . .

> 'I marvel not her love should fetter me (she sang)
>   Unto such beauty none hath e'er attained;
> So courteous, gay, and fair, and good, is she,
>   That for her worth all other worth hath waned.' "

"Quiet!" he gritted. "You don't understand. I would do anything for her, any kind of toil, danger, suffer anything—"

"Why? Does not her king have that privilege? Cannot he command his armies to protect his queen?"

At his fierce glare she involuntarily moved a few steps away. But some imp within her drove her to taunt him. "I commend to you the words I just sang to you," she told him, laughing brightly. "I forget the rest of the tune, but it is the words which you should heed.

> 'Unless your word will heal right speedily
>   Mine head's confusion and mine heart's sore pain,
> Your two bright eyes will slay me suddenly,
>   The beauty of them I cannot sustain.'

Remember that, Sieur Aimery. Especially the part which says, *'Mine head's confusion'*—"

To his surprise, as much as hers, he grasped her roughly by the shoulders and pulled her to him. His lips fastened upon hers, warm in spite of the cold wind that whistled around the corners of the castle walls. A long kiss, stirring, tingling, melting her. Involuntarily she pressed herself to him, responding, obedient to the sudden pounding in her temples.

And then, much too soon, he thrust her away, loosening his hold so that she staggered against the stone wall. His face darkened until she was afraid of him, almost.

He looked as though he could kill her. Then, abruptly, he laughed, a short bark. "Go on your way. Jump if you want to. You'll take only yourself to perdition. At least then you won't drag me down with you!"

With a whirl of his cloak he was gone through the doorway into the stone corridor. She looked after him, and then followed, more slowly. She realized with a start that night had fallen over the city, and even the cross on Saint Stephen's Church above was lost in the darkness.

15

The castle at Bourges was filled to the walls, and the town below nearly spilled the over-supply of humanity into the rivers winding around the rock below. The king's presence always meant innumerable servants, nobles, knights, hangers-on, and *their* hangers-on. But the approach of Christmas and Abbot Bernard's visit brought even more throngs to the town.

Barons, counts, and lesser nobility all were impelled to spend Christmas with their liege lord. And no knight or baron traveled alone. Even Mehun de Mowbrai, for once wary of giving offense and reluctant to make a display of his newly-attained state, traveled with what he considered a minimum. Mehun and his lady brought a train of merely twenty men-at-arms, and their servants, besides personal attendants for themselves and a string of sumpter beasts to carry the packs and boxes that held clothing and other necessaries.

As Christmas approached, the ways grew crowded with travelers, many in much greater estate than the de Mowbrais, clamoring for quarters for themselves and, if room were available, for their servants as well.

The bishop's stewards wore worried frowns and evermore-harried expressions, as the wood supply dwindled, the foodstuffs become sparse, and the king's hunters had to travel farther and farther for sufficient game to grace the king's table.

And of course the heralded presence of the great abbot of Clairvaux, Bernard, brought its own crowds of churchmen, high and low. It was widely reported that Bernard would have a special message for Christmas mass this year. And since even on low Sundays Bernard was a powerful preacher, this Christmas sermon raised great expectations.

Jehane had arrived from Belvent and joined the maids serving Countess Alis's ladies. It was good to hear the news from home. Mahaut missed Solange, but she had two new grandchildren to take charge of, and she was ordering everyone around as usual. Jehane's perspective was a bit jaundiced, Solange remembered. The girl had felt the rough edge of Mahaut's tongue more than once.

In some way known only to herself, Petronilla had wheedled a few coins from Mehun, and had secretly given them to Solange. "You'll have need of these, and it's only your right to have Belvent money."

Solange could not help but be moved by the atmosphere of excitement and celebration. Lady Alis, knowing the practical remedies for grief and turmoil, brought out another weapon from her healing arsenal.

"Solange, my dear," she said. "I confess I am doubtful about what to present to the queen as a Christmas gift. Do you know of anything she especially wants?"

"No, Lady Alis. I am sorry."

"You could ask Aimery, I imagine."

I wouldn't ask him for a crust of bread if I were starving, she thought. Aloud, she said, "I have not seen him for several days."

Lady Alis had found out what she needed to know. "I have heard that there are travelers in the courtyard who have brought wares from the east. Will you go with me to look at what they have? Perhaps some bauble will strike us as the right gift for Her Majesty."

Lady Alis believed that thinking of someone else's needs did wonders for putting one's own in perspective, but she could not have guessed how well she would succeed in her endeavor, this time.

Since the gift-giving of Christmas was approaching, the town of Bourges welcomed a fair, by the king's license. This allowed the merchants to put up their stalls inside the outer ward of the palace. Usually a fair was held in summer, in fine weather, outdoors.

Merchants traveling to the court rode under the king's peace, as well as that could be enforced, and willingly paid the many tolls on the roads and bridges in hopes of making a good profit from the wealthy people clustering around His Majesty.

The countess and Solange descended the stone stairs into the courtyard, followed by Jehane and Lady Alis's two servants and a groom. The little party struggled through the seething crowds to a sort of improvised shelter where the pedlars had spread out their wares.

Everything in the world was here for sale, thought Solange. The fairs she had been to before were poor things compared to the wealth of exotic goods brought to Bourges. There were booths of silk fabric from Syria, another of brocades from Venice. There was a small booth where the trader sold only dyestuffs—vermilion, indigo, rose madder, viridian.

There were wonderful glass vessels, to be used carefully, and handed down to one's heirs; leather goods; furs from Muscovy. Coppersmiths displayed cunningly contrived items, and there were perfumes and buckles and golden girdles and necklets studded with jewels, and laces and fine linen to be made into wimples, and enameled boxes and inlaid jewel-set caskets.

It was enough to make Solange's head swim. She had only a small store of coins, and she kept them tightly in her hand.

Lady Alis was enraptured by the assortment. She was knowledgeable about quality and price, Solange noted. But

Solange herself had less interest in the goods. Not even the pet monkey, shivering in a small cage placed near a fire, could intrigue her for long. Instead she began to wonder what sights these merchants had seen on their many travels.

Had the eyes of that one, with the great hooked nose and dark beard, rested upon the blue sea that lay beyond France? Had he, possibly, seen the Holy Land itself?

"Not I, lady," he said when she timidly asked him. "But over there, you see? There is a band of pilgrims just back. Bad news, I fear. A great battle was lost."

Murmuring thanks, she left Lady Alis and moved, as though drawn by a long thread, toward the pilgrims who were huddled beneath a makeshift shelter. Jehane protested but, waved to silence, followed her mistress like a dutiful shadow.

The returning pilgrims were housed in a rickety stable, a lean-to with a slanted roof and one side open to the weather. There was straw for bedding. It was not as much as a war horse would need, but enough, so the stewards had thought, for six exhausted men returning from Jerusalem, most maimed, destined to die before they reached home.

She stopped short a few feet away, halted by the stench that was a barrier strong as a curtain wall. The light was already failing in the outer ward, the sun already sinking behind the castle walls and towers. But she could see inside the shelter all too well.

Six men—or parts of men. One lifted stumps of wrists with a pitiful cry for alms. One, nearly hidden beneath the straw in the corner, sobbed endlessly, complaining of the cold.

"The cold of death," croaked the halest of the men, limping toward her. "He will not last the night, I fear. Lady, you seek something here?"

"You—" She swallowed the lump in her throat. "You have come back from Outremer?"

"Aye, we have." The man who spoke to her leaned heavily upon a stick and she noticed his foot twisted under him. "Better we had died there. But of course, we did not know that when we went, did we?"

"You are a man of quality," she said, surprised.

"Aye. I was a knight in Rheims, and these——" he gestured toward the pitiful men behind him "——these were some of my men who followed me. We are the unlucky ones. The lucky ones died on the journey."

"I'm sorry," she said, inadequately. Who could balm the wounds of this man as he looked at those who, for love of their faith, had followed him into hell?

A confusion of words rose behind him and he turned for a moment to soothe the babbler. When he returned to her, he said in a burst of helpless fury, "I pray to God every night to take these men into His grace." He dug one fist into the other palm and turned away lest she see his tears. Mastering himself, he said, "But I distress you, lady. You seek something of us?"

"News, only," she said. "My father took the Way of the Cross five years gone. I have not heard from him for three years, since the battle of Adana. I seek news of him."

Even one word about her father, from someone who had actually seen him since he left Belvent, would be a balm to her great hurt. Her father might have spoken a word to one of these men. It was possible, wasn't it? "His banner was of yellow silk, with a blue swan swimming," she prompted.

"A lord, of course," he said thoughtfully. "I did not know many."

"Odo de Saint Florent," she urged. "You could have heard his name?"

One by one the faces, some ecstatically looking inward, some full of compassion for this lovely lady with the violet eyes, so sorely troubled, fell with regret. No, they did not know the name. There were many Frankish knights in battle, she must realize, and in the heat of the fighting there was no chance to watch the fallen banners.

Not even the yellow silk pennon with the blue swan on it?

With regret, he shook his head. Already his mind was back with the men who were his woeful charge. He must have nursed the cripples, himself crippled, all the toilsome way back from Jerusalem. And to what end? To become beggars? Their welcome at home might be cold indeed.

Impulsively, she held out her coin-filled hand to the knight. "Sir, I beg you," she said, "I can do nothing to ease your troubles. But at least you must have food this night. Take this, and spend it. . . ." He frowned, and she added quickly, ". . . for your men."

He nodded brief thanks. "God prosper you, lady," he said, and retreated into the shelter.

She was aware of one pilgrim, a minstrel, no doubt, since he carried his lute carefully under his arm, standing at the edge of the shelter. She thought to ask him, but when she left the little band of returning pilgrims, she could not find him.

She turned away. For some reason, she was not discouraged. If these pilgrims had not seen her father, there were many other pilgrims returning on the great highways of France. She would make inquiries.

She would know at last whether her father was dead. Or—her thoughts soared—perhaps he had sent word by one of his men, one of these pilgrims?

Lost in her dreams, she failed to notice that she had crossed the courtyard and stood at the foot of the stairs. Lady Alis, so Jehane said disapprovingly, had gone on ahead, and left word for Solange to follow. She was slow to move, pondering where she would find more pilgrims in this town. She could not go out alone into the town, not after her recent experience.

"Lady," said a gentle voice at her elbow. She looked up to see the slim sad face of the minstrel, the man who had vanished from the corner of the stable.

He was of slight build, thin as a wisp. His clothes were russet, and not very clean. The cross on his back, which she had noticed earlier, meant he had been to Outremer, to the Holy City itself, and now was returning home.

The names of the fabled cities of the Cross—Jerusalem, Edessa, Constantinople, Antioch, Acre—all of these might be as familiar to this man as Bourges was to her!

"Yes?" she responded. Then, after he glanced furtively behind him, she prompted him. "You are a minstrel, by your lute. You ask alms? I regret I have given my last coins to those in the stable."

"Not alms, lady. But—a moment, please—alone?"

"Of course," she agreed. "Jehane . . ."

The maid went a few steps away. Solange nodded to the minstrel. "Yes?"

"You ask about a certain knight of France?"

"Yes! Odo de Saint Florent. You knew him?"

"You have a reason to ask?"

"I am his daughter."

"Yet you speak of him as though he were dead."

"I have been told he is."

"How did he die?"

"In the battle of Adana. I was told by one who saw him die."

The minstrel shook his head. "Not the battle of Adana. I saw him, alive and unharmed, ten days after that battle. I saw him at Antioch."

She felt the blood drain from her cheeks. Her father alive? *After* the battle? Then Mehun had lied!

Her father might still be alive! Be on his weary way home even now, plodding toward Belvent, expecting to see his pretty wife and his daughter. Perhaps he was crippled, or blind, like one of those unfortunates behind her in the shelter. She stood, stricken, and roused herself only when the minstrel began to look at her with concern. Her father . . . alive!

"Where is he?" she demanded. "Is he coming home? Where did you see him?" She reached out to clutch his sleeve. "Come with me. We will find the king!"

The minstrel turned mutinous. Shaking his head vigorously, he said, "I am sorry, lady. I could not. I can only tell you what I know. But not the king. I have no liking for dungeons."

She could not convince him that he would be safe in the kindly hands of King Louis. His fear was too great.

She was in despair. Proof was so close, and yet the minstrel would not tell the king what he knew. Her thoughts swooped like a falcon, and hit upon the right lure. "Gold," she said, promising recklessly, "I will give you much gold."

He was clearly tempted. But, he said, he dared not tell

the king. She was impatient. "Tell me, then, tell me how you saw him. What was he doing?"

It took a long time, a great deal of ardent persuasion, before the minstrel would agree to meet her again. Christmas night would be filled with laughter and festival, and much coming and going. She could meet him secretly, atop the tower, where they would not be overheard. The minstrel insisted upon that much secrecy.

"And bring the gold," he reminded her.

"I will," she said. "Before you go, what is your name?"

"Call me Loriot," he told her.

"Loriot," she thought as she climbed the steps and hurried down the corridor to her own suite. Loriot the oriole.

Well, that bird would sing a very merry tune, the very next night! she thought, her heart full of gratitude. After all her great fears, all her grief, her father might yet be alive!

Book Two
France, 1146

⚜

1

Christmas Day, 1146.

The bells rang out at first light, ringing in the birthday of our Lord. The bells on the spire of Saint Stephen's sent ringing notes of celebration out into the crisp winter air, spilling down the terraced lanes of the town, across the wide river valleys and the frozen water-meadows of the two encircling rivers, to the hills beyond.

Solange woke in happiness. Christmas Day! And this day was set apart for Solange especially, for this day she would meet the minstrel. The news he had would be good. It had to be!

Suddenly she was wide awake. Throwing her fur covering aside, she reached from her pallet to poke Bertille next to her.

"Come on, sleepyhead, time to get up. It's the most glorious day in the world."

Bertille roused, at last. "Must you?" she grumbled, shaking her dark hair over her bare shoulders. "I don't see how you can be so silly this early in the morning. If it *is* morning."

Catherine was awake now, too. "Of course it is morning. You can't be so deaf you did not hear the bells?"

Bertille stopped short. "I vow I did not hear them. Well," she added reluctantly, "I suppose there's nothing for it but to get up in this frigid room. *Someplace* there must be warmth all day and all night."

"That is what they say about the realms of Satan," Solange chuckled, "and I am sure you do not intend to sojourn there?"

"Of course not!" cried Bertille, leaping out of the bed in a desperate lunge, and snatching her chemise from her stool. "Unless—do you know how handsome Satan is supposed to be?"

Catherine smothered a laugh in her throat. "Take care,"

she said, more soberly, "lest you find out. I think he might not be as amiable as Hugh de Perigoux."

"Oh, him!"

The banter went on, but Solange's thoughts drifted away to the evening ahead. She came to herself only when the candle was lit, and Bertille stood before her, dressed.

"Solange, fasten this brooch if you have nothing else to do."

Solange wore the new pale rose gown Countess Alis had given her. Of thin Syrian silk, it was full-skirted, just clearing the floor. The soft fabric was pleated throughout, outlining the soft curve of her breast, swelling slightly over the slender hips and then falling in soft folds to the ground. She put on a new jeweled girdle, of soft gold-colored leather, centering it in front and then bringing it around to the back and fastening it in the front in a double-girdle fashion. From the buckle, set with amethysts, the long ends of the girdle fell to the hem of her skirt.

She found time to bind her long braids with rose ribbons of the same color as her gown. She wished she had the metal braid cases that she had been forced to leave behind with all else at Belvent. No one needed such ornaments in the convent!

Bertille, in vermilion to set off her dark curls, and Catherine, in pale blue, were ready before Solange was. Isabel preened herself in her new green samite, cunningly cut to emphasize her large bosom and tiny waist.

Solange felt as though her feet did not even touch the rush-strewn floor. Her heart sang: Father is alive! She dismissed out of hand her mother's illegal marriage. She could do nothing about that. She meant only to honor her father's betrothal contract for her. And that meant that neither the dreadful Baron d'Yves nor the harsh convent could touch her. Not any more!

But all was not well around her. Lady Alis was sorely troubled. Brother Garin came to pay his respects to the Count de Dreux, the king's brother. And the news he brought was unsettling.

"The Kingdom of Edessa has truly fallen," he explained. "And the infidel makes strides toward pushing the French into the sea."

Robert de Dreux wheezed impatiently, "There are Franks enough there in Antioch, in Jerusalem, to deal with the infidel, aren't there? We did it before, when Raymond of Toulouse and Godfrey took the Holy City. But I truly do not see why the Byzantine Empire does not hurl the Turks back."

"I have heard that the Greeks are treacherous," said the countess. "I fear we should not trust them overmuch."

"Yet they are Christians," said Catherine kindly, "and surely the Holy Sepulcher means as much to them as to us?"

Brother Garin said, "I do not know. All I know is that our abbot has matters of great import to tell us. Great events are coming."

Lady Alis said, with unaccustomed tartness, "The abbot's great news usually means that there is a fight going on somewhere in the world."

Her lord looked at her with amusement.

The count seemed even fatter to Solange than the first time she had seen him, only a month before. "Like my father!" he chuckled in high good humor. "Had to lift him out of bed. Couldn't even get on a horse toward the last."

Usually the count hovered at his brother's royal elbow, but he was genuinely fond of his shrewd wife, and Solange suspected that more than one of the count's sharp observations originated in the head of his wife.

"My dear, all life is a battle. Against the devil, if no one else."

Brother Garin said somberly, "And the devil may be winning."

Lady Alis said dryly, "I doubt it, even if Abbot Bernard has to fight him singlehanded."

Looking around her with a sweeping glance, she collected her ladies and led their way to the church for Christmas mass.

Solange, nearly bursting with her news, moved closer to Brother Garin as they moved along the corridor. She trusted Brother Garin. He had stood up for her from the very beginning, and now she wanted to tell him that optimism had not been misplaced. Mehun had no power over her—not now!

Touching Brother Garin's sleeve, Solange whispered urgently, "Brother Garin, I have great news. I want to tell you—"

"Later, my dear," said Brother Garin, not unkindly, but with an air of distraction. "Our abbot wishes me to attend him at the service this morning. A great honor, you know. But of course I have known him for many years. It was Father Bernard, you know, who showed me the path I must take, when my brothers embraced the world. My way lies with the Holy Church."

She was speaking to a fanatic, she realized. Did Abbot Bernard have such a powerful influence over everyone?

Disappointed, she slowed to let Brother Garin escape on his hurried way to the church. Joining her friends again, she slipped into line as the procession moved steadily upward along the stone corridors, turning to climb winding stone steps, emptying at last into an upper courtyard. Here the procession stopped.

They were waiting for the king and the queen to lead the procession into the church. The air here at the top of the hill was unbelievably icy. There was nothing to stop the bitter wind, she thought, in its travels from Norway across the northern seas, swooping across the plains to Paris, and then down the valleys to this isolated rock, which the Romans and the tribes of Gauls before them had seen fit to fortify.

Overhead the stars still twinkled in the waning night. Far to the east, the sun was caught in the trees that bordered the Auron River. Fancifully, she mused, I wonder if the sun would ever get caught in the branches and not rise at all!

A sharp nudge in her ribs told her that the procession had moved ahead while she was dreaming.

The church of Saint Stephen was surprisingly simple, considering that it was the seat of a bishop. It was small, made of wood, hardly sturdy enough to bear the golden cross on its tower. It was said that Pierre de la Chartre planned an enormous church for the site at the top of the hill, but he dared not start building without more money than he had in hand. And every time he gathered a sum he deemed adequate, some emergency arose to take it all— an emergency such as the king's prolonged visit!

The procession emerging at the base of the final rise topped by the church gathered its various strands into one winding river of people, like the braiding of many-hued silks into a woven rope. The cloaks everyone wore were bright with color.

There was not enough room in the church. And yet, all those who wanted in were determined that there should be room. Solange, holding Bertille's arm, was suddenly swept away by a surge through the side door, and had to fight to keep her footing.

"Bertille!" she cried out, but Bertille too was borne away on the breast of the surging mob. The faces around Solange were mad in their desire to enter the church, to get as much of the priest's blessing as could fall on them. It was as though their immortal souls depended on getting to the altar, no matter whose vulnerable body lay broken underfoot.

She was locked in the grip of strangers who paid her no more heed than a stream in flood heeds the leaf as it falls.

There was hardly room to stand inside the church. The king's party had gone in first, and then the suite of the Count de Dreux, the king's brother. Already the church was full, with only these two groups. But crowds surged in from the open doors, and while she thought there could not be room for one more person, yet the heralds cried, "Make way! Make way!"

At last the crowds were no longer moving. Someone had shut the doors behind them to keep out latecomers. She was not tall enough to see beyond the burly shoulders of the soldier in front of her, could only see the bobbing heads, covered with felt caps, with head rails, with veils. Someone's metal braid covers dug into her shoulder.

She was alone in this great mass of strangers, in the semidarkness, lit only by the candles on the altar and the torches in sconces along the wall.

She could not breathe. The room swam before her eyes. She moved, or tried to move. She knew she could not faint, since there was no room for falling. She concentrated on her prayers.

There was a sudden commotion at the altar. The priest was coming up, flanked by his acolytes and his crucifer. The people around Solange surged forward to catch a better glimpse, and she lost her footing.

"Aah!" she breathed, and fell back against the person behind her. Strong arms came out to set her safely on her feet.

"Better lean on me," he counseled. "I will warrant your safety."

She twisted around and looked into the eyes of her rescuer, the pale glittering eyes of Conon d'Yves!

"Best learn to trust me," he said with a twist of his thin lips. "We will save time in the long run."

Full of the confidence engendered by her secret assurance that the baron could no longer pose a menace to her, she smiled confidently. She knew she would be safe in the crowd now, for Conon's mailed body crouched over her, like a falcon's over its prey.

She forgot d'Yves when the abbot came to the altar. It was hard to realize he was the same man she had met in the streets of Bourges.

Now he was dressed in his simple white monk's robe, against the background of the red and gold of the local churchmen. In this stark simplicity, he seemed to have become taller. He stood still, looking out over the congregation, waiting for the murmuring to quiet down before the mass began.

The great body of Christ's kingdom, in this church and in all the churches of the Western World, were giving thanks to God for his Son, born this day more than a thousand years before, to bring salvation to all who believed in Him and did Him honor in their hearts.

There was no reconciling this sentiment with the crazed faces of those who had stormed into Saint Stephen's moments ago, trampling any who stood in their way. Solange did not even try to understand the paradox.

Not until Bernard began his sermon did she begin to listen. Conon's arms were tight around her, but she did not even notice. There was a holy incandescent look about the abbot that pervaded everyone in the church. Even Conon, for the moment, lapsed from his worldly thoughts.

"The Holy Land . . ." preached Bernard . . . "where Our Lord walked, is again in danger of defilement. . . ."

2

The monk seemed frail, a wisp in the white robe. Yet he burned like a flame—the "Candle of God," someone declared, awed. He was sparing of gesture, his voice low and vibrant, yet it seemed to reach into every heart and strike a responding chord there.

"The dusty roads where Our Lord walked, now profaned by unholy feet . . ." He moved his audience to tears.

"Our fathers, who answered the call of Pope Urban the second, these great men of Christendom knew their duty," thundered Bernard, "as true knights, true Christians. They gave up everything for the Way of the Cross. Their names ring out like the notes of the silver trumpets: Bohemund of Taranto, Raymond of Toulouse. The great Godfrey of Bouillon, who first set foot on the streets of the Holy City, reaping the fruits of his valor against the Turkish infidel . . ."

"Getting themselves nice little kingdoms in the process," whispered Conon, gleefully irreverent. "Why don't you and I carve ourselves a realm in Outremer? Like Saint Gilles, or Baldwin?"

She had forgotten that Conon still held her. With indignation, she thrust his arms away from her. "With you?" she said, twisting to glare up into his face. "I'd not walk a step with you."

Undaunted, he said, "Then we'll stay here. A man would be a fool to go to Outremer and leave such a treasure behind."

Those around them hissed for silence, and Conon contented himself with a lingering vulpine look, as though she stood naked in his arms, pressing back against him. Her cheeks flamed hotly.

"I can wait," he said in her ear. "You belong to me. Don't forget it."

She turned away, biting her lip in vexation. She had been glad of even Conon's protection against the surging mob, glad of a face she recognized. But he must not think she was softening.

D'Yves had made inquiries since he had come to court. Certain rumors had come his way, convincing him that the king would rule in his favor. Mehun was persistent, and, at last, confident of victory. Conon d'Yves turned over his two fat fields and his goodly wood, the purchase price for Solange. He had been perhaps, a little rash, he thought, but the maid had so truly intrigued him, her dancing grace coupled with her peppery dislike of him. She was a fever in his blood. Nothing but total possession of her would ease his hot desire.

Daylight was coming outside, lightening the dusky, incense-laden air within the church. Bernard's impassioned voice reached out to stir responses in the hearts of those who listened to him.

"Men have died to keep Jerusalem holy." *Not Odo*, thought his daughter. Not my father; Loriot had said so. And Loriot will tell me more tonight.

"Will the sacrifice of your brothers and fathers be in vain? Will they call out from their unholy burial places, crying, 'Shame!'?"

The explosive movement of the crowds chanting, "No!" shoved Solange and her protector toward the walls. Ruthlessly elbowing a path, Conon set her upon a small ledge circling a pillar, above the crowd. From here she could get a better view of the monk in the pulpit, holiness surrounding him like a radiance.

Her eyes fell upon Brother Garin, looking up at his abbot, his face sanctified in reverence. No wonder he had not wished to listen to her that morning. Her affairs must have seemed jarringly trivial.

Near the altar, facing outward, was the king's party. Aimery caught her eye. He had been looking at her for some time, and he turned his glance away just too late. She knew he had seen her, and had seen, without approval, how close Conon hovered. She would be hard put to explain to Aimery that it was merely chance that had brought him to her side. Then her chin lifted. Why should she explain to Aimery at all?

She wished Aimery could go with her to hear Loriot's message. She reflected that there was no one else in Bourges whom she would trust. Not even, in his current rapture, would she bother Brother Garin. In all probability he would not even hear her.

But Aimery belonged heart and soul, and perhaps body as well, to the queen. He was treading on dangerous ground to dally with the queen of the land. The king's heirs should be of his royal body, and it would be treason to interfere. There was only one child of the royal marriage, a girl. Rumor had it that the Queen had had to promise Abbot Bernard a boon beyond imagining before he would agree to petition Providence on her behalf. And there was as yet no male heir.

Surely Aimery dared not break his vows of fealty to the king! But then, Aimery was a man of passion. And perhaps the queen, too, was playing dangerously.

Solange could not confide in Aimery. He was the queen's. Just now he was within reach of Queen Eleanor, sitting on her raised chair, the intricate wood carving behind her fair head seeming part of her coiffure, topped with the gold circlet of her rank. Her eyes roamed over the congregation, falling briefly, inscrutably, on Solange.

What was Eleanor thinking? Was she listening to Abbot Bernard? It was hard to say. The words that moved the congregation to moans left her untouched. Either that, or she did not even hear them. There was not the slightest change in her expression, except a certain speculation evident when she glanced at the king.

Someone sobbed loudly in an interval of silence. Solange recognized the woman who wept. It was her mother. She could see her clearly, face buried in her ringed hands, shoulders shaking. How Mehun must hate such a display. His scowl was formidable enough. And when he caught sight of Solange, his frown deepened.

Solange searched out her friends. The countess and her

husband sat, as was their right, with the king and the queen. Bertille's face was half-hidden behind Lady Alis, but Solange was ready to believe that Bertille heard only a word or two of the sermon. And that was a generous estimate!

She could not see Isabel or Catherine. But beyond Count Robert was Henri, so she supposed Catherine was not far away.

Even King Louis, thinking, perhaps, not of the lost land beyond the sea, where Christendom fought to keep the Holy Sepulcher from pagan defilement, but of whatever past sins lined his cheeks and made his eyes somber, buried his face in his hands and let the tears course down his cheeks.

Bernard did not finish his sermon neatly. He broke off abruptly, as though he, too, were overcome by emotion. It was maddening, she thought. He had brought them all to a pitch of excitement, of near frenzy, and he had not offered them a release for their pent-up emotions.

The sermon was over, even though it ended on an unfinished, broken note. Shaking themselves as though awakening from a trance, the acolytes and assisting priests concluded the mass like sleepwalkers.

The congregation, as one, sighed gustily. It was as though they had each been moved beyond themselves, into another sphere where the kingdom of Christ could be glimpsed and all things were possible.

The church emptied, still in that strained quiet, each stumbling as though blinded by visions of hot dusty roads, pagan hands defiling the sacred relics of the Earth. A call to save the Holy Places? But the call had not come.

Solange stamped her leather-shod foot in impatience. She was only a woman, or she would herself start out on the long road to Outremer. For the first time she caught a glimpse of the vision that had led her usually indolent father to set out on pilgrimage.

The crowd eddied toward the door and the space around Solange's pillar cleared. Conon helped her down.

"He's up to something," said Conon. "I wonder what he has in his foxy little mind. Do you suppose . . ."

The silence stretched long enough that Solange's curiosity was piqued. "I don't suppose that an earthly mind, like yours, could catch a glimpse of what *he* envisions."

Conon looked keenly at her. "You are right, of course. I concede to him his holy visions. My own dreams, my dear, are far more satisfactory, especially when you walk through them, clad in—well," he broke off sharply, "a man's dreams are his own, after all. No, my dear, I simply wonder what the abbot's earthly plans are. For he is a shrewd man, don't forget that, and always he likes to maneuver people into doing what he wishes."

"I think you're wrong."

"You have so much experience, I imagine, in reading men's hearts?"

"I have no difficulty in reading yours," she said sharply.

He laughed aloud. "I see you need my help no more," he observed. "Your countess has no doubt gone below, but there are still enough people to insure your safety." With a sketchy salute, he was gone.

The abbot was going to rule on her betrothal, and, suddenly suspicious, she wondered whether Conon would try to influence him before the meeting.

But that was ridiculous, she told herself. The abbot was not one to be influenced lightly. And besides, with her father alive, Mehun's claws were drawn. She did not wish to think about Raoul. There was no answer to that until she talked to him, asked him what had come between them.

Perhaps it was because she was thinking so strongly about the news the minstrel had brought, that she thought she saw Loriot in the crowd surging out of the church. She started to wave to him, but he was looking the other way and did not see her.

She slipped out of the door and started through the crowds after him. She caught glimpses now and then of his russet jacket, the cross on the back, as the crowds opened and closed around her. He was getting too far away. She hurried after him.

There he was, not four yards away, penned behind a fat lady, Mamille, countess of Roucy, and her pages. By the time Loriot moved around them, she had reached nearly close enough to him to call.

"Loriot!" she called.

He turned and saw her. Instead of waiting for her, as she expected, he slipped through the remaining crowd like an eel. "*Loriot!*" she cried, but the sound died in her throat.

Intent on keeping him in sight, she did not watch where she was going. Suddenly she found her way blocked by a burly knight in light mail. There was an ugly leer on his fat face that she had seen before.

The last time she had seen Baldwin, he lay as though dead on the forest floor. He stood now with arms spread out to bar her way. He had come with Mehun in his train. His experience with Solange had taught him nothing.

"Aha! Looking for me? I thought you would change your mind," he cackled.

"Keep off, or this time I'll make sure of killing you," she said stoutly. She hoped desperately he could not see the fear that made her quake.

"As you stabbed the baron just now?" he jeered. He moved closer to her, and before she could move he had grabbed her. "Don't scream," he warned her. "Everyone saw you in his arms. They'll just think you're a lightskirt, never satisfied. But you and I know better, don't we?" All the time he talked, he gripped her arms above the elbow, drawing her closer to him, until she could feel his hauberk pressing against her. She could not move to reach her small girdle dagger. His pig-eyes lit with anticipation. "You long for a real man, don't you?"

Her eyes darted over the people around her, looking for a face she knew, looking for the help that could not come.

"Let me go!" she said in a fierce undertone, waiting for the moment when he would drop his guard. That moment came surprisingly soon.

"Of all the luck!" he muttered, and suddenly let her go. "But I'll get you one day, wait and see!" He turned on his heel and was gone.

She stood panting, not quite realizing that she was free. She glanced around her, trying to see what had caught his eye, but there was no one in sight but Brother Garin in the church, talking to Sybille de Nannes. Neither was looking her way now, and thanking the Providence that had delivered her, she hurried to catch up with the crowds hastening to the castle.

Why had Baldwin followed her, seized her in broad daylight? Had Mehun simply set Baldwin to watch her, to spy upon her? Then, she wondered darkly, had he heard her call out Loriot's name?

Would it make any difference if he had heard? No matter now, for she could not warn the minstrel. Loriot had vanished.

3

Christmas at Belvent had always been a time of feasting, and even after Odo had left, taking some few of his men with him, Solange and her mother had kept the old ways. It did not seem like Christmas because she was not at home. Instinctively, Solange sought comfort from her mother.

She had no gift for Petronilla, since her last gold coin had gone to the beggars. She slipped across the great audience chamber to another tower of the castle, not as high as the tower where she was staying. She found her mother alone. Mehun was nowhere in sight.

Petronilla's eyes were still puffy, telltale remnants of her sobbing in church. Now she stool listlessly by the window, and scarcely roused when Solange appeared.

"I wish you a good day," said Solange formally.

"Thank you," said Petronilla. "How can it be a good day when you have brought so much trouble on your poor mother?"

"I!" gasped Solange. "It was *you* who lied, who denied the betrothal. Had you simply told the truth—"

"Don't talk to me about the truth," said her mother. "I know not any more what is real or what is not real. Mehun would care for me and for Belvent, according to his lights, and yet you are not content. You have done your worst, and I trust it will not overturn us all. Accusing Mehun of sacrilege—before the king and that terrible Abbot Bernard."

"Sacrilege!"

"Don't deny it! What else is it if he ignores a contract made valid by Holy Church? A deliberate provocation of the Church. And I confess I am most uneasy about the outcome of your mad defiance of us all." Then, after a few moments, she continued in an altered tone, "What is it you really want, daughter?"

"Only the truth, Mother," said Solange. "I wish only to know the truth. Because the truth will release me from that husband of yours. You care not what happens to me, do you?"

"I care," said her mother, turning toward her. "But I vow it is difficult to make you understand."

"Yes, it is," said Solange sturdily. "I cannot believe my own mother would forswear herself to hurl her daughter into the most hideous of marriages! Try to convince me that you care about me."

With a surging return of spirit her mother said, "A hideous marriage? No more so than most." Petronilla surveyed her wayward daughter with narrowed eyes. "Hideous, you say! How do you think I married your father? Do you think I had any choice? I had none at all. Your grandmother wanted my dowry, and she got it. It was too bad I came with it."

"That's not true!"

"Oh, yes, it was. For I married not only your father, but also his mother."

"I do not remember her. She must not have bothered you overmuch."

"At the beginning of my marriage. Before you came along. And I do not wish to think of it." She shuddered.

Startled at the heat of her mother's outburst, Solange searched for words. But her mother was not finished. "How many marriages are made to suit the bride, do you think? Name me *one*, my girl. Sybille de Nannes? Her brothers wed her to that gross old man. You think her marriage is happy?"

"But d'Yves' wives—," protested Solange.

"Are no worse off than many another. Besides, I defy him to put *you* in chains. He'll have his work cut out for him!"

"He will?" purred Solange dangerously. "He will never

lay one hand on me. I promise you that! Either in marriage or out of it. And I cannot think it makes any difference to him which way he takes me."

"It's a matter of property, after all," said Petronilla, restored suddenly to calm. "That is what runs the world, my girl, and don't you forget it! You are as much property as a hoard of gold. You speak of a hideous marriage! This one is no more hideous than most." Petronilla gave her a sharp glance, and said tentatively, "No one who saw you in church today would believe that you hold the baron in such disgust. His arms around you, whispering in your ear."

"That was chance!" she cried. "I was nearly crushed in the mob and he rescued me. You cannot think that I have softened toward that brute!"

"You could do worse than settle down with a husband. I cannot think what you expect the king to do," sighed her mother.

"To marry me to Raoul," Solange said promptly.

Petronilla began to nervously tie knots in the long fringe of her girdle. "How is it that Raoul has not demanded of the king that you wed him at once?"

Solange faltered in her headlong argument. Why hadn't he, indeed? She said with a rush, "I do not know how things are done at court. It may be that he cannot leave the king's service to wed or to return to Puiseaux. But he will wed me one day soon."

Petronilla had changed since coming to Bourges, thought Solange. She had been flighty, gay and laughing, even carefree, in the days before Mehun rattled across the drawbridge. But now she wore a frown which threatened to become permanent, and her disposition had turned waspish. She clawed at Solange like a feral cat defying the hounds—clawing with words instead of nails, but the wounds were deep.

"My dear child," said Petronilla, "I doubt any man would want you after you seemed so—contented—in the arms of the baron you *say* you hate."

"I do hate him!" raged Solange. A sudden thought struck her. "How could you see me from where you were?"

Her mother refused to meet her eyes.

"I'll tell you how," pursued Solange. "That man of Mehun's, the fat one, told you, didn't he? I see in your face that I am right. Mehun set him to spy upon me. He has no right to oversee my comings and goings!"

The door opened and Mehun entered in time to hear the last of the argument. He said heavily, "I have a right to see that you bring no shame upon myself and your mother. Your behavior is lax to the point of outrage."

"But it is not your affair," said Solange, smarting. "I am no concern of yours. I am a ward of the king's!"

Mehun had left the door open behind him. Lady Alis came in in a flurry of veils and long scarves. "I came to find Solange. I have need of her. Someone is asking me who is the beauty in my suite, 'the lady of the moonlight,' he says. So romantic, is it not? I must insist that you come back to meet him."

"Who is this man who wants to meet my daughter?" said Petronilla evenly. "I should like to know my daughter's admirers, to judge their fitness for her company."

"Mother! The Countess Alis—"

Interrupting gently, the countess said, "I too would like to be sure my daughter, if I had one, was safe with friends I approved of." She sighed with heavy effect. "But, alas, I have no child of my own, and so perhaps I see more clearly that grasping love too tightly smothers it. I remember when our steward at home showed me some baby ducklings under the bridge over the pond. By accident I held one too tightly. It was a lesson learned. Do you know, I still regret that poor creature?"

With a dimpled smile, Lady Alis left them, holding Solange firmly by the arm. Not until they were back in the great tower did Alis relax.

"Who wishes to meet me?" asked Solange, suddenly doubtful. The countess closed the door of their rooms behind her.

"A mere fiction," said Alis unblushingly. "To get you away from your stepfather. You should thank me, child. You are far too wayward."

"I merely went to wish my mother a happy day."

"But you should have taken someone with you. Don't

you know that Mehun is hoping you will make a mistake? I doubt not he has some information he is hugging to himself."

Guiltily Solange told her what her mother had said about d'Yves's attentions in church. Lady Alis shook her head. "I knew it. A frontal assault on a castle, or on an enemy, is not good judgment, my dear. I wonder your father never taught you better."

"I am not a castle, nor am I planning to besiege one. I am not simply a chattel, a serf, a piece of furniture, to be handed around from one man to another."

"None of us is free," said the Lady Alis. "We all have compromises to make. My father betrothed me to Robert when I was eight years old. And a fine thing it was, too. I could not have known at that age how wonderful Robert would be."

"I suppose you are telling me that Conon d'Yves, who killed his first wife, whose other wives all met with mysterious fates, would make me a fine husband? It would not be long before I met with an 'accident.' "

"No, my dear, I am not. But I do counsel restraint. Nothing is to be gained by fighting these little skirmishes with your stepfather."

"I still didn't tell him all I could have," said Solange quietly, hugging her private knowledge to herself.

The countess stared at her. "I have not known you long, Solange, but I know you well enough that I gravely mistrust that smile." She leaned forward, her plump hands upon her knees, obviously prepared to meet the worst. "All right, what could you have told him?"

Eyes dancing, Solange suddenly smiled. "A mere nothing," she said, lightly, watching Lady Alis. "Only that I have proof that my father still lives."

The effect upon Lady Alis was all that Solange could have wished for. The countess allowed her jaw to drop and her eyes to grow round with simple astonishment.

Then with a masterful effort, she pulled herself together and said regretfully, "You have wished for this too long. I should have seen that you had more occupation than to beguile your hours with futile hopes."

"You think my hopes have addled my brain?" cried Solange, stung. "Perhaps the truth has. It is beyond belief, and yet it must be true."

"That your father lives? I suppose he has sent word by a dove?"

"That sarcasm, dear Lady Alis, is not like you. Listen to me." Solange crossed the room to sink down before her and place her hands gently upon Lady Alis's knee.

"I'm listening," said Lady Alis, skeptically.

"Yestereve, when we were down in the courtyard looking at the wares from the east . . ." Solange told her story.

". . . in Antioch—alive, ten days after he was supposed to have died. Alive and unwounded!" finished Solange triumphantly.

Alis's eyes lay in shadow. Only the leaping fire gave light to the small room. Alis fastened her brooding gaze on Solange, still huddled at her feet, her hands prayerfully on the Countess's knees. "My child, you believe this?"

"I must," said Solange. "I must at least learn what he has to say. And then I will know where the truth lies."

"So the minstrel has the proof," mused the countess. "I wonder why he has not seen fit to bring this before the king. Surely he has heard the story of your troubles."

"Perhaps not," argued Solange. "If he came to Bourges with those pilgrims only yestereve, then he might not have talked with any of the castle folk."

Slowly, Alis nodded. "I suppose so. But I do not like it. Who will ever ferret out just what happened?"

"Loriot knows," insisted Solange stubbornly, "and he will tell me the truth."

Alis took a deep breath. She was remiss in not warning Solange about one danger she saw ahead, having promised Brother Garin that she would keep her own counsel in that matter. But she could save the child, who was becoming increasingly dear to her, from another heartbreak. She dropped one hand to cover Solange's cold fingers, still grasping the yellow silk of the countess's pelisse. "My dear child, you have been gulled. Your stepfather swears he saw your father die!"

"But Loriot says he was alive after that battle!"

"Then you are doubly a gull if you think that a minstrel's word will suffice to counter the word of Mehun de Mowbrai."

"But there is a doubt! Even the king must see that!"

Lady Alis shook her head slowly. "There is no proof, and Loriot—what an impossible name!—will never talk to the king. It's too dangerous!"

"I will make Loriot talk to the king," said Solange stubbornly.

She did not change her mind during the entire time she was helping Lady Alis dress for the great Christmas feast the king was hosting. It would be a great occasion, and Lady Alis was surprisingly hard to please, tossing off two wimples that did not suit her, and finally giving Solange only time enough to hurry with her own dressing. Jehane's fingers flew, but she was too hurried. Finally Solange finished her hair herself.

She emerged from the inner room to find that the king had sent her a surprise. An escort stood alone at the narrow window.

The young man turned, and she gasped with delight. "Raoul! How good to see you! Did you come to take me down to dinner?"

"The king . . . the king gave me leave to come," said Raoul stiffly. Then, being a well-bred young man, he added, "You look very nice, Solange." With a quick grin, he said, "I remember you better with your hair in braids, and barefoot, when we caught frogs in the Petitmer!"

It was going to be all right! She laughed happily. She felt her ribs bursting with joy. All was going to turn out well. With a feeling of great well-being she picked up her mantle and arranged it around her shoulders.

"Come, let us go down to dine," she said with a sunny smile. "I have much to tell you."

In friendly confidence she slipped her hand through the crook in his arm. She felt the muscles beneath her fingers stiffen, and then, slowly, relax. She thought no more of it.

Chatting brightly as they followed Lady Alis down the corridor, they reached the great hall. She still had not told him about her meeting with Loriot. She was still too close to Lady Alis's disapproval to feel comfortable with her news. She would not risk Raoul's disbelief as well.

They stood together in the entrance to the great hall. The feast was about to begin. In fact, it already had at the long tables at the bottom of the room, below the salt. There were so many retainers that some must eat and give way to others.

"We'll always remember this day, won't we?" said Solange, pressing her fingers lightly upon Raoul's arm. "Even our wedding day won't be so fine!"

To her astonishment his face darkened and he pulled his arm away from her touch. "Forgive me," he said in a strangled voice. "I see the king needs me. I'll . . . there's your mother. I'll leave you with her."

In spite of her protests, Raoul left Solange quickly. It was as though some nameless fear spurred him blindly on.

4

One thing she could be sure of, she thought with a spurt of indignation, was that Raoul had not taken on the polished manners of the court!

She gazed after him, troubled, until he was out of sight. It was the throng, she decided, even though that explanation did not really convince her. There were so many people, and there was never any privacy in which to talk things over. Back at Belvent, she thought, they could have wandered out through the outer ward, into the tilting yard, or even into her mother's orchard and herb garden, and been completely alone, free to say to each other what was in their hearts.

Someone jostled against her, and said crossly, "Day-dreaming? Best get out of the way!" She looked up quickly and recognized Gauthier, one of Gervais's men, who had escorted her to Saint Vergillia's.

"Sorry, Gauthier," she said automatically, "I was in the way. Have you seen the Countess de Dreux?"

Moody even in the midst of rejoicing, Gauthier pointed toward the door. "Just coming in," he said. Then, his steady gaze never faltering, he looked at her piercingly. "Are you happy now?" The question surprised her, but he seemed to want to hear the answer.

"Happier than I would have been, I suppose," she said, giving his query its full due. "At the convent, I think I should have been dead by now."

"You fear death? Yet all arrive at that door in the end. What matters is whether it is now or next month? It is all the same in the end."

With that odd remark, he left her standing, like a rock in a stream, as the waiters and the throngs of hungry servitors eddied around her.

She made her way, with difficulty, through the rushing crowd to the door where Countess Alis and Count Robert waited for the royal summons to dinner.

"I'm starved," said Bertille as Solange came to her side. "That's the trouble with being highborn. You always eat last."

Solange's laugh was stifled almost at once. The king was approaching.

The silver trumpets had sent their sweet tumbling notes rollicking up the halls and down the corridors, summoning all to the great feast of Christ's birthday. The ritual this day, the washing of the hands in the small basins, was even more prolonged than usual. One of Bertille's many gallants took an unusually long time to dry her fingers carefully while whispering something in her ear that made her cheeks redden.

The great hall was decorated in such splendor that Solange could not weary of looking. The woven arrases, usually stored in chests, had been unfurled and hung, giving the brightness of red and gold and azure to the cold gray walls of the castle. She was also glad to notice that the arrases kept a little of the chilly wind out of the room.

The tables where the nobles and the high churchmen sat were arranged a few steps below the dais. The dais itself was raised higher than normal for this occasion, so that all the diners could see their king and queen and rejoice in their presence on this holy day.

On the dais beside the throne chairs but a little below them was arranged another chair for the abbot. He represented the Church itself on this festive occasion.

The aromas from the kitchen spits pervaded the atmosphere, even routing the smoke from the roaring fire and the fresh smell of newly strewn rushes.

This would be a truly memorable feast, Solange knew, including, perhaps, even a peacock with all its fantastic tail-feathers. She had heard of such a main dish but she had never seen one.

The clear horns of the heralds entering the hall announced that the king and queen were approaching. This was indeed a formal dinner. Suspended from the long silver horns were the king's pennants, and the brightly colored tabards of the heralds were a blaze of color.

There was a rushing sound as the assembly stirred to its feet on the whispering rushes. All faced the door.

The king and queen entered. Eleanor held her fingertips lightly on the king's arm and looked around her with her head held haughtily high.

Behind them, in startling contrast in his white cowled robe, walked Abbot Bernard, his eyes still focused on otherworldly things. Yet, Solange was suddenly positive, he missed nothing happening around him.

The procession passed into the room and made its way toward the dais. It passed quite close to Solange, who stood breathless with excitement, engrossed in the splendor.

To her amazement, the king stopped opposite her. Quickly, she swept downward into a flustered curtsey. "M-my lord," she stammered.

"My dear," said the king, "I wish to tell you that I will see to your little problem soon. Abbot Bernard has promised to give me counsel, and very soon we will be able to confer. In the meantime, I trust you will find Lady Alis's regimen not too strict?"

"No, my lord. She is most kind. But I beg you—"

Startled at her importunity, the king hesitated. "Yes? What is it?"

"I beg you, my lord, to honor my father's commitment. Raoul de Puiseaux has returned to your court, sire, and he must tell you that our betrothal did take place, as I said."

Something flickered in the king's eyes, but he said only, "There are matters of much greater moment to be settled first," before turning to move on.

"Come, my lord," said the queen, irritated. "The feast awaits your presence."

"Of course, my dear," agreed the king. But the abbot said something in an undertone that Solange, smarting from her temerity and its subsequent setdown, did not hear.

Surprisingly, the king turned back. "You insist that you were betrothed? Before the church door?"

Wordlessly, she nodded. She dared not speak. The king was behaving in a very strange fashion, and the queen did not like it. But it was Bernard of Clairvaux who prevailed.

"Who was the priest?" he demanded.

"Father Jean, my father's chaplain," she said, adding, "He is reported to have died with my father in the Holy Land."

"I remember him," said Bernard. "Surely there is not any doubt that the betrothal took place?"

"No, sir. Not to me. I was there, you see. My father *will confirm* that the betrothal took place," she said slowly, deliberately choosing her words, and watching for their effect.

There was a hushed silence. It spread from the little space around Solange and the king to take in her mother and Mehun, the Lady Alis and Count Robert, and even Aimery, standing beyond the queen.

Petronilla was the first to find her voice. "The child is mad!" Heedless of the king and even the abbot, she cried out, "You ungrateful child! You're trying to drive me insane. It's you who are mad. My lord," she said swiftly turning to the king, "the poor child has brooded too long on her father's death. It was a great shock to her."

"She should be put into the convent," said Mehun, leadenly. "I was right all along."

The abbot's eyes glittered. He was a man of much kindness, at bottom, but the intricacies of the problem held him now.

"But your father is dead, is he not? Have you by chance had a—a visitation from him?" He frowned mightily.

"No, sir. But I must tell you, sir, that my father did not die on that battlefield. I know—sir, I *know* that he was alive and well after that battle."

"Aha!" said Bernard. "And how do you know that?"

"He was seen, sir. Since his death. And I believe that he yet lives."

"Why hasn't he come home, then?" demanded Petronilla waspishly.

"I do not know, Mother," said Solange. "I'm sorry. But if my father lives—"

"He does not!" said Mehun with finality. "I defy anyone to say otherwise."

"But someone has said otherwise, it seems," said the king mildly.

The hushed silence that had surrounded them since Solange's outrageous claim now burst asunder. There were cries of disbelief and one or two demands that the wench be put to the ordeal to wrench the truth from her.

Abbot Bernard lifted his head in search of the originator of that idea, but there was no repetition.

Then Solange burst out, "Tonight, I am to find the proof that my father lives!"

Her eyes shone, and her unreasoning confidence spilled over onto those around her. Even the king smiled slightly, and nodded. "Bring your proof to me," he said. "I will—that is, Abbot Bernard will see justice done."

"Thank you, sire!" she said, snatching his hand and kissing it.

"No need for that," said King Louis, although he seemed pleased, "Just bring me the proof."

"This very night! I'll have it!" she promised. She didn't see Mehun's frown furrowing his black brows. She curtseyed to the king, and then, Bertille's fingers tugging at her sleeve, turned to follow the countess's party.

The menu was exceptionally elaborate. The stewards had outdone themselves to do honor to both the king and the day.

First there was the swan, arriving at their table to the sound of flutes. Resting on green pastry as though on a pond, his beak gilded and his body silvered, the swan was regal in magnificence.

The next course was roast capon, and a heavy pasty containing many small birds. The third course was served around a roast peacock, his splendid plumage spread out around him as in life.

There was a myriad of side dishes—congers, trout, herring, and dessert of peeled walnuts, figs, dates, and sugarplums.

At the last there was a cup of spiced wine to sweeten the digestion, so Alis said. She was watching her husband, who had eaten heartily ever since they had sat down. "He will need it before morning," she said with resignation. "I must make sure there is a Lazarist monk within call."

Isabel leaned across Bertille and said, in a carrying voice, "No doubt they will be busy this night with more than one patient."

Count Robert flicked a glance her way. He did not like the girl, and made no attempt to hide his feeling. He said, in mock solemnity, "One must give the monks a chance to earn their rewards in heaven. If one were not sometimes sick, monks would have nothing to do."

He speared another fat sugarplum with his knife, and paid no more heed to Isabel.

The feasters finally began to refuse the figs and the sweetmeats, and it was time for the entertainment. The jugglers had done their fantastic tricks and departed. Now, with the noise of the waiters muffled, it was time for the minstrels to sing. One followed another, but there was no sign of Loriot. Solange had not seen him since that glimpse of him after the mass that morning. Perhaps—and she stifled the thought—he had decided to leave Bourges.

The queen's favorite minstrel held the floor just now. For some misguided reason, he chose to sing a ballad that, while it might be the queen's favorite, struck no appreciative chord in Abbot Bernard. It celebrated a very earthly kind of love......

"Love's sweet exchange and barter, then the brain
Sinks to repose; (so sang the jongleur.)

Swimming in strangeness of a new delight
The eyelids close;
Oh sweet the passing o'er from love to sleep.
But sweeter the awakening to love."

The minstrel's voice died away; the last note struck from his lute twanging in discord, as he caught the warning glance from the queen's dark eyes. It was well known that Bernard had no sympathy with this kind of love, and was completely capable of stopping the feast with a sermon on the subject.

The jongleur, reddened with confusion, beat a quick retreat, and left the field to the next bard.

At last, it was Loriot.

One strum of his expert fingers on the lute, and his voice rose clear as the oriole whose name he bore. Loriot had chosen no more wisely than his predecessor, as it happened.

"Alone to sacrifice Thou goest, Lord,
Giving Thyself to death whom Thou hast slain.
For us Thy wretched folk is any word,
Who know that for our sins this is Thy pain?"

Count Robert said, with disbelief, "That man seeks suicide. That song is Peter Abelard's."

Alis turned quickly. "Surely the abbot does not still consider Peter a heretic?"

One glance at the abbot's drawn, brooding face told Solange that if anything, the abbot's dislike of Abelard was even stronger now, after his foe's death. Count Robert leaped to his feet and cried out, "Let us have no more of these sad songs! This is a time of feasting and joy. Bring on the acrobats!"

The tumblers cartwheeled through the doors as though they had been waiting for the count's cry, and soon drums and tambourines caught the rhythm. The noise was deafening.

Loriot vanished through the door into the outer hall, and Solange rose to her feet to follow him.

"Where are you going?" demanded Isabel. "Surely you cannot be weary so soon?"

Solange shook her head. "Not weary. Just cold. I'd best go get my wrap."

"I'll go with you," offered Catherine, already halfway to her feet.

"No, no," said Solange, thinking swiftly. She dared not take too big an escort with her to her rendezvous with Loriot. "I'll find Jehane at the door and send her." A poor excuse, she thought, but it sufficed, and she moved toward the door. She had gone only a dozen steps when Petronilla caught her sleeve. "Sit by me, daughter, I would talk with you."

5

Solange dared not linger. Loriot was ahead of her, perhaps already waiting for her at the top of the watchtower. Would he leave before she got there? Too afraid to wait for her, was he already on his way down from the rendezvous?

"Mother, I can't!" she cried.

Her mother grasped her waist with icy fingers and pulled her down to the bench beside her. At first glance, Petronilla seemed anxious to make up their quarrel. Helping herself to a fig from the wooden bowl before her, she said almost kindly, "You're a fool to make such a fuss."

"About what?" said Solange coolly. "A mere trifle such as a broken vow? Or a lie by my mother?"

"What do you know about broken vows?" said Petronilla, her voice shaking. "You are so young. I sheltered you too much."

"Perhaps that is true," said Solange through anger-tightened lips. "Perhaps you should have taught me before now not to trust anybody."

Her mother had taken a bite of the fig, dropped it on her trencher, and forgotten it. Her fingers clenched into a fist and she pounded the table. "Trust? You aren't so superior that you can throw rocks at me. You could have gone to the convent and trusted me to get you out. You don't think I would have let you stay in that hole? All you had to do was submit to Mehun, and trust me."

Solange forgot Loriot in her flaming indignation. "That would do fine!" she stormed, quivering with the need to keep her voice down. Even so, she caught curious looks from their neighbors. "You couldn't even keep me out of the convent in the first place. What made you think you could get me out, once I was in?"

Petronilla ignored her outburst. "But no," she continued as though Solange had not spoken. "You take up with the first man you meet in the forest—"

"A Cistercian monk is hardly a vagabond," Solange pointed out. "And you said nothing about getting me out of the convent. I recall not a word. Perhaps you would refresh my memory?"

What Solange had taken for hurt feelings in her mother was actually shaking anger. When her mother turned to reply, her blue eyes flashed sparks. "What possessed you to claim that your father is still alive? Don't you know that none of the men who were with him returned?"

"Surely that is some proof in itself that he lives," retorted Solange. "Surely all of them could not have been killed. One, at least, should have come back to tell us of my father. Do you not find anything strange in this total silence?"

"I do not accept that," Petronilla said. "You hear of great massacres all the time. Mehun himself barely escaped with his life, and only the handful of men he brought home with him survived out of his whole troop.

"You know that if your father lives, my marriage to Mehun is sinful," said Petronilla, "or had you thought of that?" She looked at Solange's pale face, and added, "I see you had not. You were ever thus, thinking of your own wishes and not of the consequences."

"It is true," said Solange slowly, "I had not thought of your marriage. Only of my own. And if you had not given my dowry to your husband, and been ready to send me into the arms of that beast d'Yves, we should none of us be here at the king's court. And I should not be so eager for the truth no matter what.

"If my father lives, I am free of Mehun. I am so sorry, Mother, but I must know. And if I fail, then it is *my* life that will not last till Whitsuntide, in the convent or in the baron's clutches."

"I suppose you think I should have waited till someone came along to confirm Mehun's word?"

Solange could not answer. She could not harden her heart against her mother for long. Petronilla was more courageous than her daughter had thought. She was shocked by the possibility of having entered into a blasphemous marriage. She was now deathly afraid for her immortal soul. Yet she did not collapse in a faint, nor indulge in hysterics.

"But if all Odo's men were killed with him, none could come back," Petronilla reasoned.

"That doesn't matter, Mother," said Solange, impatiently. "My father lives, and if he lived after Mehun said he died, then Mehun lies. And I will have the proof of it. I am on my way now to get proof that Mehun lied."

"So you say. Why would Mehun lie?"

Solange revolved in her mind the reasons of which she was sure. For a landless knight, returning from the Holy Land with his pockets empty, having spent his substance in the hope of booty from the infidel, what looked finer than the broad, smiling lands of Belvent, and a woman who did not know whether her husband was alive?

Petronilla said softly, "Mehun was so much in love with me that he could not bear the thought of Odo coming home. That must be it."

Satisfied with her own reasoning, she allowed a faint smile to settle on her piquant features. Solange pitied her. She could not tear away the veil that Petronilla had cast over her marriage. Poor, blind Petronilla!

Suddenly, the hall became quieter. Abbot Bernard left his seat on the dais and advanced to the edge, looking out over the diners. He raised his right hand to command silence. He was a slight figure, but no less impressive now in his pale robe than he had been in the church this morning.

The throng rose to their feet as one man. His voice at last rose, and a deathly hush settled over the crowd.

Moving to the door, pausing close to the lancers, Solange looked behind her to see whether eyes were following her. She saw none. But coming toward the doorway was the one man she did not want to see. Conon d'Yves. She dared not chance his pursuing her through the halls. She shrank back against the wall.

Conon's blond head bent to speak to a footman before he turned away. He did not see her, she was sure. He gave one last glance to the abbot and to the king and queen before he went out through the door.

Waiting long enough to let him get out of sight, she slipped past the guards into the hall. The draft struck her with chilling force, and she shivered. Conon was not in sight. There was no one at all in the corridors. All the footmen and the guards were inside. Cries and shouts pulsed through the dining hall, and Solange suddenly felt very lonely.

She hesitated. The breath of winter would be icy on the top of the watchtower, and her mantle would not be warm. She hurried toward the tower stairs to pick up her fur-lined cloak before she continued to her rendezvous.

She paused at every corner, listening, but heard nothing. No one lay in wait to keep her from her tryst. She began to breathe easier. She had listened too long, she decided, to the doomsayers around her, to Alis, Aimery, the rest.

She snatched up her cloak. The warmth of the vair lining did not entirely take away her shivering.

No one lurked in the hall outside Alis's suite. She might have questioned the absence of guards or footmen in the long stretch of corridors, but this was Christmas Day and there was great excitement. All who were able would squeeze into the great hall. The abbot's sermon would make this night one to talk about for months.

She hurried, conscious always of rising upward toward the parapet. Loriot had been exceedingly anxious not to be overheard, and she could understand that. There were those who did not want Odo to be alive, including his wife.

She came to an intersection that did not look familiar to her. She halted, trying to decide whether she was on the right road. There was more than one way to reach the parapet, and she had come this far by blind instinct. Now that she looked at her surroundings there was nothing, no trace of identification, to tell her she was on the right track. Impatiently, she turned to look backward, but the corridor looked like all the others.

In the meantime, while she stood here wavering, Loriot was probably freezing at the rendezvous atop the castle. She must make up her mind. The floor still slanted upward, and the corridor to her right looked promising.

It was then that she heard the footsteps, faint and far off, a measured tread. She could not tell whether they were approaching or going away. The sound echoed back and forth against the stone walls and ceiling until she could swear it was coming around the corner before her.

She shrank back against the wall, knowing there was no concealment. She waited, the sound of footsteps mingled with the blood pounding in her temples.

She waited.

The footsteps died away. She could not tell whether they went down toward the great hall or up toward the parapet. Perhaps—she laughed shakily—perhaps it was only Loriot himself!

She turned to the right and hurried upward along the stone corridor. She was nearing the top of the castle. The air grew paralyzingly cold, a biting foretaste of the fresh winter breeze that swept the platform above. She could smell snow.

She rounded the last corner and stood in the stone-framed doorway. There was no snow in the air, only drifts left there by the storm of last week. The starlight reflected on the snow gave a better light, a colder, whiter light, than the flaring torches in the great hall. A clean light and a fresh scent—and very cold. She shivered.

"Loriot?" she called at last. There was no one on the watchtower, no one at all.

And yet she had seen him leave the great hall on his way to their tryst. What had kept him? Possibly, she thought, biting her lip in vexation, he had grown tired of waiting for her and had left.

And then she realized she had been hearing faint groans, almost under her feet!

She felt the hair lift on the back of her neck, under the hood of her cloak.

She hurried around the corner of the wall. This part of the top floor of the castle faced to the east, and there was more light from the stars. There on the snow lay a dark bundle.

A man, crumpled like old rags, his knees drawn up to his chest in a spasm, trying to ease the mortal pain that had no easing.

It was Loriot.

She knelt beside him. With gentle hands she pulled his hands away from his face. His eyes were wild, glassy; already the glaze of death was upon them.

"Loriot!" she choked. "Who did this to you?"

She was not sure he understood.

She looked around her. There was no help at hand. And, she knew surely, there was no time to get help.

"Don't know. . . ."

Swiftly she changed the direction of her thoughts. It did not matter, just now, who had struck down Loriot. He was going to die and she could do nothing for him. What was vital was to find out what he knew about her father, before it was too late.

She took off her cloak, and spread it over him. The soft fur touched his cheek and seemed to comfort him. His face lapsed into a gentle smile.

"Nice," he said. "So cold."

"Loriot, tell me," she said, kneeling beside him in the snow, trying to keep from shivering. "My father . . . you saw him?"

"Fur," he whispered. "Warmer than I was. Is hell so cold, then?"

"Loriot," she cried, "You're not going to die!"

"Fool," he breathed, softly. "I'm already dead."

"What of Odo de Saint Florent?" she said, vexed with him, and with herself for her impatience with a man she knew was dying. "It's my fault," she wept. "I brought you here."

She thought he had died. His eyes closed, and he had stopped moaning.

But he was not yet dead. Rousing himself, he fixed her with staring eyes and said, "Listen to me. I came here, and was killed. Do not you also be killed. Run. Hurry away."

"I will not leave you," she said stoutly. "I cannot go to get help for you—"

"There is no help," he said, simply. "I will not die unshriven, lady, because I sought a priest before I came up here."

"You knew it was so dangerous?"

"They would have bought my silence. But you promised gold—I won't need it now. Keep your gold."

Solange had hoped the king would give Loriot gold when she took the minstrel to tell his story. She wished she had even a single coin now, to show him that his trust in her was justified.

Loriot said, in a loud voice, "I will tell you what I know, to clear my conscience before I die. I must hold on long enough—"

Over her objections, he insisted, "Do not waste my time, lady. There is little enough breath left in me. But I will use it to the glory of God and the truth. Odo lives. Or did when I left Antioch. I was in the battle."

6

"The battle of Adana. I was in it. A foot soldier. There was no need of minstrels, you see. Snatched up a bow and arrow from a man already dead." He closed his eyes, whether against memory or against pain, she could not tell. "I had some little skill. Killed many devils." He was silent for so long she thought he was dead. But suddenly his eyes flew open. "Saint Florent was in the fray. I would have died, but for his mighty battle ax. The Turk fell with a sound like a splitting melon."

The story came out, little by little, over groans and with whistling breath. The stab wound that was taking Loriot's life had come in from the back, and the long blade was driven in with such force that it could not be withdrawn. The blade had gone through his lungs, and every breath the dying man drew bubbled in his throat.

"The battle was fierce, and I saw Saint Florent fall."

"Then he *is* dead!"

The man on the snow paid her no heed. "He rose again, but his helmet was awry, and yet he fought like ten demons. The blue swan still flew when I last saw it. But you understand, I had my hands full. The pagans came on like a flood."

"Poor Loriot!" she said, a wealth of sadness in her voice. "And to come here—"

"The man with the device was fair-haired—like your own, lady. Hair the color of cornsilk in August. That is what drew me yesterday."

"You did not see him dead on the field."

"No, lady. The battle was terrible. The Turks came down out of the mountains, swift as fiends, with arrows coming in waves. Like an arras rippling in the wind. There was no escape. Our knights held fast. Ah, the world will be proud of them! And in the end the Turks turned tail and ran."

She tucked the edge of her cloak around his shoulder. She dared not move him. She had tried once, and his cry of pain startled an owl into flight from the top of the tower.

"I crawled away," he began again, in a voice so faint that she had to bend close to his lips to hear. "I found a rock with shade, and I lay there."

Eventually, he told her, he made his wounded way back to Antioch. An infidel doctor had made him well—well enough to travel, at any rate. "There were only a handful of our knights left alive. There was—I forget the name. A bear erect on his device. And a hawk, I think. And the swan."

"My father's device," she said simply. "Then he lived past the battle."

"Long enough to fight again, lady."

A noise scratched beyond the corner, out of sight. A

rat on the crusty snow? Or someone listening to every word Loriot forced past his lips?

"Fight again?" she prompted, to cover the noise of her heart racing. She could not leave Loriot in order to investigate the sound. Nor, truthfully, did she want to. Rat or man, she feared them both. Yet she must hear all Loriot could say. Desperately, she willed him to hurry.

"Out of Antioch. Riding, with some men—a half-dozen, perhaps. Less maybe."

"Riding?" She was startled. "Then he was not wounded. But I thought—"

"Wounded, maybe. But riding fast. Along the river."

"The river?"

"The river of Antioch," he said with a trace of impatience. "Oron—Oron-something." He must realize that his time was running out. She resolved only to listen, to stay with him.

"He rode out. To the—east. Away from the city. And he rode armed."

There was so much to think about, to resolve in her mind and to try to understand. Her father riding with his men, when none of the men he had taken from Belvent had come home.

Only a handful of men left with him, riding east along the river out of Antioch. She had no real concept of the background. How she wished she knew what Outremer looked like! Did it have mountains? With snow? Was it like a garden, or a desert?

"Ten days," said Loriot suddenly, in a clear, strong voice. "Ten days after the battle. I saw him."

And then, at once, Loriot died.

Surprising, she thought numbly, how flat, how insignificant a body was once the soul had flown to meet its God. She shivered again.

She could not bring herself to take the cloak away from the dead man. He no longer needed the warmth, and she surely did. But it was a sort of shroud, and she would leave it.

She herself was to blame for Loriot's death. Had she not insisted that he come to the tryst, he would not have died. Moreover, if she had not told people that she was to get the proof she needed that very night, perhaps no one would have followed him and struck the savage mortal blow.

It had probably been someone around the king when she told him, and there were many faces who appeared again in her memory. There was a sound again in the shadows. Not a rat, she was sure. A much bigger sound, and very close. She froze.

She knew she had been more than foolish, lingering so long. She should have realized that the man who killed Loriot must also know that she was coming to meet him. What good would it do to kill the minstrel if Solange herself knew the secret? Now, of course, the assailant had heard Loriot's story and knew beyond doubt that the threat to him was not erased—not as long as Solange lived.

And that, she thought grimly, was likely to be a very short time.

She waited, huddled next to Loriot, scanning the area around her carefully, lingering over every patch of darkness. Her breath rasped noisily. Turning her head as far as she could, she looked behind her, toward the door through which she had entered the parapet walk. The snowdrift lay clean and unbroken, except for her own footsteps.

But where were Loriot's?

She remembered the other door. There were many ways to the top of the castle. She had always known this fact. But she remembered it too late.

She half-rose to her feet. The cloak that she had spread over Loriot tangled in her feet and she lost her balance and crashed to the ground. At the same time, she felt a pain in her shoulder.

Half turning, crying out with the sudden pain, she saw, hovering above her like a hawk over a rabbit, a great caped figure, whose face she could not see.

He was breathing hard, and she knew she had only moments to live. One great arm lifted, cutting off the light of the stars above her, making a shadow in the snow where Loriot lay.

She hurtled herself sideways, frantically moving crabwise on knees and hips, and was not there when the knife plunged.

The demon cursed. It was a voice she did not recognize.

She scurried farther out of reach and leaped to her feet. She ran toward the door. He pounded close behind her, and she dared not swerve. His breath was loud, close as a hound on a hare. She raced past the door that would lead to safety.

Somebody whimpered, and she knew the sound came from her own throat. Her chest pained sharply. She slipped into a bowman's niche along the wall. She had not even a dagger in her belt to mark her enemy before he killed her.

The murderer caught at her with his left hand, and pulled her savagely from her pitiful shelter. He sent her sprawling to the cement floor, and she slid on hip and shoulder to the stone wall on the outside of the tower.

As she hit the wall, she doubled her knees and shoved both feet at the wall with all her strength. The thrust sent her angling a couple of feet to the side, and the assailant was thrown off his balance. But the respite was short.

Still muttering curses, he caught up with her. He fell to his knees beside her and lifted his arm, like a great bat's wing. The starlight struck reflections from the dagger as he lifted it high above her, poising.

There was no sound but the cursing inhuman voice. She had long since ceased to whimper, and she had not yet set a prayer on her lips. For away in the yard below, raucous laughter spilled out, insane in contrast to the grim scene atop the tower.

It seemed suddenly of vital importance that she know the man who would kill her. She could not use the knowledge, but it seemed unbearable that she would die and not even know who brought her death.

Swifter than thought she reached both hands to the cloth cap-piece pulled down to hide the man's face. Snatching at the knitted wool, her fingers slipped on the smooth surface before, in one desperate second, she curved her nails into talons. She tore fabric, and felt the skin smooth beneath the wool.

The man's reaction was instant. With his free hand he struck her a savage blow on the side of her head and knocked her full-length on the stone floor. Holding her down with one hand, he raised the dagger again.

The blow did not fall.

Waiting, her mind dazed, her senses numbed, she could not believe. She dared at last to open her eyes. She was alone.

Bewildered, she shook her head, blinking her eyelids to see through tears. Where had he gone? Over her fast-beating heart she could hear sounds. Running feet, crisp on the snow.

Around the parapet she could hear the sounds of pursued and pursuer. Was that the sound of steel on steel?

She clung to the rough, cold stone, unable to move. So short a time ago she had had such high hopes. She would meet Loriot and he would tell her what she desperately needed to know. Now her informant was dead, if not by her hand, then certainly by her fault. She should not have agreed to meet him in this isolated place.

The sounds had vanished. Both men must have descended one of the corridors, still in the chase.

Then a man hurried from the far end of the platform and knelt beside the body of Loriot. She could just see him, dark against the snow. Who was he? Pursued or pursuer? She must know. She inched out of her hiding-place and approached.

The kneeling man replaced the cloak over the staring dead eyes and looked piercingly at her.

Aimery stood up and glared. With a slight gesture he indicated the heap on the ground. "I thought this was you."

"It would have been me as well," she said simply, "had you not come along when you did."

"From what I saw," said Aimery, with a sudden bark of amusement, "you were doing very well by yourself. No Viking daughter could have done better!"

"But I could not save Loriot," she said mournfully, looking down upon the broken body.

"So I see. What are you doing up here alone? A tryst with a minstrel?" His voice was harsh, demanding.

"No tryst. He knew my father, that is all. But . . . it is my fault he lies dead."

Aimery nodded. "I agree. And he is not the first man to become involved with you and come to sorrow because of it."

"What does that mean?"

"Never mind," he said sharply. "Tell me what happened."

She told him of her hurried journey to the top of the castle.

"And you saw no one?"

"No," she said tartly, a little of her spirit returning. "Not even you. But you must know that."

He nodded. Narrowing his eyes, he said, "Your cloak does him no good. You need it."

She shuddered. "I could not."

"Nonsense." He spoke angrily. He stopped to pick up the cloak. Feeling the blood under his hands, he hesitated. "Put this on with the fur on the outside. It will keep you warmer than that thin thing you're wearing."

She was really very cold, she told herself. It would do no good to freeze to death. Blood was blood, and could not harm her.

"So the minstrel had the proof you blazoned loud and clear in the great hall," said Aimery.

Her fingers faltered on the silver clasp, meant to close on the outside. With the cloak inside out, she could not manage it. With surprising gentleness, he fastened it for her.

"What good is a minstrel's word?" he cried, exasperated. She could feel his breath hot on her cheek, his warm fingers touching her chin.

"He knew. He told me—"

His hands dropped on her shoulders. She cried out with the unexpected pain. "You're hurt?" he cried. "You didn't tell me." He unpinned her cloak and swung it away from her shoulder.

When the pain had subsided, slightly, she said with asperity, "You didn't ask whether that man had wounded me mortally or not."

Surprisingly, he grinned. "Not mortally. As long as your tongue is so sharp, I wonder you did not run him through with it!" He moved her arm, testing the shoulder. "Let me get you downstairs, where your maid can deal with your injuries."

"Actually, I feel nothing now. Only a bruise, I'm sure, where he threw me to the stone floor. Aimery, I can't leave Loriot!"

"Lor—oh, the minstrel. Well, my duty is to the living. The dead are in the hands of God and His angels. Come."

"Give me back my cloak," she said. "Fur side in, this time." She lifted her chin and looked into Aimery's eyes. "I am sorry Loriot is dead. I did not mean this to happen. But I have found out that my father is alive."

"*Is* alive? This very minute? How can you know that?"

Not answering, she frowned. "How did you get here?" she asked slowly, full of sudden misgivings. "How do I know you aren't the man who killed him? He said 'they' would have bought his silence. Was it you?"

"For heaven's sake! Would I keep from killing you now? The man pursuing you had no such scruples, had he? Sometimes I think you the veriest fool in Christendom!"

He took a quick look around. "We can leave him here. I will send someone to deal with him.

"You say your father is alive?"

"He was at least alive *after* Mehun swore he saw him dead." She watched Aimery's grim face as she told him Loriot's story.

Aimery listened in silence. She was conscious of a strong intelligence moving behind his eyes. She found she was waiting almost breathlessly for his verdict.

"Such things happen," he said at last. "But you cannot prove this, not by yourself. With Loriot—"

"The king can ask."

"The king has other things on his mind now," said Aimery. Bitterly, he added, "He will scarcely take time to interrogate all the returning pilgrims. Not now."

"Ah, but I can!" she cried out. "And remember, if I can't prove my father is alive, at least, Mehun cannot prove he is dead."

7

"All your stepfather has to do," pointed out Aimery, gently leading her toward the corridor leading down, "is to keep saying he saw your father die. And also point out that you will do anything to avoid the marriage he has planned. You have given proof enough of that!"

"I suppose so," she said. "But I'm not beaten yet. I will ask every pilgrim returning from Outremer until I find one who has seen what Loriot saw."

"Claimed to see."

"Oh, no! I am sure he saw my father. He told me what he looked like. Described my father's device. My father saved his life in that battle."

She found herself leaning heavily on Aimery's arm. Her shoulder was giving her a great deal of trouble.

"Has it occurred to you that someone meant to kill you both? I see it has. Will you then lay a death sentence on all who speak to you of Saint Florent?"

"I had not thought of that."

She stopped, feigning indecision, but really to catch her breath against the pain.

"Mehun's power over me is broken," she said stubbornly. "I know he lied. And I will marry Raoul."

He glowered at her for a moment and then, his face softening slightly, said, "You said once, before we arrived here, that you would wed the man you loved. Not a man chosen for you."

"Raoul was chosen for me," she retorted. "But I love him. And therefore I will marry him."

"But what of him? I see no signs of devotion on his part." He eyed her warily. The lights from the sconces in the wall gave too much light, she thought waywardly. He can read my thoughts too well, and I would not give him the satisfaction of knowing that he has touched upon my deep trouble.

"He is kept busy by the king," she said, her voice quivering. "He loves me. I know he does."

"But you have not answered my question," he said. "Do you still love him?" She hesitated, just a moment too long. "It is as I thought," he finished in triumph. "You know your own mind less than an infant does."

"Or the veriest fool in Christendom?" she countered. She needed to defy him in anger lest, in her longing for someone to understand her, to tell her she was right, to range himself on her side against the world, she collapse sobbing on his chest.

"I wish I had not said that," he said roughly.

"As an apology," she said tartly, "it lacks feeling. But I suppose it is all I will get from you. But mark my words, Sieur Aimery de Montvert, I shall marry Raoul."

Aimery dropped her arm in disgust. "How can you be so foolish? You cannot marry Raoul."

"I suppose you have a reason? You will prevent it?"

"If I have to." Aimery seemed surprised by his own words. "I will not allow this."

"You cannot stop me," said Solange.

"You will never marry Raoul," he said angrily. "It is impossible."

The gray walls of the stone corridor swam and then steadied again. She thought darkly, I may not even be able to walk as far as the suite. And, looking around, she did not know quite where she was. She swayed.

"Here," he said sharply. "Rest against the wall for a bit." His arm held her steady.

He removed her cloak and frowned at the dried blood on her shoulder. "This blood isn't from the cloak," he said.

"I didn't say it was," she said peevishly. The wound was all at once dreadfully painful, and she was secretly appalled at the amount of blood that had flowed out onto the thin silk.

His fingers gently lifted the stiffened cloth, easing it away from the bleeding stab wound. "He hit you then." His color drained from his face as he realized how near to her heart the dagger had come. "He could have killed you!"

"I understand that was his intent," she agreed wryly.

"Is this the only wound?" he said angrily. "What else haven't you told me?"

"I did not think he more than touched me," she said honestly. "How is that possible?"

"I have seen men in battle never know they were mortally wounded until they fell dead. A strange thing, but it is true. This needs dressing. There, I've eased the cloth away from the wound. Take off your bliaut."

She gasped.

"What good is it going to do you?" he argued. "It's stained. Don't argue." He laughed sharply. "I'm not consumed by desire for you. Take it off."

She obeyed. She saw a light in his eyes that told her that if she did not do as he bade, he would tear the garment from her body. Hastily she unfastened her girdle and allowed him to help her pull the garment over her head. With practiced hands he fashioned a pad for her wound from the bliaut and tore strips to fasten it in place. The pressure eased the pain.

His touch was surprisingly deft, and gentle. But in spite of his delicate practiced ability, his fingers set her tingling whenever they touched her skin. She was conscious of his nearness, and wildly her thoughts leaped to wonder how it would feel to have his strength so close to her that they could not be parted.

She shook her head vigorously. This was mad, she told herself. She was no wanton, to throw herself into the embrace of any man. She was Raoul's betrothed, and a noble lady.

"Did I hurt you?" he asked, seeing her turn away from him. "I'm sorry, but you will feel better at once. I must get you to your maid."

"I was as good as dead an hour ago. I owe you much."

"You owe me nothing," he said roughly. "But if you wish to favor me, then give up this idiotic idea of marrying Raoul de Puiseaux."

"Why? My father thought him good enough to marry me."

"But—what's the use! Just believe me. Marriage to Raoul is hopeless."

"Hopeless?" Solange suddenly felt caution fleeing fast out of reach. She had hoped for so much.

"Hopeless!" she repeated. "That from a knight who loves the queen? You feel *your* devotion has a future? I can see it now. The queen divorcing the king of France to marry a knight with not one parcel of land. Or perhaps the queen's gift will supply that lack?"

She had gone too far. She saw the glitter in his eyes, dark with anger, and his hand strayed to the dagger at his hip. But she could not stop. "Strike down all who disagree with you. Slash everyone who will tell you what I tell you! The queen will have few vassals left, I warrant you!"

He thrust the hilt of his dagger away savagely. Perhaps she was in truth Mélusine, the witch who took the guise of mortal woman.

"I wish I had never met you!" shouted Aimery. "I wish I had turned you back into the woods! I was right. You *are* Mélusine, and I doubt not you turn into a serpent when the time is right, as she did!"

"I agree!" sparkled Solange. She really felt much better, now that he had dressed her shoulder. "At least I agree that I wish we had never met! As for my turning into the serpent at midnight—you will never know, will you?"

She turned, with an impudent smile, and walked hurriedly away down the corridor. She hoped he would not follow her. And yet, a forlorn feeling invaded her when she did not hear his footsteps ringing on the cement floor behind her.

At last he came after her. "You're feverish," he said, "from your wound. You don't know what you are saying."

Let it go at that, she thought. She meant every word of it, surprised at her own temerity. What was Aimery to her that she should care how he felt about the queen?

"I believe," he said peaceably, "that I could handle a serpent at midnight!"

"Having much practice with the queen?" she retorted in blind anger.

"You think I am enamored of the queen," said Aimery, conscious of a sudden desire to explain himself to this woman with the level amethyst eyes that could look through and see the heart of him, if he would let her. He knew he wanted to see something other than scorn in her eyes, and yet, so chaotic were his thoughts that he did not know exactly *what* he wanted of her.

"I think so," said Solange, deliberately matching his air of reasonableness. "You are not?"

"The queen is special."

"And therefore above my comprehension?" she said, delicately flicking him with her sharp words.

"If you will hold that vicious tongue of yours for a moment," he said, waiting for her nod before going on. "I want you to watch your step. I cannot be on guard all the time. Don't argue about it. There are matters of some importance going forward here tonight. Bernard is here, and he'll give the signal."

"Signal for what?"

"What do you know about Vitry?"

She raised her startled eyes to his. Slowly she shook her head. "I think someone mentioned that name, but I cannot recall."

"Vitry is a town north of Paris, in the county of Champagne," he told her. Swiftly he outlined the story of how Louis, in making war against the count of Champagne, had allowed his army full rein in subduing the town of Vitry.

The townspeople had displayed unusual courage in defending their walls. The walls, so Aimery told her, had at last been breached, and the townspeople, seeing Louis's knights in the city streets, had fled to the sanctuary of the church, pressing close to the high altar, under the protection of the host.

And then the knights of the army, the Christian warriors fighting the Christian townspeople, lost their heads. Inflamed by the stubborn resistance of the people of Vitry who were merely defending their own, the king's army lost control.

They could force the enemy into the streets, so torches were lit and, before the king's horrified eyes, the church was set alight in a dozen places.

The enemy did not pour into the streets, as expected. Instead, whether the doors were flaming or whether their determination ruled, the townspeople stayed inside the church, calling to God to save them from the flames. They

died with piercing screams and heartrending cries—
women, children, priests, old men, and boys.

"Now no one dares mention the name of Vitry. Vitry-
the-Burned, it is called, but only in a whisper. The king
has nightmares, it is said," finished Aimery. "He cries out,
thinking he still hears the cries of the dying as the flames
sweep upward."

Solange was paralyzed with horror. "He is always so
kind," she murmured.

"Kind? Thirteen hundred died there, and the king did
nothing but cry," said Aimery harshly. "Tears flowed down
his cheeks like a fountain."

"Hush! Someone will hear!" said Solange, shocked.

"It is no more than others have said," he added, but in
a lowered voice. "But I should not have told you this."

"Why not?" she said sadly. "The truth never stays hidden for long."

Aimery's face was shadowed, and she could not read
his expression. "That is why," she said thoughtfully, "the
king is often sad."

"The king has a need to expiate his sins. And he has
sent to the pope for help. Bernard is the answer."

She shook her head. "You puzzle me, Aimery. I do not
understand all this."

"Bernard is going to preach a Crusade to the Holy Land.
That's what he was talking about in the church today."

"But a Crusade? Surely a Crusade is inspired by God.
The pilgrimage comes at His call."

Wryly Aimery said, "This pilgrimage goes forward for
a simple reason—*le roi le veult*—the king wills it!

"Understand that the king will be far too busy to see
justice done for you!"

8

The king wills it!

Was so vast an undertaking to be launched simply because the king willed it? No one knew better than Solange

that the king's will was law in this land. Solange's life, too, lay in the hands of the king.

What would a Crusade mean to her? If the king went on pilgrimage, he might marry her to somebody, *anybody*, just to get the problem settled so that he could get on with the great affairs of state. With Mehun so determined to wed her to Conon d'Yves, she would be trapped and there would be no way out but the convent.

"But I will not let it be so!" she exclaimed under her breath. She glanced quickly at Aimery, but he had not heard.

He did not speak again until they had traversed the lonely corridors to the door of her suite. He took her hand. "If I were you," he said gravely, "I would not speak of the happenings of this night. Believe me, I know best on this."

"But Loriot—"

"Is dead. He will be found. The murderer will send someone to see whether he still lives. In the meantime, don't go anywhere alone. Above all, don't tell anyone what the minstrel told you."

"But if my father lives . . ." she protested.

They arrived on the floor occupied by the countess and her ladies. Someone moved, ahead of them, and Solange clutched fearfully at Aimery's arm.

Aimery left her with sword in hand, and ran quickly to the far stairway. He looked down for some time before he came back, sheathing his short sword. "A soldier, from his garb. No insignia that I could see."

"Was it—?"

"The killer? I think not. He seemed too short. But he got out of sight too quickly for me to recognize him."

He looked down at her and took her hand. She leaned back against the door to the countess's rooms, and closed her eyes. She had been more frightened, just now, than she liked. She would not allow herself to live with such fear. But just for now, she clung to Aimery's hand.

Aimery lost his temper. "What if your father is alive? Will it benefit you to know he lives while the assassin probes your ribs with his dagger?" he demanded fiercely.

She drew a quick breath. "He knows you know about him, too."

"What do I know? And if I did, what's to keep me from a dagger as well?"

"You're afraid," she taunted, to relieve her own fear.

"Only for you," he said savagely. "Who will save you from your great folly if I am not here?"

He opened the door behind them, and the firelight touched the hall. She could see his cheekbones tight against the skin, his eyes glittering deep in their sockets. He might not be afraid, she thought, but he was certainly angry.

"Get that wound tended to," he ordered roughly, "it's bleeding through the padding." He half-shoved her through the door and pulled it behind her.

Jehane was alone. A chair had been drawn up to the fire, where she had been toasting her feet. How odd the contrast between this homely scene and the wild, windswept tower. Solange, feeling the heat, began to shake from the cold and reaction to her narrow escape.

"Back from the dinner, lady? What has been happening? I heard shouts as though the Norsemen were at the gates!"

Chattering, she took Solange's cloak. The wound had bled freely, and the pale tunic was dark with the stain. Jehane shrieked.

"Hush!" said Solange firmly. "It is only a scratch. Get the countess's basket of medicines and I will tell you what to do."

Under her direction, the maid cleansed the wound and applied a yellow salve. To Jehane's questions Solange gave noncommittal answers, until the maid lapsed into hurt silence. Finally, one of Jehane's earlier remarks snagged her attention.

"What did you say? Shouting in the great hall? No doubt simply too much feasting and drinking."

"No, lady," said Jehane, eager now that she had her mistress's full attention. "A great shout."

"Well, I don't suppose Bourges has been attacked by the Northmen. My ancestors have been civilized for some years now." She longed to lie down and rest, but she must appear in the great hall as soon as possible. She must pretend that all was well, and that she had no suspicions as to the identity of the man who murdered Loriot.

"Fetch me the primrose silk bliaut, the one with the jeweled collar," she added more kindly, "and I will go to see what untoward event has taken place."

Settling the heavy embroidered collar around her slim throat, satisfied that the ornate needlework disguised the thick padding on her shoulder, Solange picked up her cloak again and went to join Aimery in the hall. She expected him to be waiting, since he told her not to go anywhere alone.

But he had not waited for her. Instead, his squire Rainard stood patiently. The lad's eyes lit up when he saw her. "My lord said you were hurt," he cried.

"What did he tell you?" she inquired, starting down the corridor toward the stairway. She needed to know what story Aimery had set current, in order to fashion her own tale to suit.

"Only that you had fallen foul of a robber," said Rainard guardedly.

"Is that all?"

"Yes," he said slowly, staying close to her. "Yes, lady." But he looked backward over his shoulder so often that she was sure he had more than a suspicion of the truth.

She entered the great hall. All seemed just as she had left it.

Conon had returned to sit near Petronilla, with Mehun on the other side of her. Like guards, Solange thought. She always thought in terms of force with Mehun, and this was not so strange, really, since she had never seen him anything but violent.

Her gaze traveled on to Lady Alis at the table near the dais, to Bertille whispering to yet another young man. Alis was watching her husband with her head cocked to one side. Solange knew that familiar pose meant that the countess was troubled.

Bernard was still standing on the edge of the dais. "Has he been talking all this time?" marveled Solange to the armed man guarding the door.

"All this time?" said the lancer. "Seems less than one turn of the glass!"

She had been gone such a short time—and yet so much had happened to her. Loriot dying, the great black arm upraised over her, and her near-quarrel with Aimery. She was forced to agree that it had been less than one turn of the sand-glass.

All heads were turned toward the dais. Except Aimery's, whose eyes fell searchingly on her. She smiled faintly, reassuringly, at him. Had he been concerned?

But all was not as she had left it. Something had indeed changed. The atmosphere in the room was alive, as though one great magnet pulled every head toward the figure of the priest. Every head, and—she caught her breath at the ecstatic faces—every heart.

The priest spoke again, "Arise, soldiers of Christ, arise, shake off the dust, return to the battle where thy fathers fought, and more bravely shall thou fight and more gloriously triumph," thundered Bernard. "Christ has many soldiers who bravely began, stood fast and conquered. He has few who have turned from flight and renewed the combat. Everything rare is precious, and thou among that rare company shall the more radiantly shine."

The candles had burnt more than halfway to their sockets. The torches in the sconces along the wall had already been removed to be replaced with freshly burning lights. It was getting late.

Solange fidgeted on the bench. The pain was not so piercing now, thanks to the salves and Jehane's tight wrapping, but the wound in her shoulder throbbed like a toothache and she could not forget it.

"Thou art fearful? So be it. But why dost thou fear where there is no fear, and why dost thou not fear where everything is to be feared? Dost thou recoil at the weight of thy arms, O delicate soldier? Before the enemy's darts the shield is no burden, nor the helmet heavy. The bravest soldiers tremble when the trumpet is heard before the battle is joined, but hope of victory and fear of defeat make them brave. How canst thou tremble, walled round with the zeal of thy armed brethren, angels bearing aid at thy right hand, thy leader Christ Himself? There shalt thou safely fight, secure of victory, safe *with* Christ and *for* Christ!"

After his words ceased, there was absolute silence for a dozen heartbeats. Then, with one accord, the response came from a hundred throats. *"Dieu le veult!"* rang through the hall.

She caught Aimery's eye in the moment before pandemonium took over. She saw the same sharp cynicism she had seen earlier. *The King wills it*!

The Crusade was called. And now the surge to the dais began. Forgetting all courtly decorum, knights, barons, squires, even the serving men still carrying their trenchers, rushed to the raised platform. Hands shaking in the air, voices shouted, "Give me the cross! The cross!"

Bernard of Clairvaux was lost to view in the swarms of petitioners. Conon muttered in her ear "Fools! Wait till the morrow! Their headaches will be monumental!"

"But if they succeed," said Petronilla, leaning across Solange, the better to talk to Conon, "it will be a true miracle. Do not blaspheme, Conon."

He bowed his head. "I do not blaspheme, my Lady de Mowbrai. I merely say it is a long and deadly journey, and these men now with torn bits of the abbot's robe in their fingers, on the front of their tunics, are like toddlers planning a boar hunt!"

The picture was graphic enough to set Petronilla back on her bench, to lose herself in reflection. "But if one's sins were to be forgiven?" she said, more to herself than to her companions.

Solange heard scarcely any of this exchange. She was caught in the grip of a powerful idea.

The priest had lost his cassock, which now, in the form of rudimentary crosses, was in the hands of many in the hall. From somewhere appeared another cassock, and in moments that too was parceled out to the company. The king watched the proceedings with a strange light in his eyes. But the queen, not one to be eclipsed, especially by a lowly-garbed priest, rose to her feet.

One hand upraised for silence, she watched her husband's people, as well as a half-hundred of her own Poitevins. She was a tall woman, dressed this Christmas day in scarlet with gold trim. How beautiful she was! thought Solange, and how little Aimery must be blamed

171

to give his devotion to the queen. The realization did not make her happier.

When all was silent, the queen began. "I wish, lords and ladies, to make an announcement. Such great eagerness to share in God's holy work is contagious, and I would not want you to believe your queen does not share with you in all things."

"What's she talking about?" muttered Alis from across the table.

"Can't stand to play second to the priest," said her husband.

"My grandfather Count William and other heroes like Bohemund, Godfrey de Bouillon, risked their lives to free the Holy Sepulcher. Many of our Poitevin barons now rest beneath the hallowed soil in Outremer. My uncle, Prince Raymond, rules even now in Antioch."

Her words were stirring, pronounced as they were in a clear ringing voice.

"My blood is as noble as theirs, and I too will take the road all the way to Jerusalem. This I vow before you all. I will follow the Way of the Cross."

Applause broke out sporadically in little clusters around the press of people in the great hall. Menials from the kitchen, from waiting rooms, even from the stables had crowded into the hall, summoned by some magical current that told of impending great things.

Queen Eleanor clapped her hands twice for their attention. "I will travel as humbly as the lowliest peasant," —this brought a snort from Lady Alis—"leading the way, at the head of my own troops!"

9

A babble of sound broke out, rising around Solange like a storm wind.

"Her own troops?"

"Well, of course, she means those Poitevins of hers, Saldebreuil of Sanzay, for one. And Guy of Thouars."

"If that's true," muttered a man without caution, "the realm will be more peaceful!"

"Hush! You want to be heard?"

Solange fixed her eyes on the queen, as though waiting for revelation. The seed of a plan had fallen on her fertile mind.

Solange would go herself to find her father, wherever he might be, in Constantinople, Edessa, or Antioch.

"I hear you, Raimond de Sainte-Coeur. I do not speak of my valiant nobles from Aquitaine—although you would be in sore trouble without them. But I'm speaking of my own troops—a company of *women*. Noble by birth and character. We shall take up arms and follow the Cross!"

Tumult took over. The uproar was deafening. Solange clutched her mother's sleeve. "You hear that? It's the chance I've been waiting for!"

Her mother turned shocked eyes to her. "You? Go to the Holy Land? I won't let you. It's not decent!"

"Not decent?" said Solange. "To go with the queen? You surely can't mean that!"

"Her reputation is not clean. Her ways are far too loose. I should not like a daughter of mine to be so indecent in her behavior."

"Indecent?" hissed Solange, furious. "You can say that? I should not like a mother of mine to marry the first man to ask her, with a husband still living! You could not wait to leap into bed with Mehun, could you? You claim to know what is decent!"

Petronilla turned pale as samite. She half lifted her hand, palm toward Solange's face, but remembered her surroundings. Conon, watching the incident with aloof amusement, intervened. "The question is, what does the queen mean to do? And will the king allow it?"

Lady Alis said dryly, "I think you underestimate my sister-in-law. I will make you a wager that this time next year she will be in Byzantium!"

Count Robert frowned slightly at his irrepressible wife, and she subsided with a twinkle. She had said what she wished to say. The queen was not the only lady in the room who spoke her mind.

Even Bernard seemed overwhelmed by the response to

his impassioned plea. But, being the preacher that he was, he must continue to exhort, even as his audience came to kneel at his feet.

He reminded his listeners of how sinful they were, how little they deserved the grace of God. "O ye who listen to me! Hasten to appease the anger of Heaven. No longer implore God's goodness with vain importuning! Clothe yourselves with your impenetrable bucklers. The din of arms, the dangers, the labors, the fatigues of war are the penances God now imposes on you. Hasten then to expiate your sins by victory over the infidels."

Finally he raised both hands to heaven, either in blessing or in exhortation. "Let a holy rage animate you in the fight, and let the Christian world resound with the words of the prophet: 'Cursed be he who does not stain his sword with blood!' "

A great groan tore the air as he finished. To think that one's place in heaven could be assured by as simple a task as traveling to the Holy Land and freeing the sacred places from the defilement that threatened them—as easy as going on pilgrimage to Saint James of Compostela. Easier, no doubt. And what a journey!

To see the far-off lands of Byzantium, where it was said silk grew on trees and gold and jewels paved the streets! And then, at the end, to receive the blessings of God Himself! The ecstasy was beyond enduring!

Petronilla had cooled and her hands were now firmly clasped in her lap. The excitement around them burst all bounds. The queen's daring proposal captured the fancy of many a lady but, judging from the dour frowns, not of their lords.

The trickle of noble ladies to take the cross became, as had happened in many another fashion the queen had set, a flood. There were many ladies whom Solange did not know, but the names filled the air as each was recognized, stepping up to kneel before the abbot, the little father of Clairvaux. Mamille of Roucy, Torqueri of Bouillon— kinswoman of that famed Godfrey de Bouillon who had refused the crown as king of Jerusalem in 1099 when the great nobles had taken the Holy City. He would not, he said, wear gold where his Savior had worn a crown of thorns.

Faydide of Toulouse, the countess of Flanders whose half-brother ruled Jerusalem now. Her sons Henri and Theodoric followed her sullenly to receive the cross from Bernard.

Conon breathed, "Solange, look at the king. I vow he is as surprised as any man here. See how he appeals to the abbot!"

Solange glanced at Conon with surprise. "I would not expect you to condone a lady's acting contrary to her lord's wishes? I have heard rumors that you made sure of submission in your own household!"

"If I was not amused," he said. "But I am sure you will always find a way to entertain me."

"It is not my intention to try," she said coldly, and turned away.

"Just remember," emphasized the baron, "I have bought you. For two goodly fields and a wood. But I would not have given up my land had I not seen you, and desired you."

"You speak of desire, but not of love."

"What is love? Something the poets speak of, a mere idea. It is not real."

Solange looked curiously at Conon. "You do not believe in love?"

He snorted. Petronilla looked up sharply, but turned away again, lost in thoughts of her own. Conon said. "Not love as the queen says. Marriage is no real excuse for not loving, according to our gracious queen. But she does not mean her husband."

"Quiet," urged Solange, terrified of being overheard.

"Desire, yes," said Conon. "An attraction of the flesh. But you, my dear, have more than that. Your strange eyes, that cool way you have—there are caldrons burning inside you, and the man who first releases them—ah, there's a fortunate man!"

Troubled, Solange turned again to look at the king. He was indeed shocked. And pained. He spoke with the priest for a few moments, privately. It was clear what he was asking. And it was equally clear that Bernard would not grant his wish.

"It is true that I must give permission for the Crusade to anyone highly placed," said Bernard sufficiently loudly for the ladies at his feet to hear. "And the queen has won my approval." Bernard permitted himself a smile. "I look forward to far greater speed in the preparations, since she will enjoin haste upon the king."

The next day Solange sought out the abbot. She had laid her plans carefully. The abbot's permission was a vital first step. She must have him on her side before she took the cross, lest Mehun or Conon forbid her to go. She could not afford a public row.

She found Bernard in a small room in the tower to which Pierre de la Chartre had removed the ecclesiastical workings of his bishop's charge. It was fitting, said Bernard, that he, a Cistercian monk, should abide with the other clerics, rather than be afflicted by the sight of courtly luxury.

It was clear she could not see him alone. The queen was present, and Aimery, Garin, Lady Alis and Count Robert. There were a couple of barons Solange did not know. She finally captured Bernard's attention.

She put her petition bravely.

"I seek permission to make pilgrimage, sir, to join the king in his mission of faith."

Bernard considered. "It is true that, as a ward of the king, you may not travel without permission—*my* permission lest the king prove too indulgent. Have you asked the king's permission?"

"No, sir. I thought I would seek your advice first." It was a shrewd answer, and Bernard evidenced his pleasure.

"But that is not quite all," he said. "I have heard, my daughter, certain rumors that your purpose may be clouded with worldly consideration, a mundane search to find your father. Can this be true?"

Bernard's keen gaze penetrated to her bone marrow.

She believed the story that he could read what was written even in one's dreams. But outwardly she did not falter. "Every Christian must feel the loss of the Holy

Sepulcher like a sword in the heart," she said. "You yourself are to blame, Brother Bernard, if you have stoked the fires of faith."

"Solange!" It was only a breath of caution, from the direction of Brother Garin.

"If a lady finds a true vocation, a calling in her soul to take the cross, then I must approve," Bernard agreed slowly.

"And only I have the knowledge of what lies in my heart," purred Solange.

"You and the eternal God," rebuked Bernard. "But you have my permission to go—if the queen agrees."

It was the queen's turn to try to discourage Solange. "You cannot know the rigors of the journey," she insisted. "I speak only from hearsay, you know, but it is not a journey for pleasure."

"I do not go for pleasure, my lady queen."

The queen, baffled, tried again to dissuade Solange. The arguments she raised could in justice be applied equally well to herself, and it was clear to them both that they were merely jousting with blunted swords.

Aimery watched helplessly as the two women fenced. If he longed to intervene, on one side or the other, one could not have known it from his expression. At last, the king spoke. "I think, my dear, that the Lady Solange must be allowed to take the cross. The journey is hard, of course. But the penance would be valueless, would it not, if there were not hardships? Remission of sins cannot be easy." His eyes grew somber, reflecting his grievous inner hurt. "Nothing is easy for a sinner."

"We are all sinners," said the queen lightly, but she placed a hand on the king's sleeve and left it there. She had urged the war which had culminated in the battle of Vitry-the-Burned, and must bear part of his guilt. "This conversation is fruitless. For you must know that I will not allow your Crusade to be ridden by disruptive influences. Were I to take twenty or two hundred ladies of the court in my guard, the result would be the same. The gentlemen would follow us like bees around a honey-pot." She laughed with delight. "So you see, my child," she continued earnestly to Solange, "I cannot allow you to disrupt my lord's serious business. All my ladies must be married. And you, it seems, refuse to be wed."

It was an effective parting shot as she swept from the room, pausing only to glance at Aimery's expressionless face, and not waiting for an answer from Solange. Aimery and Garin followed.

Solange, at first too stunned to move, collected her wits and swept out, as regally as the queen.

Aimery and his brother waited outside. Aimery grabbed her arm and swung her around to face him.

"You certainly have made a fool of yourself, haven't you!" Aimery hissed. "Pushing in where you're not wanted! That's all you've ever done."

Her cheeks burned with anger. "Push in?" she managed to say with some calmness. "I was not aware that the Way of the Cross was an exclusive journey. Fit only for whom, noble women? I am as well-born as any twenty women your Queen will find to follow her. Forgive me if I misunderstood, but it seemed to me that Bernard of Clairvaux was preaching to all. And I am to be excluded? I think not. And I don't remember giving you permission to hang on to me."

He dropped his hand from her as though it burned. Brother Garin spared a moment to be glad he was not his brother, before stretching out his hand in a futile gesture. They did not even see him.

"Do you have any idea of the magnitude of your harebrained scheme? Do you for instance have the slightest idea of the distance?"

"No less than the queen does, I imagine," said Solange, seething.

"Don't tell me *you* are burdened by great sin!" cried Aimery.

"I will not tell you that."

"Someone will have to watch every step you take!"

"There will be plenty of gentlemen to take that charge upon their chivalry," she said, mischief hot in her violet-dark eyes.

Aimery stopped short. "I would not have believed you could say such a brazen thing."

"I did not say that, my lord de Montvert," she retorted swiftly. "It was your queen who told me I would disrupt the entire Crusade, you remember. And how could I disrupt anything, all by myself?"

Words at last failed Aimery. He stood, hands on hips, apparently ready to hit her, but she retreated a step, just out of reach, and laughed.

"You—*fool!*" he forced out between thin lips, and strode down the corridor. She watched him out of sight before the tears came.

Solange could not fathom Aimery's state of mind. He had surely heard the call of the flesh. That day upon the watchtower, his kiss had been as passionate as Conon d'Yves's in the forest. She remembered Aimery's warm mouth on hers with a resentment that was new to her. Why had he kissed her so, if he did not value her?

Brother Garin did his best, but his soothing words failed of their purpose.

"What heat is this," he said finally, "over a mere nothing? For you cannot go with the queen's guard, being yet a maiden."

Solange flushed angrily.

"But I will not be maiden forever, Brother Garin," she said with renewed determination. "And after I am wed—"

"Wed!" Brother Garin exclaimed. "Not to d'Yves!"

"After I am wed," she repeated, stoutly, "the queen dare not deny me!"

10

Solange made an unpleasant discovery. It was sometimes easier to be forced to wed against one's will then it was to marry when one was willing, even eager.

Raoul de Puiseaux had left Bourges before she could talk to him again. She was convinced there was a very real reason why Raoul was avoiding her, and she could not help but be hurt. She was humiliated when she thought of how blithely she had announced her pending marriage to her betrothed, only to find that the bridegroom shied away from the altar like a poorly trained *ronçin*.

Her own feelings toward him were not as intense as they had been when she dreamed of him in her tower room at Belvent. She tried to decide whether it was Raoul himself she had dreamed of, or merely escape from Mehun. It was a daunting thought that, if Raoul had ever come to carry her away from Belvent, she would have leaped into his arms without a second thought.

But something had happened to her since leaving home. Her life had taken on new depth. The court of King Louis was full of excitement and she was constantly attracted by the entertainers that beguiled the diners every night. She was making many new friends—Bertille, Catherine, Lady Alis.

Sybille de Nannes, the winsome brunette Solange had met that first night with Lady Alis, was lodged in the other tower with her husband Olivier, and her two brothers. Raymond and Pierre de Garci hovered constantly over their sister—like ravens, thought Solange fancifully. Their black armor gave the impression of dark glossy feathers, and the image was enhanced by their heavy black brows. They were twins, it was said, but one was just a shade less forceful than the other. Pierre followed Raymond like a shadow.

"There's a pair for you, Bertille," teased Solange when, one night at dinner Olivier de Nannes made one of his rare appearances, accompanying his wife and brothers-in-law. He was so palsied that every mouthful of food was a hazardous adventure, most of it dribbling down his chin and onto his faded velvet bliaut, stained with the refuse of other meals. Sybille all but fed him. "Why don't you flirt with Raymond or Pierre? Olivier won't mind."

For once Bertille did not twinkle at the idea. "Not them," she said in a low voice. "Neither one of them. They give me chills. I don't wonder Sybille wed that old man. Anything to get away from those gloom-spreaders."

"But she's not away from them even yet," objected Catherine. "They hover over her like . . ."

"Like ravens," offered Solange.

"Exactly," Catherine agreed. "Just the right word. Henri doesn't like them very well."

Bertille said. "Then of course none of us must either." She had regained her jesting air, and Catherine was not offended. Thoughtfully, Catherine added, "I think we must all cheer Sybille as much as we can."

"She dares not leave that *old man*!"

"We could insist she come walking with us," mused Solange, "or shopping in town. She must need to get away from them all. How can she breathe?"

Catherine smiled endearingly. "You could not bear to be so pent up, could you? I wonder how you will fare—" She bit her lip and continued, "on the Crusade, where we are all subject to the rules of the journey?"

"Were you going to say, 'when you wed'?" laughed Solange. "I shall do fine, for I shall love my husband and wish to do his bidding."

Bertille said thoughtfully, "I should like to see *that*. I vow you are not the Solange I know if you bend the knee to anyone. Other than Father Bernard, of course. And the king. And probably Queen Eleanor."

"Stop!" Solange cried. "Lest you bring in the whole court for me to obey!"

Catherine joined Bertille's laughter, and changed the subject.

Raoul was expected back soon, since he had gone only as far as Etampes to speed Abbot Bernard on his way to Metz, where the monk intended to persuade the indolent Emperor Conrad to take the Way of the Cross, to lead his German knights in a Crusade of kings.

Solange must marry before the spring, else she could not travel with the queen's guard. Raoul *must* agree to the marriage. Solange refused to imagine what she would do if Raoul failed her.

On a sunny day she voiced her thoughts to Countess Alis. "I can't see why the queen won't take me."

"You can't? Then I despair of your intelligence. The Queen does not tolerate competition. And what she possesses, she keeps. Even after it has long ceased to amuse her. Remember that."

"I want naught of the queen's," Solange pointed out.

"All I want is to go on Crusade. It will not hurt her precious guard to let me travel with them."

"You have not seen how the queen watches you—and Aimery?"

"Aimery! He is nothing to me. But if the queen dislikes me, for no reason, then why can't I go with the court? I do not need to be in the queen's guard."

"A lone lady? Who then hitches up your baggage wagon? Who pitches your tent? Or cooks your meals? You are not likely to do these things for yourself! There is no lady I can send you with. All are in the queen's guard . . . all of good reputation, that is. No, Solange, I do not think you should go."

"But I must. You don't understand."

"Yes I do. You are determined to go on this journey because the problems here are not to your liking. But, my child, you will find that difficulties travel with you, no matter."

"If I wed Raoul, the queen cannot refuse to take me," said Solange, setting aside her needlework. She chafed her fingers to warm them. The sun gave little heat, but it gave the illusion that there would some day be warmth again in the world. The fire was low, to conserve fuel. The king's stay at Bourges had been prolonged and was nearly ruinous to the immediate area's stock of fuel and food.

After a pause, Countess Alis said, "What does Raoul say?"

Solange lifted troubled eyes to Alis. "I haven't been able to talk to him, not really. He is so busy, and now he's gone again."

"Has not your mind changed about Raoul? Is he truly the man you wish to marry?" Alis leaned forward earnestly. "Have you not changed?"

Solange said stubbornly, "I have known him all of my life, you know. My father thought we should marry."

Alis sighed deeply. "My dear . . ." She did not finish.

Impulsively Solange covered Alis's hand with hers. "You have been so good to me. I do not wish to distress you further. I would not ask you to intervene with the queen for me. But cannot I go as your maid?"

Alis shook her head. "My husband must go. The king commands it. But not I. I do not go."

"But I thought—"

"So does the queen," said Alis with the ghost of a smile. "She thinks she can command me, all the way to Jerusalem and back. But I do not feel strong enough to undergo the rigors of the journey. And of course you must not go as anyone's maid. My suggestion is that you commission someone—Brother Garin, for example—to make your inquiries about your father."

"And what will I do in the meantime? Mehun will insist that I marry Conon d'Yves at once."

"The king will settle the matter before he leaves," Alis pointed out.

"But he will wed me to the baron if he does not believe me about my father. No one believes that my father lives. No one cares."

"If you were wed—to the man of your choice, let us say —then would you be so anxious to find your father?"

Solange rose and began to pace the small room, warmed only by the low fire in the grate and the vermilion tapestries on the wall. "Yes, of course. My lady, you have been good to me, and I love you as I would an elder sister, with all respect. But I must go to seek the truth about my father."

She dropped to her knees before the countess and looked up beseechingly into the plump, worried face. "Truly, it seems to me that I *must* know the truth. I do not remember him well. My mother says I never really knew what he was like. But the abbot has told of such terrible tortures that befell our brave people, such fevers, such grievous wounds. . . ." Her voice broke over the sob that caught in her throat, and she buried her face in Lady Alis's lap. A comforting hand stroked her long silken hair.

"I had not thought before," Solange resumed after a while, "how it was on pilgrimage. I pictured my father as I had seen him last, riding south from Belvent, following the road that would lead to Jerusalem. Just as though all he had to do was cross a mountain or two, and he would be there."

"Not quite so simple."

"I know that now. Those wretched men down in the courtyard that day, the day I met poor Loriot. Those pilgrims had come back maimed, mad, poor scraps of the men they had been. As their leader said, the fortunate ones died."

"I can see why he said that, can't you?" murmured Alis. "Their families will not welcome those living dead with open arms."

"And that's the point," cried Solange swiftly. "I can't help but see my father . . . as just such a one. There would be none to get him home again, as that knight brought his men home, because my father was his own leader. And I cannot bear the thought that my father is somewhere out there, like those men, with nobody to care for him."

"But what can you do?" objected Lady Alis. "You are tilting at shadows, it seems to me. You have no real knowledge to go on."

"But I have the name of a place. Antioch. And, dear Lady Alis, I must get there in any way I can. Then I will do whatever I must do. I must find my father, wherever he is."

"That makes it easier," said Alis. But though Solange lifted puzzled eyes to her, she would not explain the remark.

Later that day, Solange was summoned to the suite where her mother and Mehun were lodged. It was warmer here than in the countess's austere chamber. Petronilla was not one for going without.

"About this nonsense about going to Jerusalem," Petronilla began. Mehun was not in evidence and Petronilla sent her maids away when Solange arrived.

Solange was indignant, but it would be of no use to quarrel with her mother again. She managed a creditable amount of calm as she answered, purposely misunderstanding. "You mean the king's Crusade? You were there and heard as much as I did. You told me what you thought then."

"I don't mean the king's Crusade and you know it! I mean the rumor that you are trying to join the queen. Is this true?"

"I am not simply *trying*, Mother. I am going."

"What for?"

"You know what for. To find my father." She could not resist adding, "*I* haven't forgotten him so easily."

A dull red glowed on her mother's cheekbones. "You would do better not to cling to a foolish notion. Your father is dead."

"I don't believe it."

Petronilla bit her lip in vexation. It was becoming a recurring mannerism in her dealings with Solange. "Believe me, I am only interested in you. The journey is terrible. And what will you do when you get there? You haven't the faintest idea where to look!"

"I will find out," said her daughter, simply.

Petronilla looked sidelong under her long lashes. "Suppose . . ." She moistened her lips with a pointed red tongue. "Suppose I searched my memory? Suppose I remembered your betrothal ceremony?"

Solange laughed shortly. The sound held no amusement. "Who would believe that now?"

"No one could prove different." Petronilla warmed to her scheme. "You wouldn't have to marry the baron at all. Isn't that what you want?"

It was indeed what she wanted, or had wanted a month ago. Now, she was surprised to realize, she wanted much more. Some of what she wanted was still shapeless, more a vague uneasiness than a desire. But she knew one thing. "I want to know whether my father lives."

Petronilla rounded on her. "He is dead, dead, dead! He died full of wounds, in his own blood, on the battlefield of Adana. Why can't you believe that?"

Solange was shaken by her mother's outburst. But she stood firm. "Because Mehun says so." Her mother turned her shocked face away. "Because you tell me only Mehun's words. You forget that he wishes it to be so."

"My dear girl," said Petronilla. "Can't you see I can't let you go on this foolish quest? Never to see you again?"

"Don't worry," said Solange scornfully. "You will forget me just as easily as you forgot my father. May I go back to my room now?"

Petronilla's face darkened. Deep bitterness welling up in

her, she said, "I remember far too well. You are more like the old woman than I feared you could be."

"The old woman?" prompted Solange.

"Your grandmother Saint Florent. You look just like her, you know. That pale hair, white as the snows that filled her heart."

"Am I then so cold, you think?" said Solange, made uneasy by her mother's strange mood.

"No, I do not think so. But that old woman was full of guile, and as stubborn as you are. In some ways you are like her. She rode roughshod over anyone in her way— as I was, more often than not."

"I don't remember her," mused Solange.

"She was a frightening woman."

"She would have followed my father to Outremer," said Solange. "And found out whether he lived or not."

"Yes," said Petronilla. "That old witch would have done just that, no matter what the consequences. No matter whose marriage she broke up. No matter whose soul she put in mortal jeopardy. You are quite that stonyhearted, Solange. And I need not tell you that you are breaking my heart."

Tears glistened at the ends of Petronilla's long lashes. Solange was shaken to the core by her mother's blistering accusations. Was she truly so ruthless? She could not believe so. She took a step toward her mother. Petronilla was openly crying now, and she burrowed her head into Solange's shoulder as Solange's arm went around her.

"I'm sorry you think such harsh things of me, Mother. But I have to do this. Not to make you unhappy. Not even to spite Mehun."

"Then why?" came Petronilla's question, muffled in tears.

"Because in my mind I see my father in an infidel prison. Lonely. Perhaps sorely wounded. No one to help him, not even his family to rescue him or ransom him. Abandoned. I cannot sleep for this vision."

Surprisingly, Petronilla's sobs ended abruptly. "Abandoned? Helpless? Your father?" She wiped the tears from her cheek and managed a brittle smile. "My dear child, you never knew your father very well."

11

Although Alis did her best to keep Solange occupied, there were hours when time hung heavy on her hands. She had been accustomed to riding far and wide over the fields of Belvent, and confinement in a small town with too many people in it was stifling. She dared not go too far from the tower. The murderer she had met on the top of the watchtower might follow her.

Loriot's body had been found, in due course, and buried with scant ceremony. But the man whose knife had stolen Loriot's life had not been identified. Solange had wondered for days at every face she saw, trying to picture it behind a mask. This man was too broad, that one too fat, too tall, or too thin.

But when the Crusade preparations began to press upon her, she did not think quite so often about the narrow escape she had had.

There was a new feeling in the air, in the increased purpose of the men at arms who fiddled endlessly with their weapons. In a general atmosphere of hurry, as though time itself were running out and the Day of Judgment would find the court of Louis VII unready, caught in preparation for the journey that might have saved their souls.

The queen was busy. She was, so Aimery found, too busy to coquette with him, or anyone else. She seemed always in the midst of seamstresses, silk-vendors, boot-makers, weapon purveyors.

Weapons? asked Solange, astonished. She had thought the women would carry only the small daggers that every lady wore thrust into her belt. What would they need of weapons, when each lady had a husband somewhere in the train?

There was the rub, for Solange. She must wed or she could not go. She had little hope now as to the possibility of traveling with the court any other way than in the guard.

Wed she must be before spring, when Louis would raise his banner and set out for Jerusalem.

Solange visited the church atop the city once at vespers. Dim and mysterious, smelling of the incense that seemed to be the very breath of God, the church awed her. She approached the altar. Taking her candle from beneath her cloak, she lit it carefully and set it down in the designated place. Kneeling, she breathed a prayer to the Virgin. "Holy Mother, help me please. . . ."

When at last she rose to her feet, she had made a vow to the Virgin Mary that if she would prevent Solange's marriage to the baron, Solange would go on pilgrimage to Jerusalem. To find her father, if that were possible. And failing that, to walk the streets of the Holy City to the greater glory of the Savior and His Mother.

A bargain had been suggested. And Solange would fulfill her part of it.

Before she arrived at the tower, she saw Sybille de Nannes and hurried to catch up with her. "I haven't seen you this long time," said Solange, "how are things with you?"

Sybille was thinner and looked worn. Solange wished she had not asked even such an ordinary question. Sybille turned away quickly, but not before Solange saw the tears filling the lovely dark eyes.

"Come now," said Solange, slipping her arm through her friend's. "Forget I asked you. I meant—"

"Don't be sorry," said Sybille in a muffled voice. "Believe me, there are few enough to ask me how I am."

"But your family is here, is it not?" asked Solange. "Your brothers?"

"My two brothers," Sybille said, her lips trembling before she compressed them into a tight line. "I wish they had stayed at home."

Solange drew her friend away from the tower door and toward the inner courtyard. Solange knew of a small nook, and pulled Sybille to it. Glacing upward, she noted that the first window was a mere slit and too far overhead for anyone to overhear them.

"Your brothers don't seem to help you much," suggested Solange. "I suppose they're too busy."

"I wish they were," said Sybille sharply. She seemed to consider for a moment and then, as though she had made a decision, she said, "I've got to tell somebody. You don't know how it is with no one to talk to—"

"Oh, yes, I do," murmured Solange, but the other girl did not heed her.

"I did not want to marry Olivier at all, but they made me," said Sybille. "I had the same choice as you, but I didn't fight it."

Solange touched her friend's hand gently. "I couldn't have fought back had I not been previously betrothed."

"There is one I would have wed, but my brothers would not allow it," she said. "Not enough land, they told me."

"But you loved him?"

"I loved him," she added simply. "We had known each other from childhood, and I always meant to marry him. But he went away."

"Where?" demanded Solange.

"On Crusade, they told me. I thought he loved me too, but he didn't, not enough to stand up to my brothers. And without him, I cared not what happened to me."

"But he was not worth a candle!"

"No, no. I have not told it right, if you think that of him. He simply did not love me as much as I loved him, else he would have come for me." Her fingers moved endlessly, tracing the gold disks on her girdle, round and round, until Solange thought she would scream. "I did wonder," Sybille said in a low voice, "whether they had lied to him about me, and if that was why he went away. I suppose I could ask him. I have seen him here at court. But I'm too proud, I suppose."

"Sybille! Would they?"

"You don't know my brothers," said Sybille. "They have one thing in mind, one only, and that is to get land, always more land. But this is all past, my dear. Over and done with."

Solange did not know words to comfort Sybille. But then, she thought, perhaps just talking would provide as much solace as anything Solange could say.

"Olivier's land, of course, comes to me and my heirs."

Solange slowly began to take in the import of Sybille's

words. There were no heirs. So then the de Nannes estates would revert, not to Sybille, but to the king, perhaps.

"That is what is so funny," said Sybille. "My brothers knew from the start that Olivier had no possible hope of giving me a child."

"I don't understand," said Solange after the silence drew out interminably. She was vaguely aware that something was happening in the inner ward. A troop of men were jangling through the outer ward and the gates were now opening to admit them. But she paid them no heed.

"After I was solemnly wed," said Sybille, her voice full of bitterness, "my brothers informed me that I was to produce an heir to the de Nannes estates, no matter who the actual father was. And they have brought more than one man to visit me."

Solange's mouth opened in horror. "You mean just to—"

"That's right. To provide a son. They tell me Olivier will be so pleased."

"You believe that?"

"No. He will know."

The full horror burst upon Solange. Tutored by Mehun, who was at base just such a one as Sybille's brothers, Solange could see beyond the actual scheme to provide Sybille with a child. Olivier would indeed know the heir was not his. Unless, Solange suspected, he did not live to know. She turned shocked eyes to Sybille, but her words died on her lips. Sybille had clearly not followed through the scheme to its logical conclusion. Solange would not enlighten her.

The troops jangling in through the inner ward were now recognizable. Raoul, a pale gold surcoat over his mail, led the men on their return from Etampes. Solange watched him, willing him to look up to see her. But she could not make him feel her eyes on him.

Solange and Sybille strolled back to the tower and Sybille, having unburdened herself, managed a frail smile. She bade Solange farewell at the door of the de Nannes rooms.

"If you could fight so hard, then I'll try not to give in," whispered Sybille. "All they can do is kill me, and I don't think I would mind that. Life is not so good that I wish to cling to it."

Solange watched her friend square her shoulders, as if lifting a heavy yoke. Her own problems were not like Sybille's!

Solange was more determined than ever that she would not fall into such desperate straits, not as long as she had breath in her body and wits enough to plead her cause.

She left Sybille, and sought out the queen. Raoul was back in Bourges and her wedding could not now be long postponed. But she wished not to hazard all on one chancy throw of the dice. Raoul was not dependable.

"My dear, you must see that an unmarried girl would only be a diverting temptation to the gentlemen who have far more serious things on their mind than dalliance," Eleanor purred. "Surely you would not wish to be the means by which a pilgrim arrived in Jerusalem burdened with sin?"

"There are sins other than the kind you mention, Majesty," said Solange. "There is, as an example, the dishonoring of contracts."

"What kind of contract have you in mind?" said the queen, in a deadly, low voice. "Your betrothal contract, which your mother says does not exist? Even your betrothed seems not to know his obligation to you."

Something in the queen's voice was disturbing. A kind of amusement, perhaps? Solange felt more than ever that no one took her seriously. She recognized her defeat in the queen's open dislike.

She curtseyed and left the royal presence. But she was far from beaten. Solange was desperate enough now for uncompromising measures.

She slipped through the corridors from the queen's sitting room to the office floor, just above, where the king conducted his business. The corridors here were busy, with clerks and minor clergymen running back and forth with scrolls under their arms and worried expressions on their faces. The king's Crusade demanded prodigies of work from the entire household.

Solange did not notice Isabel de la Valle, following her

out of simple curiosity. Isabel had come to visit the queen when she saw Solange emerging from Her Majesty's presence with flushed cheeks and an air of tight-lipped determination. Isabel could no more resist following Solange to see what caused such turmoil, than she could have flown up and perched on St. Stephen's spire.

The king was away from his office. There were only a handful of men in the outer rooms. When she inquired about Raoul, one of them motioned with his quill pen toward an inner door.

With caution, she opened the door to the inner room. A small, austere room, it was nevertheless the center of the king's court. It was strange to realize that decisions made in this small space could set an entire countryside on the move, could command endless trains of haywagons, great baggage-carts, and set a thousand armed knights in motion.

In the anteroom of the king's business rooms, she met a soldier she had seen before, one of the king's men-at-arms, whose name she did not know. She spoke civilly to him.

"Sir, is Raoul de Puiseaux in there with the king?"

The man gave her a strangely insolent smile. "No, lady. Raoul is there, but the king is not." His hand hovered around his girdle, straightening his tunic into regular folds. He left without another word.

Raoul stood brooding at the window. He turned with a smile at the sound of the door. His smile vanished.

"Oh, it's you," he said flatly.

"I want to talk to you," said Solange. "Lately I find it hard to see you alone."

"We've talked enough, haven't we?" said Raoul.

Surprised, she exclaimed, "How could we? We have much between us that is unsettled. Raoul, why did you deny our betrothal?"

"That's none of your business," he said brusquely. "Just let me alone."

"I came to ask you to marry me."

"How can you be so stupid, Solange? I can't marry you."

"Won't, you mean. I don't understand you, Raoul. Once you thought me fair. Have I changed so much then?"

His eyes narrowed into glittering points of light. "I suppose not. But I confess, Solange, you don't appeal to me. I can't believe you would wish to wed me . . . under the circumstances. What can I do for you?"

"The queen won't take me with her guard if I am still a maid. You see, I am honest with you."

"Even marriage does not unmake a maid," he said with a short bark of laughter. "How does the queen detect maid or wife?" He made a gesture with his fingers, so fleeting that she could not be sure she saw rightly. But she was sure of one thing. It was a coarse and indecent gesture.

"Well, if your friends have let you come to me this way, then I suppose I could go along with the mockery."

"I don't have the bride price anymore," she said, her mind busy with details. "Mehun has it, and I doubt he will give it up."

He looked at her with disbelief. "I don't want the bride price," he said at last. A queer kind of compassion lightened his expression when he looked at her. She was so young, so untutored! He hated himself for doing what he was doing to her, but he could not help it. "You force me to marry you."

"There was a time," she said forlornly, "when you thought the idea pleasurable beyond all things."

He was lost in thought for a few moments. From outside the closed door came a great shout of laughter. He turned to her. "I will make you a bargain."

"I have little to bargain with."

"Enough, I think. There is one person I should like to know better, and you can arrange it for me."

"I have no influence with anyone."

"More than you think, I don't doubt. Give me your word you will do this one thing, and I will wed you."

"Such a small thing!"

"But something I have longed for, dreamed of, long months now."

He would wed her! That was the only thing she could think of. At last, Raoul was standing beside her in the duel between herself and Mehun. He would give her the right to go on Crusade, to seek her father. . . .

His voice was harsh. "You'll do it?"

He was reluctant, but he was capitulating. She could see her way clear ahead!

Exuberant in her happiness, she crossed the space between them and threw her arms around his neck. She raised her lips to his for a kiss.

Suddenly she was moving through the air to land against the stone mantlepiece and slide to the floor. Crumpled against the wall, she put her hand unbelieving to her shoulder, where Raoul had struck her a savage blow. "In the name of heaven!" she cried out. "You struck me!"

He did not help her up. His lips tight with suppressed emotion, he leaned on the table, and watched her warily. "I'm sorry," he said. "I didn't mean to do that. But you made me."

"Raoul! You're mad!"

"No," he said sadly. "Not mad. Just . . . different."

"What has changed you so?" she demanded. "I simply do not understand at all."

"No, you don't. I know that now. I hoped someone would tell you. But I see they haven't."

"Told me *what*?"

It was difficult for him to speak, but she was past compassion for him. He had struck her, bewildered her with nonsensical hints, and denied their vow. He had humiliated her beyond measure.

She asked stonily, "Are you ready to explain, at last?"

"It is simply this, Solange. I do not wish to marry. I thought I could endure it, but you see I cannot." He indicated her body, still on the floor, and then put his hands up to his face.

"Cannot?"

"I do not care for women. The very touch of them makes my skin crawl."

She was stupefied. She had heard of such tastes, but she considered them far away, apart from anyone she knew. Now, in a flood, came back to her all the hints of her friends, the odd arrested look in the eyes of anyone who heard her mention Raoul's name. The heartbreak would come later. Comprehension came now.

He bowed his head. "You do understand?" he said.

"No, I don't," she said, summoning all her pride. "I understand nothing of that. But if not women, then— boys?"

"You hate me. But it's not my fault," he insisted. "A man like . . . Aimery de Montvert, for example. There is beauty itself."

He watched her struggle to her feet, rubbing her bruised shoulder. She was sure the blow had opened the dagger wound again. There was a feeling of moisture under her hand. But she felt nothing.

The worst was yet to come. Raoul, still a distance from her, lowered his voice in confidence. "Solange, I'll make it up to you. I'll even marry you without the bride price."

"I don't want to hear anything you can say!" she said savagely.

"Only get me that friend of yours. I'll marry you, Solange, and you can go on your precious Crusade. But get me Aimery de Montvert!"

12

She was in the hall outside the king's suite. She did not see the men-at-arms staring at her curiously, nor did she notice that one took her arm and spoke gently to her. She did not know that Isabel, disturbed by her appearance, ran to find Catherine.

Catherine was there moments later. "Are you all right?" she said softly. "Of course you are not. Come with me. Solange, you're like ice! Here, take my mantle."

Catherine had the gift of comforting. Wrapping Solange with her warm cloak and holding Solange around the shoulders, she urged her gently toward the winding stairs that traveled upward to the next floor, the landing where the King's brother and his wife were lodged.

Solange did not remember traveling the stairs, nor anything except the black yawning pit that stretched before her. Her mind refused to function at all.

Another day, it would do to look squarely at the appalling revelation Raoul had bared to her. But not today.

Somehow she found herself back in the rooms of the Countess de Dreux. She was injured, she knew vaguely, because her wounded shoulder throbbed. But that could wait.

Stunned, she said to herself, over and over, It is not true.

The Eastern vice was a perversion brought back, so it was whispered, from the pagan Orient by the first Crusaders—to the great disturbance of the Church. It was a vice the infidel indulged in without shame, and reflected their opinion of women as mere devices for making sons.

Raoul had fallen prey to this practice.

What should she do? What *could* she do?

Her thoughts wrapped themselves as though in white wool and wove around themselves like vagrant sheep. Pictures came to her—Raoul as a child, a mischievous small boy, the trees they climbed together, the fish they caught in the pools of the Petitmer. But the pictures were without depth. There was no person behind the pleasant mask he showed to the world, even to her, his betrothed. If they had wed in that moment of betrothal before the church door, could she have saved Raoul from this shame?

Probably not. And again, something told her, You never knew Raoul. As you did not know your father. The Raoul you believed in, loved, did not exist. Ever. You loved only a shadow of what you wanted him to be.

A sense of grievous loss came to her, loss of her childhood, of all that she had loved. She felt old, and very cold. The hard rain beat against the shutters and a part of her mind registered that it must be beginning to thaw outside because the snow had turned to rain. The snows on the hillsides would soon melt away, revealing the dun, unfruitful earth.

Unfruitful, like Raoul. She did not know whether she loved him or not. It had been long since she had even questioned it. He was her betrothed, and that was settled.

Lady Alis came in, kissed Solange's forehead and, sorely

distressed, clapped her hands for her maids. The fire was built up swiftly, furs were tucked around Solange.

She sat in a high-backed chair, drawn close to the fire. Lady Alis drew up another chair and sat before her, her knees almost touching Solange's. With an imperious wave she dismissed the girls, round-eyed with sympathy and excitement. "Aiglentine, stay," she instructed her middle-aged maid. She watched Solange's still features, no shadow of emotion touching them. Solange had gone away, into another place, leaving only her shell behind.

Lady Alis talked.

"My dear, I would have spared you this if I could have done so. But I was not sure. There were rumors, but I had no proof. My child, it is not the end of the world."

"How could he?"

"My dear Solange, men are such mysteries."

"He is not a man."

"It is a terrible thing, Solange, but—Aiglentine, fetch the special wine. Quickly, quickly!"

"It is not true." The words Solange had said to herself now trembled aloud.

Lady Alis said nothing until the maid brought the silver goblet of the strong wine called "Water of gold." It was considered a cure for colic, dropsy, ague, and many other ills of body and mind. Motioning the maid away, Lady Alis set to work in earnest. She had expected a reaction when Solange learned the truth behind Raoul's avoidance of her. But she had not expected this despair. Alis set forth to do battle.

"Tell me about it," she began. "Why did you go to see Raoul?"

"Because," said Solange, staring into the fire, "because I thought he would wed me, so that I might go with the queen. He agreed to marry me, without the bride price. Raoul said it did not matter."

"And then he refused?"

Solange was silent for a long time, reliving that humiliating moment, believing she could not ever tell about that, and yet knowing she must. Lady Alis would wait patiently until the story was told.

"I touched him."

Lady Alis closed her eyes. How terrible a thing for this dear young girl to live through! She reached out to take Solange's hands, still as cold as ice. She began to rub the fingers gently.

"And he recoiled?" she said at last.

"More than that," said Solange dully. She pulled her hand away from the countess's and mechanically began to rub the throbbing wound in her shoulder.

Lady Alis exclaimed, "The wound reopened!" Swiftly she went to the door and gave curt instructions. Miraculously, there was hot water, and salve, and bandages. Solange's wound was wrapped again, and dressed again, the old bliaut, bloodstained and stiff with dirt from the floor of the king's waiting-room, was bundled away for burning.

"He hit me," said Solange. "He knocked me down. It's the Eastern vice, you know," she said conversationally, but so remotely that Countess Alis looked at her in wild alarm. She whispered directions to Evart, who nodded and left at once.

"No more of that wine," she said. "It has something of a wild effect on you." Then she left Solange alone, in the quiet of the room, with her thoughts.

A tap sounded at the door. Solange did not answer. After a moment, the door opened. She did not look around. Footsteps approached, and Brother Garin stood beside her.

"You did not answer," he said, offering meaningless words while he searched her face. He stepped briskly to the door. "Bring me some firewood," he ordered, "no matter where you have to get it. From the king's own hearth if you have to."

Anonymous footsteps outside went away and then returned. Brother Garin made up the fire. He had closed the door upon the servant. The only sound in the room was his breathing, and the little soft sounds of the fire.

"You've seen Raoul de Puiseaux," said Brother Garin. It was not a question.

She nodded.

"And he told you," continued Brother Garin, glancing warningly at Alis, returning at that moment.

Once begun, Solange talked and would not stop. It was obvious to the two who listened that she did not know she was talking aloud. "The thing is," she said, "that everyone else knew. You, Lady Alis. You, Brother Garin. Aimery."

There was a long pause. Garin prompted her. "Aimery knew the rumor. None of us could be positive, although there were hints in plenty."

"Aimery," she said wonderingly. "Raoul will wed me yet, you know . . . If I bring him Aimery. Is not that a generous offer?"

"Aimery! You mean Raoul . . . admires my brother?"

"The most beautiful person he has ever seen," said Solange, still in that unearthly voice that alarmed them so much. "I do not think Aimery is beautiful. His nose is large, his eyes are too deep-set." Her voice broke. The shame of it was coming fully alive, and she longed to die. She could bear no more. No more.

Garin and Alis exchanged worried looks. "The time is ripe, don't you think?" whispered Alis. "We may yet save Aimery from his attachment."

"I will speak to Bernard at once," said Garin. Solange heard them, but did not try to understand.

Suddenly there was another posset before her. It was not wine, but she drank it to the bottom of the cup.

She yawned suddenly, and hardly knew when they laid her on her pallet and covered her with furs. "Let her sleep," said Alis. "It's the best thing for her now."

When she woke, sometime the next morning, she found Brother Garin by her side.

"That's better," he said heartily. "Now then, my girl, I want to say I'm sorry."

She sat up and the whole sordid situation came back to her. "Sorry! It is I who have caused you so much trouble."

"He is a sinner," said Brother Garin without emotion. "But even more, he is a fool. You deserve better than him."

She stirred. The fur was comforting, and Brother Garin's kindly face brought calm to her spirit. "I deserve nothing," she told him. "I have been so stupid."

"Not stupid," he told her kindly. "It would perhaps be strange if you had recognized the signs. You know nothing of such things."

"But everyone else knew. And I understand now the reasons for everyone's response when I mentioned marriage to Raoul."

"Is it this that distresses you?"

She thought a moment, and answered, "Yes, in a way. None of us wishes to be made a laughingstock. But the main thing is how much he changed. How little he repents."

Brother Garin watched her, waiting for her to work it out in her own mind. Talking would be the best thing for her, he surmised, and if he were nothing else, he was a good listener.

"No," Solange amended her own words. "I do not really know how much he repents. He said he could not help himself. Is that possible, Brother Garin?"

"I am told that is so. But God knows the heart, and He can perform miracles. Pray for Raoul, my child."

"You call me a child, Brother Garin," said Solange with a wry twist to her lips. "I have indeed been the veriest child. But, no longer."

"Better a child a little longer," said Brother Garin, "than a woman too soon."

She bowed her head in assent. Silence lengthened between them, but it was an easy quiet. He rose once to prod the embers, and again to put on another log. It was a prodigal display of fire, she thought.

"How could I have been so blind?" she said once.

"We all protected you," said Brother Garin. "Those of us who guessed. The gossip vine runs fast at court, you know. I should have told you that first day in the forest, when you spoke his name. But I did not."

"I would not have believed you," she said.

"I knew that. And I wanted to see you in safe hands first. Once we could get you to the Countess Alis, I knew you would be protected."

"But not against such news as this."

"Nobody could protect you longer against that. What

will you tell the king, now? You see, one of your choices is gone now."

"I know that. But it does not seem quite as important to me. I have only one need left in my life."

"And that is?"

"To find my father. Not for any confirmation of my betrothal. That has vanished like a puff of wind. But to find out whether he lives."

After awhile he coaxed her to dinner in the great hall. Her stomach rebelled at the thought of food, and she could not face anyone, she told him, feeling shame written on her face.

"The shame is not yours," said Brother Garin. "Leave Raoul to God, and come with me."

The great hall was almost deserted. Bertille and Catherine were still at table and welcomed her with warmth. She sat down with them and ate a slice of bread. Immediately her stomach began to settle down and cease its wild swinging, and soon she could begin to listen to the chatter of her friends. They were continuing a conversation that gave signs of having been in progress for some time.

"The strange thing is," said Bertille, racked with amusement, "that Olivier de Nannes has been drinking this potion that is supposed to work miracles on him. He says that it works, that he even . . . well—you know . . . but he doesn't remember much about it. But he sure isn't making Sybille happy with it. See, across the room? He has such greedy eyes when he looks at her."

Catherine shook her head warningly, and Bertille, glancing at Solange, subsided with flaming cheeks.

"Don't worry about me," said Solange. "I will get over the shock of Raoul, I think. You've both been so good to me."

"What are you going to do now?" asked Bertille, her bright eyes full of affection for Solange.

"I could eventually go into a convent, I suppose," Solange said slowly. "It wouldn't be Saint Vergillia's, that is certain. But first I must find my father."

"Go on Crusade?" cried Catherine. "But how?"

"I don't know," said Solange honestly. "But I'll find a way. I'm sure of it."

13

She did not see Raoul again.

Her friends had a certain amount of influence, and Raoul de Puiseaux vanished from Bourges. Some said he had gone on a King's mission to Sicily. But others, whispering secretly in corners, insisted that he had awakened from a drugged sleep, begun in his room at Bourges, to find himself in a monastery somewhere in Auvergne. A Cistercian monastery, the story went, the speaker's eyes rolling toward Brother Garin.

Solange did not question his absence. She was still numb from the shock of her discovery, and from relief that she had found out before she was truly wed.

Lady Alis kept her busy on small, inconsequential errands, trusting that the routine of simply getting through another day would work its well-known miracle once again.

This afternoon Solange had carried a note to Brother Garin in the smaller tower of the castle. The clerics of the bishop's offices assembled there, and visiting monks and priests gathered there, drawn together by their shared calling.

She was hurrying back to Lady Alis, for Bertille had planned a sortie to the Street of the Goldsmiths and insisted that Solange and Catherine go with her. "My grandmother has sent me three gold ecus, and they burn my fingers until they are spent," Bertille had explained. Her grandmother, the Countess of Neuil-Savarin, had been a close friend of Lady Alis's mother. When the old Countess developed a malaise of the bones, she sent her granddaughter to Lady Alis, assured that Lady Alis would see that the exuberant Bertille did not get into much trouble. Lady Alis was not as sure as the Countess of Neuil-Savarin that she could manage Bertille. But, as she told her husband privately, "All I can do is try. It would take all the angels of heaven to watch her properly!"

Count Robert had countered, "My dear, how do you know all the angels are not?" and kissed his dear wife. Alis had to be content with that hope for Bertille's safety.

Now Solange hastened down the stairs of the small tower. Ahead of her, she caught sight of Sybille. How pleasant it would be if Sybille joined the expedition into town. Sybille was looking far too pale and harried these days. The outing would be good for her.

Sybille was not alone. Two men walked beside her, and all three seemed to be hurrying. They turned a corner, and Solange hesitated. Perhaps Olivier had become ill, and Sybille had been summoned to his side?

Solange hastened after them. Sybille's fast pace meant trouble, she was sure. She almost called to her, but she did not want to delay her.

The trio ahead did not know Solange was approaching them. Her soft leather slippers made no sound on the stone floor. Closer, she called out to Sybille. Apparently they did not hear her, for they gave no sign. They disappeared around the corner ahead. When Solange reached that same corner, she was surprised to see no trace of her friend. The corridor was empty, stretching out far ahead. She did not see how they could have vanished so quickly.

She moved hesitantly down the corridor, puzzled. There was a door near at hand, though. Sybille must have gone through it into the room beyond. Solange was suddenly uneasy, for it was not like Sybille to ignore her. She paused outside the door. It was ajar, and beyond it, through the crack, she could see Sybille.

She stood facing the two men who had brought her this far. "So? Where is he? You said Olivier was dying! Take me to him!"

One of the men reached out to take her arm. She flung away from him. The room was lit solely by a slit in the wall, high up. Solange could see only one of the men and Sybille, through the slightly open door.

"You lied to me. What do you want now?" Sybille's voice carried a ragged edge that threatened to mount into hysteria. "What more can I do?"

The man in her view made a gesture at his face, like pulling down a visor, Solange guessed. When he turned to face Sybille, Solange knew she was right. A mask of some fabric covered his face, and she did not recognize him.

His words were muffled, but she made out a few. "An heir . . . you defy us. . . ."

Sybille whimpered, and now Solange could see the other man who held her arms behind her back. "I can't do it. Olivier is too ill."

"But we are not," growled the first man. "You know what we have to do."

Sybille cried out, a wordless scream of anguished protest, ending in a shriek of pain.

Solange did not understand the conversation, but she knew Sybille needed help. The two men might overpower Sybille, but Solange could make the struggle more even.

"Sybille, what is it!" cried Solange, coming into the room.

"No, no!" Sybille screamed. She twisted suddenly, and the unexpectedness of her struggle took her captor by surprise. She was free! She ran toward Solange, hands outstretched. "Run, Solange!"

She shoved Solange toward the door. Quick-witted, Solange turned and, grabbing her friend by the wrist, began to pull her into the corridor.

"By the devil!" snarled one of the men. "Stop them!"

Solange pulled the door wide, but a strong arm struck her on the side of her head. She staggered with the force of the blow, and the moment of escape passed. Sybille was torn from her grasp, and the second man flung his arm around Solange and lifted her from the floor. She flailed her fists fruitlessly against his broad chest.

"Enough of that, you vixen!" He dumped her to the floor and she fell to her knees. She struggled to her feet, her ears still ringing, her breath coming in heavy gasps. She saw Sybille in the grip of the other man. Solange started forward. Her captor twisted her arm behind her and the pain numbed her fingers. "You'll be safe," came muffled words in her ear. "We don't want you. But we can't let you go till this is done."

Done? Until what was done? And while she watched, helpless, there was the terrible answer.

The man went about it like a chore, as methodically, thought Solange, as feeding the hounds! He shoved Sybille to the stone floor. She sprawled, breathless and crumpled where she landed, and began to whimper like a child.

"Take your clothes off," he ordered, but Sybille only cried. Neatly, speedily, he shoved down his chausses and knelt, straddling his victim. "You're no help!" he muttered. He lifted her bliaut, turning it back over her girdle, baring the white flesh that glimmered in the gloom of the stone cell.

Solange screamed, but the sound was only a grunt under the heavy hand clamping her mouth shut. She struggled. If Sybille would not fight back, Solange herself was not so resigned. The grip holding her was mailed and powerful. She kicked backwards, but only bruised her heel on bone. Her captor pulled her against him, wrapping one leg around hers so that she was unable to move any more.

But her eyes moved, seeing Sybille twist against her enemy fruitlessly. The man covering her was massive, and determined. He arched his back over his prey.

Solange bit the hand over her mouth. A curse grated in her ears, and suddenly she too was falling—slack as a rag doll—to the floor. The impact took her breath.

A faint shriek of desolate pain burst from Sybille, and Solange knew it was too late to save her friend. Solange lay where she had fallen. Perhaps, if she did not move, the men would forget her.

She was only dimly aware of what happened next. Her captor let her go, but the first man replaced him, shoving her down to sprawl full-length on the ground.

He dropped to his knees beside her. "You will forget everything you saw," he growled fiercely, "else you get the same!" She stared back at him. For a moment, his eyes flickered over her and she stiffened but he merely grunted and pulled up his chausses.

Again came the sounds of grunting, muffled cursing, of Sybille's moaning, and a sour, pungent odor. The endless nightmare sound of mating.

So this is what it's like, thought Solange. A terrible, ugly invasion of the flesh and, more than that, a bruising cruel trespass of the spirit.

After the second man had taken his turn on Sybille's limp body, the two men adjusted their clothing, hurried through the door, and were out of sight before Solange could gain the corridor to look after them. But not before she saw the signet ring on the second man's hand.

A signet ring she recognized. Horror filled her mind.

Gazing fearfully at Sybille, Solange wondered whether Sybille knew who her attackers were. This outrage had to be told to the king, to Garin, to whoever would listen.

"Solange." It was a pitiful little cry from the woman lying on the cold floor.

"Yes, dear Sybille, I am here."

"Did they hurt you?"

"Not me." Nothing but a blow on the head, that still rang in her ears. "But you—"

"I'm glad they didn't hurt you," said Sybille faintly. "I could not have stood that."

"Then you know," Solange said flatly.

"They want the land so badly," moaned Sybille.

The scheme was stark and simple. Since Olivier de Nannes was not able to sire an heir, then Sybille's brothers would do it for him. And Olivier, believing in the potion because he wanted to so desperately, might then think the heir was his.

In futile anger, Solange clenched her fists and pounded the floor. "They can't do this!"

"But they did." Sybille moaned again. "Solange, I fear for you."

"They won't touch me. They think I don't know who they are."

"Not that," said Sybille, with impatience. "But don't you see, love is not like this. Love between man and woman— I knew it once. Gentle he was, caring . . . the most beautiful thing in the world!"

But Solange scarcely heard her. She put out her hand to touch Sybille. "We can't let them get away with this. It's a terrible sin!"

"Solange," Sybille struggled up onto one elbow. "Solange, listen to me. It's over with. I should have known better than to let them bring me to this place alone. But, Solange, they're my brothers. Promise me you will never tell this.

It would be my terrible shame, and they'd shut me up, and they'd—oh, Solange, promise me! Swear you will never tell!"

With the thin hands clasping hers, Solange could not insist upon telling the truth. Sybille was right. It was over, and could not be undone.

"But why both?" she said, puzzled.

"So that they bear the blame equally," said Sybille, mouth drawn, "and neither can claim the child is his alone. Greedy they are, and mortally jealous."

"If there is a child."

"I shall pray there is one," said Sybille simply. "If there isn't, they will do it again."

Solange kept the promise Sybille had forced from her. She saw Sybille across the room that night at dinner, but her friend refused to meet her eyes. Her brothers were not in sight, and no one missed them. But they had left their mark on their haggard sister. She looked much closer to death even than old palsied Olivier. Solange pushed her trencher away, unable to eat.

But the next day, Solange had to forget Sybille. Her own day of decision had come.

The sympathy she had received from the understanding countess and the two girls who were her closest friends, helped greatly to ease her abysmal sense of loss over Raoul, and when the summons came from the king, she felt better able to sustain whatever might happen.

She was determined to go to the Holy Land. She feared that the queen would not allow her to travel in the guard. However, Solange had many ideas to offer.

The king's outer chambers held those assembled to hear his verdict on the case of Solange de St. Florent. Conon d'Yves was there, of course, his eyes lighting up when Solange came in. Her mother and Mehun frowned indiscriminately at all but the king. The queen was there, absorbed in a small notebook containing another of the many lists she was compiling to assist in her great project.

The countess had come with Solange and, due to her rank, a chair was placed for her. Solange stood beside her, holding her hand tightly. Aimery de Montvert was present, too, to Solange's surprise.

Raoul was not there. But he was present in every mind. She could not have faced him, did not even think she could stay in the same room with him. But Brother Garin had told her that the shame was not hers, and she clung to that.

The king was speaking. "I understand that the Lady Petronilla maintains there was no betrothal," he said kindly to Solange. "Is it true that you no longer wish to marry Raoul de Puiseaux?"

How fast the gossip vine grew, she thought. Her cheeks warmed as she nodded. She did not trust herself to speak.

"Then that is one solution we may not consider," said Louis. "Tell me what you yourself feel is a solution to this problem?"

"Nothing. I m-mean, Majesty, that I do not want anything but to find my father."

The king lifted an eyebrow. "Your father? But surely this is a new direction?"

"It is something I must do."

The king shifted uncomfortably. "But your father's contract is now invalid, not because of his death but because of—of other circumstances."

"I know that."

"And I, holding Belvent as my fief, can rule on your father's contract. Overrule it, or change it, as is my wish."

"I understand, sir, but I need to find my father."

"Where could you begin?"

"I have already begun, sir. I have heard that he is alive. The man who told me—"

"Is dead," growled Mehun. "A mere minstrel, whose word is worthless."

"Yet," said Solange swiftly, rounding on her stepfather, "he was important—to someone—enough to be murdered."

The king winced. "Lady Solange, we stray from the point. Where will you, since you say you have started, seek to find news?"

"I wish, sire, to go to the Holy Land, and search there for my father."

There was silence in the room. Solange felt her breath coming in short gasps. She had not intended to reveal her purpose in such a blunt way, but there it was. All she could feel at this moment was relief.

Somehow, someway, she would make the trip. She was surprised to find that she was speaking aloud. "I will go, if need be, as a laundress with the men at arms."

"Laundress! Whore, more likely," screeched Petronilla.

Aimery took a step forward, involuntarily, and then stepped back. The king's eyes turned to him, however, and Aimery said with force, "She'll do it, sire. If she has to, she'll do it. She is mule-headed."

The queen murmured, "I did not realize that you knew her so well."

Mehun, his hand heavy on his wife's arm, begged leave to speak. When the king nodded, he said, "This is a fool's errand. The girl is simply unwilling to settle down sensibly in her proper position. If you will remand her to me, sire, I promise you she will not run away as a laundress."

"My father is alive," cried Solange.

"I saw him die."

"But there are those who saw him alive after that battle."

The battle was joined between Mehun and Solange. She faced him defiantly, forgetting the king in her turmoil.

"Who?" said Mehun with a heavy sneer. "A minstrel. So you say. I wager none other heard him say such a lie. To think the man died with a sin on his lips."

"How do you know what was on his lips when he died!" said Aimery, dangerously silky. "Unless you were there?"

"I was in the great hall," said Mehun with lurking triumph. "I was not on the tower, as I have heard you were."

"Enough." The king's quiet voice cut across the heated exchange. "My queen has a guard that she is honoring by her sponsorship, a group of ladies who will travel on Crusade. It seems most fitting to me that Lady Solange go with this group. There is, of course, no question of her traveling in any menial capacity."

"But—," Solange began, and then, feeling the queen's heavy-lidded stare upon her, bit her lip and kept silent.

"Eleanor?" prompted the king. "Your permission, please?"

The queen, surprisingly, turned a beguiling glance on

her husband. "My love, your slightest wish is my command, as you have every reason to know. But have you thought of how the other ladies must feel, with a maiden such as the Lady Solange traveling among them?"

"What would they feel?" said the king bluntly.

"Since I have insisted that all the ladies be married, in the interests of decorum, I cannot make an exception. Your subjects' feelings would be outraged, sire."

The king was adept at hiding his thoughts, and it stood him in good stead just now. Only the faintest of smiles touched his lips as he said, "I have every regard for the sensibilities of the wives of my vassals. I have reached my decision and I will give my royal command now, and confirm it by my clerk's setting it down later."

"A royal command?" said Eleanor, sure of victory. Glancing at Solange, she added, "We must all abide by your decision."

"Without exception, my lady," said the king to his wife. "The Lady Solange will travel with the queen's guard. As—," he lifted his hand to cut off her remonstrance "—a married lady. And I will myself stand sponsor to the bride, in my vassal's place."

Solange could not breathe. He was giving her to Conon! There was nobody else. After all the king's kind words, he was betraying her. Brother Garin caught her eye and shook his head slightly. Conon moved closer, the light in his eyes anticipating triumph at long last.

"Solange de Saint Florent will marry as I bid her," said the king. "As my ward, in the absence of her father,"— he glanced at her sharply before continuing—"either on earth or in heaven, as God decrees, I must myself arrange her marriage."

He looked around him with his accustomed air of mingled surprise and shyness that, as Solange was about to learn, masked his real thoughts. "Solange will marry my vassal, a knight of my own household, Aimery de Montvert."

A soft sound, as of breaths released. The king, thought his queen, was not so blind as she had thought. Imagine the fool, to notice Sieur Aimery's constant devotion to her, a devotion that, multiplied many times by as many knights as she could charm, was the bread of life to her. He had humiliated her in public! But she was more than a match for her weak husband, or so she thought. Aimery de Montvert, by giving his queen the devotion that belonged by right to a wife, would titillate Eleanor even more.

But anger at her husband's impudence paced back and forth in her mind. He would pay for this. They all would, she vowed.

Book Three
France, 1146

❧

1

Solange read nothing in the queen's frozen smile. She could only hear the thunderous throbbing in her mind. Not Conon. *Not Conon*!

Somehow they all bowed themselves out of the royal presence. Solange knew she should say something, but words died on her tongue. Alis held her tightly by the arm, and imperiously waved away Petronilla. Even Brother Garin fell back as the countess, with inexorable determination, propelled Solange through the door and back upstairs to their suite.

The girls were waiting. When they heard the news, Bertille cried out, "You'll be married before us all!" Her cry was cut short under the countess's frown.

Someone brought a jeweled cup full of wine. Alis stood sternly over Solange, demanding that she drink it to the dregs.

The empty cup back in her hands, Alis said crisply, "That drink is by way of celebration."

"Celebration?" It was the first word Solange had spoken since the king's royal command had been pronounced.

"Celebration," repeated Alis firmly. "You got exactly what you wanted."

The wine loosened her tongue, and Solange sputtered. "Just what I wanted! How can you say that when you know how much I loathe him?"

"Just because you quarrel," said Alis serenely, "is no indication. When you came, you remember, your sole ambition was not to marry the hated baron. I wonder if you do remember that? It seems to me that you are forgetting the brighter side of this. You will be able to travel with the queen's guard, you know."

Alis had to marshal all her considerable tact before Solange was convinced that she had come out well. She was not to marry Conon d'Yves, nor was she to enter the convent. She was able now to go in pursuit of the will-o'-the-wisp that was her father.

Said Alis, "If you must submit to Aimery, that is little enough price to pay."

"I shall not need to pay such a price," said Solange, more calmly. "He is the queen's lover, and he has only contempt for me."

"So?" It was a soft little word, full of meaning. It spoke of the futility of a hope which never materializes. A man loves a queen in spite of her marriage vows, and all accept the fact. . . .

Except the king. Solange would one day be amused at the neat way in which the king had disposed of his rival. Looking back, she now saw the whole game.

The king knew of his queen's dalliance. He insisted that Aimery take the cross with him, so the king could know that Aimery was not dallying with the queen while he was gone. The queen had countered that move by declaring her own Crusade. And now the king had moved again, immobilizing his rival with a wife.

Was it checkmate? Solange did not believe so. And she would not be a pawn in anyone's chess game, royal players or not.

She was going to the Holy Land to find her father with a husband who had called her every kind of fool. Well, she was not fool enough, no matter how Aimery saw her, to believe in this marriage. It was no more important to her than a baggage cart to carry her boxes in. This marriage was a means to an end, nothing more.

Alis broke into her thoughts. "Maybe you can draw the man away from this infatuation for the queen."

"Me?" said Solange. "He dislikes me intensely, and I feel the same for him. If he is fool enough to chase after shadows, then I think little of him. The queen can never give him what he wants."

"He does not know what he wants," said Alis impatiently. "It is up to you to teach him. You will know how to beguile him from his mistaken attachment."

"Never," said Solange. "Never." But with a rush of affection toward the countess, she added, "I am so grateful to you for your concern. I do not doubt that the king's command is for the best. I am indeed thankful that he did not force me to the convent."

"That would be harder on the good nuns of Saint Vergillia," said Lady Alis with dry amusement, "than on you, I fear. Come now, Solange, you cannot deny that you do look upon Aimery without disgust?"

"He is a tyrant," she said simply. "He disapproves of everything I do, everything I say. He mocks me when I say I believe my father lives. He called me 'the veriest fool in Christendom.' He told me I should go to perdition my own way, and not take him too. I confess I don't know what he meant by that, but you must agree it is not the best way to start a marriage?"

"He said that?" marveled Lady Alis. "I wish I had known this sooner. There is not a doubt in the world but what you are well suited."

Solange was struck by a note in her voice. She said accusingly, "Did you have something to do with the king's decision?" Lady Alis could no longer smother her laughter. "My dear child, it was not I alone, believe me."

Solange drew a deep breath. She reminded herself of the great debt she owed Lady Alis, of her constant affection. This withered the blazing words that trembled on her lips. She said instead, "I cannot thank you for this, countess. Better I had never come here than to come to this."

"Your friends," said Lady Alis, still with that mirthful twinkle, "see a bit more clearly than you, perhaps? At least give us credit for believing you spoke the truth when you told us you would rather die than marry Conon d'Yves. You must remember that the king received much advice on this question. And, in the end, it was his decision."

But although Solange had said she did not doubt the king's wisdom, in reality she doubted it very much. How could it be good to wed her to a man who had nothing but contempt for her? A man, furthermore, who was in thrall to the queen?

Eleanor of Aquitaine had such charm, such vivacity, such brightness that all other ladies faded like stars in the presence of the sun. And if the queen were more masculinely commanding than her husband, apparently that very imperiousness held charm.

Solange could not now remember what expression had flickered over Aimery's face at the king's announcement. She had been immersed in her own concerns. He had not come away with her, and Solange decided that he must even now be plotting a way to avoid his fate.

She owed him much—her rescue in the wood, her introduction to the countess and her protection, and rescue from the assassin who had killed Loriot. Surely, she thought in a rush of gratitude, she could repay him in some part by making him a good wife.

But he did not want a wife. That was most apparent. Likely she could do him better service by refusing to wed him. Her thoughts swayed back and forth like reeds in a river current, now rebellious, now resigned.

After a sleepless night ridden with visions, she slipped away from matins and sought out the Abbot Bernard of Clairvaux.

She found him in his austere, heatless cell, unattended.

"Sorry, Father," she said, stammering slightly. "I thought you would be at matins and I decided to wait for you here. I apologize for disturbing your devotions."

"My child," said Father Bernard gently. "I know of course what happened yesterday. I expected you to come."

"I supposed Brother Garin had told you."

He put her into one of the two chairs with backs and himself took the other. "You may have guessed that Brother Garin was there as my representative."

She shot a shrewd glance at the frail abbot. "And was the king's decision yours as well?"

He bowed his head in assent. "It seemed the best way to solve the problem."

"But which problem?" she cried. "That is my question. The problem of the king with his queen and her knight— or my problem?"

"You are acute," said the abbot. "With God's help, it will solve them all."

"And the Crusade will go ahead."

"God wills it," said the abbot simply, "and all will work out for the best, even though our mortal eyes do not see how." He tented his fingers and eyed her. She thought rebelliously that the abbot might possibly have mistaken his own wishes for God's, but she shivered at the sacrilegious thought.

"The Crusade is a great work for the Faith," explained the Abbot. "To liberate the Holy Land where our Lord walked and taught! There is nothing to compare with this lofty purpose. Men are becoming too fond of their leisure, of their lands, and of their fighting—constantly fighting! Do you know how much a good Toledo blade costs?"

He seemed to be launching into a sermon, one he had given many times, so smoothly did the words come forth. But then he caught himself up short. "My daughter, I do not need to preach the Crusade to you."

"A great work for the Faith," she mused. "But is it not important to count each of us, as well? What of the individuals who fall into temptation? Will the Crusade make better souls of us all? What of those who fall into temptation along the way, who would be happier staying at home, and perhaps never be sorely tested? What of them?"

He looked at her with what might have been respect. But he would not deign to argue with a woman. He said, "It is the motive for the struggle that is the important thing. If we go on Crusade to liberate the Holy Places, God knows that. And he also knows," he added warningly, "if we have other, less honorable motives. It seems to me, daughter, that there is much rebellion in you. It is clearly the will of God that you go on this Crusade. He has brought you this far in safety, and led you to this place, where His great work is taking shape. And yet, you doubt. You seek to place your own will against His. And I tell you, beware these traits—stubbornness, willfulness. I see much of them in you."

It was so simple for him, she thought. He had only to listen to his God, who spoke, it seemed, directly and unequivocally to him. She, on the contrary, had to hear advice from her mother, from Mehun, the Countess Alis, and anyone else she might name. And none of these, she was sure, was a spokesman for God. Not even the saintly Father Bernard.

Nonetheless, when she left the abbot she wore a white

cross on her breast. Bernard of Clairvaux, holding the door for her, said gently, "To search for one's father is not dishonorable, and the search may lead you to a secure faith, to your Holy Father. I shall pray for this."

Yet her visit had not brought the peace she had sought.

2

Aimery found himself the subject of much goodhearted raillery, and not a little envy. How much had it cost him to be named the husband of that captivating silver-blonde with the strange violet eyes? Or, hinted the malicious, had he first established his "rights" on the long journey to Bourges? Had the marriage been arranged only just in time, to avoid scandal?

No one who believed the second story dared to mention it in Aimery's hearing. Aimery de Montvert was known for a chancy temper, and the hours after the King's decision saw his friends and foes alike giving full room to the bridegroom in a foul mood.

But Aimery was at base a realist. Certain things occurred to him now, things he had overlooked before. Some hours of reflection brought him to the realization that he did not resent the idea of marrying Solange after all. The maid had a strange hold over him, compelling him to protect her, to watch over her. Many a marriage had been built on less emotion than that.

Besides, he had a strange feeling that he had discovered her, that night in the woods, as one discovers a rare jewel others have trodden in the dust. And the right of discovery was, almost, the right of ownership. By nightfall he was in a much better mood.

Brother Garin, who had stirred the pudding to good effect by the advice he poured into Bernard's ear, awaited the results with some trepidation. If Aimery had found out that Garin had meddled in his affairs, well—it didn't bear thinking about. So, as Aimery's mood lightened, Brother Garin's relief grew.

The strange thing, Brother Garin noted as he moved through the rooms of the king's temporary household in Bourges, was that the announcement of the approaching marriage of Solange and Aimery seemed to touch off a frenzy of matchmaking that reminded him of finches in April. He kept his amusement private though, and did not permit himself even the ghost of a smile as love bloomed around him.

"Love!" Bertille was saying explosively at that same moment to her friends in Lady Alis's sitting-room. "What does love have to do with anything? I myself have been in love a dozen times. And I'm not through yet!"

Catherine chuckled. "Nor will you be, even when you take a husband!"

"I should hope not!" said Bertille, indignantly. "But if I ever make up my mind—"

"Have it made up *for* you," said Solange, sourly. "There are all manner of men here who know what is best for *everyone*. Turn your question over to them. You'll have an answer at once!"

Catherine was pained. "Solange, dear, you could do so much worse, you know."

"I do know it," said Solange with contrition. "And I thank you for putting up with me in this foul mood."

"What did you really expect?" asked Bertille, always practical.

"I don't know. Don't mind me. I'll get used to the idea."

"And you can go with the queen's guard, after all," consoled Catherine. "Henri and I will marry very soon now, probably when we get to Etampes, so that I can go with him on Crusade."

Bertille was much struck. "Of course! That's why she did it.'"

"Isabel," she clarified after awhile.

"Isabel?" Catherine and Solange demanded at the same time, "What's she got to do with it?"

"I'll tell you," said Bertille, savoring her secret a moment longer. "Isabel has it in her maggoty head that she wants to go on Crusade. Though what sins she has to re-pent of I don't for the life of me know, since she obviously has never been tempted."

"Bertille!" cried Catherine. "That's not fair!"

"Probably not," agreed Bertille serenely, "but wait till I finish before you decide what's fair. Isabel, you see, must marry. And nobody wants her. Her own people have washed their hands of her. That's why they sent her here to her cousin the queen—to get her married."

"Then she can't go on Crusade," said Catherine. "The queen surely can't take her when she has refused Solange."

"Nor does Isabel want to go unwed, when all the other ladies have husbands. You remember that tall blond knight in the blue cloak with silver roses embroidered on it? He came to town three days ago."

"I remember," said Catherine promptly. "He doted on every word Millicent de Pons said, I noticed."

"And so Isabel wrote him a letter—"

"*Isabel* did?" said Solange, her interest truly caught now.

"Geoffrey thought it was from Millicent, and wrote back, offering to meet her at a secret rendezvous."

Catherine said slowly. "A foolish thing to do."

"A great jest, according to our lady queen. And Isabel went, disguised. And Geoffrey offered marriage, in glowing words hot from his heart, or so I heard. And Isabel accepted."

"What idiocy!" said Solange. She was prone to say exactly what she thought, and deviousness did not amuse her.

"And—listen to this and tell me I should be fair to that *wench*. The queen is holding Geoffrey to it."

Solange's marriage faded into the background in the face of this scandal and Solange, weary of Isabel, and even of Bertille for the moment, slipped into the outer room. Catherine followed her.

"Don't let Bertille's frivolous gossip worry you," suggested Catherine. "The story can't be true."

"It must be true," said Solange sadly. "It sounds like Isabel. You would believe it too if you weren't so good that you never see unpleasant things in anybody."

"I see only that you are miserable about marrying Aimery," responded Catherine. "And that makes me unhappy. Can't you look on Aimery with some affection?"

"I'm not sure that I don't feel more than that for him. In truth, I do not dislike him at all. But he will think I tricked him somehow. Just as Isabel tricked Geoffrey. Believe me, Catherine, I don't know what to do. I wish . . ."

"You wish what?" prompted Catherine, when Solange fell silent. But Solange could not put into words her deep longing, her wish that somehow there could be love for her.

That kiss, in the bitter cold atop the tower, told her that Aimery was a man of deep passion. But she was sure that, since he had flung her away that day, his love would not reach out to her. He certainly hadn't rushed to tell her he was overjoyed at the prospect of marrying her.

It had not truly taken overly long for Aimery to seek out his intended bride. He had been stunned at the king's pronouncement, but realized there would be no appealing the royal decision. This was not the solution he would have chosen for her, he thought with a grimace, but he could not wish Solange to wed either of the other men—d'Yves or Raoul—and, as he had told her, he would not allow it.

Solange herself, he decided, must be overjoyed at the king's decision. Not because she was in love with him, but because she had been saved from Saint Vergillia's or d'Yves.

He found her in the small sitting room where Countess Alis's attendants often gathered. Solange was sitting on a bench next to the window, looking out at the dark day. Catherine evidently had been talking to her, for she was leaning over her with an air of beseeching. She glanced up with a startled look and saw Aimery.

"Here is Aimery, Solange," she said, stating the obvious. "Now you can tell your wish to him."

"Tell what to me?" said Aimery, advancing into the room. The signs of feminine industry were about him, and he trod warily through an embroidery frame, a pile of shirts for hemming.

Catherine gathered up the shirts—Henri's, no doubt—and scurried out of the room. "I've got to see someone," she explained hastily. She left.

"Someone?" said Aimery thoughtfully. "More likely,

*any*one. You and she must have been having a deep discussion." He crossed the room to stand looking down at Solange. He said, after a bit. "We know each other well enough."

She came to life suddenly. She lifted her head sharply to glare at him from those strange amethyst eyes. "Well enough, Sieur Aimery? You are quite right. Better than many a bride and bridegroom, I imagine. To be called 'every kind of fool' certainly leads to better acquaintance!"

"I seem to remember," said Aimery, stiffly, recovering from the surprise of her attack, "that you have said some unflattering things about me. But that was in the heat of argument."

"Which we seem to have a goodly share of," interrupted Solange.

"And I should think," he said, deliberately stifling a surge of temper, "that, since we both have things to overlook, we could start afresh."

"I suppose this marriage is your idea?"

"Before God," said Aimery with heartfelt sincerity, "it is not."

She blinked back sudden tears, turning away so that he would not see her hurt. One of the things she had hoped was that Aimery might have told someone he wanted to marry her, and that word of it had got to the king. Now, thanks to his honesty, she had to believe that she was simply an unwanted bale of goods.

"Well, then," she said, her words muffled.

"Well, then, what?" said Aimery heavily. "Believe me, I had not thought to receive such a tear-stained welcome."

"What did you expect?" she said with returning spirit. "That I would fall into your arms for joy? No, Sieur Aimery, I shall not. More than that, I doubt the marriage will ever happen."

His eyes sparkled dangerously. "You think I would refuse you?"

"Refuse the king's instructions? No, I did not think that of you."

"Well, at least you grant me a sense of honor."

"But," she said assuming an appearance of thoughtfulness and reason, "I wonder whether the queen will agree."

"Leave the queen out of this!"

"How can I?" wondered Solange. She had recovered from her hurt sufficiently to lash out at him, to inflict on him at least as much pain as she herself had sustained. "Either the queen does not want you any more or she will not let you go."

Her eyes were still full of tears, but she looked up at him in all innocence. "Either way, I am not sure I should take the queen's leavings."

His fury rose like a crossbow arrow shot into the sky, swift, forceful, heedless as to the target. "I am no man's or woman's leavings. I have agreed to wed you. An act of Christian charity, maybe, to save you from a fate that you have told me you dreaded worse than death. Now I see that you dread it less than marriage to me."

She faltered, knowing she had gone too far in her desire to wound him. She put a hand out in an appeal that he found pitiful in the extreme. This woman had a strange power to move him to compassion.

"Well," he said heavily, "the decision will be yours. I have nothing to gain by this marriage. Remember that."

He turned on his heel and left her alone in the room. Catherine, watching for his departure, ventured in and found Solange kneeling on the floor, her head cradled in her arms on the bench, sobbing bitterly.

3

Solange was now a true member of the court, and where King Louis commanded that court to go, she and all the nobles, the king's guard and queen's retainers, attendants, men-at-arms, clerks, and menials went.

Solange's wedding, under the aegis of the king himself, became a court function.

Petronilla, prodded by maternal affection and by Mehun's insistence on appearances, strove to take charge of the wedding. And Countess Alis, whose hand had been in on the decision to marry Solange with Aimery, chose to serve as surrogate mother.

The combination was not amicable. Petronilla had selected white samite for the bride, a long flowing bliaut trimmed in silver, a dress of moonlight like Solange herself, cool, white and silver.

Countess Alis voted for amethyst with a gold thread running through the fabric, to give Solange a little color, the look of a happy bride. "Enough of the Mélusine look," said Countess Alis with some irritation. "She is a flesh-and-blood woman, and I will not be surprised if Aimery does not find her more passionate than he expects."

Solange was caught in the middle. Trying to make peace between her mother and her benefactor, she ran back and forth between the two suites bearing messages and carrying samples of fabrics and leather. The two women refused to meet and talk. The Countess took refuge in her rank, and would not make the short trip to Petronilla. Petronilla felt that, as mother of the bride, all things should come to her.

Solange, wearying of the constant bickering, did not wait this one time to take one of the girls with her on her errand. She simply picked up a length of rose brocade shot with silver and hurried toward the stairs leading up to her mother's rooms. Petronilla had bought it for her daughter, and Alis had grudgingly approved the choice.

Intent on her errand, she did not heed the sharp sound of boot on stone that meant someone was on the stairs. She had rounded the spiral halfway up to the next floor when she realized she was not alone.

Footsteps rang on the stone below her. She told herself severely that there were hundreds of people in the king's train who had as much right on the stairs as she did. Nonetheless, she climbed faster. The footsteps gained on her, though, and she turned.

The man below her on the steps gave her the smile she had loathed from the first time she saw him, in the wood at Belvent. Conon d'Yves enjoyed her discomfiture.

"Had you known," he said, genially, "that I have been

trying to talk to you alone for some days now, you might not have ventured out by yourself."

"What do you want?" she demanded in a low voice. She regretted bitterly the false sense of security that had brought her to this lonely stair.

"To talk to you." The smile that touched his thin lips did not reach his cold eyes.

"We have nothing to talk about." She turned to climb the stairs again. She dared to turn her back on him only because she could not descend past him to safety.

"Oh, but we do," he contradicted her. He grabbed her wrist and held her fast. "Don't try to run away from me."

"Let me go," she said with all the dignity she could summon.

"My touch defiles you, I suppose? I fear you must suffer my hands on you, for the moment, at least."

She stood still, willing herself not to quiver with revulsion at his cold touch. If she ignored him, concealed her dread of him, he might drop his guard.

"What do you want with me?" she said, coldly.

He laughed, a small chuckling sound that somehow wrapped them together for a moment in a kind of abhorrent intimacy.

"You know what I want from you," he said lazily, the very words an obscene caress.

She pulled away with a muffled exclamation of disgust, but his viselike fingers held her fast. "I do not like the king's disposing of my possessions without my consent."

"I was never your possession," she said hotly.

"I bought you. You seem to forget that you are worth two fields and a wood to me. And I will get my money's worth, believe me."

"Don't touch me."

"I won't. Not now." His lips drew back in a smile that held only menace. "But I will. Sometime when you will not be able to summon the king's army to your aid."

"Aimery will kill you."

"I think not," said Conon d'Yves. "Aimery may not have as long to live as he hopes. And I regret that for him. He will never get his fill of your charms, but such is the fortune of war." He moved past her on the stairs. She shrank back away from him.

"You're disgusting. Let me pass. My mother is waiting for me."

Surprisingly, he stepped aside, inviting her to pass him on the stairs. She hesitated, but at the challenging light in his eyes, she lifted her chin haughtily and moved past him. She held her skirt tightly.

"You fear my touch would defile your skirt?" he taunted.

She bit her lip, refusing to be baited. She fixed her eyes on the curving stair. He dared not molest her further, not when he knew that Petronilla was expecting her. Or so she devoutly hoped.

He made no motion toward her. Only when she reached the top of the stair did he call her name. She turned.

"That day in the forest. Had I won then, things would have been different."

"No doubt," said Solange tartly. "You would never have agreed to wed me."

"Ah, but I already had, you know. You forget the fair fields and the goodly wood. But I would have brought you such delight, there in the forest, that you would be bound to me forever."

"Or until you tired of me."

"Perhaps. But you would have come to me willingly. For once you taste the exquisite delights of love, my dear, you will never tire of them."

He spoke with such earnestness that she stayed to listen in spite of herself. Perhaps he was right, but he would never know anything about her reactions to love. Not he.

"I truly love you, Solange. Never did I think I would say this to any woman. You're like an unlit white candle, cool and silent. But I could kindle a flame in you that would set the night to blazing!"

"Only," said Solange, unmoved, "until you had control over me. Then I would have to watch my step, wouldn't I?"

His face darkened. "I am a patient man. I can wait for you. But," he moved closer and lowered his voice, "Your worst enemy is not me."

Something in his voice impressed her. "No? Who then?"

"The queen. And watch your step, my dear. She is a

woman of great power, and I wouldn't like to see that pretty face of yours—"

He drew his finger graphically across his throat. With a return to his airy manner, he said, "Take care. I mean it, Solange." He was gone, leaving her shivering.

She went on to her mother's room, slowly, breathing hard. When she got to Petronilla's door, she was still shaking.

Her mother was prickly with resentment.

"Here's the girdle I brought from Belvent. Perhaps you won't scorn it now," she said, tossing the beautiful gold mesh belt with inset jewels toward her with a wave of her hand. The belt fell on the floor between them. "You know what the stones mean. I don't need to tell you that."

"Carbuncle for happiness, emeralds for ease in childbirth," recited Solange, dutifully picking it up. "Thank you, Mother."

"You wouldn't need all these," cried out Petronilla, "if you gave up this goose-chase idea."

"Goose chase?" said Solange, purposely misunderstanding her mother. "To follow the king's command, when that is why I came to the court?"

"You know what I mean. This jaunting off to the Holy Land. It is so perilous, I shudder to think of what will happen to you."

"Nothing will happen to me, Mother, that wouldn't have happened here if Mehun had had his way. I can't believe you love Mehun, Mother. Why then do you parrot his words?"

"For my sake, give up this search." Tears shimmered in Petronilla's eyes. Solange felt pity stir.

"Odo died. Do you have any idea how soon the wolves would have begun circling Belvent? As soon as the word came that Odo would not be back, you would have seen d'Yves, and Sayette, the Count of Saint Victor—and how many more? All anxious to own Belvent, and every one of them knowing that the easiest way was to own the widow. I could have, by force of arms, protected Belvent for a week *at best*. No longer! And then the spoils of the siege would have fallen to the victors. And not only me, my girl. You too."

"We could have held them off—Belvent stood many a siege in the past."

"For what purpose? To keep it for a man who was not coming back?"

"You did not know that."

"I knew it. Mehun told me so. And believe me, my girl, to fall spoils to a victor is less pleasant than an honorable marriage. At least now I can pretend it was by my own will."

"Honorable marriage!"

"You can laugh at it," said Petronilla. "You fill your voice with scorn. But I tell you, I sold myself to Mehun for the safety of my daughter and of Belvent. What are you selling yourself for?"

Her mother's words stung long after Petronilla had swept out of the small room. Slowly Solange lifted the heavy jeweled girdle and held it, thoughtfully, not really seeing it.

She had not understood her mother's desperation until now. Was her mother right? *Had* she taken the only way open to her after Odo's death, or supposed death? If so, then Solange had treated her most unfairly!

4

Four days after Christmas, Solange's wedding day dawned with a furious snowstorm.

On the thin edge of awareness, between waking and sleeping, she dreamed of the orchard at Belvent with the harvest tables spread with venison pasties, roasted fowl, an ox turning on a spit, and strong country beer. Her father led the black mule with the golden trappings from the great hall to the church door. Raoul awaited her there with love in his eyes. . . .

She awoke with a start. Sick at heart, she knew her dream had been false, unreal as her marriage to the king's choice.

Her long pale hair was braided into two long plaits. Then she was dressed. Her chemise was of fine linen so airily woven as to be like thistledown. The pelisson came next, bordered with vair as Countess Alis insisted. It was a double garment, the inside of fine gold-colored wool, the outer layer of violet silk. The fur border swept her ankles seductively.

The bliaut was of amethyst-colored silk floating delicately, weighted with gold embroidery in the shape of lilies. The sleeves were long, and there was even a train. Lady Alis had done wonders in such a short time, everyone had said so.

Petronilla's girdle held Solange's bliaut tight around her slender waist. Gold circles, each framing a magical jewel, it was the second time she had worn it.

Over all was the mantle, simple but fashioned of the finest fabric, a heavy Marseilles silk. All that was left were the violet leather slippers and a small lavender veil, held down by a golden circlet. Solange was ready.

It was not the usual kind of wedding. There would be no long procession to the door of the church for it was too cold and stormy for that. Solange did not ride on a fine mule, nor was there much of a ceremony at the church door. The king was too busy, it seemed. There was no need to recite, as was the custom, all the items of the dowry Solange was to bring to the marriage, for she had none.

The ceremony at the church door was simple but legal. After a few words by the bishop, the newly wedded pair went into the church of Saint Stephen's to hear the solemn words of the mass of the Trinity, and to receive the bishop's blessing. Aimery moved to the altar after the Agnus Dei, and received the kiss of peace from Bishop de la Chartre. He came back to where Solange stood, frail as a candle in a high wind. The rich color Lady Alis had chosen for her brought only the faintest pink to her cheeks. Aimery looked deep into the inscrutable violet eyes raised to his. Then, his one-sided smile of reassurance warming her, he transmitted the bishop's peace to her. Now they were truly wed.

After the cold church, the great hall was stiflingly hot.

The great fireplaces had been piled high with the last of the logs, for the court was leaving Bourges in two days.

The wine flowed as from a well-spring, and the whole court, perhaps with the rigors of the coming Crusade in the backs of their minds, chose to let mirth and jollity loose once more.

Solange, like a puppet, stood, sat, turned on command. After fighting her own battles and making her own decisions for so long, she once again belonged to someone else. Thanks to words she had not really heard, she belonged to Aimery.

The wine in his goblet was replenished time and again, and his face grew more flushed. Solange had hardly touched hers, but suddenly she reached our for Aimery's goblet. It had just been refilled, and her impulsive grasp spilled a few drops on the table.

"What are you doing?" he demanded.

"I follow your commands in every way now, my husband," she said sweetly. "And if you are to be drunk, then perhaps I must find my own courage in the bubbles." The last words were under her breath so that only Aimery could hear them. His face darkened, and many a curious eye around the long trestle table sparked with speculation.

But the wine waiters plied their trade, and soon Aimery whispered, "Let's get out of here, while we can still walk!"

A rowdy group followed them to the door of Aimery's rooms, set aside now for the newly married couple. Aimery bantered with them, his words only slightly slurred, and finally shut them out and dropped the wooden bar into place.

"Now, wife," he said, a naughty twinkle lighting his eyes, "we are alone. This is the first time. We were not even alone in the forest that first night, were we? And yet, I was sorely tempted even then."

"I would have killed you," she said quietly.

"But now, you see, you have given me leave. I warn you, I am impatient. Here, give me your mantle."

She let him unfasten the silver brooch set with an amethyst of great size—the king's gift—and slip the mantle from her shoulders. She shivered in the sudden chill.

Aimery prodded the fire, and threw a couple of extra logs onto the blaze.

"There, that's better," he said with satisfaction. He glanced up at her, from where he knelt at the hearth. "Afraid?" he said softly. "I had not thought you afraid of anything."

She watched him with unwinking eyes. Afraid? In a way, she was. Aimery was her true husband, wedded to her in Holy Church, and he had the right to do with her what he would. She could only trust in his gentleness. She remembered suddenly that brief, savage kiss he had given her atop the watchtower.

The room, lit by the fire, glowed alluringly, with furs spread on the hard pallet. Aimery lifted his arms to invite her in. She took a step toward him, and then another. But she could not take that last step.

If he hadn't flung such harsh words at her, if he hadn't sworn devotion to Eleanor the queen, if he hadn't scolded Solange nearly every time he had seen her since he met her in the forest, all might have been different. She might have followed her growing desire and leaped into his arms in a very unmaidenly way. But she was afraid, and so she did not.

All this went through her mind with the swift wings of a flying swallow, beating against her longing to be warm, to have strong arms hold her against the cold, against the lonely hurt of the weeks after Raoul's unmasking. She longed for Aimery. But she could not take that step.

"Come to me, Solange," said Aimery. The tenderness in his voice rode atop an underlying firmness, and it was just that hint of command that touched a perverse chord in her.

He would have to come for her! Lurking in her mind lay the jealous thought that he would have crawled on his knees to his queen.

"I am no serf," said Solange, "to come when you bid. I have noticed"—the wine loosened her tongue—"the way things are done here at court. The lady beckons, so it seems, and the knights trot to her like foals on a training string."

"I thought that last flagon was too much for you," he said, in a conversational tone. "I don't know what maggot has got into your head, but I suppose I've displeased you in some way. But I'll make it up to you."

He made no move toward her. He unfastened his heavy girdle, and dropped it to the floor. The metal sheath of his dagger struck a clang like a bell from the stone floor. He pulled his bliaut over his head, hastily, and tossed it into the darkness away from the fire.

"You say nothing, wife?" he prodded her. "I think you are right. This is a time for deeds, not words. And we're wasting time."

His woolen chausses dropped to the floor and he stepped out of them. Watching her with narrowed eyes, he took off his last garment and flung the linen undershirt away from him. She smothered her involuntary gasp. Her thoughts were a muddy turmoil, but she knew one thing. A prickling flame ran along her skin, and started a trembling deep within her, promising more than she could imagine. *She wanted him.*

She crossed the space between them and lifted her arms in a pathetically childlike appeal. Clasping her hands behind his neck, she moved against him, molding her quivering body to the length of his bare limbs, feeling his hard chest against her thinly covered breasts.

He drew a deep shuddering breath. His lips touched her forehead, almost in a kind of blessing, before they fastened greedily upon hers. For a moment she stirred, moving against him, conscious of the warmth spreading from his body to hers. A subtle throbbing started in her blood.

He took his arms away to fumble with hasty fingers at the clasp near her throat. The sudden release made her sway abruptly, and he laughed in his throat. He guided her to lie upon the furs, and knelt astride her.

The fire was hot upon her cheek. Aimery swore at the tricky gold pin at the neck of her tunic. She pushed his fingers away and undid the pin herself, with a laugh that sounded like a sob. He let his weight lie heavier on her thighs, and lifted her fingers and kissed them, one by one.

A shadow passed over his rough features as he looked with mock sternness at the violet silk that lay like a barrier between them. He lifted his weight to his knees and, cupping his hands beneath her buttocks, he struggled with the tangled mass of her bunching skirt and tunic.

The touch of his hands splintered the fragile happy moment into jagged fragments, sharp as daggers. She remembered the picture of Sybille, as vividly as when it had happened. She could see her dear friend ruthlessly bared and hear the horrible rhythmic grunting noises.

With a muffled cry she tore herself away from Aimery. She heard fabric tear, and knew it was her own garment. She whirled away from him and snatched up something from the floor. It was a dagger. Aimery's?

"Don't come near me!" she snarled.

"What's got into you? Put that knife down!"

"I'll put it down all right. Right in your ribs."

It was the drink, the great goblet of wine she had drunk too fast before they came upstairs. It was weeks of uncertainty, accusations that she was selling herself while knowing that Aimery loved someone else. He was pretending to go through the duties of a husband, pretending he loved her when, of course, he did not.

"You've had too much wine," said Aimery. "Put down the knife."

Although the knife slid in her fingers, she did not lose it. Aimery, angry now, and slightly mad with impatience, made a grave mistake. He lunged toward her and bore her to the floor.

There was nothing under her but the stone floor, like it had been for Sybille. He tried to reach her mouth with his lips again, but she twisted away. "Get rid of that damn thing!" he muttered, grabbing the hand that held the knife.

They struggled for the weapon. He pinned her hand to the floor, and her nerveless fingers relaxed on the hilt of the dagger. He looked deep into her eyes as he knocked the dagger away with his hand. His body lay half across hers, and his breath came in hot gasps.

She tensed herself, willing herself to endure whatever came next.

And then she was free. Aimery sat up. She felt the tension still in him, but his quivering sigh and the grim hurt in his face betokened a change in him.

Drawing great breaths, he pulled himself from her and got to his feet, leaving her on the floor. For a few minutes, the only sound she could hear was his shuddering breathing, and the metal clinks as he dressed, fastening his chausses, slapping his gilded leather hauberk into place.

He came then and looked down at her. "You can rest easy," he said, in a voice she did not recognize. "I shall not come near you again. Not until you come to me. Until you lose that loathing for me that burns in your eyes."

He walked away heavily to the door and went through it. She listened, sick at heart. She had failed. He has gone to the queen, she thought. And she could not blame him.

She might have slept easier if she had followed him—as Trotti, serving his queen, did—and seen his slow ascent to the roof of the castle. He leaned his arms on the parapet and looked out over the sleeping city.

He saw nothing of the snow-covered roofs, of the buildings that cascaded down the rock beneath him. He saw only a future bleaker than death itself.

5

Solange woke. Her head throbbed, her eyelids burned. She had slept heavily, after all, thanks to the great amount of wine she had taken.

Close on the heels of the recollection of the wine came total recollection. She was wed—disastrously.

Gingerly she turned her aching head toward the window. The sky was little lighter than the gray stone of the wall. Through the narrow slit she could see yesterday's heavy white snowflakes coming relentlessly down, piling up in the embrasure. There would be no exodus from Bourges tomorrow.

The fringe of her mind dealt with the snow, with traveling, for the great question in the center of her thoughts did not bear scrutiny.

She began to remember. Aimery belonged to the queen—

perhaps. But last night he was truly her own, wed and sealed in Holy Church. She had stood on tiptoe like a child outside a door ajar, wondering what would be within, knowing that there was light, and love, and laughter just beyond.

And now she had nothing. She could remember little of the feast of yestereve. Only that, in her great tension, she had sought to ease her screaming nerves with wine, as Aimery had done.

Had he really had to drown his senses with wine, to keep from realizing that he was married to her and not, as he must wish, to the queen?

It was this realization, perhaps, and not the wine or the memory of Conon or the recollection of Sybille's agony that had made her snatch up the dagger. It had not been fear that had caused the fury, but her blind jealousy of Eleanor of Aquitaine! She shook with shame at her childish behavior. Where was Aimery? She must find him. She threw back the furs.

Aimery was there, in bed with her. Fully dressed.

As, she discovered, she herself was. Even her jeweled girdle was still clasped. But someone—Aimery, of course— had carefully covered her with the warm fur, and crawled in beside her.

She did not remember any of that. How late had it been when he returned to her? And where had he been in the meantime?

She wished she could think logically, but her mind was vague with the reddish fumes of last night's wine. She had rarely drunk so much as a small glass at one time. To drain a whole goblet!

She covered Aimery again, and began to slip out of the bed. But he was not asleep. His hand shot out to grasp her wrist in his iron fingers.

"Come on back," he said sleepily. "It's too early to get up. What a night!"

"What a night?" she cried, tugging her wrist loose from his grip. "A most entertaining night, so it seems? I wish I had been there."

Her head throbbed and, in response, her stomach lifted and settled down again, somewhat awry, so it felt to her.

She longed to sleep again. It was not just the wine, but the sense of mourning for something lost. She could not stop her tongue from lashing out at Aimery. She simply could not bear the thought that the blame was hers alone.

"What a night," she repeated. "I wonder where you spent it?"

Fully awake now, he raised himself up on one elbow and stared at her. "I can't believe you care where I spent it, so long as it was not with you. Quite a warming welcome from my new bride—a dagger at my chest. Or don't you remember it?"

Tears coming to her eyes, she said, "I remember." She longed to apologize to him, to beg him to forgive her for her unforgivable behavior, but she could not find the words readily. And before she did find them, it was too late.

"Let us," he said harshly, "pretend, at least for the moment, that all is well between us. As, of course, you must admit that it is."

"I don't understand you."

"Let me make it clear, then. You come out of the forest claiming your wicked stepfather is sending you to a convent. Perhaps this is true."

"It was true!"

"You want Raoul, that—*nothing*! And then, for good reason, you spurn him. You get a man killed because of your insensate desire to find your father. Against all reason, against all witnesses who say Saint Florent is dead. But you—I swear my brother's mule has more sense!"

He stormed around the small room, kicking the furs out of his way as though, she thought sadly, he were kicking away the shreds of whatever hopes he might have had for this marriage.

"Aimery—"

He turned to glare at her, his eyes hot with anger and hurt. "Well?" he said after a moment. "You have something to say?" He gave a snort of laughter. "I think not. You wanted to travel with the queen's guard. You have managed that. You wished to be safe from your stepfather, and you are, now. All that remains is to reap the harvest of your planning. You've got everything you wanted. I was a fool to think you would give anything in return." His mouth twisted as he said, in a quieter tone, "It's your way to take. I realize it too late. Take, not give."

She buried her face in the coverlet. His words stung her like whips. She had once seen a thief flogged at the Boisceau fair, the blood streaming down his back in rivulets. He had screamed without ceasing. Her wounds bled silently, but she bit her lip in anguish. She would never give him the satisfaction of knowing how much he had hurt her.

"Somehow," he said with a long measuring look, "I believed you when you said you would marry only for love. You would kill yourself, I think you said, before you would allow any man to bed you without your wanting it as much as he did."

Remotely, she watched the tears fall on her amethyst bliaut, staining the violet cloth in dark patches, like blood.

"Your scruples, I confess, do not make sense to me. You will wed, in church, a man you loathe. And you do not scruple against that. But when it comes right down to it, you will have none of wedded life."

"It wasn't like that," she protested weakly.

"Perhaps you have a logical train of thought on this," he said, throwing the pelts into a corner and putting on his leather hauberk. "I confess I do not see it. To me, and to any fair-minded outsider—don't gasp, Solange. I shall not tell this outside of these walls. The shame is mine."

"No, no."

"I was fool enough to think you meant the things you said. That you would not have promised to wed me had you not had some feelings for me. The more fool, I."

"Aimery, I did not mean—"

"Don't tell me. Don't bother me with what you mean and what you think. I can see what you do, and that is the proof."

"You went to the queen last night," she guessed at hazard.

"Why shouldn't I?" he countered.

"Did you?"

He looked at her quietly. Then, with a mocking laugh, he said, "I shall not deny it."

She closed her eyes for a moment. It was true. She had

so little charm that she could not hold her husband even on their wedding night. Unreasonably, she told herself that Aimery should have understood her better.

She buried her face in her hands, smothering her sobs. He came to stand over her. "Look at me."

She shook her head. Eventually, knowing he would not go away until she did, she lifted her eyes to him. Tears swam in them and she could not see him clearly. But it did not matter.

"Crying?" His voice was harsh, and she did not know him well enough to detect the pain that lay beneath. "Do not fear that your reputation will suffer from this night. Our—coming together, in a manner of speaking, will not become common gossip. I shall not confess that my bride met me with dagger drawn."

"Nor I," retorted Solange with returning spirit. "But can you be sure that your queen will not boast that she could crook her finger and lure a man away from his marriage bed?"

He gave her a long brooding stare, whose meaning she could not fathom. He laughed, then, a short bark that told her how far she had driven him from her. "I must be quite a man, they will think. To satisfy two such demanding women in one night!"

"Aimery—"

"Your demands, my sweet wife, are far easier to meet than the queen's. And I will satisfy them. You will not be troubled with my—requirements, shall I say?—again. Not until you beg me to come back." He fastened his girdle, and found the dagger on the floor. He gazed at it as though he had not seen it before and then, with a jaunty air, thrust it in its sheath. "I can't help but feel my knife is safer in my own keeping. And now, wife, let us face our friends and well-wishers, and trust that we can put a good face on what has obviously been the greatest mistake of our lives."

Somehow Solange got through the day. She had a strange feeling that the man she had married was not the same Aimery de Montvert that she had viewed with scorn because he was in thrall to the queen.

He had told her some unsettling truths. Truths about herself. But she was too hot with resentment, and with a deadly feeling that she had ruined both her life and Aimery's, to be rational.

She had all she could do to forget the throbbing headache that nearly blinded her, to smile when she remembered to, and to face the gathering of the court. It was noon when they arrived in the great hall, and the meat and bread were already on the tables. Aimery pushed aside his regular companions and seated Solange next to him on a bench too close to the queen for Solange's liking.

She scarcely touched her food. The nearness of it turned her stomach, and she had some inkling now of why her father had been so cross after an evening spent with his hard-drinking cronies. She scarcely knew what was said to her, or what she replied.

The feast left nothing to be desired, according to those who had appetite for it. The great hall was filled. The steward in a bright red tunic entered, waved his white wand of office, and—while cymbals rang and trumpets sounded —a long train of servitors appeared, each carrying at shoulder-level a huge serving platter piled with food.

An enormous haunch of stag was set before the king, while Steward Guyot carved the meat himself, gripping the bone in his fist and delicately cutting thin slices of venison.

The wine-stewards filled the flagons, but Solange did not touch hers. She had had enough of wine the night before, wine that had addled her and led her to destroy her life.

There was mallard, pheasant, beef, mutton, swan, and boar's head.

Rabbits, woodcock. Salmon, lampreys, and shad. Stewed fruits, dried figs and dates, all washed down with a spiced wine called *hippocras*.

Solange seemed split into two people. One watched the food served, heard the dogs growling under the tables as the diners tossed meat to them, and the excessive lip-smacking of the happy feasters. The other had gone away into a small cell of her mind. Cold it was in her mind, with stone floors and gray walls, and only the dim light of winter to see by.

She remembered, later, that Bernard of Clairvaux pronounced a special blessing on the newlyweds from the dais, after the meal was taken away. And she recovered sufficiently to hear the king's benevolent pronouncements.

"Our dear friends, Aimery de Montvert and his amazingly beautiful wife," he began, "I wish at this point to add to your great happiness as you begin a new life together."

The king waited until Aimery, his hand firmly urging her forward, brought his bride to the dais.

"Aimery de Montvert," intoned the King, donning a more formal mien. "I endow thee with the barony of Pontdebois, and all its appurtenances, estates, honors, and duties. In addition, the barony of Aliquis, and its honors and duties. These seigneuries are a beginning, my son, and I call you therefore to sit in my council among the other barons of my land, and advise us well on our coming journey to the Holy Sepulcher."

The king's last words were drowned in a great shout of approbation. Aimery was popular among the men and women of the court. In addition, the romance between the new bride and groom had touched the fancy of many, starved as they were for the excitement that love could bring. The Court of Love was all very well, and many clung to its precepts with all their hearts, but true love right before their eyes in the form of such a handsome couple, was more to their taste.

Solange was furious. How dare Aimery chastise her for her motives in wedding him? When he, who hungered for land of his own, was to gain his heart's desire? She knelt before the king, with Aimery, as the king invested them with the honors. From the side of her mouth, she whispered, "You had nothing to gain, you said?"

His hand tightened painfully on hers, but she did not even grimace.

"Of the fiefs in my gift," said the king. "We have found it hard to decide which is most suitable. My queen and I, in fact, sat up the whole of the night to make our decision, while you were more pleasantly engaged, I trust." The king gave what was, for him, a bawdy smile. In truth, it was scarcely a twitch of the lips.

All night! The king had been with the queen all night! Where then had Aimery been? Solange turned impulsively to her husband, whose jaw was set. She had accused him wrongly. Then why hadn't he denied it?

The gathering left the hall, to go their own ways, to pack their goods, for the king had said that the weather would not keep him from setting out on his way to Etampes. In the press at the door Solange lost sight of Aimery. She had much to say to him, mostly groveling apology, and she even toyed with the idea of begging him to let them start anew, together.

The Baron d'Yves was jostled next to her in the doorway, and she looked up to find his insolent dark eyes far too penetratingly on her. "You would not look so forlorn today," he said, his lips close to her ears, "had I been the man in your bed last night!"

6

The weather was no respecter of royal demands. The snow that had begun on the morning of Solange's wedding began to come down even more heavily. By that night the road across the marsh was drifted shut. No one could leave by the gates. What was worse, no new supplies could come in across that howling wilderness of storm and wind.

Aimery de Montvert, baron of Pontdebois, baron of Aliquis, member of the king's council by right of his landed holdings, plunged outright into his new responsibilities. He talked with his new dependents, who had originally come to render service to the king in place of their nonexistent overlord. The small room where Aimery and Solange were quartered was filled with scrolls showing the layout of various fields and woods and villages. The estates had been neglected while the fiefs lay vacant, and Aimery was full of plans for their improved prosperity.

The payments of the villeins had not been collected. It seemed that the steward Faucon had been a hard taskmaster, and probably dishonest. Between the lines of Faucon's excuses, his new lord read that Faucon feared to enter many of the villages to make his collections. This fear was certainly due to his own cruelty, and the villeins' response to it. There was money due, and Aimery must collect all he could in order to meet his obligations imposed by the king's Crusade. The gifts of eggs, poultry, and lambs were of lesser importance for the moment. Aimery must go to his new estates to set all in order, but first in the responsibilities he had assumed was the duty to accompany King Louis on Crusade and take his place among the council of barons.

"I'm sure the cottages need repairing and new thatches provided," mused Aimery. "And the fields must be allotted anew."

They were alone. Aimery shoved away the offending scrolls, and leaned back in his chair.

"But that is Faucon's duty," objected Solange. "How can you take the time for this?"

He turned silent for a moment. "All my life I have longed for just such a fief for my own. A small world all to itself, raising all the necessary articles for life, right there. A cluster of people who dwell together in harmony."

She held her breath. Never before had Aimery talked of what was in his heart. She feared to break his mood. "My father could not gain the affection of his people. And I could see so many of his mistakes. I promised myself that I would not make the same mistakes. If you knew, Solange, how I yearned for a place of my own, to settle down and have my sons growing up around me."

Abruptly his mood changed. Savagely he pulled the scrolls back and unrolled the top one. "That, of course, is out of the question now," he said, tight-lipped, "and you will do me a kindness if you forget my lapse. I did not intend to bore you."

Two days later, Bourges was still wrapped in winter. Solange idled her time away as best she could. Their belongings were still in the chests, ready to travel to Etampes. Her sewing was packed away as well, and it simply was not worthwhile to unearth it.

Aimery paid her no heed. Apparently regretting his

confidence, he made up for it by scarcely speaking to her at all. She spent hours in the company of Countess Alis, aware that her presence put a damper on the girls' lively gossip, but so miserable that she didn't care.

It was nearly twilight when she returned to her room. Aimery and Faucon were deep in discussion over the estate records. Aimery looked up when she entered.

"Good, you're back," he said. "Just in time. I want you to listen to this, for you must deal with the estates if I am killed."

"For the heir," smirked Faucon. Solange stared icily at him. His face reddened and he turned away. For the heir! She averted her glance from Faucon and by chance met Aimery's level gaze. His eyes for a moment held an expression that she could not define, before his lips tightened and he turned back to his factor.

Solange waited until the two men were bent once more over the plat of the demesne, and then slipped out of the room.

An heir to Pontdebois, to Aliquis. It was out of the question.

By an obvious association of ideas, she recalled that she had not seen Sybille since yesterday. The attack had been only ten days ago, but Sybille had faded drastically in those ten days. Solange had been caught up in her own affairs, yet she had managed to speak to her every day, and even to visit her in the tiny room she shared with her palsied husband. What went on behind the door to that room was nobody's business, but Sybille's brothers had spread the word that the new potion was making a man of their brother-in-law, emphasizing their meaning with a broad wink and a smirk.

This day, the old baron was sitting by the fire in the outer room. He looked no better than before. His eyes were rheumy and his hands shook dreadfully. He was bundled in furs before the roaring fire, and Solange wondered how the brothers could credibly put over their deception. This man was barely able to eat, let alone sire an heir.

With a word to the nodding baron, to which he did not respond, Solange pushed open the door to the next room.

"Sybille?" called Solange softly.

Her friend needed the sleep she thought, as she knelt beside the fur-covered pallet. The dark shadows under the closed eyes were sooty. Solange yearned over Sybille, helpless to help, yet unable to forget.

Sybille stirred, murmuring protest. "Let me die. Don't bother me."

"You're not going to die, Sybille," said Solange firmly. She straightened out the furs over Sybille's bare shoulder, and her hand came upon a small object among the blankets. She drew it out. A small vial, containing . . . nothing, now. But what *had* it held?

"Sybille! What did you take?" Solange shook her shoulder roughly. "Wake up, Sybille!" Alternately calling, shaking, and coaxing, she got Sybille to open her eyes. "Sybille, what have you taken? Hurry! Tell me at once!"

Sybille shook her head. She sat up with difficulty, clutching a fox skin to her, shivering in the sudden cold as the air struck her naked back. "I took nothing."

"Tell me," begged Solange. "You can't do this, Sybille."

Wearily, Sybille shook her head. "Don't worry, Solange. When it came down to the test, I could not drink the poison." She twisted her lips sourly. "I'm just so weary. I think . . . I think they will not need to . . . arrange another time."

Solange understood. They, of course, were the brutal brothers, and already Sybille must suspect she was with child. But it was too soon to tell, wasn't it? "Did you take anything, Sybille?"

"There is no earthly medicine that could help me. Either to do away with—*it*—or to cleanse me from the shame. I took nothing, Solange. See, here where the fur is discolored? I spilled the poison. The vial is empty so I will not be tempted again. And now, Solange, if you could manage it, I should like to be let alone."

I'm the only one who knows, thought Solange, and she cannot think of anything but her shame as long as I am near. She got to her feet and tiptoed from the room.

Solange did not see Sybille the next day, and Bertille informed her that the de Nannes train had moved out early that morning toward the south, where the traveling would be better in the softer climate.

"The last of those brothers, thank goodness," said Bertille, and promptly forgot them.

The Crusade stood still these days. Even the king seemed to take the word for the deed. Now that Louis wore the symbolic cross on his breast, proof that he intended to go to the rescue of the Holy Land, his face had lost its melancholy strain.

One hardly heard the Crusade mentioned any more, Solange realized. Her own spirits drooped in consequence. Had she given up her freedom, put herself in the hands of a husband who loathed her, simply so she could be named among the queen's guard? Who knew when the Crusade would begin?

Bernard of Clairvaux, impatient to be on his own way, saw the lethargy that affected the court. What they needed, he believed, was a good hard ride for hours in the fresh air. But since that was not possible in this weather, he decided to take a few steps himself.

The second Sunday after Christmas Bernard mounted the pulpit and stood silent, a wisp of a man with burning eyes. By his demeanor, every soul in the church knew that something of moment was about to transpire.

Bernard did not let them down. Fixing them all with the piercing eyes that made each one feel he spoke to him alone, Bernard began to speak.

"My eyes are blinded by the glory," he began, on a soft note. "Not the glory of our Lord Jesus Christ as would be fitting in this holy church, but by the glory of the satins and samites. The jewels of the ladies before me. The immensely expensive mail worn by the knights of the court. The Toledo blades, the double-edged battle-axes. Even the crosses you wear are just another adornment to you. To take the cross in vain is a deadly sin."

Solange touched her jeweled belt guiltily and glanced at Aimery, standing stonily beside her. He was tenacious in duty, she had learned. He was with her a great deal, protecting her, making their friends think all was well between them.

Bernard had progressed in his peroration. "And all of this great expense is for naught—for naught, if it serves only to enliven a forbidden tournament. You know that our Holy Father has forbidden tournaments.

"But if these expensive accoutrements were put to a good use . . ."

A huge sigh settled over the audience. Bernard paused. "If these blades, this golden mesh armor, these destriers, could drive the paynim back into the desert whence they came to desecrate the streets where our Lord walked—"

The response was overwhelming. Shouts, raised hands, jostling, a burst of song by the door. And all at once, as one voice, came the cry of a hundred throats, "*Dieu le veult!*"

Outside the church the cry was echoed by the hundreds gathered in the bitter cold, "*Dieu le veult!*"

God wills it, Solange thought. And if God wills this too, I will find my father, no matter where I must go!

Bernard did not let his anvil cool. He struck again, by riding out with Brother Garin on their long journey to Metz. King Louis had urged that the Crusade would be more effective if the Emperor Conrad of the Germans also took the cross. Bernard's mission was to persuade that indolent ruler to set out for Byzantium.

In the meantime, the queen was forming her guard. Now that the Crusade was really under way, she officially named those whom she would allow to join her. Solange, of course. Catherine de Charpigny, who would wed her Henri at Etampes. Bertille de Savarin and Isabel de la Valle, being yet spinsters and not even formally betrothed, would not be among the company, not unless they produced husbands.

But one name surprised Solange. Petronilla de Mowbrai was to join!

"For the good of my soul," said Petronilla, still not reconciled to Solange's purpose. "You've stirred up things so that I can't let it rest now. If I have sinned with Mehun, if your father is in fact alive, then I will gain absolution when I set my eyes on the Holy City. And if I die before I get that far, then the Holy Mother will have mercy on me for my intent."

"You sound different," said Solange slowly. "Not like my mother."

Bitterly, Petronilla agreed. "You've changed the lives of everyone you know. I'm not the same. Mehun fears to come near me, lest he sin too."

"Perhaps he knows more than we do about my father's existence," suggested Solange dryly. Quickly, she perceived Petronilla's deep hurt, and hurried to apologize.

"Perhaps he does," said Petronilla flatly. "He has not said more to me than he has said to the king. Mind you, I still think you are wrong. But you've stirred up our lives like a cat among the pigeons, and we'll never be the same again."

Sturdily, Solange said, "Perhaps that is all good."

"Things are not good," mourned Petronilla. "Mehun is desperate."

"For what?" marveled Solange. "He cannot do anything more to me. I have a husband who is wealthy and who will protect me. What more does Mehun want?"

Petronilla stepped lightly to the door and listened. Opening it a crack, she peered into the corridor. Then, satisfied that they were not overheard, she came back and took her daughter's hand. "It's Conon. He wants his land back, the land he bought you with. He says he was cheated. Either give back the woods and the fields, or give him the girl."

"But Mehun can't give me back!" said Solange, beginning to be angry. Was she *never* to be free of Mehun's grasping malice?

"Not so long as you are wed to Aimery," said Petronilla cryptically.

"Well, then, it is simple." Solange pounded her fists on her knee. "Give back the land."

"He won't," said Petronilla, whispering conspiratorially. "Mehun won't give up one acre of land that has ever been his."

"He never would have had Belvent—"

"Don't remind me," said Petronilla sharply. "We've been over that and what's done is done. But Conon is getting nasty. And Mehun won't give back the land. You don't understand him, Solange. He never had anything at all."

"Spare me that," said Solange dryly. "I can feel no sympathy for him."

Petronilla glanced at her. "How is it—your marriage, Solange? You have never told me."

"There's nothing to tell," she said flatly, hoping her mother would not guess she spoke the literal truth.

The queen's guard, of course, were not alone. Many others had joined the Crusade and now wore crosses pinned to their tunics. Mehun was going, to keep an eye on his wife. And Brother Garin would go, probably as Bernard's agent.

Conon d'Yves took the cross. "To keep an eye on my investment," he told Solange in a low voice.

No, things were truly no easier now that she had married. No easier at all.

7

Mehun considered that the king had dealt his hopes and his pride a battle-ax blow. Aimery de Montvert now held fiefs enough to satisfy most men, but surely would not give up the idea of owning Belvent. If Mehun could be dislodged, then Aimery's right to Belvent would quite likely be upheld by the king and the council.

Mehun, in the few days after his stepdaughter's wedding, plumbed the depths of greedy despair. He had no fear that Odo de St. Florent would return. When he had seen him last, the soldier had been surrounded by what looked to be a whole Turkish army. No man could survive that kind of attack. So Mehun was fairly certain of his rival's death.

Besides his uneasiness about the future of his fief, he was beset by the importunities of the Baron Conon d'Yves. He had made a bargain with the baron, and he could not now deliver the one nor would he give up the other. Was ever man so upset by troubles?

And besides that, his wife had turned against him. That

troublemaking girl of hers, prattling of her father, had turned Petronilla's thoughts to sin. He was growing to expect tears and recriminations every time he saw her.

The measure of Mehun's desperation was taken the next day. Gervais sought out Aimery, who was endlessly poring over the accounts that Faucon had left him.

"I can't believe all this," said Aimery, fretfully throwing the papers down on the floor beside him. "I should like to set someone to look into Faucon's accounts. I think he is not telling me all there is to know."

"You suspect him of knavery?" asked Solange. She was mending a rent in her husband's favorite pelisson.

"I'm not sure. I know little enough about these things. My brother was well instructed, but not I."

"Garin?"

Aimery looked oddly at her. "No, I meant my true brother, who now has the family estates."

"But I thought . . ." She paused in her work to stare at him.

"Garin is my half-brother," said Aimery shortly. The dark look slid over his face, the one that warned her not to say more. She bent over her sewing again. She had not known that Garin was a half-brother, and yet, there had been no need for her to know.

"I can't send Rainard," Aimery said, softly, as though to himself.

"Why not?" asked Solange, simply. "If he carried your writ, he could certainly get answers to your questions."

"And find out why they planted winter wheat two years in a row, and tilled the field the third year too? Why it is that there is no fallow land around the village? Where am I to get twenty mounted men and sergeants and foot-soldiers and grain and money for supplies for the Crusade?"

She finished mending the tear and inspected her work. "If Rainard is clever enough to serve as your squire, then he can surely ferret out what you want to know."

He considered her suggestion. Shaking his head, he said, "He's too young."

"As you say, my lord," murmured Solange submissively. He glanced at her suspiciously, but her eyes were intent upon her work, smoothing the darned fabric endlessly. He crossed the room to stand before her.

"What do you have in your mind?" he demanded.

"I think I pulled the thread a bit hard here," she said innocently. "But if I stretch the cloth this way—" She stopped short.

"The cloth go to damnation!" he burst out. "You are not usually so domestic, wife. I tell you, I need Rainard."

"Of course, my lord," said Solange. "What does it matter that Rainard chafes for more demanding service, for experience beyond polishing your mail? You need Rainard, and that is all there is to it. I shall try to explain to him that his needs do not matter."

His fists clenched and unclenched, no more than a double hand-span away from the tip of her uptilted nose. She hoped he could not hear the blood pounding in her ears. She was encouraged by his discussing estate business with her. It was an admission that they were bound together now. It was a start.

She rejoiced to see his thoughts center around his new responsibilities. He had less time for the queen now, and perhaps his new lands might win him from Eleanor completely. It was chancy at best, but it was the only hope she had.

"I need Rainard," he repeated stubbornly, almost daring her to argue with him.

"I am sure you do," was her only comment. She smiled sweetly up at him. The sudden spark in his eyes took her breath away.

"You think to rule me," he challenged her, "by your spicy tongue? I will not suffer your impudence forever."

She folded her hands stiffly in her lap, stilling their trembling. "I agreed with you. I wonder what you would say were I to defy you?"

He strode back to the rude worktable. She had not looked at him with that special light in her eyes, the light he ached for. It was no use. They were mismated, and yoked forever. He flung the scrolls into an untidy pile and marched to the door. He had to get out of this room, out of her sight, before he forgot himself entirely. He would not beg her.

He flung the door open, and exclaimed in surprise. Gervais stood in the doorway, his mailed fist raised for knocking.

"Well, Gervais, what brings you here?"

"A message, sir Baron. From Mehun de Mowbrai."

Aimery chuckled. "Mehun de Mowbrai has never before failed to say himself what was on his mind. Tell me what your lord wants."

"He begs me to challenge you to a duel. You have sorely injured his honor." Gervais spoke tonelessly as though reciting memorized words.

"Me? Duel with Mehun? You're joking."

"Not duel with Mehun. With me instead, as his knight."

Aimery looked long at him, measuring. Solange cut the thread between her white teeth and dropped the pelisson on the edge of the chest. Coming to stand beside Aimery, she said, "Gervais, would you give Mehun your life? For Aimery is—"

"By your leave, lady, I know the baron de Pontdebois is mighty in the field. But I must do my lord's bidding."

Aimery shook his head. "My lady wife is prejudiced as to my prowess. Sir Gervais, too, is a dangerous man, Solange. But I do not duel, Gervais. I have taken the cross, and jousting or dueling is forbidden me."

A slight smile, whether of relief she could not tell, touched Gervais's lips. He looked younger and more human. Aimery was saying, "Your loyalty does you credit. I have need myself of such an honorable man. There would be land and substance for one who was loyal to me. Someone must look into the lands I have recently acquired. I cannot now leave the king's council." He waited, deliberately giving the other man time to consider. "Would you know of such a man, Gervais?"

The invitation dangled before Gervais. For a moment, Solange thought Gervais seemed tempted. But he said, "I dare not. Were I to break my allegiance thus, you would never be sure I would not do it again."

Bowing, he left. Aimery looked after him. "I wish he were not right," he said. "But of course, he is."

"I do not think him happy with Mehun," said Solange slowly.

"Nor, do I." Aimery thought for a long time. Then, rolling up the scrolls carefully, he tied them with cord. "Tomorrow I shall send Rainard to Pontdebois." She looked up with a glad smile, but he refused to meet her eyes. He left the room at once, carrying the scrolls.

If he did not love her, would not bring himself to forgive her, at least he had taken her advice in this one thing!

8

By the next day the weather had begun to clear. Bernard said pointedly, "Even God Himself clears the way for his armies." By noon the court began its slow progress down from the rock of the bishop's palace. The procession moved through the city, inching out the west gate to cross the frozen marsh. The footmen marched out first, for it would take them longer on the road. The first officer of the vanguard, mounted on a cob, took the very same road Solange had traveled in coming to Bourges with Aimery and Brother Garin.

The king and his court were on their way to Etampes. The Crusade had become the most urgent of purposes, almost, Aimery grumbled, as though the Turks were crossing the Rhine River at that moment.

Aimery rode beside Solange that first day. He was concerned for her well-being, and he made sure she was warm and fed. But his eyes were cold. She kept her lips from trembling and allowed the silence between them to stretch into hours.

She concentrated on the thought that every step her mount took, every twin plume of steam her palfrey expelled from frosted nostrils, took her a bit closer to the Holy Land, and to Odo de St. Florent.

Bernard, and Brother Garin with him, must already have arrived at the Metz court of the Emperor Conrad. King Louis had sent messengers before Christmas bearing letters to Manuel Comnenus, the emperor of Byzantium, and to Roger, king of Sicily, telling them of the Crusade. Answers were expected to arrive in a month, and the king would be at Etampes to receive them.

The third day out, they reached a ford that was frozen over. The baggage carts, traveling ahead, had been forging a track for the lords and ladies to follow. But at the ford, the carts had simply broken up the ice and the water churned around the jagged ice, too formidable to venture into. A knot of riders formed.

Aimery spurred ahead. Solange could not see through the throng, but she gathered that Aimery and a few others got the queen's palfrey across the dangerous ford. When it finally came Solange's turn to cross, she looked in vain for her husband.

Surprisingly, Gervais took her mare's bridle and coaxed her across. On the far side of the ford, she thanked him.

"I have little claim on your gratitude," said Gervais, solemnly. "It went sorely against me to think of you entering the convent gates."

"I understand," said Solange. "Vows of loyalty are hard to break."

He studied her for a moment. "My own vows to Mehun, you mean. I was thinking of vows made to me by a lady I once knew. She broke them as easily as breaking bread." He glanced quickly at Solange. "Forgive me, lady, for mentioning my affairs. But—I honor one who keeps her pledge."

She did not know how to answer him. She had kept her pledge, that was true.

"It is more than vows to Mehun, lady. He saved my life once, and I owe it to him." Then, releasing the bridle of her mount, he said, "Mehun is loyal to his own vows. But loyalty to others—look to yourself, lady." He touched his helm in salute, and rode off.

He had unsettled her.

The court spent a week on the road to Etampes. It was a cold journey, and the women complained much of chilblained fingers.

The day's ride had been through brilliant sunshine,

throwing an illusion of cheerfulness over the countryside. Till now they had all ridden muffled to the eyes and speech was impossible.

Solange threw back her fur hood and breathed deeply of the sparkling air. Aimery had seldom left her side during the journey. She found little comfort in his company, his lips set in grim anger and his eyes fixed ahead. But even if his thoughts were absent, Aimery himself was in her sight, almost as though he were really her devoted husband.

This, she realized, was his purpose. To show all the king's court that his marriage was as it should be, and not the sad farce it was.

She reined her palfrey closer to Aimery. "It might help your plan," she said, lifting her chin, "if you were to smile at me. Not too often, of course, for the queen might hear of it."

He turned a stony gray look on her. "My plan?" he said at last.

"You wish to appear the devoted husband," she said flatly.

"Appear?" was the only word he spoke. But it was the strange, wry smile that touched his lips that sapped her confidence.

The last night of the journey to Etampes, Solange and Aimery were lodged in a room by themselves instead of on pallets, with the rest of the higher-ranking court, in the Great Hall of the host castle.

A storm had begun. The wooden shutters of their small room in the tower moved in and out with the fitful wind.

She was glad to have a room to herself. The journey had been long, and she was so weary she could hardly think.

Aimery came in, bringing with him the cold spiciness of the outdoors. He dropped his mantle to the floor just inside the room.

"I didn't start the fire," said Solange. "I waited for Jehane."

"Your maid will not be coming to tend you tonight," said Aimery shortly. "I will deal with the fire."

He worked quickly at the hearth. Wood was plentiful here, and soon the fire roared. The storm begun to whisper against the shutters.

"I fear you are cold," said Aimery. "Best climb into the bed for warmth."

She eyed him with misgiving. Tired she was, but not too weary to wonder about his sudden change of mood. At the beginning of the journey he had been civil, as he had been after the first day or two of their marriage. But recently he had accused her of relating the intimate details of their marriage to others. He had grown hard and bitter since then. Did he really think she wished to shame him?

"I think I would like—"

"It matters no longer what you like," said Aimery, interrupting her sharply. He unbuckled his girdle, dropping it to the floor. Next came his pelisson.

"Take off your clothes," he said, glancing over his shoulder, "and get into the bed."

She still didn't move. She clutched her own mantle to her, in futile protection. When her husband had doffed the last of his garments, he turned to face her. "Perhaps you did not understand me," he said in an even voice. He took a step toward her.

"Aimery—"

He crossed the short distance between them, as he had that first night. But this time it was different. There was no soft kissing, no gentle stroking.

This time there was only the swift unbuckling of her belt, the lifting of pelisson and chemise over her head. A harsh thrusting hand shoved her down onto the furs before the fire.

She wasn't ready. "You promised—," she began, before his mouth covered hers.

She knew only the pounding of sleet at the wooden shutters, the cold invading the room, her husband's probing kiss, angry, ungentle, pinning her so she could not move. His fingers gripped her wrists, his body was heavy on hers. Then came the flooding pain.

Later, he said, "Now, *wife*, you can sleep in peace. But you know you have wed a man, not a shell."

There was no difference, then, between Baldwin and her husband. No love was part of this.

Yet, Aimery held Solange in his arms, warm against the storm, as they both fell into the sleep of exhaustion.

9

The next morning, Aimery buckled on his hauberk and glared down at Solange. "You can pass the word now that you are truly wed."

"Is *that* why you forced me? To save your reputation?" she cried.

"And yours, wife. I would not have it said that you repel me." He grinned, wolfishly.

"And I don't?"

He did not answer at once. And when he did, she did not understand him. He said only, "No man is enticed by a snow maiden." Then he added, "You ought to have wed Raoul. More to your taste." She gasped. "We will be in Etampes this day," he added. "And no doubt we shall be forced to share a bed again. But you need not worry. I shall not bother you."

"Perhaps you will not need to," she said, thinking of Sybille.

"For everyone to see you with child would enhance my reputation considerably." He laughed briefly. "After all, it is what one might expect, is it not?"

"I do not wish to serve merely as a brood mare," she said icily. "Your love belongs to Eleanor, and I will not take second place."

As though he had not heard, he said, "I shall not bother you again. Not until the snow maiden has melted."

She snapped, "That day will come when you bring all of yourself to me, not half to me and half to . . . someone else."

He finished dressing and turned to leave without another word.

Aimery did not ride with her that day. She sought the gentle companionship of the countess and her ladies. Their raillery slipped past her like chuckling ripples in a shallow brook, while her thoughts lay within her as heavy as stones. A snow maiden . . . fit only to wed a nullity like Raoul. The words sounded in her brain.

She did not know of Aimery's conversation with his brother when the court reached Etampes. Brother Garin had developed a grievous wound on his thigh, and Bernard had ordered him to halt at Etampes until it healed. Garin chafed under the order, but his protests availed him nothing.

"Bernard wouldn't listen to reason," Garin complained to Aimery. "I was perfectly well until that foolish mule stumbled on the ice."

Aimery's smile held little amusement. "Mule? Perhaps you will agree now that you should never have taken the Church to your bosom. Armor becomes you better, and at least a palfrey is a fitter mount."

Brother Garin lifted a hand in a weary gesture. "You take pleasure in reminding me of my friar's limitations. But when your Crusade arrives in Outremer, you will be glad of my special talents."

Aimery sat on a stool drawn up next to Garin. "You persist in your determination to join the Order?" he asked in an altered voice. "I have much feeling for you, Garin, and I like it not that you swear yourself into sudden and inescapable death."

"We all do that," Garin reminded him. "Your crusading vows are as perilous as those of the Order of the Temple. You know that Bernard has stood sponsor with the Holy Father for the Templars. He uses me as a messenger, that is all."

"But," countered Aimery shrewdly, "must you be a Templar to carry a message?"

Garin closed his eyes. "Do not press me, Aimery. I have taken the vows, and I may not retract them."

Aimery pressed his lips together and looked hard at his brother. Even though they did not share the same father, yet Aimery loved this half-brother rather more than Simon de Montvert, whose blood was the same as his own. "Remember what happened to Thierry de Galeran," said Aimery with an attempt at roughness.

"If manhood is the only part of myself I must give up to Holy Church," said Brother Garin with a rueful smile, "I will consider simply that my vow of chastity will rest more lightly on me."

Aimery sprang to his feet with a resigned laugh. "So be it. I vow you are beyond my ability to change."

"That is so," said Garin. "And since you relinquish the attempt, I should not preach to you, either. But Aimery, I do not like this hard, reckless armor you wear on your spirit."

"Your fancy plays you false," grated Aimery. "Sick men are prone to dreams."

"I do not ask the cause," said Garin.

"Very wise," said his brother, eyes stormy.

"But it seems to me you are not using your great experience with women to win the woman you love."

"Love? Solange?" hissed Aimery. "The king got his revenge on me, yoking me with that she-wolf!"

"Yet you are yoked," continued Garin earnestly, "and I did not notice that you protested overmuch."

"For the queen's sake," muttered Aimery.

"Truly? It is my belief that you love the Lady Solange," said Brother Garin.

Aimery glared at his brother. "I? It is not I who plead her cause, who claim to know her thoughts, who—" He stopped short, his eyes narrowing. "Not I, brother. Is it seemly that a monk of Clairvaux cast his eyes upon his brother's wife?"

"Is it better," said Garin hotly, "to love a queen? Another man's wife?"

"You, Garin, have little to say in this regard," said Aimery, his eyes incandescent with fury. "For your father was such a one."

Garin turned white. "You have never brought that up to me before."

"I have never had a wife who spurned me before," said Aimery, freely, out of the depths of his misery.

"Now that you have brought it up," said Garin sturdily,

"You must remember that your father mistreated our mother."

"I remember no such thing," said Aimery but his voice lacked conviction. He remembered all too well.

He sank into a chair and covered his face with his hands. His mood was so black that he hardly heeded Garin's touch on his shoulder.

"Our mother," said Garin softly, "was a lady of much virtue and grace, pushed beyond her endurance. Take care, dear brother, that the Lady Solange is prevented from the same misfortune."

Aimery did not move and, at length, Brother Garin closed his eyes as if to sleep, not trusting himself to speak. But the monk was troubled to the depths of his soul.

At the end of January, the court still lingered at Etampes, but not because of the amenities of the castle, which were few, or because of the rigors of further journeying, which were many. The Court was waiting for a decision.

Garin was well acquainted with the politics of the day. The Cistercian order was far from cloistered out of the way of the world. It was Bernard himself who had, a few years before, set the nine knights on their way, headed by Hugh de Payens, to Jerusalem on pilgrimage. Those men were now called the Knights of the Temple.

Brother Garin explained to Solange. "As soon as the king decided to take the cross, he sent messengers out. The messengers went to ask advice from King Roger of Sicily."

"Advice? About going on Crusade?"

"Not exactly. Advice on the best way to go, whether by sea, with the help of Roger's many ships, or by land to Byzantium."

"And the answer?"

"Is to come here. Also, perhaps, word from Manuel Comnenus of Byzantium. And Bernard is to return from Germany, also, with news of the emperor's intentions."

"When will we start?"

"You are anxious. Can you not find comfort in the days before the journey?"

"No, Brother Garin. My father is alive, somewhere, and I must find him. There is nothing else in my mind."

Garin hesitated. Should he speak? Or should he let Aimery work out his own troubles? He could not for long resent Aimery's taunt about his father, who was not Aimery's father. Aimery, two years older than he, had been a good friend to him, a brother without equal. The oldest of the three sons who bore the name de Montvert had felt his mother's dalliance more profoundly than Aimery. Simon was barely civil. Garin, having had no real home, found his home in Clairvaux, in the Cistercians, and in his faith. This should have been enough. Yet the sad eyes of Solange haunted him.

"Not even my brother?" said Garin softly.

She glanced at him through half-closed eyelids. "I do not know what he has told you."

"Nothing," said Brother Garin promptly, if inaccurately.

"But I will tell you this. Had I not needed to be wed in order to travel with the queen, I should never have married him."

"You have no feeling for him, then?"

She bit her lip to still its trembling before she could answer with even an appearance of firmness, "None whatever."

"And yet, methinks you watch him much when he is nearby, too much for a woman who cares nothing for him. And," added Garin slyly, "there is a look in your eyes that might well set a man's heart to pounding."

"He has no heart," retorted Solange, adding, with a creditable impression of casualness, "Not that I would want it if he had, for it would belong to the queen."

"Are you sure?" said Garin softly. "The queen demands much, but gives nothing in return. And no man stays where he receives nothing."

"But he stays," pointed out Solange.

"Where else can he go?" said Garin. She looked quickly at him. What did he mean? Did he mean she was at fault for not welcoming Aimery with open arms? She was not having any of that. The blame was not hers.

"He must decide that for himself," she said. "It is," she added with a struggle, "none of my affair."

When at length King Roger of Sicily replied to King Louis's letter, he did so thoroughly. No simple royal messenger brought the reply. Instead, Tancred of Palermo rode in full panoply, with a guard of twenty knights and a retinue of over a hundred. The armed troops gave the appearance of a state visit, or an invasion.

Roger was the fighting king of the realms of Sicily. Born an Hauteville, he inherited from his father a small county, and his burning ambition was to amass more land than anyone else in his family. He was ruthless.

Sicily had become, under Roger's influence, the greatest maritime power in the Mediterranean. Such a powerful fleet must not go to waste, so Roger seemed to think, and Bernard strongly suspected that Roger's next aim was to revive his ancestor's Great Scheme, and conquer the Greek Empire to make it his own.

All this was well known in Western Europe, Brother Garin told Solange, and the Frankish barons eyed Roger's emissary with wariness.

A council was called to hear Roger's answer. Aimery returned to their rooms to dress with the elegance befitting his new status.

Solange spoke timidly. "What does King Roger know about the Holy Land? His country is hardly closer than we are."

"Sicily is on the direct sea route from this country and England."

"Then he would know many returning Crusaders?"

"I suppose so. Where is my green silk tunic?"

"I'll get it."

Helping him on with it, her hand fell on his shoulder, and she felt him stiffen. Did he hate her that much? She steeled herself to ask, "Then it is possible that Tancred might have word of my father. Could you ask him?"

"And make a fool of myself? No."

"But I cannot approach him myself," persisted Solange.

"I am glad you recognize that," said Aimery harshly.

Tears filled her eyes and dropped from her cheek. He made a short gesture toward her but it fell short. "Tears. A woman's weapon," he said and left her.

She went out to find Brother Garin. Fortunately, she

caught him before he entered the great hall to join the barons. Solange put her request to him.

"Always Odo," he said, shaking his head. "If you spent as much of yourself on Aimery . . ."

"He hates me," said Solange simply.

"My child, I doubt that," he said. But she brushed his words aside.

"Will you ask?"

Finally deciding not to pursue what was clearly a painful subject, he nodded. "I will ask in good time. But are you sure?"

"Sure?"

"Sure you will want to know the truth after all?"

10

"**T**ruth?" echoed Solange. "Of course I want to know the truth."

"Whatever it may be?" persisted Brother Garin.

"What could it be?" she wondered. "Either my father is alive or he is dead. I must not abandon him. Don't you see?"

Brother Garin hesitated.

"Look," urged Solange. "The truth can hurt, I know that. The truth cost Loriot his life. I still have the mark of the murderer's knife on my shoulder."

Brother Garin nodded.

"And you will remember what a fool I made of myself not knowing the truth about Raoul. Believe me, it did not hurt the less because I was ignorant."

"I suppose you will have to pursue this truth about your father."

"I must."

Brother Garin bowed his head in acknowledgment, or in silent prayer. "I will see what I can find out. Do not wait here. I will come to you." He vanished.

When at last Brother Garin came to her in her room, his somber face and grave eyes told her of his message before he spoke.

"I asked many a man of Tancred's suite," said Garin. "You must know, dear child, that many of these with the ambassador have not been to Outremer. They are young, and straining to fight, but so far their lances have not been tested except in tournaments."

"And they know nothing of my father?"

Brother Garin hesitated. There was one grizzled sergeant who thought he remembered seeing, in Antioch itself, the man with hair the color of spun flax who had a swan on his banner. Should he tell Solange this faintest of hints? Should he stoke the fire that burned in her?

Brother Garin took only a moment to weigh Solange's nigh-hopeless quest against his own conviction that she would do well to concentrate on winning Aimery, rather than trying to find her father.

"No," he said sturdily. "There is no one who knows Odo de Saint Florent."

"No one at all?"

"I inquired of every man I could reach," he sighed, dropping onto the stool before the hearth.

"Let me give you some wine," she said, curbing her massive impatience. When she handed him the jeweled cup, he gulped greedily. "Thirsty work."

"No one knew my father?" she insisted.

"It is very likely that your father would have gone through the mountain passes to Venice, to take sea passage, no doubt. In all likelihood he never touched Sicily."

She reflected. "We did have a letter saying he had traveled part of the way by water."

"Very possible."

"Has none of these men from Sicily been on Crusade?"

"Most probably not," said Garin, draining the cup to the bottom and removing the lees from his tongue with a delicate finger. "All those whose tongue I could understand said they had been fighting Byzantines."

"Byzantines? But they are Christians!"

"Christians, maybe. But not like us."

She hardly heeded him. Her disappointment was severe.

Brother Garin, with heavy conscience, took pity on her. "Remember, child, that no word is good. Good news is possible as long as there is not proof of bad news."

After he had left her, she put another piece of wood on the fire and pulled her stool closer to the blaze. Garin was right. Even no news at all was better than word from one who might have seen her father's dead body.

She was so absorbed in her moody thoughts that she did not hear the timid tap on the door. The door opened to admit Petronilla.

"I saw your husband downstairs, so I ventured to come," said the older woman.

"Sit down, Mother," said Solange tonelessly. "A drink? Some wine?"

"Nothing, thank you," said her mother. "I came to learn the news."

"News?"

"I saw Brother Garin cornering Tancred's men. And, knowing you, I doubted not that he was on your errands. Was there word of your father?"

"None. Did you expect any?"

"I don't know what I expected any longer. You believe that friar?" Something in Petronilla's voice struck Solange.

"Why not? He is Aimery's brother," she said.

"But he is the minion of that terrifying Abbot Bernard," Petronilla pointed out.

"He is merely a monk." Solange said. "What is important is that I must find out whether my father lives."

"*We* must find out," said Petronilla. "You have stirred up a hornet's nest, and now we must find out. I believe your father is dead. But I cannot forget the sin of bigamy until I know."

"Then you aren't sure any more about Mehun," said Solange, startled.

"I was sure. Mehun still insists he is right. But—I don't know."

Solange looked up sharply. She caught her breath at the sight of her mother's face. Turned away from Solange, her features caught the light of the afternoon sun, through the west-facing window. It was, suddenly, the face of an aging woman.

"Mother!" cried Solange. "What am I doing to you?"

Gathering her dignity around her, Petronilla rose from the stool. "You might have thought of the consequences to us all before you embarked on this fanatical idea," said Petronilla lightly. She paused, lifting Solange's chin with one finger, studying her face. "It's not easy for you, either. I can see that. But take care, daughter, lest we all come to disaster through your stubbornness."

The fragrance of lilies lingered long after her mother left. And so did the unguarded look of momentary anguish on her mother's face, still clear in Solange's thoughts.

But when she saw her mother again, at the banquet for Tancred of Palermo, she thought she must have imagined it.

The banquet was sumptuous. The king was determined to give honor to the Sicilian king's representative.

When Tancred rose to speak to the assemblage, Solange had her first good look at him. He was not over average height, with dark brown hair and compelling eyes.

Tancred's blood had doubtless been Viking at one time, but now there was an admixture of other strains, indicated by his dark hair and olive skin. Even his volatile gestures and exaggerated speech were too flowery for one of northern blood.

Tancred spoke for a powerful king, and the southern route he proposed for the king's Crusade had its advantages.

"I am sure," said Tancred, letting his dark eyes rove over the assembled company, "that I need not tell you what is happening in the Holy Land. Father Bernard has told you. But I speak to you now as a military man. The Crusade is a journey of faith, but the soldiers among you know that faith alone will not provide ships, or food, or safety along the way."

His message from King Roger, at last, was simple:

Roger could not take the cross. Nor could he spare men. But he would furnish ships—for a price—to convey Louis and his Crusade along the sea lanes.

"Through the warm seas," he said. "No mountains, no rivers to cross, no enemies to repel—just sunny days on deck, warm nights at sea."

"It's that talk of warm air that will do the trick," said

Count Robert. "I wager many a romance will blossom in the summer air. And the queen favors the southern route."

"Back to Poitou for her," said Alis, adding with surprising waspishness, "I wish she had stayed there!"

11

𝕿ancred's proposal met with great enthusiasm. And the queen was determined upon the southern route to Outremer. The plan devised by Sicily's king was simple, at least the way Tancred laid it out:

Through France to the Mediterranean was an easy trip. Much of the way lay through Queen Eleanor's own lands, where the reception would be warm and there would be many excuses for tarrying along the way.

Thence by ship to Sicily and across the sea to Antioch. "Where my uncle rules," boasted the queen, "and I would see to it that we would be given all help."

The queen seemed certain her wish would prevail. When she met with her guard, as she did daily, she spoke with certainty of the sea journey.

"We must travel light, you know. We will need our pavilions to shade us from the sun, and a goodly supply of ointment for the skin."

"But what about the storms?" quavered Millicent. "Geoffrey told me about the great waves on the sea!"

"We will be traveling in spring," said the queen serenely, "and not in the season of storms. Now tell me, ladies, what you think of the costumes I have devised?" The perils of the sea were forgotten.

Tancred, gallantly paying discreet court to Eleanor, whose influence upon the king was clear enough to even the most obtuse, believed he had succeeded in his mission. His spirits soared, and he found much to talk to Eleanor about.

Solange shrewdly suspected that the queen's infinite and incontrovertible stores of information about the southern route came directly from Tancred's lips.

Aimery seemed to his wife to be greatly unhappy these days. She had come almost to feeling sorry for him. The king depended more and more on Aimery's good sense, so he said, but Conon said slyly that it was as good a way as any to keep Aimery away from the queen. It must be true, she thought, for surely Aimery gave all the signs of a frustrated lover. Her mood grew darker.

No word had come yet from Bernard of Clairvaux on his mission to the Emperor Conrad.

Perhaps it was because another storm rattled around the tower this night, reminding her of that other night, in the inn, on the road to Etampes. But, for whatever reason, Solange felt so lonely she could not abide it.

"Is it settled then? We go by sea?" she asked Aimery when he finally came in.

It was late, and for once he had returned before bedtime. He answered civilly, "I doubt not that Tancred thinks so. Not all the council favors the sea route."

Encouraged, she continued. "It sounds much more pleasant."

"Tancred makes it seem so. But Robert de Dreux, for one, fears that Roger has his own reasons for such a generous offer. And until the council knows what that reason is, they will not consent."

"What do *you* think best?"

His mood broke abruptly. "It makes no difference to me where I go, or what I do." His voice sounded as lonely as Solange's own. He turned away to poke unnecessarily at the fire.

Solange was aware of bitter rage rising in her. How dare the queen be so callous, riding roughshod over a man like Aimery, trampling on his devotion?

Although Aimery said no more, Solange was very gentle as she arranged the furs on the bed, tucking them in around his shoulder after he slept.

The next day, the answer to the barons' doubts came to court in the form of a half-dozen men riding fast from the east, bringing word from Byzantium. Suddenly the court was in an uproar.

"We come in advance of our lord Erik of the Long Lance," announced the leader. "He follows half a day behind us, with a message from the exalted Emperor Manuel Comnenus, august ruler of Byzantium and Europe!"

"Not quite all of Europe!" muttered the queen through taut lips, her eloquent eyes full of anger.

Tancred stepped forward as though to challenge the eastern messengers, but a glance from the king stopped him in his tracks.

The king purred, "We are glad to welcome Erik of the Long Lance." He gave orders for the messengers to be fed, and turned to his barons. "It is possible that there are advantages to the land route that we have not heard from Tancred, whose thoughts lie with the sea."

Tancred exploded. "Advantages? The road is leagues longer and there are hazardous mountains and swarming savages. The Greeks will deny the dangers, I doubt not, but—"

"We will abide by our barons' advice," said the king calmly. "When Erik comes, we will hear him."

Already, the queen and king, so gossip had it, had quarreled bitterly over Tancred's route. The queen was going by sea no matter how the king traveled.

Tancred, barely holding his temper, said, "Trust not the Greeks. I beg you, sire, do not listen to the Greek ambassador. Someone in your court has betrayed you, sire, sending to Constantinople—"

The King bestowed a calm glance on Tancred. "It is I who wrote to my royal friend, the emperor of Byzantium," he said mildly. "But you need not worry. I shall listen with caution, and my barons will give me good counsel."

Tancred was forced then to subside, but his darkening glances gave proof that he was sorely disturbed. If the Franks did not come to Sicily, Roger the king would take it gravely amiss. Tancred alone knew how ravenous was the beast called ambition that harried Roger. And part of the scheme was, in truth, to entice the king of the Franks into Roger's alliance against the Greeks.

Every man, woman, and child turned out to greet the

messenger from the great king of the Byzantines. The route their Crusade would follow was of great importance to everyone.

A line of soldiers guarded the way, holding back the villeins and the other lesser folk, and joking rudely with them. But when the trumpet sounded from the turret atop the donjon, the soldiers in the street sprang to attention.

Solange and Bertille, wrapped in their warmest mantles, scurried to a small niche at the base of the tower. Bertille had already decided that would be the best view. "And who knows?" she said. "Perhaps there might be a handsome Greek in the train. I cannot make up my mind about Pierre, for Guy is wealthier. But I must wed soon, or the queen's guard will go without me."

"Handsome Greek?" smiled Solange. "They are not Greeks at all, but Norsemen."

"How do you know that?" asked Bertille. "From the name Erik?"

"Aimery told me," said Solange. "Erik is a Varangian, a Norseman. He had no patrimony in his country, being a younger son. So, with his friends, he sought service in Byzantium. Look, Bertille, you can see the tips of the pennant standards, where the sun catches them."

"I thought Aimery was too busy to explain things?"

"He is. He is of the king's council, and I rarely see him. But once in a while he talks to me."

Bertille was not listening. The emissary from the Greek Emperor was trotting up the hill toward the barbican gate. It was an impressive sight. The pennants of red and gold and green snapped in the crisp breeze. Two standard bearers and at least twenty armed knights surrounded Erik. That meant at least eighty servitors to care for men, armor and beasts.

Up the hill they came, in heavy armor. All but Erik. He carried his helm on the saddle before him, careless of danger, giving the impression that he was invincible. Arrows would fly past him, battle-axes would be raised over his head in menace. And yet, so it seemed, Erik would laugh, as he was laughing now with the sheer exuberance of living. A ripple swept over the crowd, a murmur of admiration that traveled along the street and up the hill to where Solange and Bertille stood watching. Bertille leaned over the wall, her lips slightly parted in wonder. Isabel spoke from behind them, just now arriving.

"Quite a showman, isn't he?" she said in derision. "His men armed to the teeth, but he is secure as a pagan god. I say it's blasphemy!"

Erik seemed conscious of the effect he had upon the spectators. His glance slid over the mass of faces. Approaching the gate below the three, he looked up. Erik saw them. He bowed to the dark-haired Bertille, but his gaze riveted on Solange. He was caught by surprise, it seemed, when his eyes fell upon the slim girl with the moonlight-colored hair.

In that moment, when their eyes met, Solange stirred, uneasily pleased by the flattering attention. There was a fraction of time when he raised an eyebrow slightly and seemed to send a message to her. Solange, feeling her breath grow short, tried to look away but could not. It was as though a physical tie bound them. Then she took a long breath and the foolish fantasy was over. It was a silly impression, she thought. When Bertille turned to hurry into the castle to the reception room, Solange shook her head. She did not want to see that man again.

Her determination was for nothing, however, for she met her mother. "You saw them?" said Petronilla. "I have an idea. Do you think that man knows anything about your father?" Her mother plucked at her sleeve. "Do you think he might know about your father?"

"I don't know."

"Ask him."

Solange glanced sidelong at her mother. Petronilla wore again the look of anguish, but she scarcely tried to hide it now. If her mother's conscience plagued her thus, Solange knew she herself was much to blame.

"All right, Mother," she said softly.

"Don't send Garin," said Petronilla. "Go yourself."

Solange hesitated. No one else had seen that exchange of looks between her and the stranger, or felt that magnetic pull she had felt when he looked directly into her eyes as though he saw—far more than he should. She feared him, but she feared herself the more.

"Go yourself," repeated Petronilla, impatiently.

"All right, Mother." She heard the pounding in her ears. "All right. I will."

12

Erik was not the only important visitor to come to Etampes. But where Erik came in all pomp and glittering show, the other came quietly on a mule with silver harness and tinkling bells, accompanied only by a handful of friars. The Abbot Suger, the king's financial counselor, arrived from Paris.

He was a sand-colored man, to the hair around his tonsure, eyelashes, eyebrows. He had known the king for nearly twenty years, since they were both small boys at the priory of Saint Denis de l'Estrée. He knew the queen well, too, having accompanied Louis on his journey into Aquitaine to wed the young Duchess Eleanor. He was the abbot of Saint Denis, now, and guardian of that storehouse of precious relics including the revered *oriflamme*. It was clear that he had come to give his friend the king weighty counsel in the matter of the Crusade. Money would be needed, and vast supplies, and, it was said, the abbot knew how to get it.

He did not arrive in time to attend the reception the king gave for Erik, but that was a purely formal occasion. "The king," Aimery said, "will hear both sides of the discussion in council this afternoon." He scarcely had time to tell her that before he rushed back to the king.

Erik of the Long Lance and his Varangians were given suitable honors, in accordance with the rank of their master, Manuel Comnenus. While Manuel might not be emperor of all the world, as Erik's herald had tactlessly suggested, yet the Comneni held sway over much of the Asian peninsula bordering the inland sea, as well as much of eastern Europe.

The Greeks were a turbulent people, and Manuel was not the first emperor to mistrust his own subjects. Hence the Varangians, an imperial bodyguard of troops from the northern countries, the land of the Vikings, were trusted emissaries.

The King made a state affair of his council's audience. All assembled in the great hall. Solange was tightly sandwiched in behind Countess Alis, seated just below the dais, and Catherine. With white-knuckled fingers clutching the back of Alis's chair, Solange let her glance rove around the room.

Surely the emissary must be impressed by the grandeur, the glitter of this court! She herself had never seen anything so fine. The king himself, Eleanor at his left hand. Baron d'Yves, at ease in maroon satin. Geoffrey de Guiscard, Jean de Loches, Henri de Villiers, Count Robert de Dreux.

Aimery was the handsomest of all, except for the lines of care that were picked out by the harsh sunlight. Had he had those lines when she first knew him, in the forest? She thought not.

Erik's men entered first, a handful only, fanning out to stand near the door.

Then Tancred's men escorted the Sicilian into the room.

Solange thought, How long it takes anyone to do anything in the king's court! The Crusade route, while important, was still undecided. Only now, after weeks of planning, had the Abbot Suger been summoned to see about raising the money for the journey. Erik of the Long Lance had been here at Etampes for a whole day, in constant conference with the king, and yet Louis still could not make up his mind. It was the queen, someone nearby murmured, against the barons. She wanted the southern route, by sea, and the barons did not trust Roger.

She was conscious then of a concentrated stare directed at her. An uneasy feeling prickled the nerves at the back of her neck. She let her eyes move over the crowd, hardly moving her head, until she found the source of that stare. It was Gauthier! Of the men who had been with her on the trip to Saint Virgillia's, Gauthier was least predictable; stormy, moody, sullen. She stirred uneasily. Then she realized that Gauthier was not staring at her. It was Jehane, behind her, on whom his gaze was fixed.

Solange had little time to consider that, for the king rose and silence fell over the crowd.

"My loyal people," he began. "As you know, we have promised to journey to succor the Holy Places, to relieve them of the heavy hand of the infidel. Our brother Roger, king of Sicily, has sent us promises of aid, inviting us to travel by way of his lands. Now, in answer to my letters, the emperor of Byzantium has taken notice of our intent. He urges that we travel through his territories."

Tancred moved uneasily, scowling. He glared at Erik, who did not seem to notice. Instead, Erik's glance roamed the room as though searching for something . . . or someone. His eyes rested momentarily on the countess and her attendants before moving on.

The king had invited the two men to speak. Tancred was first.

Surprisingly eloquent, Tancred spoke well, of ships promised, of escorts, and of a short journey. Count Robert shuffled his feet impatiently. He had been against the sea route from the beginning.

Erik's turn came. He was not eloquent, but in a short time he had his audience persuaded.

"The land route offers room to move. You will not be cramped in the hold of a ship, suffering seasickness, and wild tempests." He made it seem a dismal prospect. But it was the man himself who was convincing. Strong, manly, open-faced, he inspired trust. A traitorous thought came to Solange: like Aimery when I first knew him. Before Aimery turned cruel and unfeeling. And yet, one kindly touch of Aimery's hand would, she realized, make her forget all the stormy weeks since their one night together.

The assembly broke up. Erik and Tancred left by different doors. The ladies and men at arms left. Only the king, queen, and the barons' council remained to discuss the problem.

The queen favored the southern route, through her own lands, and directly by sea to her uncle's principate of Antioch. Many agreed with her that the Byzantine emperor, like all Greeks, could not be trusted.

But the Count de Dreux, and a good number of others, did not trust Roger of Sicily. He could not build sufficient ships in the time left—and if he had ships already a-building, then for what purpose? "We would find ourselves fighting Roger's battles for him, since he wishes war with Manuel, and we would never get to the Holy City, nor even deserve it," cried Robert de Dreux, "if we let ourselves fight Christians rather than the infidels!"

So ran the arguments. Countess Alis, of course, sided with those against the queen. "But," she said, once again in the privacy of her own rooms, "mark my words, there will be trouble."

13

Sybille de Nannes was back at court. Olivier had stayed home as he was, so it was hinted, so worn out by the energies consumed in begetting an heir that he was now on the verge of dying. "In fact," said Sybille confidentially to the Countess and Solange, "he is already near dead. He doesn't even know me. I could care for him, I suppose, but I've been so sick myself."

"I see you have been," said the countess kindly. "But while I am glad to see you . . . could not you have stayed until the end?"

"My brothers thought it best that I come to court. To be here to claim my rights to the fiefs, they said. But in truth, I was glad enough to come. I wish to ask your indulgence, Lady Alis. I need a favor."

Solange was consumed by pity for her friend. Sybille had been so lovely, so witty and lively. Now she was thin as though she had not eaten for the entire two months she had been with child. The circles under her eyes looked as though a finger had dipped into soot and then smeared across her cheekbones. But the anguish in her eyes was the worst.

"My dear girl, of course. You know I will do anything for you. Tell me what it is you wish."

"I wish to go with the queen's guard to the Holy Land."

The two were struck silent. Sybille de Nannes looked as though she could not get as far as Metz. Solange wondered how she had managed to get to Etampes. The Holy Land? The trip would kill her.

"My dear . . ." began Lady Alis, a bewildered look on her kind, plump face. "You must know you could not survive such a trip."

"I must go. I do not wish to kill the babe. But I cannot live this way. My brothers——" She could go no further. She fell to her knees and buried her head in Alis's lap.

Lady Alis queried Solange with a lifted eyebrow, over the bowed head she stroked. Solange shook her head. If Sybille wanted the truth told, she would tell it.

Broken words came from Sybille. "They guard me. They will kill me after the babe is born. They expect to be named guardians of the child. And they will kill me lest I tell."

"Tell what?" said Alis, coaxingly. "Believe me, it will be best if you tell it, and not let it fester inside you."

Sybille sat up. Wiping her eyes, she gulped her sobs away, and faltered, "You see, my brothers married me to Olivier after my parents died. They wanted to have me taken care of, they said. But what they really wanted, they told me after I was wed, was Olivier's land. They could only get his fiefs through me."

There was no sound other than her voice. Solange had heard it before, and Lady Alis believed in total purging as the only cure for a troubled heart.

"But you know Olivier was too old, too ill. He never—he could never—you know . . . I think my brothers did not quite realize how far gone Olivier was. But then they began to hint. They wanted an heir to the fortune, no matter whose blood ran in his veins. They wanted me to accept another man—any man, and claim the babe was Olivier's. After all, who could prove otherwise?"

Bit by bit the words came out, haltingly, but as the story proceeded she began to talk faster and faster, until at the end, she spoke the fatal words so quickly that her audience was at pains to understand her. "But I wouldn't do it, you know. It wasn't right. And so—and so, my brothers took it upon themselves to provide an heir for Olivier. They took me by force. Both of them."

It was said. Lady Alis lay back, her eyes closed, for the space of half-a-dozen heartbeats.

Sybille got to her feet, and now stood glaring defiantly at them. "Say it. Tell me I have such sin on my soul that you cannot stay in the same room with me. Say it. And I will jump from the window!"

"My dear, of course I won't say it. I'll help you in any way I can." Lady Alis's voice was shaky but her words were gallant. "We'll see what can be done. I see no real reason why you can't go on Crusade, my dear. There will be others in your condition before we arrive, I'm sure. But for now, you had best stay here with me. I'll send Evart for your clothes. I vow, I will not put you back in the hands of your brothers. The *devils*!"

She was still talking, comfortingly, of warm drink and a bigger fire, of a posset to make Sybille sleep, as Solange tiptoed out. Lady Alis had a sure hand with solace!

When she left them, it was late in the afternoon. The winter night had drawn in. It was too late to seek out Erik of the Long Lance. But Jehane had a message for her. Her mother had come to see her and been upset to find her absent.

"Lady de Mowbrai asked for news," reported the maid. "I did not know what I should tell her. I knew of no news, Lady de Pontdebois?"

Solange considered. It wasn't too late after all, perhaps. But she dared not go alone. "Well, Jehane, I know of none either. But let us look for some."

She must seek out Erik of the Long Lance and ask him whether he knew anything about Odo de St. Florent.

She searched in her chest for the right attire—a turquoise bliaut trimmed with amethysts and a miniver-lined cloak of the same color. Bidding Jehane dress her hair, she searched out violet ribbons to lace into the long braids.

Finding Bertille, she outlined her plan. "Please come. I dare not go alone to the Varangians!"

"I should think not!" agreed Bertille, who was always most proper. It was for this reason that Solange had decided to ask for companionship. Erik might be dangerous, Solange felt, and Bertille was a safeguard. "But, Solange, must you go? Cannot Aimery ask for you?"

Solange lowered her eyes. "Aimery has done enough. I've promised my mother that this time I would go myself to make inquiry."

"I'll make ready at once," said Bertille. "Will you want me to take my maid?"

"Jehane waits outside. The fewer who know, the better."

It was a long way, down stone steps, echoing with their footsteps, along the rooms where the men at arms roistered. Known by the King's men, they suffered no indignity. Finally they crossed the courtyard to the barracks where the foreign soldiers were lodged.

There was a door facing inward toward the bailey, and the barracks were free standing, apart from the outer wall, so as not to provide anyone scaling the wall with a made-to-order platform on which to ease his descent.

"You're sure you're right?" whispered Bertille. "Isn't the ambassador in the castle itself?"

"I made inquiries," explained Solange. "Erik wanted to be with his men."

Muttering, Bertille pulled her cloak closer around her face. "Jean'll kill me if he finds out."

Since Jean de Loches was much in love with Bertille, Solange gave this statement the attention it deserved, and forgot it.

The Varangians had taken over the entire barracks, as they could hear long before they arrived. If the Norsemen had any misgivings at being in a foreign land, these were not apparent. The sounds of revelry exploded into the outer court from time to time. Solange nearly faltered. Bertille was ahead a few steps before she realized that Solange had stopped.

"What is it, Solange?" she objected sharply. "You need to see the man, don't you? Then let's go." She softened her words hastily. "Sorry, my dear. I'm just as nervous as you are, but it's best to go ahead and get it over with, without thinking too much."

"No doubt." Solange's mouth was dry.

"That's what I'm going to do when I get married. Jean

doesn't know it yet, but I rather think I fancy him most."

"What of Guy? And Hugh?" Solange answered automatically.

"It's Jean. Unless I meet someone tonight," said Bertille with unquenchable optimism.

Solange hesitated only a moment. She felt her courage running out like an ebb tide. She opened the door quickly, before courage vanished altogether. Jehane pulled the door shut against the cold, but kept her hand on the latch.

Little by little the voices stilled as the men became aware of the two noble ladies and their maid. One of the men, apparently prodded in the back by his fellows, stepped forward.

"I have come to speak with Erik," Solange told him in a firm voice. The men were enormous, she thought, the room much too small. "Erik of the Long Lance."

The door at the far side of the room opened, and Erik stood in the doorway. He had taken off the mail he had worn even at the king's council that afternoon, and now was dressed in a deep maroon leather hauberk with a gold design around the bottom. The hauberk was tight around his neck, revealing the strong column of neck that rose from the broad shoulders.

He looked at Solange with a gleam in his eyes. He surveyed the room without haste, and then bowed to Solange and Bertille. "Now I see the vision that has struck my men tongue-tied," he said. "I confess their sudden silence had me worried. I must apologize for the dumbness that has afflicted them all." Advancing a few steps into the room, he fixed his eyes on Solange. "Lady, I am at your service."

"I should like to speak to you, Sir Erik, if I may."

He inclined his head, and opened the inner door wider. She spoke a word to Bertille, and advanced to Erik. Turning back, she saw that Bertille had already been provided with a seat in the midst of a respectful circle. Jehane was already eyeing a willing soldier.

Solange was inside Erik's quarters. Far from cell-like, its walls were hung with thick rugs of exotic design. Rugs of squares and diamonds in brilliant clear red, blue, and cream, covered the floor. A fire roared in the grate, and two chairs were drawn up before the hearth.

"Surprised?" he said, enjoying her gaze. "Simply because we travel in a primitive country does not mean I choose to mortify my own flesh."

"All this came on horseback? I see why you do not wish to lodge in the castle."

He nodded. His eyes never left her face. "As you see, I am no monk."

Catching an unsettling note in his voice, she hastened to say, "How lovely these hangings are. They must be rare."

"Indeed, these are simple things of little value, but of great comfort. In my palace in Constantinople—ah, but you think I am boasting. Don't deny it. I read your mind, you know."

She glanced sideways at him. "You know what I am now thinking?"

His laugh rang out. "You think I am far too sure of myself. Maybe I am. But we shall see. In the meantime, I must urge you to visit Constantinople one day. What you see here is not fit to pave their streets. I should be happy to show you much there that will please you."

He handed her to a chair where the warmth of the fire beat upon her face. She threw her hood back.

"I may take advantage of your offer," she smiled, more at ease. "I will be in Constantinople in the summer."

He paused in the act of pouring wine into a jewel-encrusted goblet. "You? This year? Then—"

Enjoying his surprise, the dimple high on her cheek caught the light. "Yes," she assured him, "You are right. I go on Crusade."

"For your sins?" he said, incredulous. "I laugh." He did, a ringing sound of pleasure. "You have so few sins. You are too young to know what you speak of."

"I go with the queen's guard," she said, avoiding discussion of her sins.

"Then," he said promptly, "that means you are married."

The atmosphere in the room altered.

"But I did not come to you to talk about the journey. I should tell you at once, Sir Erik," she said mischievously, "that my mother sent me."

His open mouth gave her the answer she expected. He

had indeed thought she was placing herself at his disposal. She continued, "My mother thinks that you may be able to help us."

He had recovered from his surprise. "I shall try. But I cannot imagine what your mother thinks I can do for her."

"My mother thought you would listen to me, and that is why she did not come herself."

"A shrewd woman." He poured wine into the second goblet. "Although, if you resemble her, she must be a beauty." He stood looking down at her, eyes laughing, each hand holding a goblet. "Your mother would have been safe enough in my hands."

"You're teasing me," said Solange. "Perhaps I have overestimated you. I had thought that anyone entrusted with a mission from such a great ruler as your emperor would be a man of judgment."

"My apologies." He took a deep breath. "I should have perceived at once that you were not—what I thought. Or, permit me to say, what I hoped. It is not often that I see a lady who could have come directly out of my long-house in Glia. That pale hair, your regal bearing, like the ladies of my nearly forgotten homeland." He was serious. "My wits were addled. We have much to say to each other, lady, but let us see about your mother's errand first."

"I shall tell you, but you and I can have nothing else between us."

He studied her for a long minute. "I laugh. But you will see. The Norns have spoken to me. You know, the goddesses of fate."

This was a wild conversation, she thought. What had she to do with his Viking homeland, even though her own ancestors too had come down from the frozen seas? And what had she to do with his pagan goddesses? She might have crossed herself against his goddesses, but she did not think that would be right. He was Christian. It was only his way of speaking, she told herself.

"I seek my father."

"In my Varangians?"

"No, no. My father was—is—Odo de Saint Florent."

"Was—is? Strange."

"Not really. My father was reported dead, in the battle

of Adana. But someone said he was seen alive and well after that." She fidgeted with her cloak. "Do you know of him?"

Erik was grave enough now. He handed her the goblet, and lifted his own to his lips. "Why do you not ask your informant for details?"

"You think I would not if I could?"

"Your informant must be where you cannot reach him."

"Dead."

She finished half the wine before he spoke again. "I think," he said earnestly, "that I know the name. I truly do. But I must try to remember. In the meantime—"

"In the meantime," she countered, "I will leave you to think. I shall send to ask." She got to her feet. The room revolved and she nearly fell.

Erik held her by the elbows. Looking down into her eyes, he questioned her silently.

"It's the wine," she said faintly. "Too strong."

"It's not the wine," he said, and took her forcefully into his arms.

14

Astonishment poured over her. Not at Erik's holding her. She was not surprised at that. What stunned her was her blind response to him. It was as though another Solange had lived all this time inside her slim body, watching with lonely eyes, yearning for something lovely just beyond her reach.

And that silent Solange had bided her time, building up a tension, a driving urge that searched for something she did not recognize.

Until now.

When the spring was touched, when the nearness of Erik with his laughing eyes and his caressing hands reached that inner Solange, she melted like ice under August sun.

Slowly at first, then all in a rush, like the Petitmer in spring spate.

Far off came the thought—maybe Conon was right. Perhaps she was indeed a passionate woman.

The restlessness that had driven her for weeks exploded with Erik's touch. He pressed her close to him, closer, until her entire body pressed against his warm flesh.

Her cloak clutched at her throat, and she fought with fumbling fingers to free the clasp. She knew only sweet relief when the warm mantle fell to the floor around her feet.

Erik's hands, moving urgently on her hips, burned through the thin wool of her tunic. She heard a small whimper, and knew it came from somewhere deep inside her, from that silent Solange who was just now waking.

She slipped her arms around his neck, pressing her breasts against him, pulling his head down to her. *Don't let me go*, she cried silently. He unclasped her girdle with knowledgeable fingers, bunched her bliaut up around her waist, lifted her chemise—

She lifted herself up as though willing her body to become one with his. Her mind screamed, *Hurry, Aimery, Hurry!*

The spell was broken. The fever raging in her blood subsided. She pushed him away. His possessing lips set her free, but he still held her close.

His hands tightened on her bared waist, but she shook her head. She pushed away from him and his arms fell to his sides. She took long shuddering breaths, groping blindly for her cloak.

Erik reached to the floor and picked it up. "Here you are." His low voice caressed her. She looked up at him as he settled the cloak around her shoulders.

"I—I must go."

"I suppose so," he agreed. "For now."

Startled, her violet eyes flew open and she stared at him. "Not just for now," she told him firmly.

Aimery's hands should do this. Aimery's hard strong body should delight her with sweet pain and shared pleasure. Her husband should be leading her down the path to ecstasy, the surer because it would last all their lives.

"Never another time," she said again, unnecessarily loudly.

Erik's face was in shadow, and she could not tell whether he was as shaken as she, except that his hand trembled slightly as he took the goblets and set them on a side table.

"You are married," he said at last. "I know this. But—just now you told me much more than that. He is no husband to you.

"You are a true woman of the north, my own country, and blood runs hottest where it is cold."

"Is that true?" she asked. She was sufficiently recovered to converse with him a bit.

He eyed her with respect, measuring her. "Next time . . ." he said with a joyous grin.

"No," she fastened her cloak, slipping her braids inside. One ribbon was loose, she noted, but she would fix that later. "I came to you to ask about my father," she reminded him. "I shall tell my mother that you do not know anything."

"That is not the truth. I shall make inquiries. I seem to remember hearing the name. Odo de Saint Florent. I shall find out." He grinned. "I'll send word. Or you can come to ask."

"I shall send my maid," she said.

"Your maid may become a toy for my men," said Erik, "and I am sure you would not wish to send her into such danger."

"You're laughing at me."

"And so I am, my darling. You will be back. You know it. Why should we fence like this? You think you will not come. But sooner or later, when your foolish husband neglects you one more time, you will remember me, remember this room, and the bliss that waits for you here. You will remember what almost bloomed between us. And you will know what will yet be."

He lifted her hand to his lips and kissed it, turning it over to kiss, lingeringly, her palm. She felt the tingle all along her arm. As though her hand were in a flame, she snatched it back.

"Sir Erik—," she began, intending to sear him with her rebuke but, meeting his kindling eyes, found she could not.

"Tomorrow night," said Erik softly. "To find out about your father."

She bit her lip and shook her head. But she could not look him directly in the eyes and refuse. She must know. And she was not sure she could keep from following along the path he was inviting her to travel.

She must leave now, must find Aimery.

She would even beg him to come back to her. Back, she thought quickly, meant back from the queen. But she would swallow her pride, for Erik was too close, and she was too vulnerable. Aimery would be her salvation.

She stood clutching her cloak at the throat, holding it together. "I must go."

But Erik was not listening. Wary as a fox, he was listening to noises far away. He heard raised voices, running feet, even the sharp clang of steel on steel.

Arrested, they both listened, heads bent.

"It sounds like fighting!" said Solange.

Erik nodded. He had changed from the soft lover to the hard soldier. "Trouble, I don't doubt, with the Sicilians. I must get you out of here."

Erik strode to the door leading to the larger barracks room, and spoke sharply in his own tongue. Question and answer, quick and staccato. Erik turned back.

"Tancred cannot control his men," said Erik contemptuously. "They are fighting in the streets, and foolishly seek to overcome my Varangians."

"What shall I do?" Solange opened her eyes wide. She must get back to her rooms.

"I must see that my men do not kill the Sicilians. I fear your good king might not like bloodshed in his streets. But I will get you home safely."

"Bertille—"

"Oh, yes, the lady and your maid. I think it best for you to avoid the ruffians in the streets." Standing in the doorway he beckoned to Bertille and Jehane, and they sped to the inner room.

"Solange, they're fighting! How will we ever get home?" Bertille looked with sudden interest at Erik. "But I think we'll be safe in your hands!" Her dimples appeared, as Erik eyed her with amusement.

"I think," he interrupted, "that you ladies must get back to the castle as best you can. I'll send Viktor with you, but you must hurry."

"What is it, an invasion?" Bertille cried.

"No, my lady," said Erik, "Tancred's Sicilians have been foolish enough to tackle my Varangians in the streets. A trifle, but I must see to it." His eyes laughed at Solange in the firelight. "Too much wine."

She jerked, startled. But Bertille had noticed nothing. Erik led Bertille and Jehane to the far wall of the inner room. Sweeping aside the tapestry that hung there, he opened a hidden door.

Jehane went through first. Bertille, with a muffled exclamation, went gingerly after her. Solange could see in the starlight a tall figure with helmet and shield, sword at the ready.

"Viktor," identified Erik in a murmur. "He will see you safely back." He paused, looking down into Solange's shadowed face. "My secret door comes in handy, you see. To get you safely away from the fighting. Or," his voice dropped, "to let you in. Mark it well, for you will have need of it."

"Never," she said flatly.

"I see the Norns have turned my fate over to the future. But Skuld, then, will not fail me," said Erik.

"Skuld?" Mystified, she stopped short.

"The goddess of the future."

She shuddered. "You're no Christian!" she exclaimed under her breath.

"A Christian, yes. But my father was not, and the old ways of speech die hard."

She eyed him warily. To have dealings with pagans was forbidden, but he said he was a Christian. An untamed one, at all events. His hand under her elbow urged her into the street, and the door closed silently behind her. She was alone with Bertille and Jehane, and the enormous treelike column of armor that answered to the name of Viktor.

She followed Bertille and Jehane, hustling after the tall Varangian guard toward the castle. She could still hear Erik's chuckle as he closed the secret door behind them.

There was fighting in the streets, but she was hardly aware of it. Led by Viktor along the lane toward the bridge over the moat, they were sufficiently remote from the fighting save for one time when a sudden explosion of milling men staggered nearly to her feet. In that moment she recognized one of the men, and he was not a Sicilian. Baldwin, his face shining with an unholy light, sprawled full-length at her feet. Then, heedless of anyone around him, he sprang up from the ground and with savage pleasure raised his mace and waded into the knot of fighting men.

Viktor hurried them on and she saw no more fighting.

Erik was sure she would return to him. She would not. Fixing her thoughts on her husband, as a wanderer watches the star of the north, she stumbled after Bertille until they were safely inside the castle walls and Viktor had left them.

15

The sudden eruption of violence the night before went almost unremarked the next day. It was ignored, as though it had been only another skirmish of the same kind that poured nightly out of the taverns.

Solange had slept little that night. Aimery's even, calm breathing beside her had not stilled her own thoughts. No matter how much her mother importuned her, she would not go to Erik again. She would send Jehane, or Brother Garin.

She stood now, in late afternoon of the next day, at the narrow window, looking down over the gray roofs of the castle, to the barracks. The sun was hidden by leaden clouds, for the weather was turning gloomy again, and the promise of new snow hung heavily in the air.

The narrow slits of windows in the tower where Solange lodged let in only the barest light even on sunlit days, and now the rooms were full of shadows.

She fancied she could see the light spilling from the open door of the barracks onto the snow, and, without her bidding, her memory took her through that inner door to Erik's chamber. What had come over her?

All through the day her mind warred. She must tell her mother that there was a possibility of news of Odo de St. Florent. But she dreaded her mother's penetrating glance.

Further, she knew she could not take the chance of overlooking what might be real news.

Shaking off her growing depression, she went into the outer room to give Jehane instructions. "When my lord comes, tell him I have gone to find my mother."

"My lord," said Jehane, "is with the queen—I mean with the king, lady."

"I did not ask you where he was," said Solange icily, "and I advise you to watch your tongue."

Jehane dropped her eyes submissively, but not before Solange detected a knowing gleam. Solange hesitated, the words of dismissal ready. But the spark gave her pause. How much had the girl guessed about the incident in the Varangian barracks? It had been a mistake to take her along. But that was past mending now.

Solange hurried along the corridors to the rooms of the de Mowbrais. Solange and Aimery were lodged closer to the court these days—thanks to Queen Eleanor, no doubt.

She found Petronilla huddled before a small fire. Her hands were tucked into the long cuffed sleeves that Eleanor had made fashionable. She scarcely looked up when Solange entered.

"What's this, Mother?" exclaimed Solange. "It's cold as Norway in here!"

Hurriedly she built up the fire. "Mehun keeps enough wood for you, I'll say that for him."

"He likes his comfort," said his wife tonelessly. Then, rousing in response to Solange's activity, she said, "Where have you been? You act as though you had done something you shouldn't. I know the signs."

Solange felt a cold chill. Turning slowly, she realized that her mother was not possessed of secret knowledge, only a recollection of years past, when Solange was a child.

"I've been doing what you asked of me," said Solange soothingly, covering the shock she felt at the change in her mother's appearance. Shock—and guilt. For if it had not been for Solange's insistence that her father lived, Petronilla would not be prey to devastating doubt, and a conviction of sin.

"What did Erik say?"

"He says he thinks he knows something of him."

"Not much, is it?"

"Something, though. He will let us know."

"You believe him? Does he know anything?"

Solange thought. He had seemed sincere. But had it been only to keep her there in his room?

"I don't know," she said slowly. "But it's a chance. And we didn't have that before."

"Don't tell Mehun," begged her mother.

"You fear him." It was a statement.

Petronilla nodded. "It is best he does not know. Best for Erik."

"Erik can take care of himself," said Solange dryly, and then, seeing fear leaping in the blue eyes, she promised. "I won't tell him."

"I wish," grumbled Petronilla, "this journey would get started. I never could stand waiting much."

"I don't like it either," said Solange, "but the king must make up his mind, and the supplies and money take time. I heard that Abbot Suger does not like the whole idea. He says that the king will do better to stay and care for the kingdom that God has left in his care," said Solange, repeating the gossip she had heard. "But the king will not admit that as God's will."

"I care not what the king says," Petronilla roused herself to retort. "He has so little judgment that I set no store by what he does."

"Dear Mother," said Solange. "Can you not stay here, and wait for me to send word of the news I find in the Holy Land?"

"No." Petronilla's pretty face wore an abstract look. "You don't understand, child. My marriage, such as it was, is over. Mehun has the land, and as long as I live there will be no question of his keeping it. He is trying to get the king to confirm him in the fief, but the king never has time for Mehun. So Mehun has it in his mind to follow the king and keep after him until, in sheer weariness, he allows Mehun to do homage for Belvent."

"Aren't you afraid of the journey?"

"No. For if I die on the way, I die with my face toward Jerusalem, seeking absolution. It is all I can do."

"Mother, you won't die! I won't let you!" cried Solange, her heart rent by her mother's quiet resignation.

Her mother spoke as though she hadn't heard Solange. "I think it likely that I shall die on the way, child. I shall take my store of medicines and perhaps, in good deeds, I can serve God in one way as well as any other."

"Mother!" Solange put her arms around her mother. After a moment, Petronilla returned the embrace. They stood thus, together, when Aimery came to find his wife.

He burst in, as though he had not enough time to do all he must. He greeted Petronilla briefly and turned to Solange.

"The king wishes us to sit near him at the feast tonight for the foreign emissaries. We have little time to dress."

On their way back down the hall to their rooms, Aimery's stride was too fast for her. She slipped her hand through the crook in his arm to hold him back. He slowed his pace at once to match her slower step. The feel of his hard muscle under her hand sent shivers running through her. She caught her breath.

Didn't Aimery feel anything for her? Had that dreadful start to their wedded life destroyed his desire for her? If only they could start over, she would be everything her husband wanted.

She tightened her fingers convulsively. Startled, he looked at her in surprise, but she had turned away and did not see his expression. Hesitating a moment, he placed his hand over hers, drawing her closer to his side. Thus together, they regained their rooms.

Jehane had, to regain favor in her mistress's eyes, laid out Solange's attire for the evening. The bliaut was the one she had worn at her wedding, but there was a new pelisson. This was of figured silk, lavender and silver, the fabric brought from the Champagne fair, so the seamstress had told her. The silver threads in the cloth flickered in the firelight. On the floor beside the chest were small boots of gilded leather.

The wooden bath was drawn up to the fire and as Solange entered, Jehane poured hot water into it and put another log on the fire. She set a screen around the tub to hold in the heat, and Solange slid into the welcome warm water. The soap was fragrant with meadowsweet. Even after she had rinsed it off, she lingered long in the water, reluctant to lift herself out into the cold. But she must. She stood up in the tub, water streaming down over her slim thighs.

"Jehane!" she called. "I'm ready."

"Are you?" The voice was Aimery's. He stepped around the screen, holding the warming sheet. Before she knew it, he had wrapped her in it, lifted her from the water, and was holding her closely.

"Aimery, Jehane will come."

"I sent her on an errand," he said.

A rush of gladness swept over her. Here was where she belonged, with her true love holding her, teasing her with little nibbling kisses on her ear lobe, on her cheek, down her throat.

"You changed your mind?" he said, gently, ceasing his kisses and looking into her eyes. He set her on her feet. "You took my arm there, in the hall, as though you were glad to be with me. As though—as though you really wanted me. Is it true?"

At last it had happened. Aimery was her own true husband, and her world was set aright again. Her skin tingled, her happiness bubbled almost from her toes as she moved against him. "Yes, yes!" she whispered breathlessly with anticipation. "Oh, Aimery! Yes, please!"

His arms tightened around her, heedless of the dripping towel, and his kisses moved from her lips, to the little hollow in her shoulder, murmuring little sounds that she understood without knowing how.

Far off, a gong sounded, and Aimery cursed. "We've not more than a few moments. I must let you go." He did not move to release her.

She stirred. "We must not be late," she whispered.

"Already too late," he said, kissing her earlobe. "But after the banquet . . ." He smiled, his eyes promising everything she dreamed of.

She smiled back, the towel dropped to her waist, and she reached for the white linen tunic. Suddenly glancing up, she saw his unwavering eyes watching her, feasting like a starveling upon her naked body.

"Later," she promised, eyes dancing. "But not too much later."

16

The banquet went past her in an interminable blur. She could not have told what there was to eat, nor what filled her goblet of which she drank very sparingly.

For once, she thought with gratitude, all was right in her world. The sun shone, right here inside the great hall. Even the queen could not upset her anymore.

She was conscious only of Aimery beside her. Aimery's promise set music playing in her mind.

Down the table sat Conon d'Yves. After one glance at her, he frowned into his trencher and didn't look her way again. She suspected that happiness must be plain on her face, and she resolved to be more discreet. There was no need to advertise to the world that her husband had turned to her at last.

Her mother caught her eye, as the servitors brought in a great roast boar. Petronilla's gaze was hooded, warning. Against Mehun? His face, as he turned to speak to his wife, wore an inscrutable expression. Solange paid it no heed.

Once she looked up to see the queen's eyes on her, full of speculation. Tearing her glance away, she caught Erik's stare—amused, knowing and confident. She had escaped Erik just in time. If she had consented to Erik's lovemaking, she could not now be looking forward so ecstatically to this night with Aimery.

What might have been was best forgotten. With Aimery's love all hers, she could laugh at Erik's glance, intimate even across the trestle table. But she laughed inwardly, not wishing to hurt his feelings. Instead, she summoned a sunny smile to show him there were no hard feelings between them.

The speeches began. Tancred, whose men sported bruises and cuts, spoke first, extolling once again the sea route to Antioch. Then Erik told of the luxuries and warm welcome to be found in Byzantium.

The banquet, unending as it seemed, came to an abrupt halt. Benches scraped back, a babble of voices rose like a tide, and she turned to Aimery. He wasn't beside her. Searching for him, she found him at Queen Eleanor's side. The queen was talking earnestly to him. His back was toward Solange, so she could not see whether he wore again the look of infatuation she knew so well.

Tasting the sourness of renewed doubt, she turned away, nearly stumbling over the bench. Erik gave her one inscrutable glance before he turned away to Countess Alis and, smiling, moved away.

Aimery caught up with her before she left the room. "Wait, Solange. I will be with you in a little while," he said, hurriedly. "There is something the king needs me for."

"But I thought we—"

"Yes, yes, I know." He brushed past her objection, either because he felt guilty over delaying their time together or to hurry back to the king. "But something has come up. Tancred has some new word from King Roger, and he wishes to discuss it with the council."

"Tancred? But what of the Varangian?" She dared not utter the man's name, lest her voice reveal her emotions.

"Him?" Aimery looked surprised. "He has nothing to do with this. He had given the king the message he came with, and that's an end of it."

She knew people were eddying around the two of them, halted inconveniently in the doorway of the hall. But though she was aware of the curious glances turned their way, she did not care.

"Come, Solange," said Aimery with a touch of impatience. "I must hurry to the council chamber or I shall be late."

"The council? And I suppose that means the queen?"

Something flickered behind Aimery's dark gray eyes, and was gone. "Sometimes the queen sits with the council. But that makes no difference."

"I suppose not," said Solange, lifting her chin. She knew she was making a stir over nothing. Aimery loved her, and he would hurry to her as soon as he could. They had the rest of their lives together. "All right, Aimery. But hurry."

"I'll break away. In less than an hour by the steeple bell, I'll be with you." He searched her angry face. "Believe me for once. I do not make promises lightly."

She melted under his beseeching eyes. "All right," she said, adding with mock severity, "one hour by steeple bell. I warn you, my patience is not endless."

Singing to herself, she hurried back to the tower. Through the shutters she heard the church bell ring as soon as she came into their room. She had one full hour to wait, until the bell should ring again.

It rang again . . . and again . . . and still Aimery did not come. Yet another hour the bell signaled. The fire sank to embers, and still Solange sat alone, the knobby back of the chair cutting into her flesh.

The wait for Aimery was the longest period of time she had ever known. She had too long to think. She knew the queen was sitting in council with the king and the barons. Perhaps the council meeting had broken up, and Aimery and the queen were left, together.

Her imagination showed her much more than she wished to think about. The queen and her Court of Love, so beloved by the troubadours, and beginning to hold fast more and more of the knights of the realm as well as the ladies, did not believe in married love. A knight's highest love belonged to a lady who would never allow him to touch her.

But Aimery was too robust a man to be satisfied with a love like that. She had believed this all along, and tonight, seeing desire hot in his eyes, she believed that she had won him. But now he had deserted her. For the queen.

The window was slightly ajar. Faintly there came to her the throaty laugh she knew well: the queen was amused by something. And Solange had a strong feeling it was not council business.

But he didn't come. Once more the bell in the tower rang the hour, marking the passage of time, marking the progress, so the priest often reminded them, of all souls toward that great day when all hearts would be opened.

And Aimery's heart would show an image of the queen. The queen on her throne inside Aimery's heart, while his dutiful wife waited until her master had need of a hand-maiden on which to ease his masculine needs.

When Aimery finally decided he needed her, Solange would not be waiting.

The queen had won again. A word from her and Aimery stayed away from his wife. Broke his promise to return to Solange. His desire for her was a thing of the moment, no more. Titillated by the sight of her undressed, his man-hood had been stirred.

The queen, by a word, could dampen that ardor, quench it with a laugh perhaps, or even slake it herself.

Chilled to the bone, and stiff from sitting so long, Solange got to her feet and crossed to the window. Opening the wooden shutters, she looked out upon the sleeping city. Faint light below attested to the fact that the queen was not asleep.

Beyond the great keep, below her, was the area of the barracks. She could see the building, dark against the new snow, where the Varangians stayed. She had come behind the building, through that narrow way, using the small gate.

As she had come, so could she go.

Thankful that she had long since dismissed Jehane to bed, she found an old cloak, a cast-off one of the girls had given her when Aimery had brought her to Alis. She held it in her hands, looking at it as though she had not seen it before. Quickly, she put it on. She drew the hood close to her cheeks and held it tight at her throat with one hand.

Quickly, before she could change her mind, she closed the shutters and left the room.

It was like sleepwalking, she thought, or like a particularly vivid dream. She passed through areas she knew. She was aware of cold beneath her thin leather boots, of the moonlight upon the snow, the chill wind upon her face.

She came to an abrupt awakening when she entered the narrow path between the barracks and the outer wall. A figure loomed at the far end. She gave a faint cry. She stood rooted to the ground as the menacing figure in armor, sword in hand, visor closed, came toward her.

It was Viktor. He recognized her first and put up his helm. He motioned to her and led the way. Obediently, she followed. He rapped on the secret door, and when it was opened, gestured her inside. The door closed behind her, and she was alone with Erik.

He showed no surprise or, to give him credit, any triumph either. "How brave you are," he murmured, taking her hand. "And how cold!"

He led her to the roaring fire. "I have gotten used to heat," he said, half apologetically. "In Byzantium—ah, but you will see how it is."

Talking continuously, he slipped the hood back from her face. He did not try to kiss her. He patted her cold cheek. Drawing a chair nearer the fire, he gently pressed her into it. Judging rightly that she scarcely knew what she was doing, he fell silent.

He brought her a drink. "Here, this will take the chill off." She took it in nerveless hands. He built up the fire, and brought great fur rugs, made of Russian wolf pelts, and spread them on the floor before the fire. Kneeling before her he pulled off her boots, and gently rubbed her feet until they felt warm.

Sitting back on his heels, he caught her intense gaze. "I don't remember," he said, "that the Norns had eyes of amethyst."

"So?" she said.

"Aha, you are returning to life. You were icy to my touch, cold as our frozen homeland. I truly believe you are my own Fate. Daughter of the Norns, you are, sent me for my—salvation."

He got to his feet and took the empty goblet from her hands. He took her cloak from her, and the gold belt. The violet bliaut was pulled deftly over her head, the movement bringing her so close to Erik that she could feel his woolen tunic, thick and warm through her linen chemise. Her silver pelisson slid away from her hips, and Erik's hands stroked downward from her waist, gently, possessively.

She thought vaguely, I stayed dressed for Aimery. His hands should be doing this.

But Aimery was with the queen. And she was here.

He drew her to him, and she could feel the hardness of his leather chausses. Then, suddenly, the leather was between them no more.

She was, she noted with mild surprise, on a deeply furred rug before a fire. She did not remember when the last of her clothing and Erik's had vanished. Fur was soft against her back, fingers played delicately on her. Lips kissed lightly. Just before she thought she would die of bliss, he fitted himself to her.

If she longed for Aimery, the rest of that deliciously prolonged night, she would never tell.

Book Four
The Journey,
1147

1

Winter, as winters do, waned, fading under the bursting vigor of the delayed spring. The only difference the change in the season made to Solange was that the back lane behind the barracks was paved, not with snow, but first with icy slush and then deep mud.

The estrangement between Solange and Aimery was complete. Safely back in her room, much later on the night of his broken promise, she had fallen asleep at once and did not heed his explanation that the queen and the others had conferred on supplies for the Crusade until dawn.

Intent on her own emotions, she paid little heed to his. She was happy, for the first time she could remember. She hummed to herself, silly little snatches of long-forgotten songs.

Aimery, who was stormier than ever these days, came to their rooms one day when she was not expecting him. He found her sewing on a new braid-holder, a smile on her lips.

"I am glad you are recovered," he said, watching her with a queer hungry look in his eyes, "from your disappointment over my broken promise."

"Well," she said generously, "one must attend the queen, after all. I cannot blame you. A knight's duty . . ."

"There's something about you," he said, puzzled by compliance where he was accustomed to fiery accusations. "As if you—"

He stopped short at the look in her eyes. She pricked her finger. Was he going to accuse her of loving Erik? Had he learned, somehow? She could not bear to have her secret ripped away and exposed to view.

"As if I what?" she repeated. Her wits scampered like rabbits pursued by a ferret, until they found safety. "Probably because I have word of my father."

"You what?" He stopped short in his pacing.

"Poor Loriot wasn't the only one who saw my father after he was supposed to have died."

"Who?"

She could not face the direct question. But she told as much of the truth as she could. "One of the Varangians believes he knows what happened. He will make inquiries for me."

"Better hurry then," said Aimery. "For the Varangians lead us only partway down the great river before they hurry on to Byzantium."

"How far will they go with us?" she asked, her voice faltering.

"Probably a month's travel. Long enough to ask questions about Odo, I should think. There are, after all, only fifty men in the troop."

How short a time she had left!

She had counted more than she realized on traveling with Erik through Europe, the land route, all the way to Constantinople. She knew they would have to part someday. She knew that Erik was self-centered, ambitious. He was an adventurer, a rover, as her own ancestors had been. But where Rollo, William, Harald, Godfred, Horik had searched for lands on which to settle, Erik sought only the adventure of the search itself. She was merely a piece of delightful booty he had earned by carrying the message from his emperor.

But Erik was honest enough about her appeal for him. Aimery was too complicated for her to read him as well as she could Erik. There might be much of worth in the study of her husband's character. But after that night of waiting for him, while he dallied with the queen, she considered Aimery a stretch of forbidden territory. She would not poach on the queen's property!

"Tancred has the right of it," Aimery was saying, "but the king won't listen. The queen will see to it." Aimery sat down and smiled in satisfaction. "She is very persuasive."

The moment the words were out of his mouth, he knew he had made a mistake. It was too late to retract the remark. And yet his wife only smiled sunnily and said, with pointed meaning, "Yes, she is, isn't she?"

Baffled, he left her alone, and thus did not see the sudden tears slipping down her cheeks.

The queen, it developed, had no trouble persuading her newly formed guard to trust her judgment. She was very serious in setting her standards for the guard. She drew up a document entitled "Rules of Decorum," and read it aloud to the small inner circle she referred to as her elite guard. Solange, surprisingly, was among this number.

The queen's attitude toward Solange had altered. She spoke most kindly to her, and Solange felt the change meant only one thing. The queen had shackled Aimery to herself with such strong bonds that Solange was no longer any threat to her.

The queen now wished Solange to attend her daily, and sought her opinion on which salves to take, how much pot rouge, what would be the simplest way to wear one's hair.

"For you must know," said Eleanor, "that a great many people set store by your ideas, as I do. Such an unusual kind of beauty you have. Your hair is much lighter than mine, and your skin is a trifle too pale, but then, one cannot help these imperfections, can one? It is too bad that the dictates of beauty require dark eyes, and not that very unusual shade yours are."

But Eleanor's barbs, even under the guise of friendly intimacy, could no longer hurt Solange. She let them slip away unheeded. Not so, Countess Alis. She eyed her sister-in-law with mistrust. "Mark my words, Solange, that woman is not to be trusted. She has led her husband a merry dance, and there will be trouble in that direction before too long. There is no heir, you see, and it took Abbot Bernard's intervention with God to bring that tiny Marie to birth. Now, it looks to me as though the opportunity to produce an heir is passing by."

If the queen shared Louis's bed, it was a well-kept secret in a court that had no secrets.

Bertille's wedding would take place in a few days. She had finally made up her mind, saying farewell with lingering sighs to Guy and to Hugh. Jean de Loches had won out over his rivals, and stalked about wearing a slightly dazed grin at his good fortune.

"Because you and Aimery are so happy together," said Bertille. "I thought at first you wouldn't be, but just lately there is such a bloom on you that I hope a little of it will rub off on me. Besides," she added with a sudden descent to practicality, "Jean dotes on me."

"That is plain enough," said Solange with a laugh. "I swear he does not know where his feet are. He put them on my skirt yesterday, while he talked about how wonderful you are, and left great muddy tracks on my best silk!"

Bertille laughed. "Now I will go with the queen's guard, with you and Catherine, and we'll never be parted at all!"

A shadow fell upon them, where they sat in the window sewing—at least Solange and Catherine were sewing. Bertille held a needle in one hand and her work in the other. The shadow was gone quickly, as the cloud passed by the sun. "I will not let an omen frighten me," she said stoutly. "My old nurse would say—"

"And mine too," said Catherine swiftly. "And who could expect more from them? Fortunately, we know that God has blessed this Crusade—so Abbot Bernard tells us—and we travel under his banner."

"That's right," said Bertille, smiling again. "I wonder what the queen wants us to wear on the road. I tried to bribe one of her seamstresses to show me a sample, but it was no use!"

"The queen," said Catherine, "is very serious about this Crusade. She wants all to be just right."

The costumes were only part of it. The Queen borrowed the king's seneschal, who drilled the guard in the proper care of horses and weapons.

"The short sword is your valuable hand-to-hand weapon. You hold it *so!*" He demonstrated with a quick, fierce, downward thrust. A faint scream from Lady Saldebreuil was the only response. He looked over his class with scarcely hidden amusement.

The queen intervened. "I think, Seneschal, that the ladies have had enough instruction for the day. Leave us now to practice what you have taught us so well."

Bowing, he took his leave. The queen said, "Now, Alicia, such a fuss over what is really nothing. You do not suppose we will have to fight the pagans?"

A murmur rippled across her assembled guard. "But it is a dangerous journey," objected one.

"If we have to carry weapons, I'm not going," said an unidentified voice, under cover of the crowd.

"Nonsense!" said the Queen sharply. "It is no more than some of us use to hold off unwanted caresses." Her eyes fell upon Solange. Did the queen refer to Solange and Baldwin?

Or did she refer to that first night of her marriage to Aimery? If so, then no one but Aimery could have told her.

Later, cozily warm in Erik's room, she amused him by narrating the events of the day.

His heavy wooden chair was drawn up to the fire, but she chose rather to sit on the floor, the furs spread wide to cushion her against the bare wood. Leaning her back against the chair, she toyed with the goblet in her hands.

"Yet it seems to me," she said musingly, "that we are not ready for the trip. Not if we are to go as a true army."

"So," he said, eyes glittering, "the ladies balk at using knives? I laugh! What will they do when the pagan hordes rush at them with scimitars raised? Oh no, a knife is too fierce a weapon for a lady to use!"

She roused, struck by the scorn in his voice. "I doubt not that such an occasion would wash away any scruples."

"It's a harebrained scheme! A horde of women on the march over hundreds of miles. It's a hard journey, over mountain passes, through rugged country."

"You think we should not go?"

"Not delicate, fainthearted women. They have no business on the road."

"Nonetheless," she said quietly. "I am going."

"Of course you are!" He dropped to his knees beside her. "I cannot let you go out of my life."

"Not so soon, at any rate," she said with wry humor. She took another sip of the powerful wine. She was strangely unsettled, thinking long thoughts about the future.

A future without Erik would be cold indeed. But a future without Aimery was no future at all.

The note in her voice alerted him. He gathered her in his arms. "Fainthearted, I said," he reminded her. "There is nothing fainthearted about you, my darling. I wonder how it is you are brave enough to come here as you do. How do you manage?"

"No one cares where I go," she said frankly. "So I make no excuses."

He kissed her, lingeringly, before he let her go.

"A dangerous journey?" she bantered. "When you have assured the council it is safe?"

"Comparatively," he grinned. "Compared to crossing the sea in those peapods the Sicilians call boats!"

She was still thinking about the queen's guard. She must get to Antioch. And if the queen's guard did not make the journey . . .

"If I had you in *my* keeping," Erik murmured in her ear, "I would carry you safely through anything."

"You will lead the Crusade to Byzantium?"

"Only part of the way."

"Then we can be together a little longer," she said. "The court goes to Vezelay next week."

Erik studied her for a moment. "Drink the rest of your wine," he advised her. He stretched out on the floor, his head in her lap.

"You seek to overturn my defenses?" she laughed lightly. "I have become inured to your wine."

"Wait until you taste the potent drink we have in Constantinople," he warned her lazily. "Besides, I didn't know you had defenses against me."

He reached up to slide her gold braid-holders off her long plaited hair. He toyed with the ends of the hair until she set the empty goblet down with a tiny click of finality.

Then, burrowing his head more deeply into her lap, he reached up to unfasten her girdle. "The bailey wall. Your first defense, and I have breached it, you see." He tossed the gold mesh into the shadows.

Sliding the silk of her bliaut from under his head, he pushed it up as far as her waist. He pillowed his face against her thighs again, and began to rain kisses here and there, nuzzling under the folds of the feathery silk tunic. Through her chemise she could feel the prickling of his short-cropped blond hair, the warm moistness of his open lips upon her.

"This inner ward resists me," he said at last, smoothing the damp linen. "But not for long, my Viking princess. Will you cede me the donjon,"—he raised himself on an elbow and looked deeply into her eyes—"or must I take it by storm?"

"You well know the way into the keep, sir," she said with a demure twinkle, "and your vassal is not moonstruck enough to resist."

With both hands she lifted her chemise over her head, and let it fall unheeded behind her.

2

Lent was over. The May flowers bloomed and died away. The birds nested in the trees outside the town of Vezelay, and still the court lingered.

Abbot Bernard had come in triumph back from the Germans. He had persuaded Emperor Conrad to take the cross, overcoming Conrad's well-known lethargy and the suspicions of his barons, who mistrusted all things Greek. He had left Brother Garin to keep Conrad's purpose hot.

The preaching of Bernard breathed new life into the king's council and, suddenly, like a wave rippling ripe grain, the barons and the king were in a fever to depart, to take the first steps of the uncounted millions of steps ahead of them.

The queen too entered into the tumult of last-minute planning. Never enough time to drill, she complained. The leatherworkers going mad—all this, Solange reflected, seemed too petty to be a part of this great magnificent Crusade for the greater glory of God.

Judging by her own motives, she wondered how many of the hundreds wearing the cross on their breasts had God in their minds.

Certainly an inordinate amount of time was taken up by packing clothes, and unpacking again to take out and replace them with new garments. Boxes of creams against the hot sun. Cleansing lotions to take away the dust of the road. Veils to shield delicate complexions.

Lutes to beguile the long, leisured evenings. Rolls of poems, of songs, writing material.

Jewelry. How much was appropriate on a journey of holy purpose? The pope said none. The queen answered flatly, "Take all you can. In case of emergency, a diamond is worth more for its size than all else."

The day of departure was set for June fourteenth. At the king's insistence, the queen's guard was to display their accomplishments to the entire court.

The queen's anterooms were barred to all but the ladies of the guard and their maids. The excitement rose, urged on by the twittering maids and the scolding ladies. Solange allowed Jehane to dress her without comment. Her thoughts dwelt on Erik's prophecies. Were these noblewomen, the fairest the kingdom could produce, with all the advantages of birth and education, simply not fit to undertake a journey of this magnitude? She did not agree with Erik. She herself would make it to Antioch, God willing, no matter how hard the journey.

Suddenly, she was aware that the laughing, chattering women had one by one fallen silent. They were looking at each other in dismay.

The queen had wished to give her army the appearance of true soldiers marching their way across the land to fight for the Savior's city. But, being the queen, she could not envision her ladies—or herself—in armor of chain-link mail, or in visors. Eleanor was too conscious of her own beauty to permit such a sacrifice.

The costume she had devised for them was a compromise. The close-fitting white tunic carried the bold red cross on the front and the back. On one sleeve had been sewed the curious embroidered device that identified the queen's army. The tunic was gathered in at the waist by a belt of leather, broad enough to ensure that the wearer sat upright in the saddle.

The belt carried only a short dagger. The Queen had decided, apparently, against arming her ladies too formidably.

But the boots were the spectacular item, vivid red leather up to the knee, where the turned-over cuff, flaring widely, displayed a bright yellow.

The tunic, for ease in riding, was slit on either side to the hip. It was only incidental, so the queen said, that the slit revealed the tight-fitting hose, outlining rounded thighs in a most seductive manner.

Bertille said, innocently enough, "I do think I look fine in this. I think we may well set a new fashion!"

Finally Marguerite de Rehan, a kinswoman of Eleanor's, spoke. "I had no idea we would look so shocking. I've seen whores stoned off the streets wearing more seemly clothes than these."

"Making us look," said Petronilla, "like what we are, or will be, before the journey is done."

Petronilla was now a full member of the queen's guard. She believed in the remission of sins as promised by Abbot Bernard.

Her words struck Solange with the force of a revelation. If the queen's guard appeared to be a collection of women of loose morals, it was no more than the truth in many cases. The queen herself devoured devotion like a succubus, draining the men who offered it and casting them off.

Petronilla would find herself a bigamist if Odo lived.

Solange herself, respectably wed to Aimery, spent as many nights as possible in Erik's embrace.

Her lips twisted. Now, looking down at her rounded scarlet thighs, her garb aping the dress of the streetwoman, she was dressed as the world would see her—without morals, without reputation. Worse, she knew that Erik's love would not last forever. But at least it existed for now. And without it she had nothing.

Petronilla whispered at her left hand. "Pluck up, child. Look cheerful. Do you want the queen to know you disapprove of her choice?"

Solange straightened her shoulders. Just then the silver trumpets sounded, and the Queen moved out at the head of the two hundred ladies of her guard. All were mounted on silver housing, on the finest palfreys the kingdom could afford. The May sun struck sparks from the steel weapons and silver harnesses.

The costumes struck sparks of astonishment from the spectators—astonishment that turned quickly to disapproval. Even the king frowned as he spoke to his wife. Solange was not close enough to hear the exchange but Eleanor soon wore the secret triumphant smile that told she had won, once again.

The king scowled, but the reaction of some of the other men was more obvious. Count Robert was frankly agape. He usually gave the impression of great good humor, but not at this moment. Now his chubby face wore a scowl that transformed him.

"Good God, Louis, you're not going to let her get away with that?" he ejaculated. "It's indecent. That woman—"

The king turned quietly to him, and Robert came to himself. "I mean . . . the queen wishes the journey to pass without incident, is it not so? This is why she wanted all the ladies to be married, or so I thought. But if we have no trouble on the journey, it is not because they didn't ask for it!"

He turned and stomped away, making no secret of his disgust. Others frowned, too. But not Jean de Loches, Solange saw with surprise. His intended bride bounced up to him, pirouetting in her costume for his benefit, and still he wore that fatuous grin. Surely Bertille would be able to do what she wanted with that man!

Erik the Norseman stood a little aloof, as befitted his role as spectator. A woman's figure was not strange to him, much as it seemed to be to the Franks. Had they never seen a female form before? And then he realized what he should have guessed in the beginning. It was the husbands of the guard who objected. Take Aimery, for instance. He doubted not that Solange was going to hear something from that ferocious frown.

Solange scurried to her room, aware of the glances that

followed the women as they separated, each to bear whatever remarks her husband might deliver. Aimery cared so little for her that she doubted if he noticed. The queen wore the same garb—slit perhaps even a little higher. Eleanor's figure was shown off to great advantage. Aimery would have had eyes for none but his queen.

She unbuckled the girdle as she came through the door. It was a relief, and she dropped it on the chest just inside the door.

"Jehane!" she cried as she came through the door. And then she saw Aimery. He was waiting for her.

"I don't wonder that you want to get out of that—that harlot's outfit. What on earth possessed you to agree to that?" He was white with anger.

"It seems to me you have it wrong!" she retorted, stung by his attack. "I was not *asked* to agree to wear it. I was *told* I must wear it."

"And you didn't refuse?"

"Nor," she pointed out, "did any other lady refuse."

"You will not wear that costume in public again. I forbid it."

"Forbid it? Why do you not start with the queen? Forbid her to wear such a costume in public? Or perhaps it doesn't offend you so much on her, being perhaps more modestly clothed than—" She stopped short at his forbidding frown. She had gone too far.

She would not apologize. He had much to ask her forgiveness for, and until his debt was paid, she would say what she pleased. And do what she pleased.

"You know not what you are saying," said Aimery in a heavy, suddenly lifeless voice. "But I do not wish my wife —and you are my wife, no matter how you feel—to look like a harlot in public."

An imp she did not recognize took possession of her. "You forbid your queen's ideas? I wonder what her Majesty would say when she learns that one of her vassals has defected."

She danced lightly toward Aimery in her red boots, the slit of her tunic opening provocatively. "Or maybe it is your queen who is the harlot, and this costume suits her very well."

She set her red-shod foot upon the stool, the red pantaloons provocatively tight on her thigh.

He reached out, palm flat, ready to strike her. She retreated hastily. But her imp was not so easily daunted. "You wish the costume out of your sight. I think, *husband*, I understand your meaning now. I do not understand how I could be so mistaken. Your desire for me never stops, does it? Or perhaps I should say, it hasn't started yet? Which is it, Sieur Aimery?"

She stood defiantly before him, her feet apart. She stooped swiftly to take off her red boots. The stone floor was cold against her wool-covered feet. She advanced toward Aimery until she was almost close enough to touch him. "You do not answer me?"

He stared at his wife, a creature, so it seemed, he had never seen before. Whence had she come by this delightful tantalizing way she had? Was she truly offering him herself, forgiving his broken promise, which he had regretted since that night with every breath he had drawn?

With a swooping movement, like a bird, she pulled her tunic over her head and stood naked to the waist before him. She challenged him with her eyes. Apologize to me. One word, Aimery, just one word! One word, and I'll forget everything except that you are my husband, and I belong to you.

The word didn't come. "The tunic is out of your sight now. Satisfied? Shall I take off my pantaloons for you, Aimery? Or will the queen call?"

He made a gesture, furious, but strangely appealing. He laughed mockingly. "You don't need a knife to protect yourself any more. Your tongue is sharp enough to deal a fatal blow."

He turned and stumbled toward the door. She stood, unable to move, watching him through the door, wincing when he slammed it.

3

The king removed his council and his household from Vezelay to Paris. It was one more step on the journey to the Holy Land, though just now they traveled in the opposite direction.

King Louis's plan was to turn over his realm to deputies whom he would appoint and the barons approve. This would be done in Paris. Then the party would proceed to Metz on the Moselle River, from which city the Crusade would officially set forth.

Brother Garin returned from Metz, bearing exhortations to the king from Abbot Bernard. "I'm going back, of course," said Garin to his brother. "He has asked me to accompany the Emperor Conrad, whose resolution he is not certain about."

"And you are to keep Conrad up to the mark?" Aimery queried, lifting his eyebrows. "How will you do that? The emperor of the Germans surely will not fear one Templar."

Brother Garin looked swiftly around him. "Keep your voice down," he ordered. "I have taken the vows, yes. But Bernard is sending me to Jerusalem with—certain instructions for the Grand Master. And he prefers I go as a simple monk. As of course," he added, virtuously, "I am."

"There is something secret going on, I suppose. But perhaps you will tell me one day, perhaps when we meet in Jerusalem?" said Aimery.

"There is something," Garin assured him serenely, "although I do not know myself what it is."

Aimery and Solange watched Garin, on his way east to join the emperor, until he was out of sight. The pokey little mule with Garin astride, feet dangling nearly to the ground, made slow progress indeed.

"I had not thought I was so fond of him," mused Aimery. "But now I feel that my right arm has left me."

"But you will see him again, won't you? In Byzantium?"

suggested Solange. They stood atop the battlements of the ancient castle, and the wind from upriver Seine tossed her hair.

"Jerusalem," Aimery answered absently, his eyes fixed on the small black dot that was Brother Garin on his mule. It vanished, and Aimery turned to his wife. "If, of course, I get there."

"God willing, we will," said Solange, her own thoughts running ahead. How long would she have Erik nearby?

"Garin said Metz is almost unrecognizable," Aimery said in a conversational voice, as he led her down from the battlement.

Metz was, indeed, rapidly becoming a great storehouse of four-wheeled carts, staunch horses, sacks of grain, live chickens, ducks, geese, all ready for the start. Also, although less noticeable, were great chests of spare tents, rugs for the pavilion floors, blankets, fur-lined garments against the cold, airy sendal canopies in case it grew warm —all necessities for the queen and her guard.

Louis, however, had not lost sight of his noble purpose. There were those who scoffed at his venture, saying the king was merely dangling the lure of the East before his restless wife, hoping to beguile her into better humor with him.

But those closer to Louis remembered how he had wept as the church at Vitry burned. They knew the king needed to be shriven of his great sin. Only great atonement would be enough, or great deeds.

Louis, in preparation for his spiritual journey, visited religious houses in Paris, systematically asking blessing, and viewing—perhaps for the last time—the holy relics in every monastery and church.

The last visit was saved for the great Abbey of Saint Denis. This church possessed stained glass windows of great value, newly designed and installed. They showed, for those who could not read, the battles of the First Crusade.

Solange, as the wife of a baron of the council, was part of the retinue following the king's ceremonial visit to the abbey. She marveled at the vivid blues, purples, and scarlets in the glass, and then became entranced by the pictures themselves. The battle of Dorylaeum, the first great battle, where outnumbered Frank rallied to beat back the Turk.

The battle for Antioch, where the Queen's uncle now ruled.

There were even portraits of the great Crusaders whose names kindled a fire in the soul: Raymond of Toulouse, Godfrey de Bouillon, Bohemund.

She thought she could never weary of looking at the glass windows, the colors glowing like fire in the June sunlight.

A stir in the assembly brought her back to the present. The king was stepping forward, and now the real business of the visit was about to begin. A thick silence fell over the chapel.

The king, a humble penitent now, moved forward to the sepulcher of Saint Denis, patron of France. Prostrating himself before the sepulcher, his voice rose in quavery prayer for the success of his venture to the Holy Land. Even the scoffers fell silent before his heartwrung sincerity. Solange breathed a silent prayer of her own, "Let me find my father, whatever has happened to him. Just let me know what has become of him."

The Abbot Suger, whose church this was, escorted the king to a small golden door at the side of the altar. The crowd drew in its breath as one man, but Solange could not see what moved them.

Aimery, standing dutifully beside her, whispered, "The relics of Saint Denis are in that silver coffer. Can you see?" She shook her head, but decided it made no difference. She was not close enough to see the relics and venerate them, and the king was performing the rite on behalf of them all.

Then came the high point of the ceremony. The sacred banner of Saint Denis was brought forth. It could leave the church only in the hands of the king. This was the first time many of them had seen the banner.

On red silk, a line of birds, probably swallows, flew diagonally across the banner. The flag was attached to a gilded pike. When it was at last put into the hands of the king, the silk caught the June sunshine and it moved like a live thing.

The rest of the ceremony was short. Abbot Suger invested the king with his pilgrim's staff and the pilgrim's pouch, to symbolize the humble bearing of a pilgrim traveling to atone for his sins.

Then the king moved through the crowd and all followed him into the open air. There on the steps of the Abbey of Saint Denis, the king lifted the banner to catch the air. The crowd gave one great shout. It was a highly emotional moment, and Solange's were not the only eyes filled with tears.

The procession rode slowly, solemnly, back to the dim old palace hallowed by footsteps of Merovingian kings.

In three days, the king's Crusaders would set their faces toward Jerusalem.

The day of departure dawned. The queen's guard assembled, less self-conscious now than before. Whatever arguments had taken place over the costumes, these had not been altered.

The carts, piled high with trunks and boxes and tents, had begun moving out before daybreak.

Solange had spent her last night in Paris alone. She knew Aimery was with the king's council, going over the last-minute arrangements with Abbot Suger. The king was leaving him in charge of the finances of the expedition, and the count of Vermandois and the archbishop of Rheims would be in charge of the safety of the realm.

Countess Alis bade Solange a tearful farewell. "I'm too infirm to go on this trip," she had said all along, although Solange could see no signs of infirmity. She suspected, but was too fond of Countess Alis to say, that Alis was eager to spend some time alone on her estates, relinquishing the struggle with Eleanor for a time.

Her last words to Solange were, "Beware your enemies."

"Do you mean Conon?"

"Not necessarily. Nor Mehun de Mowbrai, although he too will bear watching. But the devil uses many tools in his work, and surely it will do no harm to be on your guard."

Solange let Jehane dress her that last morning, putting on the scarlet pantaloons, which seemed to fit more loosely than at first; the red boots, the white tunic. Jehane was coming on Crusade too, but she would ride ahead with the servitors and the baggage train.

"Are you not anxious about going, Jehane? There is still time to turn back."

"No, lady. It will be something to see the world. And perhaps pick up a husband on the way."

"Do you think we will ever come back to our own country?"

"I do not know. But I have no kin, except my sister at Belvent. She has so many children that I would just be in the way. No, lady. It is better to go where it is all new. There is nothing left here."

That was one way of looking at it, Solange decided.

The procession started out. Solange, putting aside the question of what lay ahead after she had found her father, was caught up in the color and excitement of the undertaking.

At the head of the procession rode an armed troop of knights on their palfreys, their squires leading the valuable destriers.

Behind the bodyguard rode the king, his aide bearing the standard on which fluttered the banner of Saint Denis.

His barons rode behind him and Solange caught sight of Aimery in the throng.

And then the queen's guard urged their mounts forward to clatter across the bridge, and follow in the wake of the van.

The procession was long. The bright colors marked their progress along the road, as far as one could see, the winding blue, red and gold. Even as the first riders vanished over the hills far in the distance, the last of the cavalcade were still crossing the bridge.

It seemed as though all of Christ's kingdom was on the move, marching in His name to take back the Holy Places from the defiling touch of the infidel. And all these were sinners, hoping for the grace of God to take their burdens from their immortal souls.

The queen's guard crested the far hill behind the van. It promised to be a hot day, with the late June sun on their backs. The costumes had not been designed for protection from the sun, as one or more of those near Solange remarked frequently.

The guard was protected on all sides—the barons ahead and another contingent of knights at the rear. And on the sides rode Erik's Varangians.

It was mid-afternoon before the Varangians ran into trouble. Exuberant and boastful, they seemed to believe that the queen's guard should be grateful for their protection. More and more French knights, drawn by the charm of the ladies, rode up from the rear, and inevitably jostled the Varangians. And one or two of the young French knights took exception to the overbearing Varangian escort.

Small scuffles arose between Frank and escort, and threatened to break into a full-fledged contest. Conon's voice rose over the rest, calling the French knights to desist.

Erik, hearing the scuffle from his position in the van, spurred his horse and arrived in the midst of his men. "What comes? We have barely started," he said in his northern tongue, "Not the first night yet, and already you fight with the Franks. Stupid!" Solange could follow thus far, since she had learned some of the language from Erik.

Conon said coolly, "I do not know what you are telling your men, but I trust it is to the effect that they should keep their distance from the noblewomen of the French court."

"You think your noblewomen are too good for my men? Let me tell you that nobody is too good for a Varangian. And you will remember this later, before we have gone very far."

"I will leave that question to the ladies and their husbands, but in the meantime, I think our men had best be kept apart."

"I agree," said Erik promptly. "The ladies need no escort thus far, at any rate. But I will hope that your men and mine will not travel hundreds of leagues with daggers drawn."

Conon bowed civilly, and turned to his countrymen,

speaking to them in a low voice. Erik's men galloped on ahead, and were quickly out of sight, over the ridge.

The first day's journey was short. They rode only a dozen leagues before they topped a rise and found, spread out below them, the first night's encampment. Already the pavilions were taking form, the turquoise silk of the queen's blooming in the midst of the cerise, green, and gold silk of the ladies' pavilions.

Solange realized she was more weary than she had thought, and welcomed the early stop. She was excited, rejoicing over having taken the first day's journey on the way to her father. She had dreamed of this for half a year.

4

The cavalcade soon settled into a routine of sorts. The traveling day was short, because of the women, and complaints began to rise. The women took too long to get ready in the morning, dressing and choosing jewels. The women, for the most part, had been reared in luxury. It was hard for them to abandon habit.

Mass was celebrated every morning before the day's journey began. Erik was a soldier by trade, and he deplored the lax discipline involved in moving so many people across the land.

The four-wheeled carts were so numerous that it seemed impossible that any could be left in France to serve the country! The wagons were made of heavy wooden planks, built to stand up under the ordinary usages of farm work. Built to hold hay, grain, fowl, even furniture, their makers had no conception of traveling league after league over roads that in many places were no more than dirt tracks.

The ladies' personal possessions were stowed in iron chests or wooden boxes with iron straps to hold them closed. Tucked in and around the chests on the carts were rolled-up tents, carpets, small stools, fur bedcoverings, all covered over by heavy canvas to protect against rain and sun.

Thus traveled the women of the court, with one or two carts for each lady, drawn by big-haunched draft horses straining in leather harness.

Guarding the wagons against damage or thievery, rode men-at-arms, guarding both the carts and the chamber-maids who rode with the wagons. Pope Eugenius had in-veighed against the luxury he feared might slow the Crusade—forbidding ermine and vair, jewels, personal at-tendants—yet league after league the wains, the furs, the maids, the coffers of jewels moved away from Metz, facing east toward the Holy Land, traveling in the luxury the noble pilgrims loved at home.

Scattered throughout the train, jostling for the best posi-tions, were the persons of low standing. There were smiths, armorers, miners for siege operations, pavilioners facile in pitching tents, cooks and stewards, musicians with long pipes, drums and glittering instruments. There were fletchers, surgeons, chaplains, and solemn clerks of the household of the king, with packhorses laden with rolls and boxes. For the operation of the realm must continue, even though its royal master was not at home.

Behind the wagon train came those on foot. The jails of France had been emptied, the streets of the cities had been scoured. All these took the road of the cross. Famine had struck France the winter of 1146, and the promise of the king's bounty lured many where faith might not have moved them from home.

"It was all Abbot Bernard's fault," said Conon sharply, after a long day of trying to hurry up the foot marchers. The king had charged him with guarding the rear, for this first part of the journey. "He opened the Crusade to all sinners, and they swarmed in. I wish he were here for just a day, to see how they behave."

"He would say," said Gervais calmly, "that the meanest sinner is no worse than the king, all being equal in the sight of God."

It was amazing how fast the pilgrims actually did move, no matter what Conon said. They averaged at least ten miles a day, even though many straggled in after sundown.

Some good days, where the road was wide and level and the mountains were either rising ahead of them or receding behind them, they even reached prodigies of speed that moved the cavalcade along as much as twenty miles per day.

The king made no attempt to regulate his followers. What if the Bull of Vezelay forbade falcons, hounds, rich clothing? What though the pope expressly denied the Crusaders the solace of concubines, troubadours, and personal servants? The pope was not required to convince Eleanor. And what Louis could not deny his wife, he dared not deny his followers.

Solange herself was provided, by Aimery's orders, with two servants to put up her tent, to watch her wagon against thieves, to care for her mare and the spare mount that the queen had required of her. Bagge had come from Belvent, brought especially for Solange at Petronilla's insistence. Chauve was an ill-favored villein of sturdy build and little wit. But he was a marvel with the horses.

Jehane cooked her lady's meals, cared for her clothes, and managed to flirt with every man in sight below the rank of count.

Bagge, because he and Jehane came from Belvent, tried to keep a protective eye on her. But she grumbled and told her mistress, "It's like being in jail. He watches me every place I go."

"You might be glad of it one day," said Solange, remembering the mob that had spilled out of the tavern in Bourges. "That's a rough crowd accompanying us."

"I know that," Jehane tossed her head impatiently, "but I can take care of myself."

Shortly after that, Solange became aware that Jehane had a purse full of coins that she kept hidden in the small bag where she kept her personal belongings. Gold coins? Where would she get so much money? Solange thought, with some humor, the maid is doing better than her mistress!

Bertille and her husband, Jean, seemed possessed of unnatural exuberance. Daily they rode ahead of the caravan, galloping along the road in high spirits and returning full of laughter and energy. Solange wondered where they got all that zest, for she herself was growing weary—weary of the traveling, of the constant packing up and moving on. Sometimes Antioch seemed an impossibly dim and shadowy goal.

Catherine and Henri never flagged in their devotion to each other. The ugly Henri was nearly beautiful when he looked at his wife, the devotion in his eyes so vibrant that he was transformed. Catherine grew thinner from the constant riding, but she never faltered and no word of complaint ever came to Solange's ears as they rode side by side, for miles.

Erik's fury nearly burst when the entire march was halted because a lady could not find a diamond bracelet of some value. Messengers were sent back to search without success until some one thought to check the clothes she had worn on the previous day. There it was, caught in the tight sleeve as its owner pulled off her bliaut. No one dared even speak to Erik for the rest of the day.

The first days had been beguiled by song as one group after another raised their voices in songs of praise to the God whose work they were about. But at nightfall, the court settled down to more mundane celebration. Camp was usually early, and supper was served as the sun set. Lights twinkled in the blue twilight, and around the queen's campfire were always found the best singers, the most adept lute players. Once, after they had skirted the mountains and arrived in German territory, a celebratory dance was held.

The expedition wound its way across the lesser mountains, like a long worm—its head the great laden carts drawn by slow-moving oxen, its center the brightly colored royal party of nearly a thousand, and its tail, drably dwindling away into peasants, beggars, the scum of the prisons.

The Crusaders had reached the headwaters of the Danube when harsh reality intruded for the first time.

A party of returning Crusaders were making their stumbling way up the river toward their Flemish home. They were brought before the king in their rags. The leader, a man clearly used to better things, groped shyly at his tattered shirt, trying to cover himself decently before the ladies. Half-a-dozen more stuck to the shadows.

The king was kind but he did not speak their language. He needed Erik to translate the curious *lingua franca* that was used widely in the Near East.

"You are hungry? We will give you to eat. But you must tell how it is ahead of us."

"Ahead," said the leader, "is nothing. You are from Champagne? There are others ahead of you."

"The Emperor Conrad and his followers. You did not talk to them?"

"It was worth my life to speak to them. They would have killed us."

"Not the Germans!"

"Possibly not. Your Majesty knows best. But the settlers, the villagers along the banks of the river, they are unfriendly. See this?" He pointed to a long suppurating gash running along his arm. "For nothing, they gave me this."

He spoke longer, but one thing he said Erik did not translate. Solange thought the meaning was "Beware of the Greeks." The warning was not translated for the king.

The returning Crusaders were given a place near one of the campfires, far enough away that their presence would not disturb the more delicate members of the court.

Solange sought out Erik. "Where did those men come from?"

"Jerusalem, or thereabouts. The cross on their backs means the Holy City. How are you getting on, love? This traveling in a great clutter of people every day is no good. I haven't seen you since—"

"I miss you, Erik. I wonder—would these men know about my father, do you think?"

"We'll ask. After supper. I'll come for you."

It was full dark before she heard his whistle from the shadows beyond the lines of pavilions. Cloak hiding her face, she hurried to him. He took her in his arms for a long, hungry kiss before slipping his arm around her to help her along the path. They skirted the foot of the small cliff, on what might once have been the bed of the river.

They stumbled for a long way, avoiding the light of the many fires lining the bank. Solange thought, surprised, that she had not truly realized the great number of people on the Crusade.

How many were traveling in despair under the burden of sins too heavy for them? Whose only hope lay in mortification of the flesh? How many would never return to their own homes? How many would come home in the same state as the men she was going to question now?

In the pilgrim encampment, the men lay in exhaustion around their small fire. Bidding her stay out of sight, Erik strode into their midst.

She edged forward, not wanting to miss anything. After a long conversation, and the passing of money from one hand into six, Erik returned to her side and reported.

"No word. They do not know of your father."

She sagged against him in disappointment. He led her back, out of sight of the men at the fire. Then he helped her up the hill till they stood on top of a rise.

From here, the stars shone brighter than the Crusaders' fires below along the darkly moving river. They moved away from the cliff edge, until the camps below were hidden from view. They were alone in the world. Not another soul lived, or so it seemed.

Tenderly, Erik took her cloak and spread it on the ground. He lay beside her, drawing the free edge of her mantle up to shield her from the damp grass. He brushed her pale hair back from her cheeks. "Don't cry. This is not such a disappointment as it seems. There will be many pilgrims coming home along the river. We will ask, and ask, and ask. In Byzantium, I may find out. There are people I know, and I'll have the answers when you arrive. Believe me, you will be amazed at Byzantium, there is so much to see, and I will show you the beautiful things you crave. And I will love you. You crave love, my dear."

His sudden frenzy took her by surprise. He was insistent, masterful, and his very urgency brought her to a clamoring, pounding, sobbing eagerness for release.

She responded eagerly to the caresses she knew so well. But she wished with all her heart, even now, that it was her husband here in the sweet darkness.

5

When she returned from her excursion with Erik, Aimery was waiting in their pavilion. He had been waiting for some time. He was sitting in the dark.

He made a commendable effort at control. "What do you and that Greek find to talk about till all hours?" he asked, mildly.

"Greek?" she echoed faintly, fearing he could hear the hammering of her heart.

"Erik the Varangian," he said with a sneer. "But Greek in his morals—which seem nonexistent." He lit a candle and surveyed her in its light. "As do yours."

"You know."

"Your stepfather has kindly pointed it out to me. He said he was right all along. You belong in a convent. Or wife to someone who can control you."

"Mehun meddles," she said flatly. "Why should anyone control me? I control myself."

"I have no doubt of that," said Aimery bitterly. "You lose control of your emotions only when it comes to stabbing your husband."

She said wearily, "It seems to me, Aimery, that what you allow yourself in the way of dalliance you forbid to me. What makes the queen different from Erik? A matter of royal birth? Yet Erik in his own land is as noble as she in ours." She took the candle from him, fitting it into a small silver holder.

He took a turn around the small tent. "If I didn't know you were cold, without passions, I might wonder about the Greek."

"I manage my own affairs," she said, "since you have shown me you care nothing about them. I run my own life."

"But not well," countered Aimery. "A scandal, reeking to high heaven!"

"A scandal? Yet you knew nothing of it until Mehun told you?"

She had been responding instinctively, but now that the first shock was past, she was able to think more clearly. She would not take all the blame for this marriage which was no marriage. She slipped off her cloak, sat down on the folding stool, and looked up at Aimery. "Scandal in this troop is no rarity," she said calmly. "So let us leave it at that."

"You've changed," he said, wonderingly. "You're far too free in your manner. You're too—"

"Self-sufficient?" she interrupted in a mocking tone. "You prefer the clinging kind of woman? I had not noticed. If I were to change, what would I cling *to*? My husband? Where is he?"

"Hush," Aimery commanded. "Someone will hear you."

"Who? Someone in this camp who doesn't know where *you* spend *your* time? That's impossible!"

He stiffened. "If you care to know where I spend my time, and I confess the question surprises me, I will tell you that Rainard arrived today from Pontdebois, bringing ten armed men and fifty footsoldiers, to fulfill my obligation to the king. In addition, of course, to wagons of grain and hay."

"And," suggested Solange silkily, "I suppose you have spent the evening checking supplies?"

"That's foolish," he snapped. "Rainard was exhausted. He reported to me, and I sent him to find food and a night's sleep."

Encouraged by Solange's silence, he tried to explain further, to bring her into the affairs of Pontdebois, to put an end to the estrangement between them. Once she had been interested in the affairs of his new estates, and he had hoped . . .

"Tomorrow we'll go over all the records, and see what more can be supplied," said Aimery. "We are already running low on food. The King has sent to Abbot Suger for more gold, but we'll go hungry before the funds get here."

Solange looked sidelong at him. "It has worked out well for you, hasn't it? You have the honors and fiefs you craved. Isn't that enough?"

326

"For me?" He pounded his fist into his other palm. He burst out, "Even Olivier de Nannes will have an heir!"

Solange, startled, dropped the candle. Hastily picking it up, she set it on the folding taboret with trembling hand. Olivier's heir! It was Sybille's secret, and Solange could not tell Aimery how mistaken he was. She sank to the pallet and buried her face in her hands. Finally she asked, in a low, quivering voice, "You want a son so badly?"

He stood looking down at the top of her head. Finally, resignation dulling his voice, he replied, "I saw you quail when I spoke of Sybille. Let us have no hostage between you and me."

She looked up quickly, struck by his tone. "Aimery, you mistook me. Sybille—"

"Is trapped," he said, harshly. "Don't fear that I shall ensnare you in the same way. What has gone wrong?" he added sullenly. "I could have loved you."

"The king saw fit to see us wed," said Solange, lowering her voice, "but he cannot command love from me. You could have. Once. If you had ever shown me any affection, Aimery. I had much to give you. Much."

She spoke more to herself than to him, and was surprised to hear him say softly, "What if I had? You want to share the fate of Loriot?"

In awe, matching his whisper, she said, "Did—she— kill him?"

"No, no. I mean, accidents happen. Anything is possible."

"You dare not love me?" she queried. "Blame that on yourself, not her. You want to be rid of me? Then you wield the dagger."

"I didn't mean that," came Aimery's tormented voice through the darkness. "What is Erik to you?"

"He is making inquiries about my father," she said calmly. "He took me to the camp of the returning pilgrims tonight. At my request."

He accepted it. She breathed deeply.

"It's dangerous to travel about the camp alone. It leads to rumors."

Aimery's statement worried her thoughts. *Like Loriot.*

And Loriot was dead by an unknown hand. Not the queen's . . . But the queen's tool? For what reason?

Shadows moved fitfully on the silk tent, looming large and then disappearing. She was glad she was not alone. She breached the silence.

"Who killed Loriot?" He did not answer. "And why?" she added.

"I don't know." He added savagely, "You were there. You saw as much as I did."

"But you hinted, Aimery. Just now. You can't believe the queen had Loriot slain. Can you?"

"It was an accident. Rumor lies."

"What rumor is that?" She reached her hand out to catch his tunic. "*Tell me.*"

"The rumor is that you were the intended victim. And Loriot got in the way."

"Then who?"

"Think for a minute, if you can," said Aimery harshly. "Who stands to lose if you live?"

"Mehun, but I do not believe—" But she did. "Loriot knew my father lived."

"And Loriot died. If you insist on this idiot's scheme of finding your father, what makes you so sure you will not also be killed?"

"Mehun has Belvent. I do not threaten him."

"Not until you find your father."

She laughed shortly. "I had thought," she said musingly, "that the king had played me false in giving me to his queen's leman. But now I see his great wisdom. He has given me a husband to protect me. Occasionally, when my husband comes to my pavilion to see that I still live, I am gratified all over again by the king's concern for my welfare."

"Hush!" hissed Aimery fiercely.

She continued. "I doubt that Mehun cares enough to extinguish my life. He has Belvent, and the king will no doubt confirm him in the fief. But the thought comes to me now that I am a problem for Mehun in a way I did not realize. Can you swear to me, of your own knowledge, that the lady we mentioned did not buy the hand that killed Loriot? That I was not the target?"

Aimery stared at her in the darkness. He could not read her expression, but the tone of her voice told him that her satire covered real doubts. "I am positive—"

"Of your own knowledge?" she persisted.

"No, I won't believe it."

"But you're not sure."

"There's no proof of anything," he said roughly. "Best drop this. Who knows who is listening?"

Solange was bent on her own thoughts. "But there's no proof she didn't. That fits in." Fitted in neatly to the warnings of Countess Alis . . . of Petronilla . . . even of Conon.

The shadows played, and Aimery watched them intently.

"And you can still love her?"

He did not answer. He gestured fiercely, but Solange mistook his meaning. He wanted her to be quiet—well, he was guiltier than she!

"At least, Erik is brave enough to be honest. He pretends nothing. He is what he is." And I, she thought morosely, am what I am.

She moistened her lips. "If you love the queen so badly, and you do not deny it, then you have no right to supervise me."

"Quiet," he warned.

"I give you to the queen," she ranted. "Go to her. Tell her I give her my husband, to have and to hold. To keep. For I have no use for him!"

"You've made that abundantly clear," he said roughly, "in every way you can."

"Have I?" she said, unable to keep from taunting him, even though she knew she trod on dangerous ground. "I am delighted. For I will tell you plainly that I will not provide you with a *present joy* while you long in your heart for *amor de lonh*. The troubadours sing of 'remote love,' but it has come to my attention that a man wants the best of both worlds—the high-flown ecstasy of worshiping a lady from afar, and the down-to-earth tumbling on a pallet with a fleshly woman."

Aimery crossed the tent in two steps. He took her by the shoulders and shook her hard. "You idiot!" he snarled. "Hold your tongue or by the saints I'll make you."

"How?" she taunted.

He struck her on the cheek with his open palm. The blow rang in her ears. She sat down abruptly, holding her hand to her face.

"Aimery!" It was the barest whisper.

"I warned you," he said harshly.

He panted. It was not the prospect of tumbling on a pallet with Solange that moved him. Rather, it was her stubborn insistence that he loved the queen. The queen meant nothing to him, now that he had the fiery Solange, with her bewildering charm, her lovely face and delicious body, her sharp mind that dueled with his every chance she got.

But he could not tell Solange so, for she spurned him with knife and sharp tongue.

"Did I hurt you?"

Not in body, but deeply in her heart, she could have told him. "No," she said. "A blow is no more than I expect from you. Perhaps there are more advantages than I had thought in *amor de lonh*. Just now, Aimery—the remoter, the better."

The sadness in her voice moved him strangely. He hesitated, longing to take her in his arms and kiss her sadness away. But he would not press her, not any more.

Aimery glanced toward the tent wall. The shadow he had noted before seemed to have moved. He had, by now, lost his illusions about Eleanor. Was that Trotti's shadow? Had the spy been close enough to hear Solange's accusations about the queen?

He turned to Solange. "Best hold your tongue," he said harshly, out of his great anxiety. "Who knows what mischief you have caused this night?"

"Who knows?" she said forlornly, thinking of other things.

He lifted the tent flap and was gone. She hurried to watch him. He circled the campfire, and made straight for the royal pavilion.

He went to the queen, she thought, in rising desolation. *He cannot stay away from her*.

Solange dropped the tent flap and turned away—a little too soon. If she had watched another moment she would have seen a misshapen shadow detach itself from the shadows outside her tent, and scurry away after Aimery.

But even then she might not have perceived that, in the shadow of the queen's watchdog, lay the reason for Aimery's anxiety over Solange.

6

That night's quarrel marked a turning point in relations between Solange and Aimery. From then on, even the pretense of amiability was dropped. They met at meals like indifferent strangers.

Solange rode in the midst of the queen's guard, a more sober troop now than had departed. No longer did they ride knee to knee in disciplined ranks. Their number dwindled, as some dropped out from illness or weariness—to the queen's unveiled disgust—or to ride at the side of husband or father.

Even Petronilla did not ride often in her assigned place, next to Solange. But Solange, seeing her from a distance at the overnight camps, knew she was not ill. She did not seek her mother out, lest she run into Mehun.

Sybille de Nannes rode with desperation within the protection of the ladies of the court. She clung to her saddle with both hands, easing the jolting of her body as best she could. She did not care any longer what happened either to herself or to the child she carried. Solange was not sure Sybille remembered the child at all, so deep was her misery. Raymond and Pierre de Garci were never far away. But not, Solange noted, to help their sister, whose condition they had caused. Their only purpose was to keep a watchful eye upon their sister, holding within her the key to the great estates of the dying Olivier.

They were nearing the great River Danube when Solange saw Sybille sway in the saddle. She spurred her mare to ride beside her friend. "Sybille, let's stop for a bit. Did you have anything to eat?"

Sybille turned dull eyes to Solange. "Eat?" she appeared to consider the question. "I think I did not remember to eat. I try not to remember so many things."

Solange said stoutly, "Let me give you something."

Sybille shook her head faintly. Solange looked sharply at her. Sybille was ashen, with a strange grayness in her face. The dark circles under her dark eyes were puffy, and looked strange when her cheeks had sunken so.

A walking skeleton! thought Solange. And the queen had paid no heed to this faithful member of her guard. As much as the queen talked about her ladies, making suggestions and rules for their welfare, yet when Sybille was quite possibly dying before her eyes, the queen had not noticed.

Solange looked about quickly. Her hand on Sybille's reins, she slowed both horses to a walk. There could be no delay, or Sybille would fall from the saddle and be trodden underfoot by the horses following. Easing them both out of the line of march, Solange was at wit's end to know what to do next. She could not quite control two horses, alight herself, and get Sybille down from her horse safely. Sybille swayed ominously, and Solange was sure there was no strength in her at all.

Holding firm to both sets of reins she looked quickly about for help. It came from a surprising direction. One of the knights escorting the guard spurred his Gascon mount and reined in beside them.

"We must get her down to the ground," said Solange tightly, "and I can't manage it alone. Will you help?"

The knight lifted his helm, and she recognized Gervais. He dropped to the ground lithely in spite of his armor, and led both horses to a grassy bank where a tree hung low, providing a patch of shade. His own squire took charge of the Gascon, and stood at a respectful distance.

Solange ripped her saddle blanket from her mount and spread it on the ground, as Gervais eased Sybille down.

She lay where Gervais placed her, on the blanket, covered by another blanket that the squire had found. Solange dug in her pouch for some bread and cheese.

Gervais held a flask of wine to Sybille's lips. She tightened her lips against it and turned her head away. Solange took the flask and presented it to her from the other side, and at length, as Gervais and Solange took turns at it, Sybille was too tired to resist.

The first swallow brought her sputtering to a sitting position, and Solange believed she saw a bit of color come into the ashen cheeks.

"Where are your brothers?" demanded Gervais harshly. "Don't they care about you?"

Solange shook her head warningly, and Sybille laughed, an eerie sound from bloodless lips.

"Let me get someone! Sybille, dear Lady Sybille, hold on. I'll get help for you. Hold fast!"

He scrambled to his feet and beckoned imperatively to his squire, who then ran off, after instructions.

"He's going to fetch a priest?" said Sybille in a breath.

"No," said Gervais loudly. "A woman to heal you. I won't let you die, Sybille."

Sybille groaned. "Too much trouble. I can't make it. I'm sorry to cause you trouble. Solange, go on. Let me lie here." With a great effort, she opened her eyes. "I'll be all right."

"Of course you will be," Solange said with spirit, but without hope. "And I'll not leave you."

Tears welled from under the blue eyelids. It couldn't be long now, Solange mourned. But she would not give up hope.

Sybille clutched Solange's hand with icy fingers. "Solange, tell him."

Startled, Solange said, "Gervais? You wish me to tell?"

"He deserves to know," said Sybille. The words came one at a time, as though she must dole her pitiful hoard out carefully. "We could have been happy," said Sybille. "Once. Before I . . ."

She fell back and closed her eyes. Solange stared, chafing the cold hands. Had death come? No, not yet.

Petronilla came running up the slope, followed with some difficulty by the squire. "Off," she gestured to Gervais. "I need you, Solange. I feared this would happen."

The next hours went by in a terrible blur of blood and strong broth, of making her hands do what Petronilla ordered them to do. Petronilla would not let Sybille die!

and Petronilla was transformed, to Solange's amazement, into an angel fighting off the last darkness with terrible sword and fiery spirit.

When Solange looked about her at last, and Sybille lay in a natural sleep, wrapped tightly in a clean blanket, Solange look at her mother with more respect than ever before.

"I don't know how you did this," ventured Solange. "I thought she was dead before you got here."

"She would have been," said Petronilla, wiping her sleeve across her forehead. "She needs to rest a day, but I suppose that's not possible."

"A good thing she lost the babe," muttered Solange. "Is it always like this?"

Petronilla eyed her sharply. "Not always. In fact, hardly ever."

It seemed strange that her mother's slight figure had only a short while ago been locked in mortal struggle for a girl's life. And, also, Solange realized for the first time, miscarriage had taken place under the stares of hundreds of the cavalcade as they marched past.

Gervais waited, out of hearing but not out of sight. His squire had brought up a four-wheeled wagon with two sturdy horses, used to the plow. Solange stumbled toward Gervais. She had a duty.

"You knew she would get better," said Solange, eyeing the cart filled with fresh straw, waiting to carry Sybille forward with the Crusaders.

"She had to," said Gervais simply. "I have always loved her, you know. And it did not seem right that I should lose her now."

"Then you are the man she wanted to wed, before her brothers married her to de Nannes."

Gervais nodded. "She told you? Then she told you that she could not wait for the riches she craved. My own fief was small, but it would have been enough. So I thought. The more fool, I."

Solange picked her way carefully. "She told you this?"

"She did not even bother to tell me. She sent her brother —that idiot, Pierre. He hasn't enough brains to breathe unless Raymond shows him how."

Solange sighed. How foolish men were! Blinded by disappointment and by jealousy, Gervais could not have looked beyond Pierre's stupid face to see the truth!

"And that didn't tell you anything?"

Gervais looked up swiftly. "What should it have told me? I've thought it over and over. I renounced my fief. My younger brother has it now. I followed Mehun de Mowbrai to the Holy Land."

"Gervais," said Solange, taking a deep breath. "She asked me to tell you something. And I must, whether you want to hear it or not."

She told him, all of it.

"I was there, you see," said Solange, finishing. "I could not help her, but this is how I know it is true. I was there."

"Her brothers?" It was an agonized croak, from a man deep in an agony he had not believed possible. "My Sybille?"

He repeated the two phrases, as though by hearing them in his own voice he could believe them. He stood up, and reached for his two-handed sword. "I will kill them. Keep Sybille for me. I will come back when they are dead."

Solange threw herself on him, ignoring the curious stares of the foot Crusaders, still passing. "Gervais!" She struggled to hold him back, tugging with both her hands at his sword hand. "Listen to me!"

Gervais said, "I have work to do." He spoke in deadly quiet, frightening her more.

"Listen! You want more sin on Sybille's head? You want her to believe that you murdered for her? You think she can live with that sin too? She is guiltless now, and your job is to make her believe that she did not sin. The sin was her brothers' and God will deal with them. Revenge is His, not yours." She spoke in a hurry and words fell over themselves.

"Olivier is dying. Sybille has a chance now. A chance to ease her soul. How can you take that away from her?

"She needs you, Gervais. Help her. Love her. Can you love her, and yet let her believe she forced you to mortal sin?"

She managed, at last, to convince him. "She needs me,"

he said dully, "I cannot do this . . . yet. I will take care of her. But her brothers will suffer for this, I vow."

"But not yet," said Solange swiftly, lest he brood too long on revenge. "Lift her into the cart, Gervais, and ride with her. Watch her carefully. She holds to life by a thin thread even yet."

Gervais lifted his love, still sleeping, into the cart. She roused long enough to murmur Gervais's name before she sank back into sleep, a faint smile on her face. Gervais looked up at Solange and said, briefly, "You have the right of it." Signaling to the carter to proceed, he swung up into his saddle. "I will stay my hand. For the moment."

His face was dark with tragedy as he rode toward the east. But he would find solace by helping his love to recover.

Solange mounted and rode on at a slow canter, dreadfully weary. She could find it possible to envy poor Sybille, for her friend was by far the richer.

7

The hundred thousand thieves and nobles, villeins, tradesmen, harlots, sincere penitents and ambitious optimists, had traveled a long distance. They had crossed the Rhine near Worms, and from there, their troubles began to increase.

The German villagers, seeing with dismay the hordes of people marching down upon them like a plague of locusts, began to take measures to insure that they themselves would not starve. Their measures were direct, and little to the liking of the Crusaders, who called the Germans ingrates when they didn't call them worse names.

A number of unarmed pilgrims, who traveled with the king for safety, became vociferously indignant at the secular character of the Crusade. They left the safety of the king's protection shortly after the Crusade left Worms, and while their absence left more supplies for the others, their outspoken disapproval disturbed many. But the queen scarcely knew of them.

The great river had wound its way through forested hills, rising at sharp angles from the current's edge, looping back on itself in broad strokes, trending generally to the southeast, toward Byzantium.

At Ratisbonne, some of the Crusaders took boat and launched themselves out on the stream. There were too few boats for them all, and the majority decided to stay with Louis, who would not abandon those under his protection.

The first meeting with the Greek emissaries of Manuel Comnenus, "the lofty, sublime, august emperor of Byzantium," took place at Ratisbonne, and the Greeks stayed a couple of days, making fair promises of food and comforts to come, before they floated back down the river to Byzantium.

Supper meat was not as plentiful as before. Erik's troops ranged the countryside, coming back empty-handed more often than not. The queen's hunger made her irritable, and Erik's disgust nearly drove him to rash discourtesy.

At length he cried, "I'll get you some meat!" His eyes fell on forested hills nearby.

"Those forests belong to our brother ruler, the Emperor Conrad," the king pointed out in protest.

"That same emperor," said Erik, "whose men have despoiled the country before us, leaving only empty barns and angry villagers for us to deal with? I doubt he will keep meat from our pots this night."

On an impulse, Solange rode with the hunting party. The hunt was exhilarating and successful. The red deer were magnificent. When the men started back, they had venison enough for a week. Erik and Solange lingered, sending the others on ahead.

They dismounted, and Solange strolled ahead, leaving Erik to tie the horses. She was curious about the gray stone outcropping ahead. It looked oddly like a man lying there, thrown away like a discarded toy. She moved closer.

"Erik!" It was a muffled scream. He ran to her side and gazed down at the pitiful, wracked remnant of a man. She knelt beside him and touched the head.

"He lives!" she breathed in wonder.

The man lay face down. Only the slight bare spot at the top of the head showed, until Erik gently turned him over to lie with staring, fevered eyes into the sky.

"Brother Garin!" she cried.

"A friar? His robe has little of the monkish. It seems to be made of saddle blanket."

Swiftly she told him who the injured man was. "With the emperor's train," she finished. "What can have happened to him? Not—not fever?"

"Fortunately for us, not fever. See, he has been beaten."

Bruises covered his body, and his sharp cry when they moved him spoke of broken ribs. Erik's grave face reflected the severity of Brother Garin's injuries.

Carefully, they got him onto a blanket and Solange rode back to the camp for help. Aimery was standing apart, drinking broth that served for luncheon. He turned hard eyes to her.

"You cannot find the Varangian? No use looking for him here." The look on her face stopped him. "What is it? Are you hurt?"

"Not me, him." She was out of breath, too frightened by Garin's peril to speak clearly.

"Erik?" exclaimed Aimery.

"*Garin.* Up there." She pointed to the hills behind them. At length she made him understand. In what seemed no time, men, horses, a litter, and blankets, were borne up the pass. Solange led the way. Aimery noticed grimly the seclusion of the glen and drew his own unmistakable conclusion. He turned to her, and although he said not a word, the question lay plain between them: What were you and Erik doing in this private place? But then Aimery turned to the urgent need of getting Brother Garin to camp.

From noon to sundown Garin lingered in the twilight between living and dying. Solange and Aimery took turns nursing him, but he grew weaker. Solange saw how gentle Aimery was with Garin, how tenderly he cared for him. How infinitely patient he was. For her, there was only a civil glance, an impersonal touch.

Petronilla came with a basket of medicaments, saying

flatly to Solange, "You're in the way. I need Aimery to lift the man. You run along."

Sent thus out of her own pavilion, she wandered, listlessly. She hardly heeded the rising wind, the swift dark clouds soaring out of the west. The rains fell, soaking the ground to ankle-high mud, miring the carts.

She had never felt so miserable in her life. Even the thought of finding her father seemed far away, hopeless. She ached, and her stomach rolled in her. She had to face it—she loved Aimery. And he did not love her. She huddled in the rain, sodden and wretched, unaware of where she was. Garin, her one true friend, was dying, and without him there was nobody.

It was there that Erik found her and took her into his tent. He made her take off her wet clothing, and gave her a fur rug. He gave her brandy, and what comfort he could.

The next day the sun shone, drying up the mud by noon, and bringing a marked improvement in Brother Garin. In faltering words, he related that he had stayed behind the emperor's train to minister to a small village in the hills. Instead of gratitude, the villagers had vented upon him their hatred of the emperor, who had swept their stored food into his supply carts, leaving them with nothing between themselves and starvation.

The cavalcade moved on, Brother Garin in a cart. They rounded the Danube bend, where the river turned abruptly south, between two ranges of mountains, to emerge on a plain so vast that the farthest reaches were veiled in the blue of distance. Traveling south again, along the left bank of the river, they reached a ford where the great river bent again to the east. Their route now must keep south, and the dangerous river must be forded.

Two days before, Erik had told King Louis the Danube would be too high to cross. "No need to hurry," he had pointed out. "Not now." It was still a bitter thing to him that the king's indulgence of his queen led to late starts and early halts. The group of ladies traveled no faster than an oxcart. "Had we traveled more swiftly, we would have reached the river crossing before the storms sent the waters over the banks."

"Had we traveled faster," Solange pointed out, "we would have missed Garin."

"Or," said Erik, "prevented his misfortune in the first place."

They camped on the bank of the great river, where they were forced to spend several days until the waters receded. Dirty clothes were brought out and washed. Cooking odors rose from a hundred pots, which were preparing food for the next leg of the journey.

Solange sought out her mother. Petronilla had her basket on her arm.

"Going to Garin?"

"No," said her mother. "He's getting on. It's the ones in the camp who need me." She surveyed her daughter. "You're hardly dressed for it. I'll see you when I come back."

On an impulse, Solange said, "I'll go with you. Maybe I can help." Petronilla gave her a dubious look, but led the way.

The lower camps were settled on the least desirable ground. As the Crusade moved along, the forerunners hurried ahead so that by the time the royal party halted, the best campground possible had been selected, the pavilions were erected, and the fires had been lit some distance from the royal compound, to keep odors from disturbing Queen Eleanor.

The forerunners, who broke up the camp and set it up again, were usually too weary to care much where they lay. But hundreds of peasants, tradespeople, burgesses and their ladies, the many hundreds who could not afford a mount or even to buy a ride in someone's cart, walked the Crusade, day after day, league after league. They straggled in after the royal party had already retired for the night.

Too tired to cook, they subsisted on what they could force down their dust-parched throats. Erik was wrong; it was not solely the queen's guard who slowed the pace. The king's concern for his weary pedestrian subjects made him decree short journeys.

There were many ailing. Solange, who had ridden all the way from Paris, had little idea of the great hardships endured by those who had walked the weary leagues. Their boots had not lasted as far as Vezelay, and their feet now wore callouses thicker than boot soles.

But the weariness, the fatigue, the waking in the morning to another day of trudging one sore foot before the other, until, in God's mercy, the sun began to set—all of this was taking its toll.

Exhaustion bred accidents and illness. A hard rain last week had brought on an epidemic of sneezing, hoarse voices, and rheumy eyes.

But without any doubt, the daily appearance of Lady de Mowbrai with her small covered basket and her buoyant smile did as much good as her dwindling supply of nostrums.

Solange was curious. Her mother had always been knowledgeable about herbs and salves, as had all the ladies of her class. Now, seeing the miraculous work her mother had done for Brother Garin and Sybille, Solange was sorry that she lacked this knowledge. She began to watch, and to learn. Her mother was welcomed heartily as she stepped through the throngs who were, for the first time in weeks, able to rest long enough to cook a proper meal and give their clothing an airing.

Petronilla had much to do. Solange helped as much as she could, promising herself that she would learn all her mother knew.

"I understand," said Petronilla, "that in the East there are many things we do not yet know. I shall make inquiries as soon as we get there."

"You like to do this? You like to deal with these ugly stinking sores, these hopeless limbs that will never be straight again?"

"It is one way," said Petronilla gently, "to His grace. Our Lord healed the lepers. I do what I can."

"What does Mehun say?"

"He cares not what I do. As long as Belvent is in his hands, I matter not to him."

Solange was touched by her mother's simple acknowledgement of a hurt that must cut to the heart.

"And you," said her mother, as they moved back toward the pavilions. "You have mended your marriage?"

"I have no marriage."

"But," said Petronilla, stopping in her tracks, "the babe that begins to swell your belly is not Aimery's?"

"The babe?"

This explained it all. Her queasiness, her lethargy. It was Erik's babe she carried.

"Not Aimery's," she whispered. They resumed their walk. "You have changed greatly, Mother," she said after a few steps. "I did not know you back there in the camps."

"You've always looked to yourself, first," said Petronilla. "Looking inward too much. Perhaps it was because you were our only child. And perhaps it was a likeness to your grandmother Saint Florent. You don't know me and never did. Nor did she. All she could see was Odo." After a silence, Petronilla added, "You didn't know your father either. You saw him with veiled eyes."

Before they parted, Petronilla touched Solange's arm. "What are you going to do?"

"About the babe? I don't know."

"Best tell your husband," said Petronilla. "At once."

"I dare not."

Petronilla looked at Solange for a long time. "You don't know *him*, either. Perhaps you don't even see yourself clearly!"

She left, leaving Solange to make her slow way to her tent. What could she do? How he would laugh! If he didn't kill her.

Nor could she throw herself on Erik's feeling for her. She knew that was as evanescent as the wind. Nor, if she were totally honest, did she want to spend her life with Erik. He was attractive, tender, accomplished in love-making. But she did not wish to marry him, even if she were free.

She stopped short. She had jeopardized her soul for a passing passion that had no true foundation. And she had forfeited any hope of Aimery's love.

There was nothing to do but keep silent, at least for a while, until she could think clearly.

When she reached her tent, she found that the camp was in an uproar. Another party of returning pilgrims had come upon them. The forerunners had brought them in and they were now with the king. She heard voices raised, and joined the others who were clustered indecently close around the king's tent.

It seemed that these pilgrims were of a higher class and much luckier than the previous group. These still had their horses, and even food. But they still had many grievances.

"Beware of the Greeks," said the leader, whose deep voice carried to outside the tent. "The emperor sayeth fair things, and yet his people did the foulest deeds."

"That is not true," Erik's voice came clearly in denial. "You have falsified your experiences, for your own purposes. I do not know what they may be. But I bear the authority of the Emperor Manuel Comnenus in this land, and I say you lie."

"I will tell you—"

Erik interrupted flatly. "You will tell me nothing. Did you just now cross the river?"

"It is in flood, as you see," said the pilgrim. "We came through the mountains yonder."

"There is no path through those mountains," said Erik in triumph. "I doubt you are pilgrims at all. Have you even seen Byzantium?"

Aimery's voice interrupted. "I think we must hear these men. We need to know whether in fact Manuel will keep his promises to us. We are relying on the grain he will send, and the help of his people."

"And little enough of that you will get," interrupted the pilgrim.

The king intervened, then, and the voices were lowered. The rest of the interview was inaudible to those outside. But Erik appeared at the door of the pavilion and looked back over his shoulder. "You speak from envy," he said, "and I understand that."

But Erik was so angry that he brushed past Solange on his way through the crowd, and did not see her.

She decided to speak alone to the pilgrims. She could not very well ask Erik to put her question to them.

"Yes," said the pilgrim leader. "I know Odo de Saint Florent. He did not die in the battle. I saw him later."

343

"Later? How much later? Where did you see him?"

The pilgrim eyed her with misgivings. "Why do you want to know this?"

"He is my father, and I have been told he was dead. But you say he is not?"

"*Was* not, when I saw him. After the battle of Adana, lady, he was in Antioch. I saw him going through the gate they call the Duke's Gate, riding through the marshes."

"Not wounded?"

"He was riding. That's all I know."

Solange was uplifted by greater hope than she had had in weeks. She was sorely tempted to tell her news, but promised herself that she would keep quiet.

For one thing was quite certain: If her father had died since Antioch, then Mehun's story had still been a lie!

8

Bagge had, like Jehane, recently come into a sum of gold coins not easily explained. Chauve's curiosity about the money came briefly to Solange's ears, but she paid it no heed.

There was little coin left in the entire cavalcade of Crusaders. The march had found that many a town closed its walls against the hungry Crusaders. At each village there were lengthy negotiations from the Franks at the bottom of the walls, and the natives at the top. After prolonged bartering, a basket would come down on a rope, and the coins agreed upon would be taken up. Then the food would come down in the basket—rarely the promised amount of food. And all the Franks could do was to shake a mailed fist futilely at the Greeks who laughed atop their great walls.

The sun shone upstream, apparently drying up the many rivers that sent their storm runoff into the Danube. The water level of the river crossing went down every hour.

The local guides told Erik that the river would be ready for crossing on the following day.

The next day, Solange was glad to continue the journey. Bagge brought the mare to where she stood, watching Chauve pack away the tent.

"Here she is, lady," said Bagge. "You're not ready to mount yet, so I best leave her and go help Chauve."

She nodded permission absently, but later on she realized that she had not seen Bagge helping Chauve.

The stewards of the company were frantic about getting the thousands of travelers across the river. The knights helped ferry the barges across, laden with baggage carts and the helpless foot passengers.

The better horsemen were impatient to cross and left the barges to others who were less able.

The river was low here, and made a wide bend. In the process of making the sweep toward the south, it left many sandbars in its wake, and only in one place was the current deep and swift enough to make the horses swim.

The king and queen went across safely. The knights were crossing, giving a helping hand to those nearby, as the queen's guard took to the water. They went from sandbar to sandbar, as the guides directed, and soon the river was full of the bobbing heads of people and horses.

The current was swift and unpredictable, the river still swollen. Heads bobbed and disappeared. There was no counting those who vanished beneath the water, for some bounced up again some little way downstream. Some, however, did not.

Aimery was in the rear, rallying the peasants whom the king had put into his charge. Erik had gone ahead, his Varangians being the first to cross, to test the way.

Solange found the crossing easy at first. The sandbars were solid and unyielding under her mare's hooves. She let the mare pick her way. She did not notice one of the barons downstream from her, who seemed to parallel her course.

She set the mare to swimming when they reached the deepest part of the river. The water was swift, and the mare had hard going. It was then that her saddle slipped sideways with a sudden jolt.

Solange felt the swift current close over her head.

She could not breathe, her lungs strained to the bursting point. The entire world was only water, rushing past her ears.

Her saddle was out of reach. There was nothing to hold to. Her fingers now clutched sand—the bottom of the river—and now water.

Dimly she knew that her mare was flailing the water in her own dread panic. Solange struck out, away from the slashing hooves, to where the water ran deeper.

The water was full of horses. Solange bobbed to the surface, but before she could get a deep breath, she was dragged under again by the current as it swept around the bend.

She glimpsed daylight again, but the water streamed into her eyes and she could not see. The current tugged at her boots, her tunic, turning ever over and over like a log. How foolish to die thus!

Suddenly she was caught on something. Her clothing must have snagged on an underwater limb, holding her fast. Lifting her.

If she could believe it, a tree was lifting her out of the water! She could breathe again. The water streamed down her face, into her open mouth.

The tree spoke, and, oddly, she was not surprised to hear it speak with the voice of Erik the Varangian.

"Hang on," he said. "I'll get you out of here."

She clung to him, bouncing in and out of the water as he fought the current. It was an endless time, full of Erik's hands on her clothing, her face full of water and, alternately, the sun hot on her skin.

Erik, with the efficiency of the experienced soldier, had piled his armor on his palfrey and gone into the river less encumbered than most of the Frankish noblemen. She slid against his wet leather hauberk. She was conscious of his hand shifting from her tunic to grab her girdle, and then she felt the girdle clasp break, and she was borne away.

Coughing, she reached the surface and began to strike out mechanically with her arms. She saw branches on the bank coming after her, coming to get her to drag her down into the dark water.

She spewed water. Erik panted, "Hang on, darling. I'll get you to shore. Just hang on."

Her foot dragged the bottom. "I can touch bottom," she gasped.

He held her while she stood once more on firm footing. The water reached her chin. She was content to stand gasping for air. Erik, too, drew great shuddering breaths.

"That was a near thing," he told her, finally. "Your king does not listen well. I told him the river should fall one more day before we crossed. Now, dearest, tell me what happened. You are too good a horsewoman to slip from your saddle."

She nodded agreement. The breath of Death on her had been too close, too hot. Steadied by Erik's hands, holding her even now against the current, she cast her mind back. There had been a sharp jerk when she stood in the saddle, almost as though the girth had given way, and she had nearly slid under the mare's belly. But the saddle had been new before they started from Metz. "It had worn through, I suppose," she said. "The girth, I mean."

"Your groom should have checked it more carefully. You could have been killed."

Thinking back, she protested. "I checked the saddle myself when we ended the last day's ride. It was sound then."

The hands that held her steady in the current urged her gently toward the shore, into the shelter of an overhanging tree. Erik smiled down into her eyes with the look she knew so well. He stroked her body, lingering on the gentle curves. Letting his hand move over her waist, she waited for his discovery.

"What have I done to you?" he exclaimed, suddenly pulling her to him and burying his face in her wet hair. He gave a long shuddering gasp then, and let her go, steadying her against the tree limb. It was an oddly intimate place, she thought, with the world outside their leafy shelter.

She stretched her arms to encircle his neck, and pull his lips down to hers. Against his warm breath she murmured, "You've made me very happy," and let her body lean against his for the only comfort he could give her.

They both knew it was farewell. The water streamed

down her face from her wet hair. Mingled in the river water was the taste of salt tears.

He left her. She felt the slight swelling at her waist, and wondered at the grasp on life the unborn already held. Surely her experience would be enough to kill most wanted children. Here the unwanted clung tenaciously to life.

When Aimery found her, she had recovered somewhat. Someone had given her a spare tunic, still wet from its plunge into the river, and her slim figure was outlined in the wet silk. He thought he had never seen her more provocative.

"I heard," he said. "A very narrow escape."

"Yes," she said dully. "I was fortunate that help was nearby."

"I am sorry it was not I."

She lifted her dark violet eyes to him. "Your people, Aimery? Did they get through?"

"Most of them. Not all. We lost many unfortunate souls this day."

He sat down beside her. "How did it happen?"

"My saddle gave way. The girth was probably cut," she said dully, and was surprised that she believed it. The last time she had looked at the girth it had been intact. But anyone could have cut it, in the hours before the crossing. "But of course," she added, "there's no way to tell, now."

"I think you must be wrong. Who would do that?"

"You might know well who would wish me out of the way."

He glared at her. "Who?"

"So she could have you to herself."

"The queen? You are mad."

"Perhaps." She turned away as though she had lost interest in the matter. His eyes traveled from her white throat, gently touched by the sun now, over the firmly outlined breasts, to gently swelling waist. And something touched him inside, something that chilled him to his marrow.

"Solange," he whispered in a strangled voice.

She looked quickly at him and saw that his gaze was fixed upon the swelling.

"As you see," she said simply.

"A child? It can't be mine."

"I never said it was," she retorted. "You have taken care that there is no possibility of that."

"Then who? I warn you, I will have the truth."

"Erik's."

The color drained from his rugged features, leaving behind a grayish pallor. A pallor, not of fleshly death, but of a grievous loss that gripped the heart. The words streamed forth like blood from a mortal wound. "I tried not to believe it. I told myself that you were simply friendly to him." He smashed his fist into his open palm.

"As you see," she said harshly, "you were wrong. What did you think I would do? Wait until my royal cast-off husband came crawling back to my tent? That I would provide virgin comfort to a fool?"

"Erik! That popinjay! He's the one—" He broke off and eyed her sharply. Solange kept her eyes fixed on the distance. She did not see his anguish. She would get through the next hour, somehow, but if she thought of something else until it was all over, it would be easier.

"Erik, and how many others? How can you be sure? To have an unfaithful wife is bad enough, but to have one whoring after the whole—"

"You know that isn't so," said Solange, remotely. "You didn't care before about me. Why now?"

The answer never came. They were interrupted by the arrival of Petronilla. "I heard of your misfortune. I'm glad to see you're all right."

"Oh, yes, she's fine," ranted Aimery. "As you can see."

"You found out," acknowledged Petronilla calmly.

"In time to know that Erik's fathered a brat in my household. But the world is going to know that the child isn't mine."

"If you don't lower your voice," observed Petronilla, "they'll know it now. You feel you must broadcast your scandal to the world? How they will laugh!"

He came to his senses. "You're right," he said at last. "No need to know that I couldn't father the child. No need to know that—"

"That you've kept your embraces for the queen," interposed Solange swiftly.

"Enough," said Petronilla sharply. "You are not entirely to blame, Aimery. I confess my daughter is sharp-tongued enough to drive away anyone."

He grunted and left. Petronilla said, thoughtfully, "I didn't know he was so much in love."

"With the queen," said Solange.

Petronilla only shook her head. "I thought you were an intelligent girl. But I now give up on you."

9

The toll was heavy. It took a long time to count, for many of those lost were known only by the names given them on the journey—Nicolas of the Short Coat, Eglantine Squint-eye, Theresa Red Shoes. Bodies lodged between rocks on the bank, bobbing up and down as the current moved them.

The horses suffered cruelly, and many pilgrims now took to their feet who had once ridden.

Solange, steeped in her own misery, still managed to seek out Catherine and Henri, who had survived the crossing, and Bertille, stunned by the disappearance of Jean. He had gone down, she said, out of her reach at once and she could only watch his dear head as it moved down the river and out of sight.

Not until nearly twelve hours later did Jean manage to make his way back to the camp, having been deposited, like sand, on a sandbar in the upstream side of a fallen tree, more dead than alive. It was the first brush with death for the de Loches, and they rode on with more gratitude than they had before.

Raymond de Garci, Sybille's brother, had drowned. His body, borne down by heavy mail, dead hands still clinging to a small casket of coins, had been fished out. He had been avid to cross, and had refused to help the poor, reported Henri. Raymond, in his opinion, had got no more than he deserved.

The crossing of the Danube had cost the Crusaders much in men, horses, and food. Spirits were dampened for some time.

After several days, the train left the great river and headed into the mountains of Bosnia.

Travel was slower now, and the queen's guard straggled as badly as the peasants trudging behind the mounted Crusaders. Solange's condition was evident now. If any doubted that Aimery was the father of the coming child, none ventured the thought aloud.

Day by day the mountains closed in around them. Leaving the vast plain, they now struggled ever upward, topping one rise to find another, even more difficult, ahead of them. As the mountains grew higher, the roads became narrower. When they thought they had gone as far as they could, there appeared before them another narrow pass over which they must struggle, breathing hard in the thin air.

From time to time Solange glanced up to find the queen's eyes somber and speculative on her. She was reminded then of Conon's remark about the queen. She could remember the sharp jerk as her foot gave way in its stirrup. If the strap had been cut, was the queen responsible? There was no answer possible. She could not even prove that there had been an attempt to kill her.

Erik's duties turned more and more difficult. The mountains rose before them, and many hearts grew faint. He was constantly cheering them on, telling the king that the way would soon be easier. He saw Solange only rarely, and even when he did she could not rejoice in him. Already, Erik's lovemaking was receding into a past that she only vaguely remembered. Too much in her mind now was physical misery, and the apparent hopelessness of her future.

She had lost her mare in the crossing, but rode her spare mount. She found riding difficult and painful now, as the child grew heavier.

She was not alone. The queen's guard had lost the lightheartedness with which they had started the journey. Many another lady was now pregnant—and the mountain terrain grew increasingly rigorous.

Sometimes an entire day passed without their reaching the heights of the mountains at whose feet they had camped the night before. They would never get to Byzantium this way.

But the king seemed to feel that his sufferings were part of God's plan. He grew more and more quiet, retreating into a serene place deep within himself. Yet his compassion for those in his care was boundless.

Petronilla, on foot now, trudged near Solange, unobtrusively watching her. She was concerned more about Solange's mental condition than her physical state. She, Petronilla, could look back and take some of the blame for all of this.

One day they reached the top of the mountain only to see another range, even higher, beyond the valley. She spoke to Aimery.

"That girl needs a cart," she told him bluntly.

"She has not asked me for one."

"You know she'll never ask for one. But if you want to kill her, there are more merciful ways than to let her suffer like this."

"Let Erik provide her with a litter," he said coldly. "I will not care for another man's child."

"Or your wife?"

Aimery was silent. He too had been watching Solange, and had marveled at her courage. But he would not relent. *Erik's child, not his.*

"You want me to broadcast," she said cunningly, "to the world that you could not be the father? You are unable to get any woman with child?"

"That is not true!"

"How do you know? At any rate, people will believe me."

He bit his finger. "You wouldn't do that. It reflects on your daughter."

"You are a fool," said Petronilla, impatiently stamping her foot. "A fool in love, besides."

The Varangians left them to cross the mountains alone. The pressure of urgent business, so Erik told the king, was taking him away. "To send back grain and horses," he told Count Robert, "which you sadly need. But I must tell the Emperor myself of your need else he will not believe it."

Erik came to say good-bye to Solange. He found her alone while her servants were stowing her tent in the cart. There was little to say. "I shall see you in Constantinople," he said.

"Of course," she answered. But all this was mere civility.

He touched her cheek with the back of his hand, and said, softly, "If ever I would have wed, Solange, it should have been you."

She smiled slightly. "We have both missed much," she said cryptically.

"When you get to Byzantium," he said, "call on me for anything you need."

She nodded, still smiling faintly.

"You remember I told you I would show you my city. That is something we shall look forward to."

"I am sure of it." Her tone was casual.

"I really meant all the things I said to you," he said, earnestly. "You mean much to me."

She roused herself to say, "Have a good journey, Erik. You helped me when I needed it, and I hope you find someone who will do the same for you if you ever need anybody."

After he disappeared, she looked up to find Aimery's eyes on her. With studied indifference, she turned away.

Shortly afterwards Petronilla came to her. "If the king thinks that the Varangians are going ahead to speed our relief, he is even more naive than I would have thought."

"Come, Mother. You don't like Erik, but there's no reason to believe he is perfidious."

"I suppose it was Erik who now sends you relief?" She pointed behind them. "Now you can ride—thanks to your husband."

A cart, filled with straw and drawn by a donkey they had picked up at the foot of the mountains, stopped beside them.

One of Aimery's men was leading the donkey. "For my Lady," he said. "My lord sent the cart. An easier ride, he thought."

"I will not take it."

Petronilla warned her with a glance. "Lady Solange is thankful to Lord Aimery," she said. "And accepts with pleasure."

Solange, mutinous, would have spoken again but her mother glared at her and she fell silent. "Just the same," she said later, "I want my own man to lead the donkey. I will have none of Aimery's men. I want nothing from him."

"All right," said Petronilla at last, "I will send Bagge to lead the animal."

All went well down the long rugged range and through the valley. The cart was truly more comfortable than walking, and she was grateful for the rest.

Surprisingly, there were no people to be seen. There were villages in small clearings in the mountains. Little churches perched like eagle's nests on the rocky face of the mountains. And, to the French priests' open disgust, the chapels inside were painted with representations of saints and martyrs. Not so different, one might say, than the abbey of St. Denis—but these paintings were not in stained glass but were drawn right on the plaster walls.

Brother Garin said cautiously, "The Greeks do not seem Christian as we are. But God knows their hearts." And Aimery, who had just come from dealing with yet another complaint about foodstuffs missing overnight—carried off by the local Greeks who could not be found in the daylight —said, sourly, "Their hearts are full of thievery!"

Near a small town called Stara Zagora, they paused to await the arrival of Abbot Suger's emissaries. The King had once again sent for money from his faithful deputy. They would not be able to go farther without the food the gold would buy. When the men came, at last, they brought news of home.

Olivier de Nannes was dead, at last. Pierre was furious. With Olivier dead, and Sybille no longer with child, there was no longer the hope of his getting the vast de Nannes lands. But Pierre would not admit defeat.

"Go home with me," he told Sybille. "We will travel with the abbot's men and hold the castle against Olivier's cousin."

"No, Pierre, I will not."

"But if we get there first, we can withstand them all."

"But we cannot get there first, Pierre. And I will not go. I shall never return to France."

He pinched her arm with savage fingers. "I say you will go. Get your things together. We leave at once."

He twisted her wrist savagely, and she cried out, nearly falling to the ground. Suddenly Gervais stood beside her. Pierre, looking at Gervais's eyes, saw something to change his mind at once. He dropped his hand, letting it linger momentarily on his sword hilt. He glanced around, but found no support anywhere. Without his brother Raymond, Pierre was only a husk.

"I'm going," he said less confidently, "I'm going back to Paris. You'll have to shift for yourself now."

Sybille rubbed her arm where her brother's fingers had bruised her. "I care not, Pierre," she said. "I shall manage to get to the Holy City." She looked at him without illusion. "And I shall say a prayer for you. One prayer— no more." She turned her back and walked away, leaving Gervais to glare at her brother, until Pierre averted his eyes and walked away.

The king, still feeling the recent defection of several thousand pilgrims who felt this was a dissolute court, kept a paternal eye on those who remained with him.

There was no money left in the pockets of the foot pilgrims, so the king's chaplain told him. And the king, once again, sent urgent messages back to the Abbot Suger in Paris, to send money, more money, all he could gather. But it would be weeks before the messengers returned. The king saw, as he rode beside the straggling pilgrims toward that evening's camp at the foot of the next mountain pass, many faces already in torment, and many whose souls would have flown upward much before Suger's money arrived.

The king sent Aimery ahead. "The last of our gold," said the king. "Take it. Surely ahead of us you will meet the emperor's supply train. Urge them, as they love us, to hasten to us. But if you fail to meet them, then buy all the food you can. Take carts and enough men to guard your purchases well."

While Aimery rode away, over the pass and down into the valley beyond, Solange mounted the cart and took her place in the long procession strung out along the narrow mountain road. She pulled her thin cream-colored cotton cloak over her head to serve as protection from the hot sun, and tried to sleep.

The path arrived at a small clearing and then soared upward, narrow as a wagon track, a ledge cut on the mountain flank. On one hand the red rock rose sheer, and on the other side the drop was equally sheer for a thousand feet.

Solange felt every roll of the cart, deep in her bones. As she lay cramped in the cart, the child pressed upon her lungs so that she could not breath in the thin mountain air. The little donkey moved slowly upward, but it took all Bagge's strength to convince him to move. She remembered Sybille's great agony as she rode along the Danube River. Thanks to Aimery she did not have to ride, or walk, either, as so many did.

She had made so many mistakes. She could not atone for them. Never could she bring to her husband the fresh, untouched love he had a right to. Always the shadow of her unfaithfulness would lie between them. But hand in hand with remorse came her insistence that Aimery had trampled her love underfoot in his eagerness for the queen. Finally, she could not stay curled in the cart any longer.

The caravan had halted for the moment, and she slipped from the back of the cart. She turned to tell Bagge she would meet him beyond the summit, when she saw a strange sight. Bagge was doing something odd with the cart. . . .

He cut the donkey's traces, so quickly she could not cry out. She took a step toward him, but the cart was already tipping over the edge of the cliff. It was gone from sight in a single instant.

Then Bagge, a triumphant smile on his face, looked behind him. He saw his mistress watching him, and the smile faded. His face grew ashen.

He stared at her, his deadly sin clearly inscribed in his small darting eyes, the red tongue moistening dry lips. Solange stepped toward him, fingers itching to claw.

Just then all the devils of hell erupted from behind

them, around them, even over their heads! Wild battle
screams, the clash of steel, the shouts of attackers. After
a moment of stunned surprise came the rallying cries of
the Franks. "The Greeks! The brigands!"

All was clashing, shouting turmoil.

The Greeks had fallen upon the Franks at a critical
point in their passage of the mountains. Most were trapped
here on the near side of the narrow mountain pass, but
many, including the armed royal party, had already traversed the narrow ledge and were winding down into the
green pine-clad valley below.

The Greeks did not venture their bodies against the
armor-clad knights. They wielded their swords with savage
ferocity on the pitiful, defenseless, raggle-taggle group
that followed the king.

The way to escape was open just ahead of Solange. She
took a few steps toward the empty path, toward the safety
of the valley below. Bagge had vanished from sight. She
could get away. For an instant her feet moved along the
narrow ledge, toward safety.

She turned back. The baggage train was in total confusion. She snatched up a long piece of wood, destined
once to be a spare ax handle.

There were Greeks everywhere. Bearded faces, savage
eyes, scraps of bright-colored rags over the head, ragged
tunics, bare sandaled feet—all this Solange noted with
one part of her mind. They had come out of the rocks like
wolves, pouncing on what they assumed was a rich baggage
train.

The air was full of defiant, angry shrieks. The savage
cries of the brigands dinned in her ears until there was no
room left for thought. She stood stunned, seeing Jehane
on her knees, praying, stunned into abject fear.

"Get up, Jehane!" cried Solange, shoving her on the
shoulder. "Pray—but *do* something!"

There were Franks around her, stumbling over the
wagons, seeking to flee ahead over the pass. They jostled
her, mad with fear, and she was knocked to the ground.
She crawled to the shelter of a rock to catch her breath.

The Greeks were overrunning the baggage train. The
battle was not yet won, for some Franks had gathered

themselves into small bands, back to back, forming a knot that the Greeks could not at once break through.

The spare ax handle she had snatched up had flown from her hand as she fell. Now she saw it, blood-covered, in a puddle of gore next to a dying Frank. Her stomach writhed. There were pools of blood covering much of the ground.

Brother Garin, everywhere at once, moved among the victims, giving absolution to all within reach of his finger. He was oblivious to the battling around him.

She crawled on hands and knees toward the bloody ax handle. She stretched out her hand to take it, but a pain coursed upward from her hips and doubled her up in agony. The next time the pain came, she barely felt it. She wiped the blood from the stout wooden stick with her tunic, and looked about for an enemy.

She did not have to look far. The Greek before her was all black rolling eyes and broken teeth, until she swung the ax handle and he fell to his knees, and then to the ground. The wood splintered in her hands. She stared at the blood trickling from his temple. He was the first man she had killed.

A Greek came toward her, his club raised. Its momentum carried downward. She dodged, and the blow struck her near her hip.

She did not feel it. She moved now with instinct, her Viking ancestors closer than she thought. She snatched up a weapon from a fallen man nearby, and waded into the fray.

She clutched the heavy sword with two hands, the only way she could lift it. The weight, added to her own strength, was deadly.

Where were the knights? she wondered. Fierce, hook-nosed Greek faces loomed, savagely baring their teeth in the exultation of the battle and the prospect of loot.

Solange looked about for Jehane. The battle swayed back and forth before her weary eyes, and she could no longer make out faces. But she knew that Gauthier was running berserk at the cliff edge, lifting Greek after Greek and hurling them onto the rocks below.

Jehane was nowhere to be seen. Solange called her

name, but she could hardly hear her own voice over the din of the clashing swords.

Swords? The knights had returned!

Then she saw Jehane. Her face jouncing upside down, mouth open in a scream lost in the battle din. Jehane hung over the shoulder of a Greek, climbing up the rocky scree of the mountainside. She pounded her fists futilely against his back. Fantastically, she was leaving a trail—a trail of golden teardrops. Solange blinked and started forward, dragging the two-edged sword behind her.

The golden teardrops became gold coins as Solange scuffed one into the dirt. With a great effort of will, her mind cleared away the red veil that stood between her and the world. Still raging, but no longer crazed with her fury, she knew she must save Jehane. The maid's purse of gold coins was now gone past retrieving, but Jehane herself was still safe.

Solange ran a few steps toward the Greek and his captive. "Jehane!" she screamed, "watch out!"

Her scream startled the bandit, and he faltered. Quick as a ferret, Jehane slid from his shoulder. At the same time Solange, staggering forward under the weight of her mighty weapon, raised it, trembling with the strain, and let it fall.

Jehane was free, searching on hands and knees for her lost wealth, and sobbing. Suddenly, there were fewer of the enemy. The Greeks, nearly empty-handed, were vanishing back over the rocks. The fresh new shouts that came from behind her told the reason for the sudden change.

The great army of knights were returning from the valley below. She heaved great shuddering gasps, in relief,

But she had relaxed too soon. Another Greek, hidden behind a cart, lifted his club. She felt a sharp blow on her abdomen. There was a great tearing feeling, and Solange knew no more.

10

The world jounced in a very peculiar way. Up and down, round and round, all centered around a hub of the wheel located somewhere inside her. She heard someone moan and knew she herself had made the sound.

What had happened? She knew this much—something terrible made Jehane's eyes swollen, red with weeping.

Solange turned her head slightly, and met Aimery's clear gray look. "Not like granite," she thought and did not know she spoke aloud.

"Solange, it's all right," Aimery crooned.

"No, no it isn't," she whimpered, "but I don't remember why not."

Aimery held her then, letting her weep her misery out against his leather tunic. Someday he would tell her what had met his eyes when he raced back up the pass with the rescuing knights—raced solely in search of Solange.

His frail wife was laying about her with a sword as big as she was, and the ground around her was strewn with the fallen. A Viking lady indeed, he thought, his lips twitching with the memory. But the word Viking came back to wound him.

It was Erik's babe she had lost. What would she feel when she knew? Would she be desolate? How deeply had she loved the man?

The battle was not really over. The Greeks had retreated, leaving the Franks time to succor their wounded. But now they had rearmed themselves, and fell once again upon the Crusaders.

"I must go," he said to Jehane. "Take care that she is put into the first cart that goes down the mountain."

Solange heard none of this. She was wandering in a limbo where weird shrieks were commonplace, where rushing winds buffeted her cheeks, where the pain never stopped.

She roused slightly, thinking she had been cradled in her husband's arms. But he was not there. She must have dreamed it. Dreamed it—and mourned for it like a child sobbing in the dark.

Aimery returned, wiping his sword before he thrust it back into his girdle. He dropped to his knees beside Solange, still lying on the ground, still as death. Jehane crouched beside her, lifting up woebegone eyes to Aimery.

"She's dying. My God, she's dying!" He thrust Jehane aside and knelt beside Solange. "Get Lady de Mowbrai!"

He glanced wildly around him. There was a cart, one wheel crazily at an angle. But there was straw in it, and perhaps it could be righted.

His powerful muscles straining, Aimery got the wheel back on the wooden axle. He lifted Solange and gently laid her, on the straw, the blood on her pelisson drying in the hot sun. Then he picked up the shafts and, in the place of a donkey, pulled his wife down the mountainside trail.

Aimery met Petronilla and Jehane coming up. Petronilla gasped when she saw Aimery's grim face and her daughter's body.

He carried Solange to the place Petronilla indicated. How had he been so blind? How had he been able to deny Garin's certainty that love was at the bottom of his feelings for Solange? From the moment he had seen her, pale and shaking in the woods, he had felt a tie pulling him toward her.

Quite a lover, he thought bitterly. The queen's Court of Love, prattling about the fine emotions, the delicate romances, the unquestioning devotion to one's love. What a comedy!

Now it was too late. Solange lay dying, and he had no chance to tell her how much he loved her.

Petronilla banished him from the hastily set-up tent, but he moved only as far as the base of a pine tree, close enough to watch the door. Inside, there was frantic activity. He dreaded the moment when it might stop, for then all would be lost.

He was still there, eyes riveted on the tent door, when word came to him that the queen wanted to see him.

He could be of no use here, he thought, following Trotti across the camp to the royal pavilion.

"I understand," said Eleanor when he arrived, "that you are concerned about your lady wife. Is she still living?"

"At last report." His voice was strangled.

"You have been faithful to the wen—to your lady, beyond the call of duty. With such provocation as you have suffered, your loyalty does you credit. Not many a baron takes his vows so seriously."

"Vows taken in Holy Church, lady, are to be reckoned with." Aimery watched her warily. The queen was a woman of uncertain temper, and she wielded much power, not only through the king, but her own power as well. More than half the knights on the Crusade were her own Poitevin vassals, and much of the money that Suger was to raise would come from the lands which called her their duchess.

Aimery held no illusions about the queen. Shrewder than the king, perhaps, he understood the queen better than her husband did. And, just now, torn apart by his love for Solange, likely dying this moment, he was wild to be back at his wife's side.

He had learned much in the last months. The heavy responsibilities the king had laid on him were exactly what he needed in his aimless questing life. He had risen to the duties of his station and grown with them, and the Court of Love, by which the queen seemed to set store, was at best a foolish notion for children.

And yet, the queen's eyes glittered just now and he was afraid. Not for himself, but for his dainty, lovely, mischievous, thoroughly unpredictable Solange.

At last the queen spoke again, murmuring silkily, "From what I am told, not every man—or woman—takes to heart vows made in Holy Church." Smiling brilliantly, she dismissed him. "I trust," she said, not trying to hide the hollowness of the sentiment, "that you will find the Lady Solange better when you return to her."

Solange recovered.

Petronilla's ministrations began to take hold after two days.

The cavalcade continued on its way. Solange rode in the cart for ten days, and then, as they came out of the mountains and saw the fifty towers of Byzantium in the distance, she left the cart and rode a mule that Aimery found for her.

The fabled city of the East rose before them in fantastic splendor, and the Crusaders fell silent in awe of the great civilization they were seeing.

It was October fourth. At Belvent the great oaks would be turning brown, the maples scarlet. The grasses along the Petitmer would already have become a tawny border to the water reflecting the matchless blue October sky.

Here in this strange land, summer lingered, stale and past her prime, but reluctant, like an aging belle, to relinquish the center of attention.

Constantinople, the capital of the east, was built on the tip of a peninsula jutting out into the great water of the Sea of Marmora. Beyond the city, Solange knew, was a fabulous indentation in the shoreline of the Bosporus, the narrow link between the waters of Marmora and the Black Sea. The inlet, for it was no more than that, was called the Golden Horn, possibly because it was filled shore to shore with ships of all kinds, bringing precious goods from lands that seemed no more than legendary names.

The city itself commanded the great waterway that separated Asia from Europe. Beyond the five-mile strait that ran between the two continents, rose the hills of Asia, great rising mounds that would eventually lead into mountains. And somewhere beyond the Bosporus lay Antioch. And Odo de St. Florent.

She could not cease looking at Constantinople, the gateway to all her hopes. The great walls that surrounded the city rose nearly to the sky, so it seemed to her, and in her weakened state they looked impassable. So might a weary pilgrim assault the gates of heaven and, finding no gate, wander the outside rampart forever.

Solange had become terribly thin. What few clothes she had left hung on her. Her state of mind was as forlorn.

Erik was in Byzantium, ahead of her. She could not even remember just what he looked like. She could, if she summoned memory hard enough, remember the feel of his hands on her, the press of his hard body calling forth her eager response. But Erik himself was vague.

Aimery now rode nearby, not close enough to be a companion, but so that when she lifted her eyes to her surroundings, he was within sight. She had not spoken much to him since the battle of the mountain. She knew, because her mother had told her, that he had fetched her down, and got the help she needed. But when she had thanked him, he brushed her gratitude aside.

The emperor sent emissaries to meet them, to bring them jewels and gold encrusted cups.

"What we need," said the Franks, "is food for our stomachs and hay for our mounts."

But the food and hay were not forthcoming in the amounts that Manuel Comnenus had promised. Back in the great hall at Etampes, Erik had delivered his ruler's promises—grain in abundance, fruit such as you have never before tasted, forage for all the horses you can bring, and a great welcome from all my people.

They had enough of the welcome, said Garin, still limping from his wounds. The monk, usually optimistic, found even his good humor was strained. The Greeks had been forced to allow Roman masses in their churches. But it did not add to the Franks' goodwill to see the Greeks hasten in, almost before the last Frank had left the church, to cleanse the altar and the church from the defiling touch of the Romans.

"Aren't we all Christians?" muttered many of the priests. Their mutterings did nothing to calm the pilgrims, smarting from the treatment they had received all along the way.

But the emissaries of Manuel the emperor seemed not to understand the Frankish tongue when the barons from the west asked for grain, even going so far as to hint that the emperor was a man of little integrity.

After the great reception for the king and queen at the Blachernae Palace given by Manuel's nobles—though the emperor was too exalted to greet them himself—Solange was limp with exhaustion.

They settled at last, the queen's guard housed in luxury. Solange, however, did not reside with most of the ladies.

Aimery was a valuable member of the king's council and, as such, he and Solange were given a palace to themselves, with its own fantastic view of the Golden Horn.

She could hardly believe such luxury existed. Used only to Jehane—often as not absent on her own lucrative business—Solange could hardly believe that she needed only to clap her hands and a troop of servants would appear and bring her whatever she desired.

A bevy of soft-voiced, dark-eyed maidens bathed her daily in a marble tub and rubbed her with scented oils.

She ate dates, figs, sweet apricots fresh from the orchards along the Golden Horn. She felt she had been born again to a new life. Gone was the nightmare of the rigorous journey, and now that she was beginning to feel herself again, she began to recollect events from the journey. Certainly the famine and the hardships had changed everyone who survived.

Now she could remember: Aimery's terrible anger at the river crossing. The cut strap on her saddle girth. Aimery tending her after the battle on the mountain, when she had lost Erik's babe. Bagge's deliberate overturning of the cart on the mountain pass.

Bagge had disappeared after the battle, probably killed. The battle itself and her dangerous brush with death afterwards had erased Bagge from her mind. But now she could remember the stricken look on his face as he realized she had survived and had seen him try to murder her. But why? Someone must have paid him. She remembered, too, that Chauve had complained about Bagge's sudden riches. Was that after the river crossing? No, she remembered, it was before. Perhaps that money was to pay for her death. But whose was the gold?

Was it Mehun's, d'Yves', the queen's? Possibly Sybille's brothers, in revenge for her witnessing their crime, had wished her dead. But she tired easily, and soon, lulled by the security of Byzantium and its luxurious living, she decided she was safe, at least for now. Aimery stayed close to her these days, and she knew he would keep her safe.

Aimery concealed from Solange a scheme that had formed itself during those days when he thought he had lost her.

He must win Solange, as though he were just now meeting her for the first time, must draw her toward him by imperceptible stages, until he saw that certain light in her eyes—the light he had seen only once before, and had let vanish.

But he must be careful not to arouse the queen's jealousy. And Eleanor had spies at all levels. Aimery did not even trust Jehane, devoted as she had been in Solange's great trouble. He did not trust anyone. There was an atmosphere of distrust throughout the city. Aimery, being close to the king, saw it.

When he returned to the palace at the close of the day and sought out Solange, it was to tell her about the day's proceedings. His heart leaped when he saw her eyes light up as he came toward her across the marble floor. Sitting together on scarlet and turquoise cushions on the balcony, looking out over the fairyland city, he looked forward to telling her what was going on.

She had a quick intelligence and her interest never flagged. When King Louis arrived in Byzantium—Aimery told his wife—he had expected to find the Emperor Conrad waiting for him.

"They were to join troops and set forth overland to the Holy Land. The Byzantines were to have a fleet ready to transport us over the waters, and the supplies for our army were to be in warehouses at Nicosia," said Aimery.

"But the Greeks did not do this?"

"Manuel sent the Emperor Conrad on ahead."

"Manuel's empress is Conrad's sister, isn't she? Does he want to have all the glory?"

"So it is thought in the council. There is a lot of feeling against the Greeks."

"You remember," said Solange, "the returning pilgrims? Every one of them said to beware of the Greeks."

"This is so. But our good king is too trusting."

"So we are to ride out soon!"

"The supplies are not ready yet, so we are told. I confess I should like to see those grain barns myself, to know what is truly in them."

"I should imagine that Manuel didn't want our army added to Conrad's in his own capital," said Solange.

"No doubt," said Aimery, pleased by her perception. "We could take the city, even with our army alone, I think."

He sipped his coffee, sweetened in the oriental way, and made a face. But it was all there was to drink in this city, except for the wines, which he did not trust.

"There are those," he continued, in a lower voice, "who urge privately that we should depart from the city, join our rabble outside the walls, and then take for ourselves the fields and orchards. They say that, as we have been promised these, we would thus be taking only our own."

"How many starved for lack of the promised grain!" she cried.

"They say the king should retrace his steps a bit, and seize the entire land of Thrace, with its fertile fields and prosperous cities and castles. Then, when Roger of Sicily comes with his fleet—as he will—take Constantinople itself. But the king will not listen," Aimery explained.

"But that is not fighting the pagans!"

"No, but there are those who say the Greeks are not true Christians, anyway. They are not Western Christians, at least. And there are those in the council who say simply —let us take the city and teach Manuel what it means to break his word."

She was silent a long time. Aimery was content to watch the sun touch the curve of her throat, deepen the dark lashes that lay thick on her pale cheeks. He would never have thought that he could restrain his ardent desire for her. But there was more at stake in his life than the next hour and the slaking of his present thirst.

"What are you thinking?" he asked huskily.

"I was wondering when we should set out for Antioch."

"To find word of your father. I have not heard his name mentioned at all."

"There was a time when I was too weak to care. But I still must know what there is to know."

"I understand how it is," he said. "And I will help if I can."

"Thank you," she smiled.

Was it possible that soon he would see the light in her eyes grow into a steady flame?

11

At last Solange felt well enough to undergo the rigors of a state reception. She dressed carefully—not in amethyst, for that color was forbidden to all but the royal family—but in turquoise and silver, the bliaut made with long pointed sleeves whose cuffs reached to the floor.

The first item was to be a religious ceremony at Hagia Sophia. The ladies were not allowed on the floor of the church at all, as was the custom in all Byzantine churches. Solange joined the queen, the Empress Bertha, Manuel's niece Theodora—a young woman of surpassing beauty and an awareness of her own charm quite equal to Eleanor's—and the other ladies of the queen's guard in the north gallery of the church. The church was so beautiful that Solange thought heaven itself could hold nothing finer. She could not take it in all at once: the glass mosaics, the columns topped with sculpture so deeply cut that they seemed like lace made of stone.

But above all, the great dome seemed the very vault of heaven. Cunningly devised, it seemed to float in the air without resting on the church structure at all.

She hardly noticed the beautifully carved marble screen before the altar, or the silver gauze curtain behind the screen. Nor the chanting of the priests, nor the candles and oil lamps in the magnificent, crown-shaped chandeliers. She could almost feel the blessing of God resting upon her head, and she hardly knew when Bertille plucked at her sleeve and told her the service was over.

From there they were escorted to an official reception at the Sacred Palace, and she got her first glimpse of the great emperor. He was tall and built like an athlete, his complexion sun-browned as befitted a man of action. It was said he was an able fighter, and his weapons were said to be so heavy that most men could not lift them.

Solange saw his eyes resting more upon the ladies than his councilmen, or even King Louis, his honored guest. The boldness of his stare reminded her of someone, but just now she could not think whom. But it would be a strong woman who could deny that charm. And, if rumor were true, very few did.

The reception was fantastic, and after they had bowed themselves in and out again, the Franks gathered in the Blachernae palace which Manuel had placed at the disposal of his guests.

They had been in Constantinople for ten days. Already the snows were falling on the mountains beyond the Bosporus, so it was said, and Louis was in a fret lest the snows clog the passes and prevent him from accomplishing his mission this year.

There was much to discuss and, surprisingly, the king did not retreat into privacy with only his council. Instead, he told the assembled nobles what Manuel had suggested.

"He feels that the rigors of the journey, the great danger in the battles, are too much for the ladies to undergo. And certainly, we have firsthand knowledge of rigorous travels! So—"

The queen could not wait for her husband to finish. She interrupted, saying, "So the emperor wishes us to stay here. The queen's guard, he says, are too precious to endanger."

King Louis looked sidelong at his wife. Solange had not seen them together for some time, but she now thought she could detect friction between them. But the king, if he were annoyed, hid it well.

The king's nobles also chafed to leave the city of so many delights and so little progress. The emperor promised, his servants promised . . . but there was no sign of horses, of supply wagons, of boats to take them across to the Asian side of the water.

And the soldiers, camped outside the walls because Manuel dared not let the Crusaders all inside at once, were growing restless. The Greeks were charging outrageous prices for provisions.

Louis decided it was time indeed to move on. Besides,

certain bishops who had come all the long way with Louis, and had watched the religious fervor of the expedition as it waned, had already remonstrated with Eleanor for her lack of pilgrim's demeanor. Eleanor, waspish, had defied them. It was time to journey onward.

"The queen's guard," said the queen, "will go on Crusade with the rest of the army. I have promised a convent to the glory of Our Lady if I once see the Holy City. And I must, of course, keep my vow."

Her dark eyes flickered over Aimery, Solange thought. But she for once agreed with the queen. She herself was going to Antioch. To find her father. After that—she did not want to think what she would do after that.

"It seems to me that Manuel had some points on his side," said the king. "It is rigorous for the ladies."

"He wishes us to stay as hostages," said Lucienne de Beçu. "For your good behavior in giving over the cities you take."

Immediately a babble arose, most of which seemed to be in Lucienne's favor.

"No matter," the queen's voice cut through the noise like a knife. "I have decided. I will go, and my guard will accompany me. Unless anyone is too ill to travel." It was not a question. She looked directly at Solange.

Solange was spared the embarrassment of answering as Lucienne fell into an argument with her neighbor. Soon the meeting, such as it was, broke up in confusion.

Not until Solange was back in her palace did she begin to lose her anger with the queen. There seemed little doubt that the queen wanted Aimery to herself all the way to Jerusalem. But Solange would go.

Later in the day, the sun was setting to the west of the city, glinting on the Golden Horn, on the gold-covered domes of the hundreds of churches.

Aimery had left her, to return to the king, where the discussion was to continue.

Jehane slipped into the room with an air of great stealth. Solange looked up in surprise. "What is it?"

For answer, Jehane gave Solange a slip of paper, folded and sealed. "Where did this come from?"

Jehane said, "I do not know the messenger, lady."

Breaking the seal, Solange read and gasped. " 'News of Odo,' " she read. " 'I cannot write it. Come to me and I will put you in touch with a man who knows.' " The missive was signed "Erik."

Erik!

He had not sent word to her in all the time she had been in Constantinople. She had thought he had forgotten her. But he had remembered her quest.

"The messenger is waiting, lady," said Jehane.

"Get your cloak. We will go at once."

She hesitated for a moment, after Jehane had left in search of the wraps. Should she send word to Aimery? He said he understood her search. But he might not understand Erik. No, it was best to tell him after she returned. There might not be much news.

Jehane returned with dark hooded cloaks for both of them. "You wish me to go?" said Jehane doubtfully.

"You are afraid?"

"Oh, no, lady," she said, moistening her lips nervously.

The messenger was waiting. She thought she might know him, but he was a stranger to her—a silent stranger, at that. He beckoned and they set out through the dark streets.

It was a long way to their destination. The great hordes of wild dogs that rooted in the streets at night bared their fangs as their guide made their way through them.

In daylight, the city was beautiful. But now at night, the water running through the filthy streets, the dogs, the smell that told them they were heading downhill toward the shores of the Golden Horn—all these lent an air of conspiracy to the expedition.

They passed shadowed doorways, and Solange was aware of other silent shadows in the street. Once, she stopped short. Jehane bumped into her from the back, and her guide went a few steps beyond before turning back. She thought of returning to her own palace, and going to see Erik on the morrow.

But she reflected that maybe Erik's informant was not able to wait until the morrow, and she wanted to talk to him herself. And she realized, looking back, that she did not know her way back. She could not find her way through the maze of streets, not without her guide.

Although she did not trust him overly much, he was all she had just now.

She gestured to him. "Go on, we will follow."

He turned then and began to walk very fast. Very fast indeed. And then she saw the shadows gathering around.

There were shadows around them on the street—the shadows of armed men, with lifted arms, and unmistakable intent.

Her scream died upon her lips.

12

It was all over in a moment. Solange saw the fleeing guide running down the cobbled street, turning the corner of the next street before being swallowed by the dark.

There was no time to reflect upon the perfidy of the guide. She had been foolish in the extreme. But it was too late. Her assailant wrapped her in her own cloak, pulling down her hood to muffle her screams. Cursing as she wriggled, the man wrenched her arms behind her, and painfully lifted her from her feet.

Where was Jehane? She listened carefully, but there was no sound from the girl. Only from the man who followed her own attacker. "A nice piece," he was saying in that strange *lingua franca*. "I didn't expect two of them."

"You can have her," said the man who was carrying Solange. "I'll take the money for this one, and buy my own."

They went through winding streets, Solange trying to remember the twists and turnings as they went. But there were too many. She did notice that they kept going downhill, toward the river. She knew, from her previous excursions around the town, that there were many beautiful palaces lining the river. But it was not likely they were going to one of them.

At last they arrived at their destination. She was set upon her feet, still muffled in the cloak, on a marble floor.

The sudden light, when they took off the cloak, was blinding. She did see, though, that Jehane was taken away, and she herself left alone. Her attacker said simply, "Wait."

The moment he was out of sight, she turned to flee. But her way was barred by a broad hulk of a man, silent as a mute, with a large curved sword.

Soon another servant, as mute as the guard, came and bade her with gestures to follow him.

There were many rooms, but no one was in sight.

Her curiosity finally was piqued. If this were Erik's idea of a joke, she would have a thing or two to say to him. After all, she had not been hurt, and Erik's humor had sometimes been of the more boisterous variety.

The room her guide finally stopped at looked no different from the others. He motioned her inside the door, and she obeyed. The door was shut behind her with ominous finality.

She had heard wild stories about the domestic arrangements of the infidels. The savage Turks had many, many women, and were able to handle them all, one after another.

Here were silken cushions, of size enough to form a bed. Wall hangings of delicate silk, spun fine so that the slightest breath would make them move, revealed a rainbow of color.

The curtains swayed slightly as the door opened and closed behind the last man she had expected to see.

"Ah, Solange," said the Baron d'Yves. "At last."

"Your palace?" Her blood hammered in her head. She had nearly forgotten the deadly threats this man had made, his insistence that she was his. He had not forgotten, though. "How came you by this"—she gestured with both hands—"this harem? Even your robe is fashioned in infidel style."

"Not quite a harem. This is all designed for only one woman, Solange. The woman I own."

"No one owns me," she said vigorously. She must keep

him at bay while she thought of something. Anything. For there was no possibility of rescue from this trap. She was the fool of the world to have fallen into it!

"I have bought you. You do seem to forget that."

"I can't think why you feel I have changed."

"I don't suppose you have. But the question is, have I? Yes, I think I have changed. I am tired, for one thing, of waiting for you to come to my arms."

"You may wait forever."

"I think not, my dear. I don't have forever, you know. I weary of this incessant traveling, and I am quite sure the delights of the road to Jerusalem—whatever they might be—would pale besides the infinite variety of experience to be found in this city."

She was startled. "You mean you're not going on to Jerusalem with the king?"

He laughed, an odd rippling sound that chilled her. "I never was *with* the king. I came along for the company. Yours, particularly."

She must keep him talking, keep him at arm's length. She said, "I suppose you found as many willing women as you wanted along the way."

"Oh, yes. Even your maid served me one night, and I confess she had a trick or two I didn't know about. I wonder where these peasants learn these things. . . ." He sighed elaborately. "Possibly from the animals around them. But no matter."

"Aimery will kill you," she said stoutly, "Surely one night with me is not worth your life?"

"But your husband does not know where you are. We have the entire night before us, and I am sure you will prove worth the waiting."

"And then—you will send me back to my husband?"

"If he wants you. Although you will be, I regret to say, not as you are now."

"Wh-what do you mean?" Solange felt the blood drain from her face. "I knew you were evil, but—"

"Wait and see, shall we? Who knows? You will be amazed at some of the things I have learned since we arrived here."

Solange said defiantly. "From what I have heard, you already were a master of the unsavory."

"Ah, but they have refinements here. One of the emperor's cousins has taken me under his wing, and we have sampled some of the night life along the waterfront. In disguise, of course. Although he does seem to be well known, especially in the back rooms where all manner of things go on."

"You are vile!"

"Perhaps so. But you are a woman of passion, and not averse to dalliance with a man not your husband. Perhaps you might even learn to like some of these things I have in mind. The most delicate of sensations, the pain so fleeting that you will hardly notice it, I promise you."

"You will never see the day!" she cried.

"I do like a little resistance," he said, a smile touching his lips, but not reaching his eyes. He made a sudden movement and there was a knife in his hand.

"All right," she said suddenly. "You have checkmate. What will you take to let me go free? You are greedy for money, I know, Conon. How much will it take?"

"This night is not for sale at any price," grinned Conon. "The first thing—"

"The first thing," she said, with an air of concession, "is a drink of water. I have had nothing to eat all day." She eyed him warily, to see whether her ploy might work. "You would not want me to faint dead away, would you?"

He stopped to consider. "No, I think not. Although I have learned some interesting things to be done—but perhaps later. Now I have wine here, and I urge you to drink of it."

He had handed her a small glass of amber liquid.

"Is this drugged?" she asked airily. "Although I suppose you would not tell me if it were."

"Drugs would only veil the exquisite sensations you will feel, very soon. Drink the wine, Solange. I become impatient."

With misgivings she dared not show, she swallowed the drink. She hoped he was truthful about the wine. Logic told her he probably was. He would want to extract every ounce of pleasure from her—suffering or ecstasy, either one, he wanted to savor it all.

He came to take her glass away and set it on the table. He came close, but his eyes were too watchful for her to make any move away from him. He set the glass down, and the knife beyond it. "You will have no chance at the knife, Solange. I remember too well your expert handling of even a small dagger."

The lamp flickered, throwing its flame high when Conon moved toward her. In the sudden light she could see his odd eyes, tiny pupils startlingly dark in the glazy pale iris. "Where is Jehane?" she demanded.

"Jehane? Is she here? I didn't really know. Enough," he said with an alarming change in his voice. "I think it's time."

He stood stock still, arrested in motion. He made a quick, obscene gesture with his hand. "Oh, yes," he said, still in that strange eerie tone, "it is time. I should like to tell you, Solange, just what I shall do to you. Or perhaps it will come better as a constant series of delightful surprises? But I feel that delay may defeat my purpose."

With a sudden movement of his shoulders, the flowing robe fell to the floor around his feet. He stood naked before her, and she could see that, as he had said, it was indeed time.

He started for her.

All the refinements of torture he had mentioned were forgotten as he flung her back on the cushions, sobbing with emotion in her ear, unable to subdue the rising urgency of his lust. His torso toppled upon her. He lay heavily, as though unable to lift his arms, simply sobbing uncontrollably. He gasped out her name.

A warm rivulet ran down the outside of her thigh. Then he lay spent, shuddering great breaths, his weight pinning her, unable to move.

Slaked, he rolled to one side, one hand heavy on her waist. His laugh was self-condemning. "You see? Now I will have more leisure to arouse an equal delight in you. A refinement, I confess, I had not planned."

He loosed her to wipe his beaded face with his free

376

hand. Instantly, she slid from the cushion and was on her feet facing him.

"You devil!" he said, scrambling to his feet. "Don't you know you'll not escape me? There's no place for you to go!"

Her wild, dark eyes staring at him, she backed away, step by step, as he stalked her. She skirted the smaller of the cushions on the floor, and he followed her, his eyes fixed on hers like a ferret's on a rabbit. She had no plan, but fear drove her. She kept backing until she could get the cushion on the floor between them at the right angle.

Then, with a quick thrust of her foot, the cushion shot out into the path of the baron and he could not avoid it. Suddenly, he fell, and his arm doubled beneath him. She could hear something crack—a bone, probably—and he cursed.

"I'm hurt—," he cried. "I'm bleeding! Get help! I'll bleed to death! The bone—right through my flesh!"

She hurried to the door. Outside, barring her escape, was the great guard. Swifter than thought, she gestured toward the fallen baron, holding his arm and rocking back and forth. The guard was startled out of his wits. Rushing to his master, he dropped his sword and reached out both hands to lift him up.

And the scimitar lay unwatched on the cushion behind him.

Solange, armed with the great curved sword, tiptoed out of the room. She did not try to close the door behind her, for the noise might alert those within. She blundered down one hall after another.

Jehane—where was she? She could not leave without her. She had deep suspicions of Jehane, who seemed overly gullible in the matter of the note. But she could not leave a girl brought up on the lands of Belvent to an uncertain fate in the baron's palace.

She found her tied to a chair, waiting the further pleasure of the man who had carried her this far. He had already torn the girl's tunic, and ropes cut cruelly into her flesh.

The scimitar served its purpose quickly, and the ropes fell away.

"He's gone for more drink," sobbed Jehane.

"Then we won't wait," whispered Solange.

Out into the night, through the back door, through the shadowed grass and trees. They were in one of the apricot orchards along the water's edge.

With any luck, there would be a gate in the walls surrounding the palace. And with even greater luck, no one would be guarding it.

"Come on," hissed Solange urgently. "We've got a little way to go. But we've got to hurry."

13

They found the gate, a small door in the whitewashed wall surrounding the palace. Solange stopped, gasping for breath. She still held Jehane's wrist in a tight grip, and the scimitar in her other hand.

She loosed her hold, and Jehane rubbed her wrist, whimpering. "What are we going to do?"

Solange looked back at the palace they had just left. Lights were springing up at various windows. The guard was summoning help. For Conon, of course, and then, no doubt, to search for the woman who had felled their master and made her escape.

"We're going to leave here," said Solange, praying she was right.

She found the latch to the gate. Surprised at its simplicity, she lifted it and the gate swung inward.

It stuck, not open enough to let them through. She dropped the scimitar, somewhat surprised to find that she still carried it, and used both hands to tug at the gate. It was no use. She could not get through an opening only a handspan wide.

Impatiently, she moved the gate closed again and then pulled it violently toward her. This time it opened easily and she nearly fell to the ground. "A twig underneath the bottom," she guessed. "Come on, you go through."

"I'm afraid," Jehane whined. "It may be a trap."

"Do you have any other ideas?" gritted Solange.

They would simply have to trust in the Providence that had guided her escape from the horrible fate Conon d'Yves had prepared for her.

"Look!" cried Jehane. "They're coming!"

Torches now bobbed in the darkness along the palace, spreading out into the dark orchard. There was no more time. Without hesitation, Solange slipped through the gate.

There was no one in the street beyond. Conon had felt secure enough that he had not bothered to set guards at the gate.

The river lay on her left. Therefore, the way home must lie to the right. Solange pulled her maid along with her. The street of the palaces lay above the waterfront, she knew that. And there would be streets that rose upward away from the shore. She must make their way ever upward, until at last they were on streets she knew.

They turned yet another corner. Jehane was whimpering constantly now. Solange hissed, "You got us into this. I should have left you there. If you don't shut up now, I'll leave you here in the alley."

Jehane's moan held a wealth of fear. She followed more quickly, and almost stopped whimpering.

But the dogs had found them.

The dogs of the city ruled at night. During the day they slept, or slunk away when a human approached them, but the night was their element and they snarled and fought and cleaned up the carrion left in the streets, and battened upon the helpless.

It was said that sleeping babes had been carried off and eaten by the dogs, and there were whole areas of the city, in the hovels and the tenements, where no man walked by night for fear of the dogs.

The two women heard the barking, snarling, guttural grunts of the dogs, and Solange's heart failed her. She had come so far to be downed at last by a pack of dogs!

"Run, Jehane!" she urged, starting to run and pulling her maid behind her. But it was no use. The dogs were nipping at their heels, and Jehane cried out with pain. Suddenly Solange remembered.

"I've still got this!" she cried. "Stand aside, girl!"

The scimitar in both hands, she swung, and swung again. Swung until the night was filled with yelps, howls of anguish, and, finally, the sound of fleeing dogs.

Jehane began to whimper again, but this time Solange said, "They've gone, Jehane! Cry if you want to. I might even join you!"

"I want to go home," wailed Jehane.

"Believe me," said Solange with distaste, "I wish you were there. Come on now, lest I leave you behind—for the dogs."

Solange thought she saw a wider mouth in the narrow street. With a few more steps, they would emerge at the wide plaza where there were people. She could already hear voices!

But the voices ahead were rough and harsh. Solange and Jehane held together in the shadows, scarcely breathing. "It's the Norsemen!" breathed Solange.

They stepped out into the light. Solange realized their appearance did them little good.

"Aha! Here's fair sport!"

"I vow I starve for a blue-eyed damsel once again!"

"I am no damsel," said Solange with dignity. "Take us to Erik."

The mention of their leader struck one with amusement. "Yes, yes! He likes the pale kind. Remember the woman in France? This one is like—"

"I am that woman!" protested Solange. Too drunk to listen, they herded the women across the plaza to a smaller building. Once inside, she recognized Erik's predilection for austerity on the outside and luxury within.

"Why shouldn't I have a woman like Erik!" It was the drunkest of the lot. They turned up the lamps. She now recognized someone.

"Well, Viktor?" she said. "You tread dangerously in your master's footsteps."

"By Thor, it is the lady," he muttered, stricken.

"Take me to Erik," she repeated.

For answer, he rapped on an inner door, and opened it. "You, lady," said Viktor. "Not her. She stays."

Jehane looked numb. She looked at her mistress with mute appeal, but Solange could offer no help. She faced ahead and moved through the door Viktor held open.

The effect her unheralded entrance had upon Erik was most satisfactory, Solange decided, after he had closed his open mouth and got to his feet. Then she detected a certain wariness in the back of his eyes.

Mischievously, she took advantage of his surprise. "Do you know why I'm here?"

"My good angel has brought you," he said promptly.

"You did not send for me?"

"I had not the courage. But now you are here—" He moved toward her. She stepped back automatically.

"I came here in answer to your note," she told him. "Telling me you have news of my father."

"I sent no note," he said, mystified, "and if I had word of your father, I would bring it to you."

Satisfied, she sighed. There had been a lingering fear that Erik might have given his help to Conon, for whatever price, but now she no longer believed that.

She paid no heed when Erik came closer to her, and placed his hands on her shoulders. Drawing her close to him, he tilted her chin toward him and kissed her, a long, probing kiss. She stood unmoved in his arms.

At length he drew back and looked down into her wide eyes, quizzically. "You do not respond?"

"I'm sorry, Erik."

He released her and took a quick turn around the room. "Was it because I left you carrying my child? I thought it best. Besides, I had orders to return."

"It was not that, Erik. You have not asked, but I lost the child."

"I knew that. I have kept track of you, you know." He filled a cup and brought it to her. "You see, I still care about you."

Strangely, she believed him. She had a faint glow of something very like gratitude for him. He had been what she needed at a critical time.

A sharp sound of rolling laughter came from the outer room. "My maid, Jehane!" she cried. "Your men—"

He strode to the door and spoke a few words. The laughter died. "They will find their amusement elsewhere. But how came you here?"

Briefly she told him of her journey through the streets, and Conon's trickery.

"I'll take care of you," said Erik. His eyes said more than his tongue, but she was grateful to him again for his restraint. Their paths could never cross again, and he was wise to know it.

Just the same, he took the greatest care to get the two women back into the side gate of her palace. Hurrying to her room, and obedient to the arrangements she had made with Erik, she lit a lamp and placed it on her balcony, so he would know she and Jehane had arrived and all was well.

She could hear the faint clatter of horses as Erik and his men rode away. She and Jehane were safe, and never again, as Erik had warned her, would she be so gullible as to trust an unfamiliar messenger.

A messenger brought by Jehane? She blew out the lamp, and lay down gratefully on her cushioned bed. She wondered. Had Jehane been involved in Conon's plot?

Yet Jehane herself had been tied up. Jehane had learned a lesson, perhaps, and it was all past. Solange had come away from Conon's without injury, when she had feared not to come away at all. Now she thought more generously about her maid. She would talk to her in the morning, and then forgive her.

14

Solange had not yet fallen asleep when Aimery entered her room. She roused quickly, suddenly aware that she had not bathed or changed her clothes since her excursion into the night.

"I did not expect you back tonight," she said, flustered. "So I gather."

"What does that mean?" She quickly realized that he was furious. Something must have gone wrong at court, she thought. She moved to take his cloak and was stopped short by the anger in his eyes.

"It means," he said, deliberately cruel, "that as soon as I tell you I shall be away, you take advantage of my absence, and frolic around the town."

"Aimery, you're mistaken. I did no such thing."

"Frolic, I suppose, is too mild a word for your activities? I judge by your streaked face and soiled gown that there was more to this evening than frolic?"

His sarcasm was knife-edged. She was bewildered. He was much as he had been at the beginning of their marriage. Whatever had happened to change him back?

"Aimery, I wasn't frolicking. It was all a terrible mistake."

"I am not surprised to hear that. Who was your companion this time?"

She was conscious of a rising anger in herself. She had had quite an evening, one way and another, and she had considered herself fortunate indeed to reach home alive. She had not expected to be accused before she had opened her mouth.

"I think you will apologize," she said, with as much calm as she could, "when you hear what happened tonight."

"I'll retract nothing," he said roughly. "I can imagine what happened tonight."

His imagination, fueled simply by his own strong desire for her, ran riot.

He took a turn around the room. "Perhaps I was hasty," he said, offering a mere olive twig. "I have spent a very hard night with the council—"

"For which I am to blame?" she asked.

He looked at her with something like appeal in his eyes. Memory pained him. He had suffered another wound like this, long before Solange danced into his life, long before she was born. His mother had played his father just this falsely, and their two-year-old son Aimery had clung bewildered to his mother's skirts, crying, when his father, austere and cold, had plucked him away, saying that his mother was soiled and could never be clean again.

He thought he had forgotten that, assumed he had come to terms with it. He knew the fault lay in him and in his old wounds as much as in Solange.

"What happened?" he asked bluntly. "Where have you been?"

With impish malice, she told him the truth. "I have been in a number of places this night, husband. I have been in a room looking much like a Turkish harem, from which I managed to escape by means of wielding a scimitar. Then I frolicked through the dark streets."

"Solange!" It was a groan.

She appeared not to hear. "And then I spent an hour with the emperor's bodyguards, but of course they were very drunk and might not remember just what happened."

"But you can't blame me," he was saying, "for thinking the worst."

"I can't?" she cried.

"Men are always bringing you home to me in a state of disarray."

"That's outrageous!"

"I will not tolerate such behavior," he was saying. "I will not be a laughingstock."

Furious, she lashed out at him. "You are the queen's. Don't tell me what you will tolerate. I have a few things of my own to say to you."

He started toward her and her words died on her lips. Then suddenly he stopped, holding his head in his hands.

"Solange, Solange!" he groaned, turning away. "What has happened between us? Can we not somehow put this back together?"

"Once," she said sternly, "I thought we could have. I even thought, in recent days, that we might become friends. I have long wished for such a friend, Aimery. But . . ."

She was silent so long that he prompted her. "But what?"

"But there's too much wrong between us now. I suppose, in time, I could have forgotten the broken promises. The unfortunate penchant you have for running when the queen crooks her finger. Your willingness to always believe the worst of me."

He interrupted sourly. "And I suppose you always see the best in me? I think not."

She scarcely heard him. She was growing weary of this constant battle with Aimery. She waved her hand vaguely, brushing aside his words. "I have seen too much of what happens, Aimery. Today one lives, and tomorrow one is dead. And I tell you this, husband. The king has wed us. For his own reason, as everyone knows. We have taken vows in church, and I will keep most of them. I do not believe, though, that church or king can direct my love to one man or another."

"Solange—!"

"Hear me out, Aimery, for I will not say this again. I will remain chaste. Erik was the only man who possessed me, and I went to him gladly. But none other. And I shall not take a substitute for my husband again. I promise you. But love you, I cannot."

He stood, the color draining from his face. The finality of it twisted in his belly like a sword. Not the words so much, as the lonely, desolate tone. It was eerie.

He would not allow this. He would make her love him. He would shake some sense into her.

He came toward her, his intent clear on his frowning face. She backed away, again. "Solange!" he groaned, clenching his fists in plain agony as he saw her flee, frightened of him.

But suddenly, she could fight no more. This was not Conon, not Erik. This was Aimery and she was his. If he killed her, she would not really care.

She sank down onto a cushion and buried her face in her hands. "No more," she murmured, "no more."

Aimery's suspicions flared anew. No more what?

A rap on the door froze them both where they were— she on the cushion in a posture of despair, he bending over her, hands balled into fists.

"A messenger from the court, my lord," said the servant. "It is demanded that you return at once."

The sound of mailed heels on the marble floor disappeared into the distance and then Aimery, too, was gone.

Gone to the court, thought Solange, gone, without a doubt, to Eleanor.

She sobbed herself to sleep, her head on the cushion, her body on the cold marble floor. She hardly noticed.

Science, just now, would have spoken again but h mother glanced at her and she fell silent. "Let me come one, she said later, "I want her own man to lead the double I will have none of ⟨M⟩cleut's men. I want nothing fro him."

"All right," said Samuela at last, "I too have fug

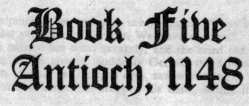

Book Five
Antioch, 1148

1

Spurred on by Manuel's good wishes—he was sincerely glad to see the last of the turbulent Frankish knights—and the fear of some of the king's barons that the Emperor Conrad would garner all the spoils of battle before they could join the Germans, the Crusaders made haste to leave the eastern capital.

The vanguard of Conrad's army straggled toward them on the outskirts of Nicea. The Franks lifted arms in glad welcome, but their shouts died away on their lips as they took in the sight before them.

The raggle-taggle troops of the Emperor Conrad were in rags. Sorely wounded, these starvelings were the fortunate ones. The unlucky nine-tenths of the German Army had left their bones along the way, mingled with broken horses, pieces of weapons, all the debris of the vanquished.

"I've had enough," said Conrad to King Louis. He looked now little like a great ruler. His fat had vanished, and his once-blond hair was now streaked with gray. His childlike blue eyes held the wonder of a man who, having always had all he wanted, had suddenly come upon adversity and failed to understand how this could happen to him.

"Enough? I should think so," said Count Robert. "Stay with us, and we'll merge our strength."

"Enough!" exclaimed Conrad. "I have had enough of this godforsaken land, where no man's word is worth anything, where the ground itself fights us. I think we are not meant to succeed with this Crusade, friend Louis. I think there is a curse over this land."

The innocent eyes darkened for a moment. "The guides, you know. They told me we would need a week's supply of water and food. *Gott in Himmel!* They lied—lied! It was a desert. No water. No food. Nothing but arrows coming out of nowhere! And then the guides left us, crept off during the night. I ask you, Louis! Would honest men do that? I think my precious brother-in-law arranged the whole thing. He's no Christian. I'm going home to Bavaria!"

It took strenuous efforts to make Conrad change his mind. And even after the barons thought they had convinced him to join his pitifully few troops to theirs, they found that he had again counted up the cost of the crusade in terms of soldiers, and the job had all to be done over.

"We took the road from Byzantium that the caravans take. But we didn't see any of the caravans. Not enough food and not enough water for my men. Horses died every night, and some of the men did too. Later, we fought all the Turks in the world!" Conrad went on. "Those little ponies they have are hardly bigger than dogs. They may *be* dogs for all I know. The Turks bark like hounds. And those drums, and the sheets of arrows—like a curtain they were, and they never stopped."

Conrad buried his face in his hands. His agony moved the men around him. The same Germans who had plundered the villages of the Danube, looting and killing, had now left their bones in the mountainous defiles of Asia. Even the stoniest among Louis's nobles were moved to pity, and an uneasy fear that what had happened to the Germans could happen to them. Louis mingled his tears with Conrad's.

The Germans and the Franks, in council, decided to not pursue the route through Cappadocia that Conrad had taken. "They even got my royal treasure," mourned Conrad. "I suppose there's no hope of getting it back?" he ventured hopefully.

"None whatsoever," said Count Robert, with finality.

The Crusaders turned westward. It was late November, although it was hard not to believe they had been on the road for years. The route lay along the coast rather than through the treacherous mountains.

The days stretched into weeks, and the season of rain and snow came upon them.

December saw them following the footsteps of the apostles, and now the spirit of faith that had brought them thus far flared up again, lighting them to new purpose and dedication. At Ephesus they saw the very site where Saint John the Evangelist had preached, and regarded with awe the ruined Temple of Diana. Saint Paul had stood on those very stones.

By Christmas, the cavalcade was two months behind schedule. And disaster struck again. Rain from the mountains beyond their sight swept down the river, taking with the flood men, horses, gear, siege engines carried all the way from Metz. All was now lost forever in the sea. Conrad and his men turned back.

They decided to strike inland, over the mountains, to Laodicea, and thence to Antioch where the queen's uncle awaited them. It seemed a short distance on the map, and perhaps they could travel faster now without Conrad and his Teutons. And so, unutterably weary and dispirited, they came at last to Mount Cadmos.

It was early January, 1148, on the Feast of Epiphany.

The gorges lay ahead of them. Strung out as they must be, in the narrow pass, it was imperative that all of the Crusaders stay together. They would be most vulnerable to attack.

The barons took turns leading the van, and this day leadership fell to the queen's Poitevin vassal, Geoffrey de Rançon, a man more than half in love with the queen since she had been a girl. The king's uncle, Amédée, the Count of Maurienne, shared the command. He was an old man, and the rigors of the journey were beginning to tell on him.

There was a bare tableland looming ahead just below the mountain's summit, spacious enough to provide room for a bare encampment. Geoffrey's orders were to stop there for the night.

As it was vital to keep the cavalcade together, it was decided that the van would camp halfway up the mountain, and wait for the rest of the train.

But the queen rode on beyond the tableland, exhilarated by the altitude and the difficulty of the ascent. She turned her brooding eyes back down the trail to where her husband was striving to get her baggage wains up the impossible defile, hurrying his cavalry to get through the pass before nightfall.

Ahead of her lay an inviting green valley, water flowing through the middle of it, lush and cool. "Geoffrey!" she called, and pointed ahead of them. "It's just the place to camp." She looked around her at the bleak tableland, her mouth drawing down at the corners. "Not here! I won't do it."

"My orders—"

"*My* orders," said the queen gently, and rode on ahead, down the track toward the meadows below. Geoffrey muttered. But seeing that his queen was proceeding without him, and thinking that the Turks might fall on her unprotected person, he spurred his horse and followed her.

The ladies cantered down into the valley, following Eleanor. Soon the green grass blossomed with the exotic colors of the ladies' garments.

Behind them, in the gathering dusk, climbed Louis and his knights, without their armor. The mail would have boiled them alive in the heat. The men toiled, encumbered by baggage wains, pilgrims trudging upward with their last ounce of strength, the cavalry traveling single file. The men struggled up the mountain pass, straining to arrive at the tableland where there would be food and drink, and rest.

When they arrived, there was nothing. The tableland was bare. Louis passed a hand across his eyes, unbelieving.

The tableland, where he had ordered his queen and the vanguard to halt for the night, was empty. He looked back down the steep pass his men had just traversed with such difficulty. He was chilled by the realization that his army, without armor, was strung out for more than a mile and, ahead of him somewhere was his queen with only a handful of armed knights to protect her and her ladies. Louis stood for a moment while the enormity of the situation bore in on him. At that moment Louis understood that his lively wife was a curse to him and to his people.

Then the Turks fell upon them. Lurking in the hills, they had been waiting for the moment when the army would be helpless. Now there burst from every rock, every ravine, swarms and swarms of Turks. They came in whirlwinds— as Conrad had described—their tomtoms and their tambourines and their odd animal yelping sounding like all the fiends from hell let loose.

Baggage wains, horses, riders, all tumbled into the gorge at the lip of the pass.

Aimery sped to his king's side and, with a few others, held off the Turks for a while. Darkness fell and the battle raged. At length, the beleaguered king climbed into the stub of a tree. His men guarded him below until, weary of the battle, the Turks rode away.

And the queen first learned of the tragedy when scouts brought news the next day of heaps of bodies lying in windrows up the mountain.

At daybreak, the dazed king of the Franks rode into the valley on a wounded cart horse, and the roll call was taken.

The toll was incredible. Hundreds were gone, dead from the fall into the gorge, or with Turkish arrows in their unarmored bodies.

Because the king's uncle had been commander along with Geoffrey and must, therefore, share the blame, the only punishment levied against Geoffrey de Rançon was that he was sent home to Poitou. He lived the rest of his life with a vision of bodies, knowing that, but for him, those men would have lived.

When they reached Laodicea, it was decided to continue to Antioch by ship. The way would take only a few days, so the Greek guides said, and there would be many ships to carry the Franks from the port of Satalia.

There were only a handful of ships, as it turned out. Enough for Louis and Eleanor, and sufficient for the army to provide an escort, but hardly more. The king could not afford to pay the passage of all the followers in his train, so many paid for their own way and their servants'.

But there were simply not ships enough—the Greeks had lied. Also, they had lied about the length of time it would take to skirt the land and arrive in Antioch.

The only consolation in the three-week miserable voyage was that the journey would have been much longer and more perilous by land.

2

It was March. It had taken the Crusaders five months to cross Asia Minor, and at last they had arrived on friendly soil. Antioch was in the hands of the Franks, and they could rest safely until they began the last stage of their journey to Jerusalem.

The harbor town bordered the sea in a crescent-shaped gathering of houses on either side of a river.

The voices raised on the shore belonged to the Frankish nobles of Antioch, summoned by a lookout posted to sight the first sail. The welcoming party had galloped ten miles in glad haste to meet the Poitevin queen and, incidentally, her husband.

The welcome was elaborate, and for the most part sincere. The residents of Antioch poured over each boat as it landed, seeking news of their families left behind.

The distance between the port and the walled city of Antioch was covered in stately procession. Leaving the port below them, they traveled inland over constantly rising ground.

Solange sought a glimpse of Aimery in the council around the king. He was taller than most, and rode with a certain unmistakable grace. How he had changed in the months since she had come out of the forest to his campfire! He was now a great noble, trusted by the king. A man one could count on forever.

Solange saw the walls and towers of the powerful city on the Orontes River through a blur of tears. If she could live her life again . . . she blinked the tears away. No time for tears. She had vowed to reach Antioch, and she was here.

Antioch was an ancient Roman city, with ruins of a theater where, it was said, the mighty Caesar had sat in the front row.

It was a great walled city, the wall so wide that four horses abreast could ride it. The city sat astride the ancient caravan routes, in a series of terraced gardens, setting a green border around the church spires.

The welcoming banquet given by Prince Raymond to his royal guests equaled anything that Manuel Comnenus had set before them, including artichokes in silver dishes, stuffed kid, caviar, fried frog. The wines came in airy-thin, colorful glasses. Silver boats on the table held spicy sauces. And the newest thing to the Franks was the two-pronged fork. Such a tool had never been seen in Paris!

Seated a short distance from the dais in the banquet hall, Solange and Aimery sat together at a low table. Bertille and Jean were beside them, and Brother Garin, thin and pale, sat nearby.

Jean narrowed his eyes at the munificence of the feast. "I trust we will not overdo. This, after our voyage, may overtax us."

Bertille eyed the dish of caviar greedily. "I fret not about overtaxing my stomach. There has been nothing in it for three weeks—there's plenty of room!"

They were merry, like shipwrecked sailors coming ashore after fear of death. Aimery was thoughtful, watching the prince. "What is it?" whispered Solange.

"I like it not. He wants something. Mark my words."

Whether Aimery was right or not, Solange could have sung. He had spoken to her in confiding tones, as he had in Constantinople before that fateful night without rancor, even as friend to friend.

Solange sought out her brother-in-law the next day. Brother Garin was lodged near the outer wall of the palace. He stood outside his room, blinking in the hot sunlight. With him stood Rainard, who had led his troop of ten knights to join the army in Byzantium. "This is the place," Solange said after greeting them both, "where my father was last seen."

"You still believe that?" said Garin, searching her face.

"Yes," said Solange with satisfaction. "I've told no one but Aimery about this, but one of the pilgrims returning from Crusade said he saw my father, too!"

She persuaded them to go with her into the city. When she rejoined them, in a plain borrowed robe, she found Brother Garin searching a map.

"I've learned the map of the city," he told her. "We'll start our inquiry in the bazaar. Many travelers find their way there, so that's the best place to start."

After two days of questions, of frustrations, of the conviction that many lies had been told her, she returned in discouragement to the rooms she shared with Aimery.

When he came in later, he found her still in darkness, the lamps unlit. "You've been overdoing," he reproved her.

She flared at him. "With your brother. Perhaps he is trustworthy enough to believe?"

Surprisingly, he answered mildly. "I know where you've been." Feeling her glance sharply at him, he explained. "I want only to know that you are protected. It is not safe to haunt the bazaars alone."

"But it is there I am apt to hear news. The merchants come from all over Asia, and surely some day I shall hear something."

"And then what will you do?" he asked heavily. "When you find out he is dead?"

"Then my quest will be over."

"I know your quest will soon be over, whether your father is dead or alive. But what will you do then?"

"I don't know."

"Will you go on to Jerusalem?"

"I suppose so."

"To take the veil as your mother says she will?" There was a rough note in his voice and Solange turned to look squarely at him. But she could not read his expression.

"Perhaps," she said. "What does it matter to you?"

"It matters," he said briefly. "What did you find out?"

"A good deal of nothing." She told him all she had learned.

"Not much," he agreed. "All this is old news, isn't it?"

"Yes, old news."

He changed the subject. "I must go away for a while on the king's business. I don't know when I'll be back."

She could not bring herself to ask him where he was going.

3

Eleanor had found her spiritual home at last.

The queen's guard had forgotten their drilling, their smart appearance, even, so it seemed, their morals. There were langorous afternoons, when certain of the ladies retired with headaches, and returned hours later much refreshed. By coincidence, said Brother Garin, the plague of headaches seemed to afflict the Frankish army as well.

Aimery seemed no longer to be a member of the king's council. Had the king finally allowed his resentment of Eleanor's feeling for Aimery to overcome his appreciation of his ability? Solange wondered, but she could not ask.

Aimery himself disappeared for a day or two at a time, without explanation. Once, she even thought she saw Aimery at the bazaar. But, of course, that was impossible. The man, wearing a flowing Arab robe, turned quickly away, but he moved with that grace she knew well.

She started to follow him, to demand what he was doing dressed like that, but he paused on the edge of the bazaar and looked back. She stopped short at the warning in those gray eyes. It was Aimery, and clearly he did not wish to be recognized.

What was he doing in disguise in the city where he could walk as freely as the prince himself?

He returned that night, very silently, carrying his robe beneath his arm.

"In a way I'm glad you saw me," he said pleasantly. "Now I can keep my robe here in our rooms. Much handier."

"But why?"

"Don't ask questions, Solange. You care not whether I come or go, nor in what garb."

"But that doesn't mean I don't care what happens to you!" The words surprised her as much as they seemed to astonish him, sounding as though they had been forced from her lips.

"Let me see if I understand you. You do care what happens to me?"

Her lips quivered. "Why must you tear every word of mine apart?"

He appeared to consider the thought. "Perhaps I do. I had not noticed. But I wish to understand exactly what you want of me. I have made all the mistakes I care to, by taking too much for granted."

She could think of nothing to say, and dared not speak lest she pour out all her jealousy and desperate loneliness upon him. She would not so lower herself again.

The next day, tired of haunting the bazaars for news she did not believe would come any more, Solange dressed in pale apricot silk shot with silver threads, and joined the queen's party on the terrace outside the prince's palace.

It was a fantastic place, even in daylight, in the clear light of the sun. A lattice overhead for shade—flowers everywhere. The constant music of the fountains. And the queen and her uncle, and some of his court, whom Eleanor had known as a girl, were taking full advantage of the fine weather.

The queen and Raymond had lapsed from the first moment into that peculiar dialect that was spoken in the Duchy of Aquitaine, which was incomprehensible to those of the king's court. But the queen cared not.

Eleanor had grown lovelier, if possible, during the stay here in Antioch. Gone was the paleness, the gaunt look of the journey to Constantinople. Gone was the weathered skin suffered at sea.

She had blossomed like an exotic tropical flower, the jasmine climbing up the pillar at her side, the many exotic roses that flourished in pots along the terrace edge.

And as she blossomed, so Solange fancied, so Louis withered.

Always frail, he seemed to be even wispier than before, his frown not due entirely to the Crusade he was leading. Solange saw his frequent glances at his wife and her uncle.

Bertille whispered. "They say she—you know—is very

friendly with her uncle. And any of the handsome Turks, too."

Solange protested. But, later, watching the two, she wasn't quite so sure their intimacy had a limit.

The prince was not all courtly dalliance. He had a simple goal—to use the Franks to recapture Edessa the fallen. Antioch could not be safe so long as Edessa, a short distance away, was in the hands of the infidel.

"Why should we," railed Count Robert, "conquer a city for him? He has wealth aplenty, he has men and barons. Let him do it himself!"

Lurking under the wrangling was Raymond's suspicion that Queen Mélisande of Jerusalem had made a secret alliance with Louis that he should come to her aid.

Louis was proof against them all. "I have vowed to go to Jerusalem," he said mildly. "And I shall go. I have been too long away from my own country, and I have little time to spend."

"I will leave Antioch as soon as possible," said Louis. "The Emperor Conrad is even now on his way to Acre, and the count of Toulouse also. We will fulfill our vows."

But the struggle was not over. The queen had yet to take a hand in it—so Bertille said. It was a constant surprise to Solange that Bertille was so knowledgeable about the queen's business. But Bertille was seldom wrong.

Whatever the truth of the relationship between Eleanor and her uncle, it was nearly finished. A quarrel broke out between them; sudden, hot, and without warning.

"I will not do it!" cried the queen. "Totally beyond my scruples. I came here a Christian queen, to worship in Jerusalem. And nothing else."

"Nothing else!" said Raymond, with malicious amusement. "I ask you to do nothing that you don't already want to do. Merely divorce your husband, and God is my witness that you have mentioned it every day since you set foot on the soil of Antioch. A divorce is nothing, you say. Your do-nothing husband is a cousin of sorts, too close a relative for marriage. You can break this alliance without any trouble."

Eleanor's dark eyes flashed dangerously, "Not so close as—"

"But we are not talking of *marriage* between such close relations as you and I, are we?"

"*You* were talking about marriage to a heathen. Some sultan?"

"You heard me, Eleanor. I confess I had not thought you to scruple overmuch about a liaison with a Turk, so long as he is a sultan, and wealthy. Does this not intrigue you?"

Struggling to maintain her control, she said, "Why, Raymond? Why this sultan, whoever he is?"

"Because, Eleanor, your husband will not help me recover Damascus. And the sultan of Iconium will. It is as simple as that."

"Simple!"

"But of course he will want some kind of reward for his services. And I can think of no better prize to insure his loyalty to me."

"I am queen of France!" she raged.

"But not working overmuch at your duties. I confess I had hoped you would have more influence over your monkish husband, but you cannot even persuade him to join my armies and take Damascus."

"He'll delay his journey to Jerusalem. I have one more weapon—"

Raymond's eyes flashed with appreciative malice. "A delightful weapon, but methinks your husband is as well armored against your wiles as I am. Unlike certain desert-robed sheikhs who find you irresistible."

"You can't prove that!" She paced back and forth. Raymond was hitting too close to the truth for comfort. She was beginning to realize that her capricious seductive charm was no longer working on Louis. Certainly she could not bend his mind to fit Raymond's scheme.

Raymond picked up a small cup of hammered gold and pretended to examine it. But beneath his dark lashes he studied his niece carefully. He had made a mistake just now, a slip of the tongue, and he hoped she had not caught it.

" 'As I am?' " she echoed in a low, vibrant tone. "You speak of your armor against my wiles."

He sighed. He had not intended to bring a halt to this

exquisite dalliance, but the day would have to come, and he might as well seize the opportunity.

"My dear niece—"

"Don't 'dear niece' me, when I am accustomed to hear other words from your lying lips!" The glass bowl of fruit sailed past his head, far too closely.

"My dear, I take comfort in the fact that I tried in vain to teach you to throw a ball when you were ten—" But Raymond, prince of Antioch, had had enough. He clapped his hands and at once two large servants stood inside the door. "I should be loath to apply force, dear child. But I really cannot permit you to demolish my room. Not that my trifles are valuable, but it would be fatiguing to replace them."

His niece stood gasping with anger before him, but her own royal pride was bringing control back. After a few moments he nodded at her in satisfaction, and the servants left.

Eleanor managed a taut smile. "Perhaps, Raymond, I said too much."

He shook his head. "Not too much, Eleanor. Just enough. I shall have your apparel and your pavilion set up in the meadow to the south of Saint Paul's Gate before nightfall. You will be most comfortable there, I am sure."

"Raymond?" she quavered. "You forget—"

"I forget nothing, my dear," said Raymond quietly. "I wish I could."

The queen, skirts awhirl, swept from the room with what dignity she could muster, nearly overrunning her husband who had come to see his host. She didn't recognize Louis.

Louis stepped hesitantly into the room, looking back at his fleeing wife. "When I first saw her she wore a skirt fifteen yards around, and it whirled just like that. At the time, I thought it entrancing," he said mildly.

"But no more?" said Raymond dryly, joining him at the door.

Louis did not deign to answer, but said only, "She will think better of her anger."

But Raymond, a strange look in his eyes, responded slowly, "No . . . it's all over now."

4

Bertille was full of gossip. The story was that the queen had changed her mind about leaving Raymond's presence, having gotten over her quarrel with Raymond. But the king, advised by the eunuch Thierry de Galeran, prevailed at last. Seeing the Crusade falter through his indecision, Louis gave word that the queen was not to return to court.

So the queen's guard was moved outside, and, rumor had it, the queen herself was taken through a side gate by force.

The queen's guard were unhappy. Many of them had had no wish to leave their castles and familiar surroundings in the first place.

Some of them had become pregnant on the long journey down the Danube, and many had miscarried. They had climbed mountains on foot, fought off bandits, been wounded. Some had lost their husbands in battle. The privations and the terrible dangers had taken their toll. Some were ill. Some limped now, and would forever, from bones broken during the journey.

And on the grassy meadows outside the city walls, the sun beat down fiercely, and the ladies wilted like lilies. The feeling against the queen rose daily, like a tide lapping at the walls. Discontent was hidden no more.

The king's Chaplain, Odo de Deuil, thought it well to remind the Crusaders of the reason for taking up the cross in the first place.

The Crusading fervor was renewed at the service. Those hundreds who drowned in the Danube, the scores who were starved or died of thirst, all were memorialized. The constant loss of those in the train, shot by arrows from unseen killers, those left behind when the King took to the sea, and those lost in the ambush in the pass of Mount Cadmos, the toll was sounded for them all.

Unfortunately, with the reminder of Mount Cadmos, the chaplain roused more animosity toward the queen than he quieted.

Solange reported this to Aimery. "The queen should be convinced to let us move inside the walls again," she fretted. "No good can come of this privation, as though we were still climbing the mountains, when just beyond the wall is comfort. There's constant grumbling. Even Bertille is jumpy and cross."

Aimery toyed with the idea of telling Solange what had happened in the queen's tent that very day. The scene unrolled before his mind's eye.

Eleanor had changed. Flirtatious as always, there had been a different quality to her gaiety that morning. She had dropped her regal air, and allowed herself to become wholly feminine. Once, that femininity might have moved him. But he had been schooled by Solange, and he could discern more than a subtle difference between the two women who had ruled much of his recent life.

"You sent for me," he began in a neutral tone.

"Since my favorite baron has not come to me of his own will, I had to." She toyed with a jewel suspended from her neck by a thin gold chain. "I thought you would welcome a respite from duty. Is it so, Aimery?"

"My duty," he said carefully, "is also my pleasure."

For perhaps the first time in weeks she looked at him with care. There were new lines framing his lips, wrinkles crinkling at the outer corners of his eyes. He was a man with great control over his emotions. It might be fun to test that control, she told herself. To see just how far she could tease him before he would erupt into violence. She was not afraid of violence, for she had only to lift a royal eyebrow, and any importunate noble would cringe.

"One of the first knights," she sighed, "to subscribe to my Rules of Courtly Love. I fear you have forgotten."

"I forget little, madam," he said, wondering where all this was leading. She had had no time for the Rules of Courtly Love while she romped through Byzantium with Emperor Manuel, or dallied with her uncle in Antioch. Now she was seeking to resurrect what she must know was very dead. His love—better called devotion—had not the strong adhesive of physical passion to bind him to her. Whatever charm she had once possessed no longer touched Aimery.

" 'It is well known,' " she quoted from the Rules she had herself formulated, " 'that love is always increasing or decreasing.' Tell me, Aimery, can your love be induced to increase again?"

He thought hard. Was she trying to seduce him? *Now?* She had spurned him when he had been feverish to possess her. He answered stiffly, quoting another of the Rules, " 'No one can be bound by a double love.' "

The light in Eleanor's eyes flashed with dangerous heat. "I cannot doubt that. But surely you have no love for the wife that my foolish husband foisted upon you? You give no sign of loving her."

The relationship between Solange and him was not to be tarnished by any of Eleanor's sneers. He did not know his face darkened to match his thoughts.

Out of a sheer whimsical desire to pull the strings that would bring Aimery to kneel again at her feet, Eleanor began to realize that she had nearly lost him. Once again her greed for sway over men asserted itself. When she was through with him and his footling devotion, she would dismiss him. When *she* chose.

Just now she chose to pull the string a bit tighter. If he grew angry, so much the better. She never doubted her power over him, and she would enjoy seeing him swallow his fury.

"You haven't bedded the child since—"

"I did not realize," interrupted Aimery, "that you keep such close watch on the ladies of your court."

"My Amazons?" she said lightly. "They do very well, don't they? I must say I am proud of them all." She sighed. "They all have such happy lives. They are all loved, and love in return. But I—I am a prisoner of my own foolishness."

She glanced at Aimery under her long lashes. He was startled. The queen surely had lost her touch. This was flirtation of the most blatant kind, and he had always admired her finesse. Even when she had held him at arm's length, he had appreciated her deft style.

Something lay beneath all this, he guessed—something that worried her, that gnawed on her self-esteem, that eroded her pride. He thought it would be well to walk very warily.

"A queen is never foolish," he ventured.

"This queen is," she responded swiftly. "I have staked my happiness on a set of rules that were designed to make men happy—and women, too. Life is so harsh in our Frankish castles. I have learned much here in the Eastern empire."

He watched her silently, willing to follow her lead, within limits.

"You men are always fighting—if not wars, then tournaments. A noble woman has a hard time making her gentle voice heard above the sharp clash of metal."

"Your Court of Love has worked wonders."

"But it isn't enough." She whirled to face him squarely, her exceedingly full skirt belling around her ankles before it settled, outlining her slim, well-shaped legs. "A *love remote* does not fulfill needs. I am sure you know that."

"You will always have my devotion," he said, when the silence lengthened embarrassingly.

She moved a step closer to him. "I could reward well a knight who remembered my Rule Twenty-Six."

Lord, what *was* that Rule? He had known them all at one time, and had even recited them as a monk does his breviary. But no longer. She was prompting him. " 'Love can deny nothing to love.' And yet you deny me . . . yourself."

"I am not free," he said, desperately casting about for an argument that would serve his purpose and yet not anger the lady he was, in truth, rejecting. "My fiefs came from the king—"

"And I have equal fiefs to grant. One in Provence—villages, a fine castle, vineyards . . ." She went on to describe the prize she dangled.

Suddenly he realized the extent of the offer she was making him. "That's Geoffrey de Rançon's holding." The man who had granted her whim to camp in the meadow, against his orders. Who was even now on his way back to that fief in disgrace. She would even dispossess the man whose shame was equally hers.

"So it is," she said silkily. "And you know the worth of the fief."

"I don't deserve," he said, "this generous offer you make. And I dare not accept, for it would not be long until you would see I am not the man you think me. I should not like to disappoint my queen."

"Let me be the judge," she began.

"I dare not," he repeated, thinking swiftly. She had grown less subtle, and he must follow her example. Usually a man of few words, he must find sufficient to obscure his very real disgust with this entire interview. "I dare not chance your displeasure, for a shaft from those incomparable eyes would strike me dead. 'A man in love is always apprehensive,' you remember. I could not live under your displeasure."

That, he reflected, might have some truth in it, for the lady was regal in her anger, capable of—much that he did not want to think of.

"Aimery—"

"I must return to the king," he lied. "I have leave for only a few moments. But I am grateful for your kindness in granting me this opportunity to reaffirm my boundless admiration, my devotion, to my queen."

The smile with which she dismissed him was sweet. He was too thankful simply to bow himself out of her pavilion to notice that the smile did not reach her eyes.

After an hour in the clean air, his thoughts settled a bit. He sought Solange.

Watching her now, he could begin to forget the scene with Eleanor. Solange's fine cheekbones were visible under the tight, pale skin. Her violet eyes had darkened with privations. He would never, he guessed, know what this journey had cost her. But then, it had cost him something too.

But he knew what he wanted, and while the road he had set himself was rocky as the pass of Pisidia, he would get Solange back.

Eleanor didn't have a chance. Should he tell Solange it was all over, that he was cured of his fever for the queen? He decided not to. He had nearly ruined his chances with her by that foolish and unreasonable jealousy in Byzantium. His explosive anger then had damaged the fabric of their growing concern with each other. It had taken too much time to mend, and he dared not chance another rending.

So he sat in silence, not knowing he was making a grievous error. He told Solange all the news he could think of. The king had been asked to further Raymond's designs on Damascus. But the king's barons said that Queen Mélisande of Jerusalem was opposed to such. an excursion, that Damascus was their only friend, and if they warred on Damascus, and lost, the way would be wide open for the Turks to march in their great hordes onto Jerusalem itself. The king wished to know the truth of the matter. And Aimery, the day after his interview with the queen, dressed in his Arab robes and rode toward Damascus.

The queen knew her enemies. Thierry was one, a major one, of course. But with the entire Order of the Knights Templar behind him, she could not touch him.

She was not unaware either of the growing tide of dissidents in her guard. She looked back in her memory at the high, sunlit hopes with which they had come out of France, the long romantic nights along the starlit meadows of the Danube. The incredible luxury of the court at Constantinople—now that was the way a queen should live! The extravagance of the court of Byzantium did not speak to her of decadence. It spoke only to her lively enjoyment of beautiful things, and to her sense of what was due a queen.

And here she sat, far removed from Byzantium, even from the exciting dalliance with Raymond.

Eleanor could not touch Thierry de Galeran. But she had another victim within her grasp. A smile stole over her full lips. Aimery and his little ninny of a wife were in her thoughts much that day.

5

The Crusaders had been too long without proper food, without adequate rest, and too worried to enjoy what little they did have. At last, their deprivations caught up with them.

Whether it was borne by a pedlar from the east, or from a minstrel who had beguiled the queen's guard for an hour, or whether it was simply that they had all been through too much was impossible to say.

But the illness pounced upon them, suddenly, and with virulence. Petronilla and her basket moved into the pilgrims' camp, and Solange followed. The illness was not the dreaded plague. But it was something that defied all the Frankish doctors, and Petronilla's medicaments did little except to ease the discomfort of the patients. Soon half the queen's guard were down with the illness, along with many of the attendants who had come with them on the ships.

Petronilla stormed the queen's pavilion demanding help, and came out, her face grim and set. "That—*that* is no woman!" she told Solange. "She had me sent away, lest I contaminate her! I'd like to—"

Solange shook her head. "Don't," she said. "We must deal with this ourselves. Can you imagine the queen holding a basin for one of these?"

Petronilla barked a short laugh, and said. "No matter, we'll never have the chance to see that!"

Solange went into the city, through the Gate of Saint Paul's, to inquire daily of the newly arrived merchants. There was no news of her father. But she was able to buy salves and small jars of foul-smelling concoctions that she was assured would take away all the fever.

"Quick as the falcon flies," said one man, "the fever will fly."

"And the patient with it?" suggested Solange. "Never mind, we'll try it."

Even those who recovered—and most did—were weak for days. They crawled into the sunlight, with sunken cheeks and hollow eyes. The ladies were hardly recognizable as the flowers they had been.

Petronilla drafted many of those still well into nursing duties. Solange was soon too busy even to think about Odo. Or Aimery.

She could even be glad that the rigors of the journey had taken such a toll. Surely it was better to die in one screaming plunge from the lip of the precipice in the passes of Pisidia than to let one's life slip away like this.

Solange took a short cut with her basket of drugs and medicines from the soukhs, past the front of the prince's palace on her way to Saint Paul's Gate. There was a stir around the palace gates, and Solange stopped to watch. King Louis was entering for yet another of the conferences that took place in Prince Raymond's council hall. Perhaps Aimery might be among those following the king? She stopped, her great haunted eyes searching for him.

The king halted, caught by her solitary intentness. "Lady Solange," he greeted her. "It has been long since you have come to my court."

He took Solange's hand and smiled kindly at her. Then his glance dropped to the basket. "I fear you must expect a great plague! So many medicines!" He smiled again.

"We already have the plague, sire," she told him. "And I am on my way back to the sick."

"How is this? The plague?"

"I doubt not it is something other than the deadly plague, for many do recover, sire," she told him. She was anxious to get back to her mother with the medicines. She chafed against the questions, the answers surely known to him by now.

Or so she thought. "How is it I have heard nothing of this?" Louis turned to Robert and the others. "You knew? Or you?"

"It did not seem serious," Saldebreuil intervened. "Our own people were not infected."

Solange turned her burning glance to him. "Jean de Loches is very sick with the infection," she said. "Henri de Villiers is now recovering from it but he will not be able to take horse for at least a week. His lady, Catherine, is worn out from nursing him, and has now succumbed herself. I fear she is taking it very hard. More than a hundred are dead already. But, as you say, it is not serious."

She curtseyed slightly to the king, and moved around the cluster of nobles. She could hear voices raised behind her, but she was too angry to listen. Our "own people," indeed! Our own people were the poor, the sick—all those Crusaders who had shared the dangers and known more than their share of hunger and hardship.

And the king did nothing for his commoners!

Again, she was wrong. Within the hour, a Turk wearing a green turban and dressed in the universal Arab flowing robe, presented himself to Lady de Mowbrai. "I have been sent," he announced calmly.

Petronilla stared at him. "Sent?"

"By the great prince of Antioch, at the request of the Frankish King Louis," he said, bowing slightly. There was an undercurrent of scorn in his voice, as though his words contained a jest known only to him. "To help the victims of this unfortunate illness."

He set to work at once. Unfortunately, some of the ill were too weak for aid.

Jean de Loches was one of those. Unstinting of aid to all within his sight, he had none left for himself. He died before dawn.

Bertille collapsed with the illness as the last clod of earth fell on her husband's grave. The doctor, Abu Ibn Saud, came to the tent where she had been laid on a pallet. "An infidel," cried Bertille. "I'll not allow him to touch me."

"Are you better than the others?" asked Solange sharply. Bertille gave in, too weak to argue.

The doctor from Damascus had strange ointments, singular potions made of powders and a poisonous looking green liquid. Petronilla eyed the fluid askance.

"How do I know what is in that unnatural brew?"

"You don't," said the Turkish doctor calmly. "That is

why they have called for me. Your remedies do not work. Mine do. If you knew what was in here, you would use it yourself."

Petronilla bit her lower lip. "You can't refuse the man," said Solange. "The prince has sent him."

"And we all know how the prince feels about us," said Petronilla.

"But the prince is your host," said the Turk, "and our eastern laws of hospitality are exceedingly strict."

Petronilla capitulated all at once, striking a bargain with the doctor. Could she help him, and would he teach her what he knew?

He lifted his eyebrows in surprise. Surely a Frankish lady would not wish to take instruction from an infidel doctor?

His sarcasm elicited no more than a faint smile from Petronilla. "Yes, she would," she said firmly. "Starting now."

The two of them worked together. Solange and some of the other nurses did no more than follow them, carrying, changing linen, lifting, coaxing medicines down gagging throats.

By nightfall, those who had first taken the dosage were less feverish. A hardy one or two were even sitting up, clamoring for broth!

"A miracle," breathed Petronilla.

"By an infidel's hand," said the doctor, gently.

There was no shelter for the patients who needed help the most. Solange offered her tent. "I shall not need it," she said, "and they must be kept from the night air."

Bertille, grudgingly giving credit to the vile green liquid, was soon able to drag herself around and even help a little.

The six most severely ill patients were carried into Solange's tent. Aimery was off to Damascus, and she expected he would not return for three days. She stayed with the patients. The doctor and an assistant came in hourly to visit their patients.

Bertille was nodding on the other pallet, but she would wake at once if any of the patients called. Hugh de Perigoux was the last to be brought in, and she promised to watch faithfully over her old suitor.

Solange was enormously weary, but the satisfaction of seeing some of them improve made it worthwhile. Toward midnight, she watched the Turkish doctor leave, and then dropped the flap behind her as she returned to her charges. They all seemed easier, and she slept.

While she slept, the queen was busy. Solange herself had furnished the material from which Eleanor would weave her scheme. Soon, a messenger slipped out of the queen's tent—through the back flap so as not to be seen by the rest of the camp. He hurried to find Aimery on the road to Damascus.

"Solange is unfaithful," read the message. "All this night she has spent with an infidel, inside her tent. Not one, but two! I suggest you put an end to this scandal."

Solange had dug the pit wherein she would fall, as the Scripture said. Once unfaithful, always unfaithful—in her heart, if not in fact. So Aimery would reason, the queen was sure of it. And if Aimery spurned the queen's bed because of his marriage vows, then she would see that he was miserable for it. Eleanor of Aquitaine never gave anything up until it was her wish to give it up.

The messenger had taken the first step in the plot. Now Eleanor herself set to work on the second.

The queen's malice was served better than she knew. Aimery had been finding Solange increasingly desirable. And he knew it was not physical desire alone that rode him. It was a fascination with her sharp wits, with that sidelong glance she occasionally gave him. Her thoughtful gaze, and the darkening of her eyes when she gave vent to mischief. And above all, it was the courage with which she had met disappointment after disappointment.

He would give anything if she were truly his—heart and soul and mind. And she was not, not quite. He had told her he would try to win her one more time. But Aimery knew he would keep trying until his death.

When the messenger came, he did not weigh it carefully, as he should have done. The message struck too near the vulnerable crack in his armor. He had to get home at once, to demand an explanation of Solange.

His mission was finished. He had the information the king wanted.

The ride home, in Arab garb, was a tortured journey. He rode with jealousy gnawing at him until he was close to madness.

6

As Aimery galloped furiously out of Damascus, a royal party set out more or less secretly from Antioch. Since nothing the king did could remain hidden for long, it was soon common knowledge that Louis and Eleanor rode out together, with only a few of their retainers, on a hawking party.

It was good to see the royal couple on happy terms again, pronounced Bertille, but Solange doubted that such a deep quarrel could be healed over so quickly.

Anyone watching would have thought this jaunt was purely for appearances' sake. Neither spoke to the other. The king rode to meet Aimery outside the city, lest some of Raymond's hired ears overhear. The queen came for purposes of her own. Thierry de Galeran would not have missed the expedition for any price.

They rode slowly, enjoying the fruitful lands through which they rode. The scars left by the great siege of Antioch, less than fifty years before, were covered now. Newly planted orchards gave bountiful fruit. The meadows were green again. The land was whole once more.

The king looked about him as Thierry pointed out various points of interest. Thierry had become so thoroughly a Templar of Outremer that he could never return to France and be happy. The prospect of returning home to a family he had forgotten dismayed him not a little. More immediately, he was worried about the message that Aimery might bring. If Louis were diverted to fighting Raymond's battle with Damascus, it would bode ill for the kingdom of the Holy Places.

Thierry mistrusted the new amiability of the queen, who

had begged her lord to let her come today. Did she bring arguments from her uncle?

The queen looked up to find the Templar's gaze fixed upon her. She wished she had been . . . not more kind, but at least more discreet about the castrated Templar. She had made a formidable enemy. She moved uneasily in her saddle.

They expected to meet Aimery at a place where the river made a wide turn, where there was a grassy meadow, excellent for hawking. But they had not made allowance for the haste engendered in Aimery by the queen's secret message.

Aimery appeared as a galloping dot on the road miles before they expected him. They awaited him, consumed by curiosity. "What can he have discovered in Damascus? He rides hard," exclaimed the king.

The queen smiled secretly.

Aimery pulled to a halt. His gray eyes were hidden under the burnoose he wore as a disguise, but Eleanor noted the set of his lips and was satisfied with what she had wrought. She reined her mount to one side and waited.

"Majesty," saluted Aimery as soon as he drew near enough to speak.

"What of Damascus?" queried the king at once. "Are they friendly?"

"It would be a grave mistake to attack them," said Aimery bluntly. "They are well armed and it would be more of a battle than was expected at first. Besides, you see where they are situated."

After dismounting, he found a stick and drew a sketch on the sand by the road. "Here is Antioch, and here, Jerusalem. Damascus is far to the northeast, and poses no threat to either. But if Damascus were not friendly—if they defeated our people in battle—then they would be able to swoop down this river valley here—" He drew a long sweeping mark toward the heart of the Kingdom of Jerusalem. "And besiege Jerusalem."

Aimery stood up. There was a scroll within his robe, and he pulled that out and gave it to the king. He had completed his mission.

"The local leaders, Prince Raymond and his men, say

that Damascus should be reduced," mused the king. "But this information gives me pause. Thierry, what do you think?"

"My lord's judgment is without fault," said the eunuch. "The Holy Places must be preserved. Outremer is not a place to carve out small kingdoms for ourselves. Our duty lies elsewhere."

"My vow was to go to Jerusalem," said the king. "I had the dream again," he added more to himself, "and I *must* honor my vow, else I will never be done with it."

His subjects stood respectfully while the king brooded. At length, his face brightened. He had made up his mind. "I will leave for Jerusalem in two days time," he said, turning to Eleanor. "You will, I am sure, be ready to fulfill the vows we took together."

The vows to go on Crusade, thought Thierry, or her marriage vows? Either, he thought, were as quick to change as the weather.

"My lord's will," she said with obvious insincerity, "is my command. I will be ready."

The king's mind at ease, he wished for a day of hawking. But the queen demurred, saying she had much to make ready—so as not to keep her lord waiting. "I shall return to Antioch," she said. "If some of your men could accompany me? Aimery?"

"Not Aimery," said the king. "I wish him to have some relaxation after the fine service he has done us. Come hawking, Aimery."

It was arranged so, to Aimery's dismay. But the queen took a moment to speak to Aimery before she rode back to town.

"I thank you for your note," said Aimery between tight lips. "But I assure you your concern is unnecessary. My wife is innocent of the charges some lay against her."

"So?" murmured the queen. "You will not believe me?"

"I believe," lied Aimery, "that you were misled by others."

"With my own eyes, I saw the Turk go into her tent."

"Solange will have to tell me that herself."

"And if you hear it from her lips?" said the queen silkily. "Then?"

He bowed his head. There was no possible response. He had worked off much of his rage in the hard gallop. But the vulnerability was still there, and his shame could not be disguised.

"You will hear it from her own lips," said the queen. "Come to my tent tonight, after dark. We will talk then."

He did not trust her. But he could not yet trust his wife either.

"I must stay here with the king," he said. "I will handle this when I return."

"I will see you when you return," said the queen, and lifted her reins. "Remember, I shall wait for you in my pavilion, alone. Don't fail me."

He watched the small cavalcade escorting the queen vanish from sight.

The king bore on his wrist his new falcon, given him by Prince Raymond as a peace offering. The gift of a gerfalcon from one ruler to another would have been generous. But Raymond had outdone other rulers. He gave Louis a kind of eagle, from Mongolia, called a berkute. It was trained for big game like antelope, and Louis was as delighted as a child with his new bird.

Aimery, chafing with irritation, was forced to watch while Louis sent the berkute aloft in the lush meadows of the Orontes marshes. If he had been asked, later, to relate the details of the gazelle hunt, he could not have remembered any of it.

Aimery could not now remember what it was that had drawn him to the queen at first. If she had sought him out, to her blame, yet he had come willingly enough. Yet while the queen had been indiscreet or worse with many a man, Aimery de Montvert had not been one of those.

Aimery knew they were hawking on the meadows formed by the junction of the Kara-su River with the Orontes. That meant he was four hours from Solange. . . . and the plotting queen.

The queen's return without the king caused little comment. "The king is hawking," said the queen.

Her interview with Solange was lengthy. She sought her out and drew her away. "My dear," she said, "it is a source of unhappiness to me that you and your husband are not happy with each other."

Solange eyed her stonily.

"Your Majesty is kind to think of such a small thing," said Solange.

"Anything that has to do with my husband's subjects is important to me," smiled the queen, purring.

"But I am sure many of your subjects are unhappy," pointed out Solange. "And I am honored that you take my affairs at all seriously."

"Let us stop fencing, child," said the queen in a tone that made Solange feel she was again five years old. "You have blamed me for your husband's estrangement, I know. And while you are young and foolish enough not to know that a wife *never* has her husband's true love, yet you have suffered much on this journey. I have been sorry to see it."

"Your Majesty is kind," murmured Solange. Her cheeks were burning with indignation.

The queen smiled again, gently. "What I set awry, through no fault of my own, I shall nevertheless set straight."

Solange waited.

"It would be too bad were you to go into danger unreconciled with your husband."

"Danger?"

"The king, in his great wisdom," explained Eleanor sarcastically, "has decreed that we march to Jerusalem two days from now. The road will be as hard as the way we have come. Each one's fate is hidden."

Solange started in alarm. "In two days? Aimery is not back yet, and there are so many ill—"

The queen continued as though she had not spoken.

"I have a plan to reconcile you to Aimery. We have no privacy in this camp. I have just come from the river road, where Aimery—looking so like a Turk you would hardly know him!—is returning from Damascus. The king has kept him up the river, hawking, for one last day of sport here before we go on to Jerusalem. But how can you be reconciled tonight, with your tent full of patients?"

Outrageously, the queen winked. "I will lend you my

own pavilion tonight. I will send Trotti to fetch you, probably after dark. You know how the king loves his sport. I doubt he will start back early."

"And Aimery?"

"I will send him to you when he returns. The *moment* he returns," she emphasized, "dressed in that strange garb. I know he will be so impatient he won't take time to change."

The queen left. She had seemed sincere enough, thought Solange. Perhaps Eleanor's conscience had been bothering her, and she meant only to assuage it.

Solange turned back to her patients, but her mind leaped ahead to the night.

7

The long afternoon dragged on. Word had come that they were to move out in two days' time. Those who were too ill to travel would remain in Antioch. Prince Raymond offered safe lodging inside the walls.

Petronilla decided to stay where she was needed. "There is time enough to see Jerusalem," she told her daughter. "One of the things I will do just before I take the veil."

Solange had too much time to think. Helping the patients took up only a part of her mind. She mistrusted the queen. Certainly Eleanor had never been her friend.

And yet—it was a tempting invitation. What it boiled down to, she realized, was that every fiber in her body longed for Aimery. She thought she could not bear it if he spurned her again. And tonight would be her last chance to try to make peace with him. One more chance. That's all Aimery would give her. He had told her that.

After dark, drawn to the pavilion like a magnet, she slipped out of the tent and stood, letting her eyes become accustomed to the darkness. Overhead the stars shone brighter than anywhere else in the world, she was sure.

She set out across the meadow, where the lights inside

the pavilions shone like gems behind many-colored veils. The queen's pavilion was a little removed from the rest, on the edge of the encampment. Its back flap was open, so rumor had it, to the dark desert. This would make it possible for Aimery to enter without the entire camp being aware of it.

She hurried a bit. Perhaps he was already there.

The pavilion was unlit. The silk tent stood apart, in darkness. She halted, suddenly assailed with misgivings.

But there was a darker shape detaching itself from the pavilion and coming toward her. It was not Aimery. The crablike walk was unmistakable.

Trotti, the queen's trusted servant, whispered, "Lady de Pontdebois?" All was fine, Solange thought in unmistakable relief. The queen's own servant expected her, and, no doubt, would stay to guard the door so that she and Aimery could spend the night in privacy.

Her heart thudded, as she moved inside, through the front flap.

"No light," warned Trotti, and she nodded, forgetting that he could not see her in the darkness.

Trotti the hunchback, would die doing the queen's bidding. He had saved the queen's life, so she had said, but the circumstances were obscure. The most widely believed story had it that Eleanor, climbing the ruined tower of an abandoned Roman aqueduct, had somehow come to grief in the climb. A stone had given away, and she had clung for an hour to a perilous projecting stone which, at any moment, might give way under her weight.

It was Trotti who had come to her rescue, had caught her in his arms just as the stone gave way at last, and fell to the ground. Eleanor was cushioned from the fall by his body. It was thus that his back had become crooked. And his loyalty, in spite of his injury, was deeper from that moment. To give loyalty where there might have been resentment was a shining thing.

But Solange did not like Trotti, just the same.

She found a pallet, the cot where the queen slept. There was a faint scent of jasmine, rising from the silk cover of the cot. The queen had recently taken a great fancy to the scent.

Where was Aimery?

The moon rose. Another hour passed. This vigil was as fruitless as all the rest. She rose to her feet, ready to leave, but a sound at the back of the tent brought her lonely vigil to an end. Someone was out there. A shadow moved against the wall of the tent. The flap lifted.

Ducking his head to avoid the top of the tent, dressed in desert robes, came her love—the man she had waited for, as it seemed, all her life.

8

He was silhouetted momentarily against the silk of the tent. Arms outstretched, he came toward her. Her white tunic guided him in the darkness. Her heart lifted and soared, singing, into the sky.

With strong arms he reached for her and swept her to him in an irresistible embrace. Both arms around her, drawing her close to him, his burnoose falling over his face as he bent to her lips.

She would have spoken, but she could not breathe. Her heart hammered in her temples, and she could not even speak his name.

At length, feeling his hard body moving against hers, she trembled. At once he released her. He pressed her downward toward the cot behind her. She half fell onto the scented blankets. With deliberation he searched for the hem of her garment, lifting it over her head.

She shivered as his lips moved on hers, searching, probing, possessing.

It was as though he had come to her expecting her readiness. And in truth, she had not known that passion demanded so much of her, demanded the total, abandoned, giving of her body. She gave herself gladly.

She could not bear the growing tumult within her. Her whole being was caught in a flood, a mountain stream in full spring spate, driving downward with unstoppable force.

And yet, he held back. She moved herself upward, toward him—begging him to ease the tumult in her blood.

For this, she thought, slipping away on a roaring tide, she had been born.

Later, she lay numb with lassitude in his arms.

The man cradling her with one arm, his face hidden in her hair, spoke. "My queen."

She would kill him. It was as simple as that.

She could not forgive him this time. Never. To make love with such delicious abandon, when all the time he supposed it was his queen. Eleanor had planned well . . . to prove, finally, that Aimery was truly hers.

With a vicious shove, Solange toppled him to the floor. Sitting on the edge of the cot she glared down at him.

She felt for tinder and a candle on the table, and light flickered into the room. The man from the desert, his djellaba to one side, sprawled on the floor, dark eyes blinking from the sudden light. He stared at her in blazing fury.

Suddenly conscious of her nakedness, she snatched a blanket and wrapped herself in it.

They spoke as one.

"You're not my husband!"

"Who are you?"

The man groaned. Solange covered her face with her hands, so appalled she could not think.

The man on the floor stirred, reaching for his curved dagger.

"You tricked me," he whispered ominously. "And I do not suffer dishonor alone."

Solange paid him little heed. "Go ahead," she said softly. "Kill me. I welcome it."

"You are not—whom I expected," he said, trying to reason it out. "But why then are you here?"

"Because I'm a fool. The queen tricked me well indeed."

The Arab's eyes kindled for a moment. "Why are you here?" he repeated. "That's no answer."

"The queen told me my husband would meet me here," she said wearily. "What difference does it make now? He'll come in and find us here together—"

"He will try to kill *me*? Sheikh Njer-el-Din?" said the

Arab in a conversational tone, fingering his dagger's edge. "I think not."

She shook her head in denial. "More apt to kill me," she said mournfully.

There was a moment of silence. Then he reached over and blew out the candle.

"No, no, don't fear me," he said. "I go only where I am welcome—as I often have been welcomed in this very tent. It is clear that we have both been tricked. But your sins will be forgiven when you get to Jerusalem, will they not? I do not understand this reasoning, but this is what I am told."

"I suppose so. But I did not come on Crusade to get to Jerusalem. Not mainly."

"Then why?" He touched her arm. "Get dressed quickly. We may be interrupted by those who plotted our downfall. Tell me quickly."

Solange pulled her tunic down over her bare breasts and fastened it at her waist, explaining as she did so. "My father—I came to seek my father."

Quickly she told the man the story of her search. "And so, I cannot find him. Now, thanks to you, I have not even my husband. Or will not have, when he finds out."

"That witch, your queen," he said sharply. "She sent for me to make a fool of me. I should tell her that I found her substitute a thousand times more delightful than herself."

"Oh, no! Don't!"

He said, "Perhaps all is not yet lost. Let us see what we can do."

He reached for her hand and kissed her fingers one by one. "I must tell you, before we part, that this has been a delightful evening. I would not exchange it." He placed her hand back in her lap and said, in quite a different tone. "Now. Let us see."

Quietly whispering, shy of Trotti, who was still on guard, Njer-el-Din considered ways of punishing the queen, whose perfidy had savagely wounded him and Solange.

"What is his name? Your father?"

"Odo de Saint Florent."

"Tall, white hair—like yours. A scar on his chin, him?"

"Yes, yes! Do you know what happened to him?"

"Aha, yes. I do know. Can you face what has happened to him?"

Solange gave the faintest of cries. But she recovered at once.

"Yes," she said sturdily. "I can."

"Then," he said simply, "I will take you to him."

"We leave in two days—"

"We leave at once, tonight. As the day breaks. It is a long journey. You may not be back here in time for the departure to Jerusalem. Take what you will need."

She took a deep breath. "Dawn, you say."

"Not much time, I admit. But my men are waiting, hidden in the vale beyond the mountains. I cannot keep them longer."

"What of Eleanor?"

"That is not for you to be concerned about. I will have my revenge, and soon. It will not be meager, I assure you."

She shuddered. She would hate to have this dark-browed desert Arab as her enemy.

"Maybe," he added, "she will think we have eloped to the desert, you and I. Since I found you more desirable than she!"

Her hand flew to her mouth.

"No," he said, reading her thoughts, "this will not happen. Not unless you are willing." The memory of the hour just passed was clear in his eyes as he looked at her. "Willing, yes. But also—not misled. I should not wish to enjoy you again unless you wanted it, and you knew what you were about. But I promise you, I shall try to convince you."

With a last smile, he was gone. Flight with him was a way out—at least for the moment. What might happen to her later on was beyond thinking about.

She would go to find her father. She followed Njer-el-Din out of the back of the tent, and hurried to her own tent. She was filled with misgivings, but surely she could not remain here, not now! And perhaps—just perhaps—she could trust this man who said he knew her father.

423

Book Six
El Chorazin, 1148

1

It was well after dark before the king's cavalcade rode into the valley of Antioch. Somewhere below them, as they paused at the top of the ridge, was Solange. Aimery knew the strange lilt in his thoughts was only because of her. And suddenly the fear that had clutched at him after the queen's veiled hints grew to a terrible strength.

With only a word of apology, he left the king and spurred ahead toward the encampment of the queen's guard. He reined in before he got there, and turned aside to pick his way around the camp. There was the queen's tent, dark. He went softly by. He thought he saw a candle flicker once, but he paid it no heed. If the queen waited there for him, it made no difference. He would not fall into her trap just yet.

Skirting the settlement, he found his tent of pale lavender, lit from inside, making a lilac veil of the silk. Much activity was taking place there. With dread, he watched men carry out a litter, a figure inert and lifeless on it.

Solange!

He leaped from his horse and ran to the tent.

"Stop!" he cried. "Set it down!"

The startled litter-bearers faltered. One look at Aimery and they hastened to obey. He looked down at the body that was not his wife and exploded in amazement.

"Where is Rainard? What is this?"

He turned to see a grave-faced Turk standing in the doorway of the tent. "What happened? Where is she? If you have harmed her, I'll wet my blade—" He swung his scimitar.

"You appear to be one of us," said the Turk, "but you speak like a Frank."

Aimery had forgotten he was still wearing his Arab garb. "I am Aimery de Montvert," he said, "and I think you have some explaining to do."

427

He advanced upon the Turk. Doctor Abu signaled to the litter-bearers to continue with their errand, and followed Aimery into the tent. Aimery looked around in astonishment. The ground was bare. No bed, no stools. A single lamp was placed on the ground. Its light cast shadows upward, making the two men appear sinister.

"My wife?" said Aimery with dangerous calm. "Where is she?"

"The Lady Solange? I do not know. She stepped outside, just after dark. For a breath of air, I suppose. The order came then to take the patients into the city, and I have been busy transferring them from here to there."

"Patients?" asked Aimery, heavily.

"Abu Ibn Saud, at your service." He watched the Frank with eyes that saw much. He would not go out of his way to assuage a Frank, but the lady had been kind, and untiring.

"Lady de Pontdebois has not taken the sickness, in spite of it all. She has given herself without stint. Here, in this tent. And I have tended her patients."

Abu added, "Some of the worst cases, the Lady caused to be brought here, out of the night air, so she could watch them through the night."

Aimery's broad grin disarmed Abu. "Physician Abu Ibn Saud," he said, "you have healed me of much hurt. Now go, and tend thy patients."

Alone, he settled down onto the ground. He must find Rainard and give him word to prepare the men for the journey to Jerusalem. But first he must know that Solange was safe. He began to search among the tents, but realized that was pointless. She would return, at sometime. And he must be there when she came back.

He paused, holding his scimitar, while he thought of Solange. The queen had spoken of Turks in and out of Solange's tent. Surely Eleanor knew the tent was crammed with patients, and that Arab doctors came to see them! Eleanor's purpose was to rouse him to blind anger. Well— he thought grimly—she had failed. He understood it all now.

A sound behind him startled him. He turned, still holding the scimitar, and saw Solange.

Her eyes flew wide open, darkening until they were almost black, her face ashen. He took a step toward her, saying, "I've just been thinking about you."

Her gaze went from his face to the curved sword he held. She whispered, "Oh my God!" just before she fainted.

2

She dreamed Aimery was bending low over her, chafing her hands, kissing her forehead, her lips. But it had to be the sheikh, for his burnoose was in the way.

Suddenly she remembered. Her eyes flew open. "Aimery!" she cried. So much had happened. She lapsed into confusion. But Aimery held her hands tightly in his. The curved sword was not in sight.

"I was disappointed not to see you," he said. "But I learned you have been more than busy. You're sure that you are not sick? You haven't caught this fever? You fainted."

"I thought you were going to kill me," she said simply. "That sword—and, I guess," she added, struggling to sit up "a guilty conscience."

He surveyed her with sudden amusement. She was so pale and shaken, so clearly conscience-stricken, that he longed to take her in his arms and kiss away her fears. Something held him back.

"The sword is out of sight," he assured her, "but I can do nothing for your conscience. Tell me."

She shook her head. If only he wouldn't be so kind when she was so upset.

"Well, then," he said after a short pause, "you might tell me where you were just now?"

"J-just now?"

"My dear Solange, you were white as a sheet when you came in. You must have been somewhere that upset you."

Little by little, he coaxed it out of her. She grew more

confident, and even told him that the queen had told her she was to blame for the state of their marriage. Involuntarily she glanced up at him.

He was not angry. Instead, he turned away from her. But he said, grimly, "Go on."

Faltering, she continued. "She said I should come to her tent, so we could have a private discussion as soon as you came back."

"Why there?"

"Because she knew this pavilion was full of patients and the doctors kept coming in—" She broke off, fearing the sudden change in him.

"So. She *did* know. But I foiled her scheme. She got out of this with empty hands for her trouble!" He chortled in triumph. Then he said, "You're not amused? Solange, what happened?"

She had to tell him. "I thought it was you. Dressed like this—and I was expecting you."

"But I didn't—"

"I know that now," she said with weary patience.

"Then who?" By a miracle, he kept his voice steady.

"An Arab. But he wasn't expecting me, either, no more than I expected a total stranger in your place."

"In the queen's pavilion. He expected her—and the tent was dark."

"I suppose I do resemble her. My light hair."

Firmly he said, "Not in the least, not really. Thank God you are nothing alike."

She looked puzzled.

"I should have known it was a trap."

"Hush," said Aimery. Motioning her to silence, he stepped stealthily to the door of the tent and peered out. "No one there."

"A trap, of course," he agreed. "I need no one else to intercede for me with you. Especially not the queen. But you said the sheikh did not know you at first." Jealousy prodded him. "When did he find out you were . . . not what he had expected?"

The question lay between them, loaded with danger. How much dared she tell him? It was an instinctive decision—she could at least save him some hurt. "Quite soon," she confessed. "He called me his queen."

Aimery appeared placated.

Suddenly conscious of the passing time, Solange jumped to her feet. "But Aimery, I forgot the most important part! I've got to go—"

She began gathering things into a canvas wallet. He caught her wrist. "Go where?" he demanded. "You've not told me all!"

"He knows where my father is!"

He held her fast until she told him all of it. Sheikh Njer-el-Din knew where her father was.

"He says," snorted Aimery.

But she must meet him at dawn. He would not wait beyond that.

"He'll wait, all right! You'd make a fine addition to his harem!"

So close to the sheikh's words! Solange was startled. "But he knows, Aimery. He said so. And he asked me if I could face my father's circumstances. Aimery, suppose—" Her voice faltered.

"Suppose he knows nothing," Aimery was harsh.

"But I'm so close to the truth now. After all this, I've got to take the risk."

"You admit there is a risk?"

"Everything in life is a risk," she said sadly, "But we keep going. I have little left but to find my father. After that, it makes no difference what happens."

"Have I failed you so much?" said Aimery. "You have much to blame me for, I confess it gladly, but—" This was not the time to talk to her, to confess all that he had let come between them, to try once more.

He looked at her with an expression she could not read. Finally he came to a decision. "I shall not try to hold you back, if you are so determined to ride with this sheikh. You leave before dawn? So be it."

He let her go. Stepping out of the tent, he left her alone. Half-sobbing, she thought how angry he must be. And he might be right. She knew nothing of this sheikh, but she could not turn back now.

She packed and changed into darker, sturdier clothes for riding. Should she leave a note for Aimery? She decided against it. He knew where she was going. She picked up her bag.

Aimery stood in the doorway. "I feared you would be gone," he said. "I had to obtain permission of the king, and send Rainard to muster my men. But we will be ready in an hour." Her bewildered expression caused him to smile wryly. "You think I would let you go alone?"

Before they could depart, Petronilla entered. "So," she said crisply, "after all . . . you have word."

"So I think, Mother. I am going to see."

"Odo lives?"

Solange answered slowly. "I do not even know that. The man says he knows Father. Says, too, that I must be strong. So I know not what to expect."

Petronilla said, thoughtfully, "You will find me here when you return. I will stay with my patients."

"What of Mehun?"

"What of him? He knows where I am. He speaks only of going back to Belvent. And since I will not, he leaves me alone."

"He goes with the king then, in two days?" she asked.

"I suppose so. He follows the king like a shadow," she said with amused contempt. "He thinks that the king will weary of seeing him and, in desperation, confirm the fief."

"And you care not?"

"In truth, I care not for Mehun. Nor—even if you find him—do I wish to see Odo."

"Come, Solange," Aimery called urgently from the doorway. "My men are here. Already it lightens in the east."

Solange embraced her mother with affection.

"Find out," counseled her mother. "Find the truth. No matter what." She smiled wanly. "If I have two living husbands, I will walk to Jerusalem to expiate my sins. And then go into the convent. To sin no more—" With a sudden twinkle, she added, looking more like the Petronilla of old, "—at least not in *that* way! God go with you, my daughter."

3

They cantered slowly out of the meadow beneath the walls of Antioch. Fearful of being stopped by Raymond's patrols, Solange kept close to Aimery.

"Don't fear," said Aimery. "I have the king's pass." Suddenly he laughed. "The patrols are far from infallible. Your sheikh got through."

With a mischievous smile, she agreed. And tonight wasn't the first time.

When Aimery decided to do something, she reflected, it was done thoroughly. In that small space of time, since the sheikh had bade her prepare, her husband had gone to the king, obtained the all-important pass, and mustered his men. The company that rode out in the dark that night was powerful, made up of well-seasoned veterans, experienced and tough.

She settled back in her saddle with a feeling of comfort. Aimery was at her side.

The appointed rendezvous was more than a mile down the valley south of Antioch, beside an old stone mill. She was beset by fears that the sheikh would not wait. That, if he saw so many coming, he would fade into the shadows.

But there he was, all of a sudden, a pale glimmer in his white robe, astride a milk-white horse of the small-boned variety that belonged to this country.

Aimery saluted the sheikh in the Turkish fashion, fingertips to forehead, lips and breast. The sheikh, after a surprised moment, responded in kind.

"I did not expect an armed host to come with you," he said to Solange, adding to Aimery, "My own men are up the valley. They will be sufficient to protect the lady."

Aimery gave him a wintry smile. "But when the Lady Solange returns to Antioch," he said with faint emphasis, "she will be well protected by her own men."

433

"So be it," said the sheikh. Solange had feared he would be insulted and refuse to guide them farther.

With a beckoning gesture, he started on ahead of them. He led them at right angles to the road they had come, heading east from the valley of Antioch. Solange glanced once at Aimery, but it was too dark to read his expression. She noticed that he rode close beside her, so close that she could reach out and touch him, if she desired. She kept her hands on the reins.

They traveled east all that first day. The sheikh's party rode ahead, and a contingent of his Turks rode behind them. Aimery thought the Franks rode as prisoners. He glanced at Solange. She seemed unworried, so he said nothing. But he signaled to Rainard to keep a sharp eye out for an ambush. He did not put much faith in the sheikh's assurances.

The road wound eastward into a broad valley. Aimery had not traveled this way before, and he was surprised to see such luxuriant growth, watered by a small stream that trickled down the center of the valley floor.

There seemed to be few inhabitants. From time to time the sun touched upon small clusters of white buildings on the far side of the valley, but the sheikh's way lay far removed from habitation.

The day finally became afternoon, and soon the sheikh motioned to them to halt.

"We will camp yonder," he said, "for the night. There is ample water, and grass for the horses." A slow smile touched his lips as he added, "I am more than sorry there is not a pavilion for the lady."

"The open sky is fine," said Solange.

The campfire held the night at bay. Solange bathed her face in the river, and curbed a strong wish to remove her clothes and let the cool water cleanse her from the dust of the road. She let the water run over her wrists, and had to be content with that.

Later, as they sat around the campfire, the sheikh said, "The Lady Solange has nothing to fear from me. I have told her that. Does it mean you do not trust me, Lady, that you bring such a strong guard to protect you?"

Aimery answered calmly. "She did not bring the guard. I did. It is not, sheikh, that I do not trust you. But you will agree—a man must take care of his own."

I'm *not* your own! cried Solange inwardly. But a second thought crossed her mind—how much she wished she were!

"And yet," said the sheikh, "even a man who guards his possessions closely may find that they vanish, right before his eyes. Either someone steals, or—"

"Or what?" prodded Aimery.

"Or the possession leaves, of its own accord. Here in our land we take a realistic view—"

"Especially of women," interposed Aimery wryly. "In our land, we cherish our women."

"And yet, your cherishing appears casual. You may yet lose."

"Sometimes," said Aimery deliberately, "a man prizes most what he once valued least."

Solange looked intently at her fingers, interlaced in her lap. Did he mean it? Was he sure that, at last, he could love and trust her?

The strange duel between Aimery and the sheikh seemed to take place on several levels. Uppermost, there was the ordinary civility of conversation. Beneath that was the challenge. Aimery was throwing down the gage.

She swayed with weariness. It had been a long ride, after many sleepless nights with her patients. She fell asleep on the hard ground, and didn't even sense Aimery covering her with her cloak.

Rising at dawn, they set out during the cool of the day. They camped again early, so as to be settled before the dark, which came upon them suddenly.

The fourth camp was the last one. The narrow river canyon widened into a broad, fruitful valley. The green fields, the leafy trees, gave rest to her wind-burned eyes, and Solange was grateful. After the evening meal was consumed, the sheikh sat strangely silent.

"Where will we spend tomorrow night?" wondered Solange aloud.

"In the city of El Chorazin," responded the sheikh. "In the land where the Princess Fazia rules."

"Then we are nearly there?" cried Solange, breathlessly. "Where my father is?"

"Tomorrow," said the sheikh. "All will be known . . . tomorrow."

4

The city of El Chorazin was the capital of the kingdom of the same name, which extended as far as this beautiful valley. It seemed a rich kingdom, but her only interest in it lay in the whereabouts of her father.

The expedition made a slow start the next morning. Since that day would see them at their destination, Solange took more care than usual with her appearance. Taking out the turquoise mantle with a hood which could veil her face, she found a secluded place to change her clothes. She would enter the city with as much style as she could manage.

The journey was a long one. The towers of the city rose before them in mid-morning, but as long as they rode, the city seemed no nearer.

The road lay through pleasant cultivation. There was sugar cane, and orchards with apricots heavy on the trees.

Imperceptibly, her spirits rose, little by little, until she began to hum.

Aimery gestured to the sheikh. "Your men are leaving us?"

The sheikh bowed his head. "As you have astutely noticed. Do not fear. They do not go to bring down an army upon your heads."

"Then why?"

"Simply because I do not wish to lead an armed host into the province of the Princess Fazia. She is a gentle woman for the most part, but jealous of her rights."

"And she does not like you," finished Aimery with a wry smile.

436

"I would not like it myself, were an army to gallop upon my capital."

"You are right, of course," said Aimery. "But you yourself?"

"I will stay with you until noon."

He moved away, and Aimery could not question him further. Aimery looked behind to find Rainard looking troubled. He dropped back to relay the sheikh's words to him.

"If that's true," said Rainard, "then we're all right." But his tone was more than a little skeptical.

The city of El Chorazin took shape before them. Slowly the minarets could be distinguished, stretching slender fingers toward the sky. They were pale, the color of sand, but ornamented at the top with exquisite tile in turquoise, gold, and deep red.

"Inside the city," the sheikh informed them, "there live many people, all under the rule of the Princess Fazia. Her father was a cruel man, but she is his opposite. She rules with a gentle touch, and her people adore her."

"Then my father is not likely to be tortured under such a gentle ruler?" Solange burst out, the fears she had kept to herself seeking assuagement.

"The Princess's father has been dead only a little more than a year."

It was a cryptic remark, and did nothing to ease her worry. "Now I must leave you," he said, "the gates are in sight. You will find your way."

He lingered long, looking at Solange with an inscrutable expression. "Lady, I pray that the time I can be of service to you, once again, will be vouchsafed me. I am your servant."

She watched him ride away, fast, the way they had come. His robe billowed behind like a sail. He never looked back.

5

The gates were already open as the Franks rode up to the city wall.

El Chorazin was a seemly city. The stone houses were two or three stories high, and greenery peeped over the edge of the flat roofs. But on the ground level, the houses presented unbroken, forbidding stretches of blank walls, turning their backs, as it were, to the stranger. Beyond the market square stood a larger building with three stone stories. It held a certain imposing look, like a palace.

Aimery held himself alert and ready. It was not the safest proposition in the world to ride, in such few numbers, unheralded, into a throbbing city throng. The citizens had clearly seen them coming. The entire population of the kingdom of El Chorazin, so it seemed, crowded around them.

There was no violence. The crowd was rough, shoving, but there seemed to be more curiosity than resentment about their presence. The Franks held to their saddles. Once afoot, they would be at the mercy of the mob.

Aimery gestured to his followers. "We'd best seek out someone who can help us—the local *drugeman*, for instance." He bent from his saddle to address one after another of the men who were close enough to touch his stirrups. "We should like to speak to the princess," he repeated, in Arabic, and then in *lingua franca*. He was met with blank stares.

There were so many people. Solange felt the hair on the back of her neck stir. The horde hemmed her in and she could not move forward.

Faces, faces—she scanned them all, looking for one particular face. She was not even sure she would recognize her father. There was one man at the far edge of the throng, a little taller than the others, who caught her eye. She could not see him clearly, for he turned away quickly

438

and she lost sight of him. But there was something about him that haunted her. Had she seen him before?

It was not her father, that was certain. It was probably a traveling merchant, one she had seen in the soukhs in Antioch.

The Franks tried to edge their horses forward, into the crowd, intending to reach the gate of the palace beyond the square. Not a one of the hundreds gave way. It was almost eerie, as though these brown-faced, bearded men were not possessed of the ordinary fears of snorting horses and armed men.

Suddenly there was a stir at the edge of the crowd. Way was made freely now for a robed man, undoubtedly an official of rank. Everyone in the crowd now found his tongue. There was much shouting, in a language she did not understand.

Aimery greeted the official in Arabic. Speaking carefully, he was gratified by a glint of understanding. The official spoke Arabic.

"We have come a long distance, but we come in peace." Solange could grasp a few words. "We have come to find a man, a friend. We believe Her Royal Highness, the ruler of this land, can help us. We should like to see her."

The official answered in some length, while Solange fixed her eyes upon him. She was thankful for the Turkish custom that required the veil before her face. She could watch without being watched.

Suddenly the official gave a few short orders, and the way was abruptly cleared. Men sprang to hold the bridles of the snorting destriers and Solange's palfrey, and they were led through the city of El Chorazin.

"The princess?" breathed Solange.

"We shall see her tomorrow," said Aimery. "They say."

Their reception had been crude, perhaps, but not unfriendly. They approached an iron gate. The soldiers of El Chorazin surged out of the gates and the little party was surrounded. Aimery and Solange were cut off from the rest, and invited to dismount.

Solange stood bewildered on the cobbled pavement. What is this place, she wondered? Not a jail? But it could not be the palace.

They stood inside a courtyard, enclosed on four sides by the palace and three other buildings, all apparently connected to each other. Another gate lay at the opposite side of the courtyard. The yard itself was green, with luxurious grass, and a magnificent fountain.

She had the strange idea that someone was watching her —not her guards, but someone whose attention burned upon her. She looked around but saw no one.

They were led away from the courtyard, through another, smaller pair of gates into a building that bordered the courtyard.

A door was opened and their guard motioned for them to enter. The door clanged shut behind them, and they were in what could only be called a cell.

Aimery prowled the square room. It was larger than most, and contained rugs and a small water pitcher. There was no other furniture.

"Apparently not a dungeon," he pronounced after he had examined the walls and the tiny window that looked out onto empty sky.

"Then what?" said Solange skeptically. "This looks like a jail to me."

"A sort of intermediate jail," suggested Aimery, carefully examining the door that had shut behind him. "Very clever. There is no handle on this side of the door. There is no way out."

"That makes it a jail."

"But not, my dear, a dungeon. We are clearly not in favor with the princess. But it seems she does not wish us executed outright."

"Aimery—" Her voice quavered in spite of herself.

He crossed the few steps between them swiftly and took her in his arms. "Now darling, don't worry. We're here peacefully, and they will understand that. We need fear nothing. We'll see the princess tomorrow, and, please God, we will be on our way home in a couple of days. With the news you've hoped for."

He did not necessarily believe what he said, but her ease of mind was paramount to him.

Hours passed, and they lost track of time. It could have

been that day, yet, or the middle of that night when they heard the door clang open at last.

Starting to their feet, they watched the guard enter. He motioned to them to precede him through the door.

"To our execution?" cried Solange.

Aimery's hand tightened on her shoulder. "He's smiling."

"Perhaps that is their entertainment," she objected, but nevertheless she moved through the door. In the corridor were half a dozen other men, in voluminous pantaloons and broad smiles. It was still daylight.

The guard produced one word. "Follow."

They followed. Through the iron gate and into the courtyard. A peacock strolled upon the grass, turning at the sound of their approach. Then he spread his tail, slowly, with arrogant assurance, and the quills rattled like tiny drums.

Solange caught her breath at the beauty of it.

The guard said again, "Follow."

Their destination was another wing of the palace. But this wing was not a jail. The walls were not stone, and the rooms to which they were shown were on an upper floor. The floors were strewn with carpets, like the ones Erik carried with him. The cushions were soft and deep. And there was a balcony through which the late afternoon sun was streaming.

The transformation in their surroundings was fantastic. Deferential servants rushed to and fro, bowing themselves in and out of the room. Baths were provided, hot water, soaps, and perfumed oils.

"Honored guests," said Solange, wrapping a gossamer muslin robe around her.

The princess came to them shortly. A small, delicate woman, she was curious about them and did not try to hide it.

With an air of authority, she motioned her guests to sit. The princess then began an inquiry that touched widely on a number of subjects. She seemed surprisingly well informed, though she was clearly no older than Solange.

"And now, lady," she said, after considerable conversation, "tell me about your mother."

6

$\mathfrak{S}$olange was bewildered, but before she could ask what had prompted the question, the princess signaled an abrupt end to the interview. Before leaving them, she promised they could see St. Florent the next morning.

The next day, the princess herself led them through many rooms. One was large, without chairs, except for two at the far end of the room, placed before a colonnade of delicately arched columns.

Two chairs were arranged on a dais of sorts—one enormous thronelike chair, the other less ornate and set a trifle below the first—for the ruler and her prince consort.

They passed swiftly through the reception room to a room of mirrors, of crystal chandeliers, all swimming in the hazy faint light coming through narrow window slits. Whereas in Solange's land the windows were narrow to keep out the cold, here they were designed to keep the merciless sun at bay.

The princess turned to smile encouragingly at them. Solange said, "My father?"

"You will see."

But she did not elaborate. Instead, she motioned to a pantaloon-clad servant at the door. He sprang to open it. The princess, to Solange's surprise, took her hands. "My dear, your father is within. I wish you had not come, but you must know the truth. I understand that."

With a thoughtful look at Solange, she waved them through the door, but did not follow.

They were in a magnificent room. There were cushions, rugs, delicate brass dishes, on curiously carved tables.

The entire far wall was open. The sun did not come to this side of the building, and the air wafting in was muted by the shade. A small tree stood on a balcony beyond the doorway, its pink and white blossoms scenting the air.

In the doorway to the balcony stood a man, his back to

them. He was heavy-set, rounded with good food, and the oriental garb he wore accentuated his plump outlines. He wore the fez of a ruler, the tassel of gold hanging on the right side.

His hands were clasped behind his back, and on the little finger of one hand he wore a magnificent ruby. And on the finger of the other hand was a gold ring with a curious device. Solange sensed rather than saw that the ring displayed the swan of St. Florent.

All this she saw in the half-minute before the man turned.

He faced them. "Well, daughter," he sighed. "So you found me. I wish you hadn't."

She could not breathe. Here, in good health—in blooming prosperity beyond her wildest dreams—stood the man whom she had feared either dead or tortured beyond endurance.

And she was astoundingly furious.

"You wish I hadn't come," she said, in a tone so quiet that Aimery looked at her with alarm and stepped closer to her. "Well, I too wish I hadn't. I suppose it would have been far better for me to always picture you eaten by wild animals, suffering tortures at the hands of the infidels, miserable, dying, thinking no one cared about you."

Her father was profoundly puzzled. "Eaten by wild animals?"

Aimery made a quick gesture of silence. Solange later did not remember most of what she had said. If there had been a sword in her hands she would have swung it. She had a faint recollection later that at one point in this strange confrontation she held a brass pot in her hand, but someone—Aimery—had quickly removed it.

At last Aimery stopped her, by the simple method of standing behind her and placing his hand over her mouth. He held her thus, until she was calmed.

"All right, Solange?" he asked at last. Satisfied, he let her go.

"Now, sir," said Aimery to his father-in-law. "I think we can deal better together."

"Oh, I agree," sighed Odo. "One thing I could never stand is a termagant. What does a man need of screaming and shouting, of recrimination? A shrew, that's what she is." He sighed deeply. "Let me get you some refreshments. No, no, I insist. One's hospitality must not be impugned."

He clapped his hands, and at once a small table was rolled in. A brass pot of rich black coffee, a plate full of sweetmeats, cups inlaid with silver. Odo's eyes glinted. It was clear enough where he had gathered in the plumpness that strained at his red sash.

"Coffee? You will not refuse me, I am sure. It calms the nerves." He glanced at Solange as he handed her the cup. "And that will certainly be an improvement."

The three of them sat on deep cushions at the balcony doors, open to the breath of air that lifted the tree petals.

"My child," he said to Solange, "it pains me to see you distressed. Now, my Fazia is never stormy. She is always gentle, soft-spoken, a delight to the eye and ear."

He emptied the dish of dates and popped them into his mouth. "You could take a lesson from her."

He caught Aimery's bleak eye upon him, and his words trailed away.

"And who are you?" said Odo, finally.

"I am Aimery de Montvert," said Aimery crisply.

Odo's hand stopped halfway to his mouth. "Montvert. Your father is Simon? I remember him well. But you're not the heir?"

"My oldest brother, also named Simon. But what is more to the point, I am husband to your daughter."

"Solange?"

"Who else?" demanded Solange. She was calmer now.

Aimery continued. "And now I think we will have an explanation from you."

The two men faced each other, the one calm and demanding, the other indignant and quivering. Solange, her fury dwindling now, realized that Aimery could deal much better with her father than she.

He was certainly not the man she had thought him! Her mother's words returned to her, *you never knew him very well.* Solange needed time to put the two together— her father, and this man now glaring at Aimery.

"Don't threaten me!" shouted Odo. "Your men are not behind you now."

444

"Where are they? I confess to a great curiosity about their welfare." Aimery's tone was mild, but Odo looked up sharply with narrowed eyes.

"Well provided for. Mathieu has seen to that."

"Mathieu!" Her father's favorite servant, with him from their childhood at Belvent, had come all the way to this end-of-the-world place! "Then I did see him in the crowd."

"How else would I know you were here?" countered her father. "A harebrained scheme, sir, to ride in with your army, like—like Bohemund the Destroyer."

"We came in peace."

"Little enough peace you've brought me," he muttered. "Have some more coffee. This brown powder adds much to the flavor. A kind of sweetness, but not so cloying as wild honey. They make it here out of a kind of grass. Try it."

He watched while Aimery spooned a little into his cup and tasted it. "A strange flavor indeed," he pronounced. "We have seen this *sarcara* in Byzantium, but I am no adventurer in foods."

"Well, each man to his own *métier*." Odo took a deep breath, as though remembering that this visit was hardly a social occasion. He turned back to Aimery. "You demand explanations. Let me remind you that I am prince here."

"I wondered just what your position was," interposed Aimery.

"And I can snap my fingers and have you exterminated."

"And sell your daughter into slavery? I think not. Solange has come a long way to rescue you. We have time to hear your story—before we leave."

Solange glanced quickly at Aimery. He was unmoved by her father's boasting. He was even pleasant. But looking from one to the other, she realized that Aimery was by far the stronger. Aimery had the strength to draw from the older man the story he was reluctant to tell.

"Solange has followed some exceedingly faint clues to find you. She has pictured you wounded, in prison, tortured. But it is obvious that you are none of these."

"Tortured? Oh, yes, I was. My late father-in-law—whose name be praised!—clapped me into his dungeon, all right.

Look at these hands!" He held out his hands, fingers out-spread. The knuckles on his left hand were ugly and swollen. "Until my dearest Fazia came to my rescue."

He lapsed into brooding silence, hands behind his back, clasped to hide the misshapen fingers. Aimery let the silence lengthen, then prodded gently. "The word in Europe was that you were dead. Killed at the battle of Adana. Bodies were heaped in stacks around you." The irony was gentle. "Where did you go then?"

Surprisingly, Odo chuckled. With childlike glee, he said, "Was I killed? How delightful a way to end my life in Europe. To be a hero, fallen in the wars against the infidel! Not every man survives his death, you know."

They waited in silence. Aimery kept his eyes fixed upon Odo, but his hand reached out to touch his wife's, and the simple gesture calmed her.

"Well," said Odo, sober again. "It is clear that my so-called glorious death was not convincing. Else why would my loving daughter not accept it?" He turned to her. "You're too much like my mother," he accused her. "A formidable woman. Like you, she expected too much of me."

Solange bristled, but Aimery intervened. "So you left the battlefield and went to Antioch with your men. Then?"

"Persistent as a gadfly, aren't you?" He refilled his cup and drank it down in one gulp. "Never thought I'd have to dredge all this up again. That was all of three years ago, after all."

He began to pace the floor, driven by memories. Suddenly he stopped. "Your mother. She lives?"

Solange nodded, unable to speak.

"She is not coming *here*?" The consternation in his voice was almost amusing.

Aimery took shrewd advantage, speaking before Solange could. "That depends. She is in Antioch now."

Stupefied, Odo glared at them. "Good God," he muttered involuntarily. "What do you want of me?"

"The truth," said Aimery.

"All right, all right." He pulled himself together, becoming somehow taller and leaner. He began.

446

"I went to Antioch with Mathieu and six of my good Belvent men. The battle had gone badly and we hardly had an army left. But somehow we got to Antioch in dribs and drabs—a handful of knights straggled in every day or two for a week. The prince of Antioch—you know him?"

"Raymond? Yes."

"He still rules? A very devil of a man. He wanted us all to swear fealty to him and ride out to take Damascus."

"Damascus!"

"Had a bee in his bonnet about Damascus. Wouldn't take no for an answer. So, not wishing to gainsay my oath, I left the place. Besides, I thought there was booty to be gained along the merchant road."

Turned highwayman? Aimery wondered.

Odo hurried past that. "We went here and there. Can't tell you the names of places. Never knew them."

It was clear that Odo and his small band had harried the countryside, taking what they wanted and riding on. There were many small bands of raiders roving the hills of Asia, without discipline, in no sense any longer an army with purpose.

Sometimes the Turks fought back. And one by one Odo's small band dwindled until only he and his faithful Mathieu were left. And he, Odo, was grievously wounded.

"I came through the battle of Adana with hardly a scratch," he said with a rueful laugh. "I was nearly shipwrecked twice in the Mediterranean Sea, and then—after all that—to come a cropper from an arrow, miles from anywhere! Well, Mathieu took care of me as best he could. But when I was almost dead, he got me here."

"Then the princess nursed you back to health?" said Aimery, skeptically.

"You may scoff, but I'll take my oath on Scripture that it's true!" said Odo hotly.

"Then you're still a Christian? I wondered."

Odo's face grew red. "Well, it's hard to say what I am. But never mind. Then, when I was well enough, the old bast— that is, my father-in-law, may Allah bless him— had his fun. But my Fazia got me out of that while I could still use my hands."

447

Solange spoke for the first time, unable to sit passively by any longer. "We've come to take you back to Belvent."

Odo stared. "Are you moon-touched, girl? Belvent? It's out of the question!"

7

All this, Solange thought, and for what? All this, to rescue her father, who had so unaccountably altered that he was nearly unrecognizable. And who had no wish to be rescued.

"All this for nothing!" she said aloud. "Father—"

Odo lifted a hand in protest. "I do not wish to discuss it. I frankly see no reason why you should want me back. You've got your husband. And a good one, too, if he can manage you. I think you'd best forget all this."

Aimery laughed. "I wish you had made a better choice of words, sir. You've done me no good."

With a surprisingly shrewd glance, Odo looked conspiratorially at his son-in-law. "Skittish, is she? Well, she's got sense though, if she's a Saint Florent. It'll come right."

He clapped his hands, and a servant glided in and removed the tray. "I can't stand cold coffee," he complained to his guests. Another tray of coffee was instantly at his hand. Solange marveled at the service her father commanded.

"But, Father," said Solange, "Belvent—"

"Can't your mother run it?" he interrupted.

"It's not a question of the Lady de Mowbrai running the estate," said Aimery, deliberately.

"Lady *who*?" demanded Odo, clearly shaken.

"Lady de Mowbrai," supplemented Solange. "My lady mother."

Odo turned indignant. Fixing his daughter with a stern look, he said, "She married again? Without asking me?"

The absurdity of the question swept over Solange. She burst out in a whooping laugh, to her father's evident anger.

At length, she wiped her eyes and said, "I'm sorry, Father. But you really are ridiculous. You know that."

"Me!" said her father indignantly. But he was, at times, a fair man, and he grinned reluctantly. "I suppose that's right. But nonetheless, I'm really very angry. Who is this upstart? I suppose he wants the manor?"

"And my mother," said Solange quickly, "who was then a very pretty woman."

"I suppose you'd better tell me the worst."

Aimery realized that this meeting was going to take far too long. In spite of Odo's assurances, he was nervous about his men, and he was not at all sure of his father-in-law's intentions. It might be that he wished no word at all to trickle back to Antioch.

Aimery told a concise tale, of Mehun de Mowbrai riding home from Outremer and finding a fair estate and a fair lady. "He said he saw you die at the battle of Adana," Aimery pointed out. "And there was no reason not to believe him. I think there had been no word from you for some time."

Odo nodded morosely.

"So Mehun de Mowbrai wed the widow," said Aimery. "All might have gone without comment, had not Mehun greedily decided to betroth Solange to the Baron d'Yves."

"That pig?"

"You had already betrothed me to Raoul de Puiseaux," said Solange. "So I refused to wed another until you said I might."

"And that's how this journey all started," Aimery concluded.

"But you did not wed d'Yves. Nor, quite obviously, did you keep your contract with Raoul."

Aimery warned him with a small shake of his head.

"Ah, well," said Odo, tolerantly. "A lily, I suppose. He was never my choice, but the lass had her heart set on him."

Aimery looked at Solange with some amusement. He was pleased to see that she had recovered her self-possession.

But there was a telltale tautness around her mouth that boded ill.

Odo de St. Florent slumped morosely upon his cushion. His thoughts ranged far afield. Something struck him as he mulled over Aimery's narrative. "You say your mother *was* pretty? She is not now?"

"Not in the same way," ventured Solange. It was hard to explain Petronilla's change. Her character had begun to rule her face in the last months, and it was a more beautiful face because of that. But the prettiness had departed.

Aimery explained. "I think it is the possibility of having two living husbands that has distressed her. I think Mehun leaves her alone. But, of course, he still has Belvent."

Odo made up his mind. He rose and, stretching to his full height, said, "Daughter, I wish you to forget you ever found me. I am dead as far as your world is concerned. We can leave it at that."

"You won't come back with us?"

"How can I?" he said. "I am a prince. I am a Moslem, at least outwardly. In order to marry Fazia, I was more than willing to convert. I admit that good wine still lingers in my dreams—forbidden, of course, now."

He gestured for them to join him at the door to the balcony. "See the land out there, flourishing with fruit trees, date palms, melons? It never snows here. The air is always soft, and never biting. The people are happy. There is plenty to eat, and here in this valley no one bothers us. We have all the water we need." He glanced sheepishly at Aimery. "These Moslems have some habits I have grown used to. I've even learned to like bathing. What do you say to that?"

Aimery guffawed. "You should hear our Abbot Bernard on the subject. He says baths contaminate morals. Do you find it so, sir?"

Odo puffed his lips out. "None of your business, youngster!" But his eyes twinkled.

Shortly, Aimery and Solange were escorted back to their luxurious apartments. Solange had been unusually quiet, and the tautness around her lips had not eased.

After examining the rooms to see that no overeager

servant remained behind, Aimery made Solange recline upon the cushions, arranging them so that she could look from their balcony out to the sky.

"Now then, Solange. What do you think we should do?"

"Aimery, I truly do not know. I feel as though some giant hand had reached inside my head and twisted things around. What looked black and white to me yesterday now has all the colors of the rainbow. And things that were once so important that I could think of nothing else now seem vague and pointless."

He looked at her anxiously.

"I don't know why I thought it would be worth all we've gone through. My mother's unhappiness, my own." She glanced at Aimery under her long lashes. "What I've done to those near to me, I shudder to think about. And my father—Why, he's just a shadow of what I thought him to be. It's as though I never knew him! And, of course, that's what my mother always said."

"He has found happiness of a sort, though. Don't fool yourself that he is beguiled only by the soft airs and the luscious fruit. There's something more."

They soon found out what that something was.

At a banquet held in their honor, Solange and Aimery were seated beside the princess and her escort, Prince Odo. In the gentle light of a hundred lanterns, they listened to the soft twang of a dozen stringed instruments.

The banquet was sumptuous. Dishes of silver, cups inlaid with gems, mother-of-pearl-handled knives and, again, the two-tined forks graced the tables. There were well-seasoned meats, indescribably sweet melons, and Solange scarcely knew what else was set before her.

Princess Fazia was kind. Solange recognized that. But she herself was numb, unable to speak, even to think. She had followed her father's footsteps across Europe for so long, and when she reached the end of the trail she found he was a different man. She could not accept this strange enchantment that the Arabian wizards must have wrought on him. The land of El Chorazin was bewitched. She fought hard to keep a firm hold on her own wits.

At the end of the banquet, Fazia said, "Now I must show you the treasure of El Chorazin."

"I shall be happy," said Solange, mechanically.

But it was not a casket of jewels that Fazia brought forth. Instead, clapping her hands, she summoned a nurse-maid—who brought in a child.

The child, wrapped in the finest of garments, clearly cherished, had very light blond hair, like Solange's own. The baby slept.

"The heir to the throne of El Chorazin," said Fazia, with shining eyes, "is not quite one year old."

Solange lifted her eyes from the son to the father. Odo looked back at her with a steady gaze. She recognized her own defeat. She bowed her head to her father. It was all the submission she could manage, and she managed it with grace indeed.

8

That night the reaction Aimery had feared set in. Once they had returned to their rooms, Solange threw herself on the cushions and pummeled the soft velvet.

"How could he?" she cried. "All the while we were waiting at Belvent, watching down the road for the first sight of his banners, and he was lolling on cushions in a sultan's palace!"

"Remember the fingers," said Aimery, calmly.

"Remember my mother's anguish!" flashed Solange. "Remember how I nearly got killed—how many times? Remember that I might have been forced to marry the baron! What a fool I was!"

"Not such a fool," he said, stroking her hair gently. "You persevered until you found out the truth."

"I wish I never had!"

She alternated bouts of wild weeping with angry threats of vengeance. Aimery let her rant, now, knowing she must get it all out of her system before she could begin to heal herself.

"I'll drag him back by main force! Make him confront

my mother! See what he has to say to *her*! You've got
enough men, Aimery! We can do it."

He said, with far more amiability than he felt, "Of
course. We would drag the prince of this land out by brute
force, make the princess as much a widow as your mother.
Your anguish for your mother must be selfish indeed, if
you can call down the same feeling on another woman,
especially one who has done you no harm."

"Harm!"

"Well, what harm has she done? Did the Princess Fazia
try to marry you off to a brutal monster? Did she deny
your betrothal, before King Louis? No, I think Fazia has
not deserved vengeance."

"She took my father away from us!"

"Your father," Aimery pointed out dryly, "was already
traveling away from Belvent before he came here."

In her mind a balance was beginning to appear. She did
not quite recognize it, nor did she welcome it.

Aimery misread the signs. "I have an idea, Solange,"
he said. "Why do we not go back to Belvent and rout the
usurper? Your mother will not care, and Mowbrai will
then be punished."

To his great surprise, she turned on him, the fury now
pouring out on Aimery's head.

"Belvent! So that's it!"

Bewildered, he said, "What's it? What do you mean?"

"All this time you've come along with me, telling me
you were as anxious as I to get word of my father, and
all you wanted was to own Belvent!"

Her tirade bewildered him, but then it infuriated him.
He had learned much about keeping his temper, but this
woman had power to move him beyond the ordinary. As
his love was greater than most, so was his anger.

"Isn't it Belvent that you are after, yourself?" he gritted.
"I merely want to get your property into your hands. You
resented Mehun de Mowbrai taking over Belvent, with
his men, and his grasping hands. Now it's you who want
it, just as greedily."

"You lie!"

"Tell me, then," he asked. "Have you given a thought
to your father in all this? Are you so blind that you can-

not see he is happier here than ever in his life? A loving wife and a fine son, a realm of his own in a land he loves. You begrudge him this? If that is your idea of love, then deliver me from it!"

"You need not worry!" she cried. "You won't be troubled with it!" He paled. "I did this for my mother!" she finished in a fine blaze of anger. "Not for the property!"

"For your mother. I see." He was white with rage. "Then it was to your mother's benefit to believe her soul was lost forever? To alienate her from a husband who was at least somewhat caring? To drive her to a pilgrimage that has nearly killed her?"

She picked up a pillow and threw it at him. His eyes glittered then, and for a split-second she was almost afraid of him.

What was she doing? Aimery had offered her consolation, support, and an object for her to vent her anger on. She was damaging what she had left with Aimery. She did not know how much that might be, but surely it was less now than moments ago.

He turned on his heel and strode from the room, leaving her crumpled on the floor, reflecting on her folly between fits of weeping.

At length she began to remember all he had said. And she thought that part of his argument was right.

By the time Aimery came back, she was calm. The storm had passed, leaving her spent. She summoned a pale smile for her husband.

"Your father wishes to see you," said Aimery. "You must come."

He would not tell her why. "I've been talking with him," was all he would say. "Now he wants to see you." He felt her hand tremble in his. "Can you bear this?"

"Yes," she said calmly. "I should like to apologize for the things I said to him."

Aimery's reflective gaze lingered on her, but all he said was, "Come."

Aimery had talked to Odo with good effect. And now, after Solange had stammered her apologies, Odo announced, "I'm going to sign over Belvent to you. Mowbrai has not done fealty for it, Aimery tells me, and so it is still my fief. I can dispose of it as I wish. And I wish my daughter to have it, with the understanding that you will take care of your mother. Keep her out of that damned convent. What a ridiculous idea. I can't imagine where she got it!"

Solange looked at the paper he handed her. While it had been done in great haste, yet it was clear and unequivocal. Except for one thing—

"This says 'also, Aimery de Montvert, baron of Pontdebois and baron of Aliquis'." She turned questioningly to Aimery. "Together."

"Your man's no fortune-hunter, if that's what you think," said her father irritably. "But how else will you gain possession of your property? Can you take Belvent away from that wolf de Mowbrai? Alone?"

Solange conceded the point. As well do it with grace, she thought finally, and, with a smile, she turned the paper over to her husband. "For safekeeping," she said sweetly.

For the first time since Odo had ridden out on Crusade, Solange saw her father beaming upon her in proud approval.

The farewell to El Chorazin was filled with sunshine and rose petals, and a little sadness. The Franks stayed for two days after Odo's turning over Belvent to his daughter, and during those two days, Solange got to know her father better than she had before. She gave him her promise to tell Petronilla that they had found only his grave. "I'm a new man here," he said, strangely shy.

Fazia was gracious and warm, and Solange secretly envied the princess the obvious sway she held over her husband. She was too proud to ask her secret, but Fazia guessed what was on Solange's mind.

She said, "You have a good husband in Aimery. He is formidable. It is not the way of the woman to rule a man, but to be ruled by him."

"And yet you rule here in your land."

"In my land, yes. But in my heart, it is my husband who rules. There is no happiness in striving to be the same, the woman equal to the man, for then the two halves do not fit together as they should."

It was something to think about, thought Solange,

sharply aware that all her ideas had been given a jarring in the past few days. It would take some time to come to terms with herself again.

They rode out of El Chorazin to the shouts of her father's people. The royal guard would ride with them a day's journey, and then Aimery and Solange would travel on alone—with their ten knights and sergeants and mounted squires.

They rode hard the second day, and the third. On the third night they came to the canyon they had traversed on their way to El Chorazin. Aimery decided they would camp there.

"You thought it was dangerous," Solange pointed out.

"But easily defended, too. As Njer-el-Din pointed out."

After their supper, which included the last of the melons and the final meal of roasted goat sent with them, Solange decided to climb up to a shelf a dozen or so feet above her head. The moon was about to come up, already touching the lip of the canyon high above. She had been thoughtful all day, and now she wanted to watch the moon rise. It would be a sort of ritual farewell to the enchanted land of her father and the princess.

With some difficulty, she climbed over the scree to the shelf. Scraggly bushes grew along the edge, screening a concavity in the rock wall from the soldiers below.

She pulled her cloak around her and leaned back against the wall. Drawing her knees up to her chin, she waited, watching the sky glow with the ascending moon.

Aimery found her there, and without a word she made room for him beside her.

"Sad about leaving your father?" he asked at last. He took her fingers and interlaced them with his own.

"In a way. I've been thinking. He was not so changed as I had thought at first."

"No?"

"It was not a great change in him. It was that I never knew him. Mother told me often that I did not know my father well. I didn't notice, for instance, that he was far too lenient with the villeins. The harvest was less than it should have been, mostly because no one supervised the work. My father would rather hunt, or talk to his friends, than prod his factor."

"And yet your father was loved," mused Aimery.

"Yes, my father cast a long shadow. Over Belvent, over my mother, over me."

"And now?"

"It was a long shadow, and I followed it. But it was the shadow I followed, not my father as he truly was."

Aimery released her fingers and put his arm around her, drawing her near. She let her head fall onto his shoulder.

"Some people only cast shadows," he said after awhile, "and others are larger than life. Either way, people are frequently not what we suppose them to be.

"But," he said slowly, thinking it out carefully, "it is not wrong for us to be misled. It is what we ourselves think that truly matters. Only that is real. You thought your father was different from what he was, and that belief has made you brave, enduring, and faithful."

She stirred so that she could look into his face. "Aimery?" She dared not ask about Eleanor. But she craved—oh, how she craved!—to know.

"And when they turn out to be other than you thought—then you learn by the contrast. If, for instance, you find your fancied love is false, bitter, then you know what true love is." He gazed down into her eyes. "And value it above rubies." She lifted her lips for his kiss.

The moon rose higher. A campfire winked at either end of the canyon, where sentries stood guard.

This time, at long last, there was love.

Solange was moved to her depths, and she rose to respond. Her body arched to fit his, her senses swimming. Her passion was to melt with him—above all, to make him happy.

And their coming together was so intoxicating as to sweep away forever all memories of the sheikh.

When at last they lay spent, loath to move apart, she traced a furrow down his cheek with her finger. "It's been a long time," she murmured. "A long terrible time."

"But it's over now," he said. "We have won through at last."

She was silent. It would take a while to feel as free with him as she wanted to. She must tread carefully, building the fabric of their marriage as carefully as weaving a precious tapestry, strand by strand.

She drowsed against his bare shoulder, waiting for the moment which was coming as surely as dawn, when his hand would reach out to her again, stroking, arousing. Already she was shivering with desire.

The world exploded into crashing metal, shouts, and cries. Aimery sat up with a curse, reaching for his mail shirt and his hauberk.

His full armor was below, but there was no way to reach it. He hastily put on the light armor he had.

"What is it? An ambush?" she cried.

"The Turks were waiting for us, and bottled us up here." He buckled on his light sword. "Stay here," he commanded, "where it is safe."

9

She watched him slide down the slippery scree. Without full armor, a man could easily be killed, run through with a thin Turkish sword.

The tumult echoed off the canyon cliffs, giving speed to her fingers, fumbling with her tunic, skirt, leather boots. She could not find her gold girdle and did not take the time to search.

She crept to the edge of the ledge and peered over, using the brush as a screen.

A riot of thoughts raced through her mind. The sheikh had said he wanted her, if she would come. The sheikh believed that she was a prisoner in an unhappy marriage. Was this his rescue?

The clashing of weapons, steel on steel, came closer, down the canyon from the west.

Suddenly something occurred to her. Something should have been part of this terrible battle, and wasn't, and that was the shrill ululation of the Turkish soldiers. It was a part of the charge they always made, a cry wavering like a wolf in winter, striking terror and giving the Turks the advantage of surprise.

She had not heard it. Something was not right.

Directly overhead now, the moon shed bright light upon the battle below. She gasped. It had not been Turks who descended with raised sword upon Aimery's men camped in the valley. It had been Franks.

The attackers had every advantage. They had ridden in wearing full heavy armor, slashing, thrusting.

The cries of the wounded rose up the canyon wall. Even while she debated whether she could render service if she descended from her perch, she sought out Aimery. She found him still on foot, whirling on every side with his great battle-ax.

A knight detached himself from the rest and rode through the canyon, from the west, slowly, obviously searching for someone. She watched him, fearful of drawing attention to herself.

The knight's shield bore no device at all. His armor was darkly glistening in the moonlight, but the visor was closed.

With patience he watched Aimery dispatch two foes who had attacked him at the same time. Then, while Aimery stood still, his chest heaving with exertion, the knight suddenly put spurs to his destrier and the great steed leaped forward, hooves upraised.

"Aimery!" she screamed. The knight hesitated, and she knew she had given her presence away.

Aimery, warned by Solange's scream, stood his ground as the great enemy bore down on him. At the last possible moment, he avoided the downthrusting sword, and fell to his knees. Swifter than sight, the sword Aimery held cut the hamstrings of the destrier, and horse and rider fell to the ground.

It was not over. The unknown foe raised himself to his feet and faced Aimery. The knight of no device and Aimery, her love, were locked in a duel. The knight sustained no damage from Aimery's blows, but Aimery was clearly losing strength. He could not hold out much longer. The knight of the dark armor pressed relentlessly forward. He seemed to be in the grip of a merciless personal fury, a desperation that pressed Aimery back, and back.

Aimery had to give ground, little by little. It was only a matter of time until that battle-ax would smash through the light protection Aimery wore.

Aimery moved back, step by step.

A plan began forming in her mind. Bring him closer! She implored her husband silently. Aimery did—he was forced to.

Breathless, she watched.

And at last the time had come. Aimery, his back against the canyon wall, was just beneath her. She remembered that the ledge had protruded, and Aimery was out of sight. Only his ax moved in and out, like the tongue of a viper, and caught the moonlight.

The stone she counted on so heavily was at the lip of the stone ledge. She knelt behind it.

She looked again. The knight was looking down at something now.

Solange could almost feel the gloating smile hidden inside the visor. The right moment had come. Instinct guided her.

The armored man below began to slowly lift his mace, to deal Aimery the final, crushing blow. With all her strength, Solange pushed the rock. It did not move. And then, suddenly, it did!

The rock took with it small pebbles that fell on the knight below, arresting his arm in mid-air. He turned his visored face up to see where the rain of gravel came from. He looked up just in time, as it happened, to see the boulder hurtle through the air at him.

The great stone found its target.

10

She waited, barely breathing. Below her the knight lay heavily on the ground. There seemed to be no life in him.

Where was Aimery? She called his name softly. He did not answer. She gathered up her skirts and scurried down the scree, hastening to where Aimery was sitting up, holding his head.

"What happened?" he said. "I could see his arm coming down! Was it a thunderbolt?"

"I did it."

"Can you help me up?"

He leaned heavily on her arm. "We can leave him, for the moment. What of the rest?"

She said simply, "The battle is over. Here comes Rainard."

"You're alive? You're hurt!" cried Rainard.

"Nothing. A scratch, no more. But are they all dead?"

"No, they fled down the canyon. We thought to go after them, but no one had seen you and we came back to see what your orders are," explained Rainard.

"Wounded?" It was Aimery, the crisp military commander, who spoke now.

"Two killed, the rest wounded. Three . . ." Rainard shook his head.

"We will stay till morning, and bury our dead." He looked down at the fallen knight. "And this one."

"Who is he?" asked Solange, her voice quavering. Reaction had set in, and she realized that she had killed a man.

"Let us see who of our countrymen decided to set upon us," said Aimery grimly. Kneeling beside the fallen man, he removed the visor.

The knight was not dead. The dark eyes moved painfully, as though straining to see.

"Mehun!" breathed Solange.

"My men—" His breath came with a whistle.

"All on the way back to Antioch," said Rainard bluntly.

"I must join them . . . must hide . . ." Mehun struggled to move, but he could not. It was clear to them all that his wound was mortal.

Together Aimery and his men helped ease off the armor that confined him. They eased him back to the ground, and gave him water.

Solange leaned back upon her heels, half-hidden from

Mehun's view by Aimery. She could not believe what had happened. She and Mehun had come half the world over, carrying their hatred of each other, only to have it end like this. The ways of Providence were strange. Now, thanks to Providence, Aimery was safe and her enemy lay dying.

In delirium, Mehun spoke. "I had to do it. She wouldn't go home. She wouldn't . . ." The voice died away.

Aimery wore a look of intense concentration. "Mehun," he said in a taut voice, "can you hear me?"

"Y-yes."

"You know you are dying."

"Yes, Father. I know it."

"He thinks he's a priest," muttered Rainard to Solange.

"Mehun, you know me," said Aimery.

"Yes, Father. I confess—Let me not die with this on my soul."

He breathed heavily for some time. Aimery put out a hand to hold Solange back. He knew they must hear it all, to put an end to the whole business.

"I lied. I lied about the man Florent," came the husky words. "Father, don't leave me now. I must tell you all."

"I lied about the man being dead. I didn't know him at all. Saw him once, I think. But she believed me, and I wed her. The estates would be mine."

Even now, the darkness of death closing fast upon him, he could kindle at the thought of the fair lands of Belvent.

"Never had lands. My men too, landless. All was fine, but for the girl." Each word cost great effort, but he persevered. If there was one thing he had, reflected Solange, it was determination.

"She wouldn't obey, wouldn't believe. Threw it all into the air."

The moon had left the canyon now. The shadows were creeping out over the canyon floor, from the stone wall, over Mehun de Mowbrai. It was like the shadow of death coming to claim him, thought Solange, and shivered.

"King wouldn't confirm me, not until he knew more, he said. But the girl wouldn't give up. Should have let her alone in the beginning."

She pulled her cloak around her. The memories of Belvent swept over her and she began to weep. She could feel the tears tracing runnels down her cheeks. How far away it all was. She might have accepted Mehun—hated him, but made the best of it, had he not overreached himself by selling her to the baron. *Selling* her!

Belvent in the kindly sun of spring, in the warm russet and gold of autumn, was a fair land, and a magnet for Mehun's destruction.

"The minstrel, I killed him. The girl believed him, and upset everything. Tried to kill her. The only one who could betray me was that girl."

Aimery said, "You tried to kill her?"

"Yes. On the tower. On the river."

"You cut her saddle girth?"

"Yes. No . . . not me. Bagge. I paid him."

"Then Bagge tried again on the mountain road."

"Incompetent!" Mehun tried to struggle up to lean on his elbow. "Jehane, Bagge, the whole lot! Jehane couldn't even get the job done in Byzantium! Got her to d'Yves—everything went wrong.

"Father, I confess I did all these things. The knowledge that St. Florent lived must be erased. No one must know—don't you see?"

He was delirious, and his raving took him back to a time before he caught sight of Belvent. Long-ago battles, the booty that he took from fallen Turks and, so it seemed, from fallen comrades. Women he had possessed, and fair deeds he had done—all too few of them, though—all came out in broken rambling.

He clutched Aimery's sleeve and Aimery was content to let him rave. He sat on his heels, paying no heed to the blood trickling from cuts on his face, giving what comfort he could to the man who, only minutes before, had lifted his battle-ax to smash him.

"Father."

Aimery had to bend low to hear the words. "I confessed."

Mehun was distressed, moving restlessly. The end was very near, Aimery knew, and with sudden insight he knew what mattered to Mehun.

"I confessed, Father. . . ."

Aimery loosed one hand. Drawing the sign of the cross on Mehun's forehead and breast, he whispered, "*Te absolvo.*"

Solange caught her breath. Aimery was no priest. He could not forgive Mehun. Nor could she, for all the pain he had caused, the great mountain of suffering caused by his greed.

Aimery whispered, his eyes boring into hers, "Solange, you must forgive him."

Her lips formed the word: Never.

His voice was regretful. "Do you still hate him so much?"

She sat for a moment. Mehun had caused grief. But many things had come out of it all besides pain.

And each man did according to his lights. Who was she to judge another human being? She too had sinned, and must hope for mercy, as Mehun hoped.

She leaned forward. "Mehun, can you hear me? It is I, Solange. I forgive you, Mehun."

There was a flicker in his eyes. It was shortlived. It was almost as though he had been waiting for her words. In the next moment, his entire body shuddered as though struck by a mighty blow.

Starting up, with astonishing strength, he let loose of Aimery and threw up his arms as though to ward off a blow. With a great cry of fear, he fell back. Mehun was dead.

The terrible moment left them all silent and shaken. At last, Aimery reached for Mehun's hand. He pulled off a signet ring and put it in his own wallet. "We will need proof that it was really Mehun de Mowbrai," he said matter-of-factly.

"What do you think he saw?" ventured Rainard.

"Please God," said Aimery, gravely, "we will never know."

They buried him as the sun came up, in a hastily dug grave at the bottom of the wall. They covered the grave with rocks and left him alone. Their own dead they buried together near the mouth of the canyon, where the river sang over stones.

Then, slowly, they rode out of the canyon, bearing their wounded in improvised litters.

Solange was spent. She felt almost bereft. The search for her father was over, and Mehun was no longer a threat.

Aimery would take the ring to the king, and tell Louis all they had heard. Aimery also had the letter from Odo de St. Florent giving Belvent to Solange and himself.

And, Solange realized, her mother had no husband at all.

11

Toward the end of the day, two days ride from Antioch now, their wounded were standing the journey well. They were all almost lighthearted for once, thinking their troubles were over. It was then that they found the bodies.

Aimery, in the lead, reined up sharply.

"My God!" he breathed. "What happened here?"

Bodies were strewn over several yards of ground. Vultures flew off, flapping their wings heavily as far as the nearby trees. They perched there, waiting.

The men had been killed outright. Their armor was still on them except where the visor had been opened on each, to be sure they were dead.

There were a dozen men in armor, at least that many sergeants in leather padding, and a few squires. "Others were probably carried off," said Rainard, "as slaves."

Mehun's men, fleeing from the battle in the canyon, had come down the road to Antioch, pounding in desperate haste. But they had not made it beyond this point.

The horses were gone, probably driven off by the killers. Something flapped nearby and caught Solange's eye. She hastened to it. A rock the size of a man's fist held down a square of the material they used in this region for paper.

The words were written in a fashion that suggested the writer was not accustomed to western letters.

Aimery came up to read over Solange's shoulder. "These men had time to write a note?"

"No, it's—read it yourself. See if it says what I think it says."

"Lady, you see your enemies before you. I give you this, for your graciousness to me."

The sheikh Njer-el-Din, had given her what he could. She could not walk his ways. Nor would he have wanted her for long, she believed. And yet, there had been something between them. He had given her what he could. "Go with God," the letter finished.

After all, his God and hers were one. And had always been one. How could she not have known this? Why did the others, the rest of the Crusaders, not understand that? "Infidels" indeed! Solange was shocked by her blindness.

She recognized some faces, swollen already in the hot sun, fit now only for vultures. Stephen, Baldwin, and the mad Gauthier. Aimery's men buried them all.

They were nearing Antioch now with their wounded. They passed the old stone mill where Njer-el-Din had waited for them more than a week before. They came out of the river valley they had followed all the way from El Chorazin. Solange paused to look back the way they had come.

Petronilla was waiting for them in Antioch. How she would take the news they would bring her, Solange did not know. But her mother had courage.

Miles upstream, the water that flowed at their feet now had flowed past the walls of her father's city. She had followed the long shadow of her father all the way, until she found the man himself.

He was a far different man than she had thought, a little weak, perhaps, but not a bad man. She would think of him often, seeing him in the midst of his apricots and melons, and watching that small boy who would one day rule the land.

"Aimery?" she said, turning to him. He reached his hand out to her.

"Shadows gone?" he asked. He had carefully avoided questions about the sheikh, having a strong suspicion that he would regret knowing the truth.

"My shadows are," she said, "or at least they are fading in the light."

He thought of the queen whose strong dark influence had nearly wrecked him. And of the great mercy that had led him out of that shadow into the sunlight of Solange's love.

He gestured ahead of them to where Antioch lay in the hot sun. "See?" he smiled, and reached for her hand. "High noon."

She smiled at him then, a smile he would gladly have given the world to see, the smile he once feared was gone forever. And that miraculous light in her eyes—there it was! It was back!

Together, they galloped down the last slope to Antioch, riding too fast to hold hands. There would be time enough for that, later, for they were one, at last, in heart and mind—and body.

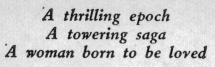

A thrilling epoch
A towering saga
A woman born to be loved

The Golden Sovereigns
Jocelyn Carew

Carmody Petrie stood on the threshold of something big—sole heiress to the family estate in England—she was beautiful and alone in a world of passionate women and bold men.

And before she could fulfill the warm, throbbing romantic destiny that her desire foretold, she would be at the mercy of a ruthless Duke, sentenced to penal servitude on the island of Jamaica, and married against her will to a brutal landowner . . . on a tumultuous sea of danger and depravity to the New World, freedom, a lush Virginia plantation, and the wild, savage adoration of Mark Tennant!

GOLD 12-76

Long ago and far away . . .
the story of a great love

*Hers is
the song of
all women.*

*It cries
to be heard
as she sings of her love
for one man.*

Listen!
*Tara's
Song*
BARBARA FERRY JOHNSON
author of DELTA BLOOD

AVON  39123 $2.25

TARA 9-78

AVON ◆ THE BEST IN
BESTSELLING ENTERTAINMENT

From the author of
Devil's Desire and *Moonstruck Madness*

THE STORY OF ONE MAN, ONE WOMAN, ALL LOVE!

AND NO LESS THE STORY OF

LAURIE McBAIN

TEARS OF GOLD

Reaching across an unending landscape of human emotion, from Paris to Gold Rush California, Laurie McBain's long-awaited new romance brings together two proud people:

MARA
She could seduce the moonlight . . .

NICHOLAS
A man who took what he wanted,
when he wanted it . . .

Through breathless adventures and dangerous charades —from vast, sunbaked ranches where Spanish land barons beckon with kisses flavored of wine, to a lush Louisiana plantation where they unite in a blaze of joy and pain—their destinies were one. For though Nicholas had sworn to kill her, she was the love he would die for!

 Avon   41475 $2.50

TEA 4-79

**IN HOLLYWOOD, WHERE DREAMS DIE QUICKLY,
ONE LOVE LASTS FOREVER...**

*"I love you," she said.
"I've loved you since the sun
first rose. . . . My love has
no shame, no pride. It is
. only what it is, al-
ways has been and
always will
be."*

The words are spoken by Brooke Ashley, a beautiful forties film star, in the last movie she ever made. She died in a tragic fire in 1947.

A young screenwriter in a theater in Los Angeles today hears those words, sees her face, and is moved to tears. Later he discovers that he wrote those words, long ago; that he has been born again—as she has.

What will she look like? Who could she be? He begins to look for her in every woman he sees ...

Always

AVON

**A Romantic Thriller
by
TREVOR MELDAL-JOHNSEN**

41897
$2.50